P9-CNB-399

By Lisa Scottoline

Dirty Blonde
Devil's Corner
Killer Smile
Dead Ringer
Courting Trouble
The Vendetta Defense
Moment of Truth
Mistaken Identity
Rough Justice
Legal Tender
Running From the Law
Final Appeal
Everywhere That Mary Went

LISA SCOTTOLINE

ROUGH JUSTICE

HarperTorch
An Imprint of HarperCollins*Publishers*

This is a work of fiction. Names, characters, places, and incidents are products of the author's imagination or are used fictitiously and are not to be construed as real. Any resemblance to actual events, locales, organizations, or persons, living or dead, is entirely coincidental.

HARPERTORCH
An Imprint of HarperCollins*Publishers*
10 East 53rd Street
New York, New York 10022-5299

Copyright © 1997 by Lisa Scottoline
ISBN: 0-06-109610-5

First HarperTorch paperback printing: September 2001
First HarperPaperbacks printing: September 1998
First HarperCollins hardcover printing: September 1997

HarperCollins®, HarperTorch™, and ◆™ are trademarks of HarperCollins Publishers Inc.

Printed in the United States of America

Visit HarperTorch on the World Wide Web at
www.harpercollins.com

40 39 38 37

For the Truly Awesome Molly Friedrich,
and for Peter and Kiki

Undefeatability lies with ourselves.

—Sun-Tzu

It started with a slip of the tongue. At first, Marta Richter thought she'd misunderstood him. She felt exhausted after the two-month murder trial and couldn't always hear her client through the thick bulletproof window. "You mean you struggled in *his* grasp," Marta corrected.

Elliot Steere didn't reply, but brushed ash from his chair on the defendant's side of the window. In his charcoal Brioni suit and a white shirt with a cutaway collar, Steere looked incongruous but not uncomfortable in the jailhouse setting. The businessman's cool was the stuff of tabloid legend. The tabs reported that on the night Steere had been arrested for murder, he'd demanded only one phone call. To his stockbroker. "That's what I said," Steere answered after a moment. "I struggled in his grasp."

"No, you said he struggled in *your* grasp. It was self-defense, not murder. You were struggling, not him."

A faint smile flickered across Steere's strong mouth. He had a finely boned nose, flat brown eyes, and suspiciously few crow's feet for a real estate developer. In magazine photos Steere looked attractive, but the fluorescent lights of the interview room hollowed his cheeks and dulled his sandy hair. "What's the point? The trial's over, the jury's out. It doesn't matter anymore who was struggling with who. Whom."

"What's that supposed to mean?" Marta asked. She didn't want him to play word games, she wanted him to praise her brilliant defense. It was the case of her career, and Steere's acquittal was in the bag. "Of course it matters."

"Why? What if it wasn't self-defense? What if I murdered him like the D.A. said? So what?"

Marta blinked, irritated. "But that's not the way it happened. He was trying to hijack your car. He attacked you with a knife. He threatened to kill you. You shot him in self-defense."

"In the back of the head?"

"There was a struggle. You had your gun and you fired." Without realizing it, Marta was repeating the words of her closing argument. The jury had adjourned to deliberate only minutes earlier. "You panicked, in fear of your life."

"You really bought that?" Steere crossed one long leg over the other and a triangle of tailored pant flopped over with a fine, pressed crease. "'In fear of my life'? I stole that line from a cop show, the one where everybody smokes. You know the show?"

Marta's mouth went dry. She didn't watch TV even when she was on, another television lawyer with wide-set blue eyes and chin-length hair highlighted blond. A hardness around her eyes and a softness under her chin told the viewers she wasn't thirty anymore. Still Marta looked good on the tube and knew how to handle herself; explain the defense in a sound bite and bicker with the prosecutor. Wrap it up with wit. Smile for the beauty shot. "What is this, a joke? What's TV have to do with anything?"

"Everything. My story, my defense, was fiction. Rich white guy carjacked by poor black guy. White guy has registered Glock for protection. Black guy has X-Acto knife. Not a good match." Steere eased back into his chair. "The jury bought it because it was what they expected, what they see on TV."

Marta's lips parted in disbelief. The news struck like an assault, stunning and violent. Her mind reeled. Her face felt hot. She braced her manicured fingers against the cold aluminum ledge and fought for her bearings. "What are you saying?"

"I'm guilty as sin, dear." Steere's gaze was point-blank and his voice tinny as it passed through a thin metal grate under the bulletproof window. The cinderblock walls of the interview room, lacquered calcium white, seemed suddenly to be closing in on Marta.

"But he slashed your cheek with the knife," she said, uncomprehending.

"He was dead at the time. I held his hand, with the knife in it."

"They found fibers from your tux on his hands and clothes."

"There was a struggle. He put up a fight. Mostly begging, boohooing like a little girl."

Marta's stomach turned over. "Tell me the whole story. The truth."

"What's to tell? A bum came at me when I stopped at the red light. He was waving a knife, drunk, screaming I should give up the car. Like I would. A new SL600 convertible. Wet dream of a car." Steere shook his head in momentary admiration. "So I grabbed my gun, got out of the car, and shot him in the head. I called the cops from the cell phone."

Marta crossed her arms across her chest. You could call it a hug but that wasn't how she thought of it. She'd heard confessions like this from other clients, and though Steere didn't look like them, he sounded like them. They all had the urge to brag, to prove how smart they were and what they could get away with. Marta had known Steere was tough-minded; she hadn't guessed he was inhuman. "You're a murderer," she said.

"No, I'm a problem-solver. I saw some garbage and took it out. The man was a derelict, worthless. He didn't work, he didn't produce. He didn't own anything. Fuck, he didn't even live anywhere. This time he picked the wrong guy. End of story."

"Just like that?"

"Come on, Marta. The man was *useless*. He didn't even know how to handle the fucking knife." Steere chuckled. "You did it better during the demonstration, when you held it under your chin. Did you see the jury? The front row almost fainted."

Marta felt a twinge as she flashed on the jurors, their faces upturned like kindergartners. She'd hired the requisite raft of jury consultants but relied on her own instincts and experience to pick the panel, ending up with a solid reasonable-doubt jury. She'd stood in front of them every day of the trial, memorizing their features, their reactions, their quirks. Fifteen years as a top-tier criminal lawyer had taught Marta Richter one thing: the jurors were the only real people in any courtroom. Even the ones with book deals.

"They're suckers," Steere said. "Twelve suckers. The biggest loser was your friend the Marlboro Man. Better watch out, Marta. He had the look of love. He may be fixin' to get hisself a filly."

Marta winced. Steere meant Christopher Graham, a blacksmith from Old Bustleton in northeast Philadelphia. Marta had learned that Graham had recently separated from his wife, so she worked him the whole trial, locking eyes with him during her cross of the medical examiner and letting her fingertips stray to her silk collar when she felt his lonely gaze on her. Still, manipulation was one thing, and prevarication quite another. "Everything you told me was a lie."

"It worked, didn't it? You shot the shit out of their case. The bailiff thinks the jury will be back by noon tomorrow. That's only four, five hours of actual deliberation." Steere smiled and recrossed his legs. "I hear the reporters have a pool going. The smart money's on you, twenty to one. There's even action

6 — LISA SCOTTOLINE

that they acquit me before there's three feet of snow on the ground."

Marta's mind reeled. The media, more lies. She'd told the reporters Steere was innocent and declined to speculate on how long the jury would be out. *I just win, boys. I leave the details to you*, she'd said with a laugh. She wasn't laughing now.

"It's almost three o'clock," Steere said, checking a watch with a band like liquid gold. "You've never had a jury out longer than two days, if memory serves."

Marta flipped back through her cases. She was undefeated in capital cases and she'd win this one, too. No tough questions of physical evidence to explain away, just a disagreement over the way it had gone down, with the Commonwealth claiming Steere had intended to kill the homeless man. It took balls to prosecute a case that thin, but it was an election year and the mayor wanted to crucify the wealthiest slumlord in Philadelphia. Marta understood all that, but she didn't understand the most important thing. "Why did you lie to me?"

"Since when are you so high and mighty? Did you ask if I was guilty?"

"I don't ask my clients that question."

"Then what's the difference if they lie to you?"

Marta had no immediate reply except to grit her teeth. "So you made up this cock-and-bull story."

"You never doubted it? One of the best criminal lawyers in the country and you can't smell shit?"

Not this time, because she had let her guard

down. Because she'd been attracted to him, though she wouldn't admit it, even to herself. "Your story made absolute sense. We went over it and over it. You told it the same way every time."

"I lied from the door."

"Even to the cops? The statement you gave them. It was recorded. It was all consistent."

"I'm excellent at what I do."

"Lie?"

"Sell."

"You used me, you asshole."

"Come off it, dear." Steere's smile twisted into a sneer. "You got paid, didn't you? Almost two hundred grand this quarter, including your expenses. Hotel, phone, even dry cleaning. Every cent paid in full. Twenty-five grand left on the retainer."

"That's not the point."

Steere's laughter echoed off the cinderblock walls of the interview room. "Easy for you to say, you're not paying it. For that much money, using you should be included. Christ, for that much money, fucking you should be included."

"Fuck *you*!" Marta shot to her feet, seething. She felt the urge to pace, to move, to *run*, but the interview room was as cramped as a phone booth. She was trapped. By Steere, by herself. How could she have been so naive? She still couldn't bring herself to accept it. "So you killed Darnton, even though you'd be questioned? Charged?"

Steere shrugged. "It was a risk, but I run risks every day. I figured the D.A. would find a reason to charge me, but that's okay. Any ink is good ink. I knew I'd hire the best and get away with it, and I will. Because of you."

Because of you. The words burned into Marta's brain. Steere had written the story and she had sold it, better than she'd ever sold anything in her professional life. Pitched it to the jury in the day and the satellites at night. And she didn't do it for the money or the facetime, not this time.

She did it for Steere.

In the split second she realized it, Marta's fury became unreasoning. She could have sworn he wanted her, he'd given every signal. He'd lean too close at counsel table, look too long at her legs. Once he'd touched her knee, bending over to retrieve his fountain pen, and her response had been so immediate it surprised even her. The memory made her feel crazy, unhinged. Unleashed. "I'm going to Judge Rudolph with this," she said.

"You can't. I'm your client and this is a privileged conversation. Disclose it and you're disbarred, ruined." Steere laced his long fingers together and leaned forward on his side of the metal ledge. "Of course, I'd deny the conversation ever took place. You'd look like a fool."

"Then I quit. I'm not your lawyer anymore. I'm withdrawing from the representation." Marta snatched her bag and briefcase from the tile floor.

"The judge won't let you withdraw while the jury's out. It's too late in the game. It's prejudicial to me, infringes my constitutional rights."

"Don't you lecture me," Marta shot back, though she knew he was right about her withdrawal. "I suborned perjury for you."

"Suborn perjury, my my. You can talk the talk, can't you? So can I. You didn't suborn perjury because I didn't testify in my own defense."

"It's a fraud on the court—"

"Enough." Steere cut Marta off with a wave. "Here's what happens next: the verdict comes in by noon and I go free. Then I hold a press conference where I tell the world that the mayor is a smacked ass, the jury system is a blessing, and you're the best whore money can buy."

Marta froze. Her fingers squeezed the handle of her briefcase. Rage constricted her breathing. She felt choked, with Steere's polished loafer on her throat.

"Then we'll go to the Swann Fountain for the victory celebration," Steere continued. "We can play footsies, just like old times. After that I'm booked to St. Bart's on a Learjet that'll take off from Atlantic City if Philly is snowed in. I love the beach, don't you? Hate the water, but love the beach. Want to come?"

Marta only glared in response. She wouldn't be used like this. Not by him. Not by anyone. She reached for the door of the interview room.

"Aw, don't go away mad, honey," Steere said.

"I have work to do."

"What work? You just proved me innocent."

"Right. Now I'm going to prove you guilty."

Steere chuckled behind tented fingers. "There's no evidence."

"There must be."

"The police couldn't find any."

"They didn't have the incentive I do."

"And you'll find this evidence before the jury comes back? By noon tomorrow?"

"They won't be out that long," Marta said. She yanked the door open to the sound of Steere's laughter, but as furious as she was, she knew it didn't matter who was laughing first. Only who was laughing last.

The Criminal Justice Center in Philadelphia is a newly built courthouse and the holding cells adjoining the courtrooms resemble small, modern offices. Clear bulletproof plastic has supplanted atmospheric iron bars and the white-painted cinderblock walls are still clean and relatively unscuffed. Elliot Steere's cell contained a white Formica bench, a stainless steel toilet, and a half-sink. Steere was the only prisoner on the floor and because of transportation problems caused by the snowstorm, would be staying nights in his holding cell during jury deliberations. He crossed his legs as he read the *Wall Street Journal* and pointedly ignored the older guard standing in front of him like a penitent.

"I can't do it, Mr. Steere," the guard said, glancing over his shoulder. The other guard was out on break but he'd be back soon. Frank didn't want to get caught standing in Steere's cell. "I tried, but I can't."

Steere didn't look up from his newspaper. "Yes you can. Try again."

"I can't. The hallway's full of reporters. They got TV, cameras, everything. They're right outside the door, all the way to the elevators. In the lobby downstairs, too." The guard shook his head. "It's too chancy."

"You'll find a way."

"There is no way. Somebody will see me. Somebody will wonder, why's he goin' in and out? You know how reporters are. They're already sayin' you got special privileges."

Steere skimmed the front page. "Don't worry about the reporters. The snow's the big story, not me. It says right here, 'East Coast Hit by Major Snowstorm.' I'm not even above the fold today."

"I can't do it, I swear. I couldn't get it through the metal detector."

"You've done it before, Frank."

"Today is different. Today the jury's out. Everybody's walking around. Watching. Waiting. It's crazy out there." The guard shifted nervously from one new shoe to another. Orthopedic, they were, three hundred bucks a pair. *Orthotics*, the doc called them. Frank had never been able to afford them before; they weren't covered on his lousy HMO. "Believe me, it's nuts."

Steere turned the page.

"Please." The guard's lined forehead shone with sweat. "I got you the newspaper."

"I think I'm entitled to a newspaper."

"Sure you are. Don't get me wrong." The guard kept shifting his feet. Not that they hurt, he could stand forever in these babies. Walk all day, even at the mall with Madeline. Didn't have to wait in the car like a goddamn dog. "The newspaper was no problem, no problem at all, Mr. Steere. But this is a whole 'nother thing. Maybe I could get you a Coke from the machine."

Steere flipped to the stock quotes and skimmed the columns. "Good news. Hampden Technologies is up two points."

"I could get ice, too. From the lounge. Take me five minutes, tops."

"Uh-oh. Potash is down another point." Steere cracked the wide paper to straighten out a crease. "Still holding your potash, Frank?"

"Yeah."

"Do you think that's wise?"

Frank Devine swallowed hard. He'd started investing small amounts on Steere's say-so when the trial started. Steere was right each time, and Frank made real money. Steere had picked up a tip on potash last month, and Frank socked all he had plus what he could get from his brother-in-law—seventeen grand—on the stock. *Consolidating my holdings,* he told his Madeline. *Big shot,* she'd said, scowling. Now his seventeen grand was worth thirty and when he cashed out he'd buy whatever he needed. Two hundred goddamn pair of shoes. Orthotics, whatever.

"Frank? I asked you if you think it's wise to hold potash."

"I guess it's . . . wise." The guard watched Steere scan the quotes, his eyes going up and down the rows, but he couldn't tell anything from Steere's expression. He never could. Steere was like a freak that way. "Do you think it's wise, Mr. Steere?"

"If you guess so."

"I'm still ahead of the game," the guard said. He wasn't stupid, goddamnit. He'd learned a lot about stocks since the Steere trial started. "It closed at thirty yesterday."

"What was it this morning? Did it dip?"

"No, sir." The guard had checked with his brother-in-law, who found out from the computer. Frank didn't know much about computers and felt too old to learn.

Steere kept reading.

"Well, uh, should I sell it, Mr. Steere?"

"I don't know. I guess you should." Steere's eyes stopped at mid-column. "Then again, I guess you shouldn't. What do you guess, Frank?"

"I usually guess what you guess," the guard said, trying to make a joke, though he felt sick inside. It was so quiet he could hear his stomach groan.

Steere turned the page.

Frank shifted his feet.

Steere skimmed the quotes.

"Mr. Steere," Frank said, "should I hold potash or sell it?"

Steere's attention never left the newspaper. "I don't know if I'd hold it. It failed to make a new high. Made an attempt, but failed."

"How bad is that?" Frank's dentures stuck to his lips. "I mean, is that bad? It sounds bad."

"It depends."

"On what?"

"On how you feel at strike two."

Frank laughed, but it came out like he was choking.

From behind the paper, Steere said, "The phone, slugger. Bring me the fucking phone."

"What are you wearing?" Steere said into the flip phone. He was kidding, but there was a stiffening between his legs just the same. He'd been in jail almost a year.

"I'm in a meeting," she said in her professional voice, loud enough for the people around her to hear. She was a star and she knew it. Steere imagined her in the meeting, every inch the career woman, at least on the outside.

"You still have that bra, the black one with the lace?"

"I can't talk now, really. The gang's all here. Movers and shakers, even a city editor. Right, Marc?" she called out. "Call me back when you have your schedule. Gotta go." In the background Steere heard hearty masculine laughter.

"Wait. I need you to do something. Get to the file and destroy it."

"What? Why?"

"Richter knows."

"That's interesting," she said, her tone even. Steere knew she wouldn't get rattled, whether an editor or a row of priests sat in front of her. She was the only woman he knew who kept her wits about her, and that was why Steere wanted her. Well, one of the reasons.

"Richter knows I killed him intentionally, nothing else. Drop everything. Get the file. Today."

"In a blizzard?" she asked lightly. "I'd rethink that. Maybe next week. You choose the restaurant. My secretary will make the reservations."

"Not next week. Now. I'm not taking any chances."

"But we may need that information."

"Don't fuck me. Do it." Steere punched the END button, edgy and still hard.

Next Steere punched in the number of a man he introduced as his driver, Bobby Bogosian. The title was left over from the days Bobby drove Steere around in a dented brown Eldorado with the cash that would launch an empire stuffed in his pocket. Steere would go from rowhouse to rowhouse in the city's poorest sections, offering the elderly $30,000 —*cash money, on the spot, no strings*—for their homes. He could rent the houses for many times that and he made money if only 10 percent of the pensioners took the deal. Plenty more did.

Steere would tell them he was solving a problem for them as he sat in their cramped living rooms with the curtains drawn. Their couches were worn and saggy, with thick roped fringe at the bottom, and

Steere sat on more springs than he could count. Still, he felt neither contempt nor affection for these couples, no matter how toothless, poorly dressed, or just plain stupid they were. They reminded him of his foster parents, and instead of running away from them, he played the role of their perfect son.

In house after house, Steere smiled and showed the face of a bright, earnest young man trying to make his way in the world. He leaned forward on his knees as he spoke, dressed in a department-store suit and tie, and honeyed his voice. They'd call him a "go-getter," a "self-starter." Steere would remind them of the kind of young man they thought didn't exist anymore and who really didn't, except in an imagination spun with nostalgia, as substantial as cotton candy.

As Steere spoke, the old couples would relax in their ratty armchairs and confide in him, their eyes glassy with fear. In these city neighborhoods, whites were afraid of blacks and blacks were afraid of whites. Blacks and whites were afraid of Hispanics, Jamaicans, and Vietnamese. Everybody was afraid of drugs and gangs, and whatever their fear, Steere played on it. Because he understood their problems, they believed he could solve them. *On the spot, here's the cash, no strings.* Bobby Bogosian would stand silently behind the couch until the homeowner took Steere's ballpoint in a bony hand and affixed a shaky signature to the dotted line.

"Yo." Bogosian answered the beep quick as a Doberman at heel. "What up?"

"Where are you?"

"Center City."

"My lawyer, Marta Richter, just left the court-house. Keep an eye on her," Steere said, without further explanation. He never told Bogosian more than he needed to know and didn't want to know more about Bogosian than he had to. Steere didn't even know where Bogosian lived and heard only through the grapevine that Bobby's probation officer had taken off his ankle cuff.

"Got it," Bobby said.

"She's gonna be busy until the jury gets back. Make sure she doesn't do anything or go anywhere."

"Anything else?"

"Nothing major. I need her until the trial's over."

"What about after?"

"Then I don't need her anymore. Understood?"

"Sure."

Steere pressed the END button with satisfaction. He felt back in control. He had unleashed Bogosian, and the man would do the job. The best thing about Bogosian was that he didn't think. Steere pushed his button and the man took off like a missile sensing heat. Locking on target, exploding like a natural force.

Steere tucked the flip phone into his pocket, closed his eyes, and sat still on the hard bench. He'd learned the stillness as a kid when he got whacked for moving, and it stood him in good stead. Steere imagined himself as he always did, like a pole at the top of the world, the pivot for the globe whirling dizzy beneath. He remained motionless as the walls of his cell spun off and flew into the ether. Around him it grew dark, cool, soundless. He listened in the silence, waiting for the rhythm of his breathing. The beat of his heart, the bubbling of his blood. Then Steere slipped inside his own mind.

He considered the situation. He'd made a mistake with Marta, but had recovered and was back on plan. He'd just sent out protections and was hiding his distance, as Sun-Tzu would have put it. *Be near but appear far*, the Chinese general wrote. Sun-Tzu, an expert in military strategy, was one of the few men Steere admired, and when Steere read Sun-Tzu's book, he realized he was already doing the things Sun-Tzu had written. Steere had already bought the key properties in the city when he read in Sun-Tzu: *Occupy first what they care about*. And he had vanquished all his enemies except the mayor when he read: *Both sides stalk each other over several years to contend for victory in a single day*. That quote had stayed with him, and Steere had built his strategy for defeating the mayor around it.

Steere smiled inwardly. Sun-Tzu talked about the nature of victory, and Steere understood the nature of victory as if he had written the book himself. He understood that victory required more than aggression, more than conflict. Victory required violence. The clean, deadly violence of financial destruction and domination, like the detonation of a distant bomb with an explosion watched on videotape, and the intimate, hot violence of murder. Shooting a struggling man on a sticky night, while his heels kicked futilely against the asphalt. Killing him while you stood close enough to whisper in his ear, smell the stink on the back of his neck, and feel the heat from his skin. Making him take the bullet while he wept for his life.

Steere hadn't known if he could really do it or how he would feel after the fact. He had been surprised in both respects. Murder had come more easily than he expected, and after it was done he didn't feel thrilled or aroused. On the contrary, after killing the man Steere thought, *That was a snap.* And if he had been curious about the extent of his powers, Steere had learned they extended even further than he'd thought. He had murdered and would go free, so there was no limit to what he could do. No boundary imposed by self, man, or law. Steere had become invincible.

Sun-Tzu said, *Undefeatability lies with ourselves; defeatability lies with the enemy.* Steere knew instinctively that his new enemy, Marta Richter, could never achieve victory over him, even though she was free to move and he was confined to a prison cell. She knew how to win a courtroom battle, waged according to evidentiary rules and legal precedent, using words as weapons and lawyers as soldiers. It was no contest. Not even a fair fight. A box cutter against a Glock.

Because Elliot Steere knew how to win a war.

3

Heart pounding, Marta pushed her way through the reporters clogging the courthouse's hallway and lobby, only to find that outside the Criminal Justice Center they were as thick as the driving snow. They mobbed her as soon as she pushed her way through the courthouse's revolving door. "No comment," she shouted, blinking against the snowflakes and blinding TV lights.

Gonzo print reporters ran alongside Marta in the snow, grasping steno pads and hand-held dictaphones, wearing baseball caps against the storm. "Marta, will they find him innocent?" "Marta, how long will they be out?" "Will Steere sell his properties to the city if he's convicted?"

"No comment!" Marta snapped, charging to the street.

"Aw, come on, Marta!" TV reporters in orange-face makeup hurried in front of her, scurrying under colorful golf umbrellas held by interns. Their cameramen and technicians aimed videocams and TV lights as they ran backward in front of her, a practiced art.

"Marta, will the deliberations be suspended because of the storm?" "Ms. Richter, will Steere be found innocent?" "What's next for you, Marta?" "Got a book in the works?"

Marta didn't stop to kiss up or propagandize. Didn't even break stride. Let them print what they wanted; her spinning days were over and she didn't have any time to lose. She elbowed her way out of the throng, and they didn't follow because the assistant district attorney, Tom Moran, emerged from the courthouse.

"The gag order's still in place," Marta heard Moran say, and felt her gut twist. The D.A. had been right all along. Steere was a cold-blooded murderer. Now Marta had to prove it. But how? The bravado she'd shown in the interview room had vanished, scattered by frigid blasts of snow and reality. What was she going to do? Get back to the office. Get her bearings. Go!

Marta hurried to the corner to catch a cab, pushing the sleeve of her trench coat aside to check her watch. Three-fifteen. How much time did she have? Until noon tomorrow? She reached the corner of Market Street, where the traffic was heaviest, and tried to hail a cab. Snow flew in her eyes. The storm was worse than she'd thought.

Snow fell in thick wet flakes, blanketing everything in sight. Office buildings, subway canopies, and parked cars were already frosted white, their outlines indistinct. Icicles like pointy daggers jabbed from the power lines. The stoplight in front of City Hall was frozen red, confounding the already congested traffic. The sky was overcast. Soon it would be dark.

Marta wheeled around at a loud screeching behind her. A shopkeeper was pulling a corrugated security gate over a glass storefront. The other stores were already closed, their lights out. Commuters flooded the sidewalk to the subway stairs, leaving work early. Philadelphia was shutting down, freezing solid. What was she going to do? She had only one night and it was in the middle of a fucking blizzard.

Marta waved harder in the gray shadow of City Hall. Traffic accelerated as it turned the corner around the Victorian building and jockeyed for the fast lane to the parkways out of the city. Cars spewed clouds of steamy exhaust, and a minivan angling for the lead sprayed snow on Marta's pumps. She spotted a cab and waved at it, but it drove by, occupied. Marta was struck by a memory appearing from nowhere.

Hey! She's standing at a curb. Waving. Cars speed by. Wind blows her hair. It's cold by the road. Winter in Maine. *Hey, mister. Please stop!*

BEEP! blared a bus, almost upon her. Marta, startled, jumped back to the curb as its massive wheels churned by, dropping caked snow from its treads. *BEEP!*

"You okay, miss?" asked a voice Marta only half heard as she spotted another cab halfway up the street. The cab's roof light glowed yellow. It was empty!

Marta dodged passersby and dashed to the cab, her briefcase and bag under her arm. Snow wet her face and eyes but she blinked it away. The cab crawled toward her up the street, its headlights shining dimly through the snow. Marta waved like a fool. As the two converged she thought she saw a shadowy figure in the backseat. Damn. The windows were too dark for her to see inside. Marta reached the yellow cab and pounded on the back window.

"Hey, hey!" she shouted, battering the pane with her fist. "I need this cab!" An old man in the backseat recoiled from the window in astonishment, and Marta became vaguely aware that she was acting crazy, feeling crazy. Bollixed up by what she had to do and how little time she had to do it in. Marta tore open the back door of the cab. "I need a ride uptown! It's an emergency!"

"No!" the old man wailed. He sunk deep into the backseat, his eyes widening behind his glasses. The cab fishtailed to a stop.

"Yo, lady!" the driver shouted, twisting angrily around. On his dashboard was a deodorizer shaped like a king's crown. "What do you think you're doin'?"

"This is an emergency," Marta said. "I need a ride uptown."

"Get out of my cab! I already got a fare!"

"Let me share the ride. I'll pay you fifty dollars."

"Are you crazy?" bellowed the cabdriver.

"Make it a hundred! We got a deal?" Marta thrust a foot into the back of the cab, but the old man edged away in terror and the driver fended her off with a hairy hand.

"Stop that! Get out of my cab!"

"*Two* hundred! We'll ride together, you drop me off. Uptown for two hundred dollars!"

"GET OUT, LADY! You're a fuckin' PSY-CHO!"

"No, wait!" Marta yelled, but the cab lurched ahead and the door banged shut, knocking her bag and briefcase to the snowy street. Marta fished them out of the snow and brushed them off. Fuck! She needed to get to the office somehow. Maybe she could call the cab service. Marta tore into her purse for her cell phone and punched its tiny ON button. Nothing. The battery had run out. Marta was about to hurl the phone across Market Street when she saw another cab coming her way. Was it empty?

She tucked her stuff under her arm and ran for it.

Across the street, a large man in a black leather duster was watching. He was hatless despite the freezing temperatures, leaning against the fake Greek facade of Hecht's department store. Marta didn't notice him. She wouldn't have recognized him even if she had, for Bobby Bogosian wasn't someone Elliot Steere would ever introduce to her.

4

Christopher Graham was tall and brawny, with big-boned features and a gray-flecked beard trimmed just short of the collar of his flannel shirt. He stood at the window of the large, modern jury room in the Criminal Justice Center, resting his callused hands deep in the pockets of his jeans and watching the snowstorm. The jurors in the Steere case had been told a storm was predicted, though they weren't allowed to watch the news because of the sequestration; no TV, newspapers, or radios for two months. The jurors complained about it all the time, except for Christopher. He didn't miss his VCR, he missed the horses whose shoes he reset and the money he'd make. The last thing he missed was his wife, Lainie.

"Okay, settle down, everybody. Settle down," Ralph Merry called out. He was a bluff, king-sized man who called himself an "ad exec," although the jurors sensed correctly that Ralph was never any type of "exec," but some sort of advertising salesman, his life fueled by scrambling and Scotch. Ralph waved the others into their order in accustomed chairs around the rectangular table. "First order of business," Ralph said, "is we elect a foreman."

Christopher tried to ignore Ralph in favor of the snow flying past the window. He'd known it was going to snow even without the TV news. He'd smelled it in the air this morning when they came from the hotel and he'd seen it in the grayness of the sky, or what was left of the sky once the skyscrapers got through with it. Out where Christopher belonged, the horses would've known it was about to snow, too. They didn't need weather radar and whatnot.

"Ain't you gonna be the foreman, Ralph?" asked Nick Tullio. Nick was the last juror empaneled, an aged Italian from South Philly. Nick had a wiggly neck wattle and a chest so spiny he looked more soup chicken than grown man. A tailor all his working life, Nick wore a suit and tie all the time, so he was curiously overdressed for every occasion. His thumb had gotten chewed up in a sewing machine accident, and Nick kept it tucked out of sight, which served only to draw attention to it. "You should be the foreman. Don't you want to?" Nick asked Ralph.

"Sure, but we gotta vote on it," Ralph said.

Nick looked sheepish. "Okay. Sorry. What do I know? I never did this before." He hated this whole thing. He wished the lawyers had never picked him in the first place. Nick couldn't believe it when they got through all the other people to choose him. Now it was time to decide if Mr. Steere was guilty. What should he do? How should he vote? Nick wished his wife, Antoinetta, was here.

"Not foreman. Foreperson. You have to say foreperson," corrected Megan Gerrity, a blue-eyed twenty-year-old with coarse red hair, shorn short. Megan was one of three jurors with any college experience. She had spent a year at Drexel University before she quit to design webpages. Her business had been growing until the Steere case, but jury duty could kill it. Megan lived on Internet time, and her clients needed their pages up and running yesterday. She couldn't afford to be sitting here. She hadn't been online in ages. She missed the sky, the sun, and the Microsoft clouds on the start-up of Windows 95.

"You don't want a man foreman?" Ralph asked.

"A woman," Megan corrected, unsmiling. She was so over Ralph. He always pulled this sexist crap, waging a sitcom gender battle with her. Megan suspected she wasn't the only juror to tire of it. The black jurors—three men and one woman—didn't like Ralph from the outset, Megan could tell. "I want to be the foreperson," she said.

"You?" Ralph shot back in mock disbelief. His large hand flew to the chest of his khaki shirt. It was Ralph's favorite shirt because it looked like the one General Schwarzkopf wore in Desert Storm. Ralph thought Norman Schwarzkopf was our greatest leader since Patton. Ralph had taped the general's press conferences from the Gulf War and had even stood in line to get a signed copy of his book. "Megan for foreman? No way. No women and no redheads.

No redheaded Micks! Everybody agree?" Ralph smiled and so did the other jurors, except Kenny Manning.

Kenny's glare was as dark as his skin. He sat at the opposite end of the table, his muscular arms folded over his broad chest. Kenny hated Ralph's jokes. He was sick of him from jump street. Kenny couldn't wait until the fuckin' case was over so he didn't have to look at Ralph's puffy pig face anymore. "Let's get this thing over with," Kenny said. "I been here forever."

"And the snow's comin' down hard," said Ray Johnson, Juror 7. Ray called himself "Lucky Seven" and sat at the end of the conference table next to Kenny Manning and Isaiah Fellers. The group of three black men routinely ate, sat, and rode the bus together, although the quiet Isaiah was something of a third wheel.

Isaiah glanced unhappily at the snowfall. Winter made him cranky, and he was living for the day when he would leave for his honeymoon in St. Thomas. Every conjugal visit, his fiancée would tell him the temperature there. She saw it on the Weather Channel. They would cuddle and talk about how they could spend all day together and drink piña coladas. Isaiah hoped they had a bar you could swim to from the pool and sit with your butt in the warm water.

Christopher was looking out the window, too, but he wasn't watching the snow anymore. He was picturing horses before a snowfall. They'd lift their heads from the hay in their stalls and swing them in a slow arc toward the window. Their dark, wet eyes would be unblinking, their gaze steady. They'd stamp their hooves, expectant, almost hopeful. Christopher knew just how they'd act because he'd grown up with horses and, like them, he'd grown accustomed to waiting. But he'd never allowed himself to hope, until now.

"I'm with Kenny," Lucky Seven said. "Let's get this over with so we don't get snowed in. Who says the man's guilty? Me and Kenny and who else?"

"Wait just a minute," Ralph said. He wielded his yellow pencil like a number two scepter. "We have to pick a foreman."

Nick Tullio watched the two of them and felt that burning in his stomach. The doctor said he didn't have an ulcer but Nick knew he did. He had to, he felt that burning whenever he got upset and he was getting all upset now. The moolies would want to send Mr. Steere to jail, but Nick wasn't so sure. He wasn't sure of anything. He wanted to drink his water but he didn't like to show his thumb, so he didn't. What would Antoinetta say?

"Fuck that," Kenny said. "We don't need a foreman. We can vote right now."

Ralph winced. He didn't like swearing around the women. He'd asked Kenny not to do it but that only made him do it more. Ralph knew there was no reasoning with them. His thin lips set in a hyphen of determination. "Kenny, we're gonna do this orderly. We all want to vote and go home but first we have to pick the foreman."

"Foreperson," Megan said, to cut the tension.

She felt uncomfortable when it got racial, and it always got racial lately. A white man had killed a black man, and Kenny couldn't see it any other way. God, Megan wanted to go home, where it was just her and her Compaq, and they never fought. "How about foreplay?" she quipped, and the jurors laughed.

Even Kenny smiled. "I'm down. Now let's vote. Elliot Steere is guilty. That's one vote for guilty. Who else? Lucky?"

"Me too," said Lucky Seven, and he snatched the verdict sheet from the center of the table.

"Hey!" Ralph shouted. "You can't take that. The foreman has to fill that out, and I should be the foreman. I nominate myself."

Megan shook her head. If Ralph were the foreperson, he'd never shut up. It would take forever. "No, I had first dibs. I'd like to be the foreperson. All in favor, raise their hands."

"People, don't fight. If we're going to elect a foreperson, it should be a secret vote," said Mrs. Wahlbaum. Esther Wahlbaum was a retired English teacher at a city high school, and she knew how to keep order in a classroom. "That's the official way to do it. A secret ballot."

Martin Fogel, sitting next to her, rolled his eyes. "Thank you, resident expert in everything." Mr. Fogel was an old watchmaker who wore steel-topped bifocals and a thin white shirt. A stripe of thin gray hair covered his head like a seat belt. "The woman is amazing. You need a plumber, she's a plumber. You want dance lessons, she does the fox-trot."

Mrs. Wahlbaum pursed her lips. "Don't start up, Mr. Fogel. Everybody knows a secret vote is more official. Just like with the regular elections."

Gussella Williams shifted impatiently in her seat, her jersey dress stretched between her large thighs. Gussella was black, a heavyset bookkeeper still unhappy over missing Christmas vacation for this trial. She'd planned to go to South Carolina to see her new grandbaby, who was growing like a weed. "I'll be damned if I'll miss his first birthday, too," Gussella grumbled, and nobody asked what she meant because they knew already. "Let's just get to voting. Secret, public, makes no difference to me. Lord, let's just vote."

Heads were nodding around the table, even of the two jurors who never participated, Wanthida Chandrruagphen, a thin, graceful Thai whose name no one could pronounce, and Ryan Parker, a shy man who worked for a yarn manufacturer. The jurors could hardly wait to have the trial over with and go home. They thought the lawyers repeated themselves and the exhibits were too technical. The experts talked down to them and the witnesses droned on forever. By the last two weeks of trial, nobody was even taking notes and crankiness had turned to hostility.

Nick looked confused. "A secret vote? How we gonna have a secret vote? If we close our eyes, who's gonna count?"

Christopher closed his eyes at their chatter. He hadn't heard as much yapping in his life as he'd heard these past two months. Since Lainie had left, he barely talked to anyone at all. At the barns where he did his shoeing, his only contact was with the horses. He avoided the rich ladies who took dressage lessons in tan jodhpurs and velvet helmets; ignored the barn managers who would steady a skittish mare as he pounded a nail into her hoof. No woman had ever really interested him until recently. Christopher felt like he'd been waiting for her his whole life, waiting like a horse for the snowfall. He turned from the window. "I'd like to be the foreman," Christopher said, and because he spoke so rarely, each face looked up at him in surprise.

"I think that's a great idea!" Megan exclaimed, because it was a compromise that would head off trouble. Who could object to Christopher? He was serious, smart, and handsome, in a lumberjacky way.

"Good for you, Christopher," said Mrs. Wahlbaum, pleased that the young man was finally coming out of his shell. It proved what she always told her class about patience.

Kenny looked over his folded arms at Ralph, who nodded back, agreeing tacitly to at least a temporary truce. "Okay by me," Ralph said. "You be the foreman, Chris."

"Thank you. I appreciate your confidence in me." Christopher felt good. He had a job now, a purpose. He'd do everything in his power to persuade them to acquit, and fast. He'd take care of her, like he did his horses. Quietly, and without fanfare or thanks. He'd see to it.

For Marta.

❖   ❖   ❖

"Okay, we're all agreed," Christopher said. "We'll take a vote to start things off. Everybody write down what they think the verdict should be. Don't put your name or anything. It's secret."

"Roger." Ralph nodded. He began ripping off sheets from the legal pad and sending them skidding around the table to each juror.

"Ain't we gonna talk about it first?" Nick asked, just to stall them. He didn't know how to vote. He looked around the table for help, but his wife wasn't on the jury. His stomach burned like hell. "Ain't we gonna discuss? Just for a little?"

Gussella shook her head firmly. "No, we're voting first, we already agreed. Why waste more time? Maybe we'll all agree on the verdict. Here's your paper." She reached across the table and handed him a sheet of paper. "Vote."

Nick took the paper obediently, and the other jurors grabbed sharpened pencils from a plastic tray on the table. Nobody skimmed the exhibits stacked in the middle of the table, tagged and labeled. Nobody gaped at the autopsy photos or puzzled over the DNA evidence. The jurors' heads were bent for only ten minutes and they handed their papers in as eagerly as kids on the last day of school. Christopher opened each sheet with care, smoothed it out on the walnut veneer table, and wrote the juror's vote on the blackboard behind him. There was complete silence as each chalk hash mark screeched on the board. It was as if Steere's fate were their own.

Christopher opened the last piece of folded-up legal paper and his face betrayed none of the happiness he felt inside. "Another vote for innocent," he announced, making the final hash mark. He stood away from the blackboard and read it aloud. "It's nine to two to find Steere innocent. Only one person abstained."

"Thank you, Jesus," Gussella said, beaming. She had a gold filling on one of her top teeth, and it was the first time she'd smiled broadly enough to let it show. "Carolina, here I come."

"How do you like that?" Ralph said, grinning, and his voice sounded like he liked it just fine.

"Who abstained?" Megan asked, annoyed. All they needed was a holdout. She was losing clients as she spoke. She scanned the faces around the table. So many old people with nothing to do. That was the problem. And the race thing. It was obvious who the two votes to convict had been, Kenny and Lucky Seven.

Mrs. Wahlbaum clucked in disapproval. "Now, Megan, we can't pick on whoever abstained. It's a secret ballot. Everybody has the right to follow his own beliefs and conscience. Even if it does keep us here longer."

Nick Tullio looked down at his thumb, embedded between the wool pleats of his handmade pants. He didn't know what he stained, but he guessed he was the only one who wrote I DON'T KNOW YET on his yellow paper. Nick was relieved Christopher had figured out a way to have a secret ballot.

"Abstaining is against the rules," Ralph complained. "The judge didn't say people could abstain."

"Rules?" Kenny jumped in. "Ain't no rules. The man don't know, the man don't know." His glare had gotten angrier since the votes were counted. Kenny figured he and Lucky Seven were the only two who voted guilty. Isaiah musta pussied out and wrote I DON'T KNOW YET. Kenny would have to talk to Isaiah when they were in the TV lounge tonight, alone. They had to stand together. "The man's allowed to take time. Make up his own mind. Goddamn don't have to rush this thing."

"That's true," Mrs. Wahlbaum said. "They still haven't sent in those exhibits about the fingerprints."

"What exhibits?" Ralph said, but Christopher shook his head. He didn't remember what exhibits they were talking about and it didn't much matter. It wouldn't be long before he delivered on his tacit promise to Marta. Christopher's chest swelled with satisfaction. And hope.

By four o'clock a foot of snow had accumulated on the sidewalks of Philadelphia and the brand-new law offices of Rosato & Associates were empty. The secretaries had gone home early and only two associates remained, waiting for the jury to come back in *Commonwealth v. Elliott Steere.* They'd been indentured to Marta Richter, who'd retained Rosato & Associates as her local counsel when Steere hired her.

"We blew it," said one of the young lawyers, Mary DiNunzio. She slumped over the conference table and buried her face in a hard pillow of correspondence. Her navy blue suit was wrinkled, her dirty-blond hair was genuinely dirty, and her compact body was worn to the bone. "We blew it and there's no going back. There's nothing we can do about it."

"The trial? No way. We won, easy." Judy Carrier was spinning in the swivel chair on the other side of the conference table. A native Californian, Judy was tall and strong, with a face shaped like a dinner plate and features that registered more honest than plain. A wedge of light hair flipped up like a paper parasol as she spun in her chair. "I bet they come back before dinner tomorrow, assuming the court doesn't close because of the snow."

"No. I mean our life, we blew our life. We had it made at Stalling and Webb, but no. We wanted to be on our own. Now we work for a psychopathic bitch. In an avalanche." Mary closed her eyes, dry with fatigue. She could feel her contacts fusing to her corneas. Tonight they'd peel off like Band-Aids.

"Hey, we gave it a try," Judy said, going round and round in her chair. The walls of the conference room were eggshell white and the room smelled like latex paint. The front wall was entirely of glass and faced the hallway. A sculling print by Thomas Eakins hung on the far wall and three more in the series leaned against the wall, yet to be mounted. The Rosato offices were unfinished, but Judy didn't mind. She liked working for a new law firm. It felt like a fresh start. "Nothing wrong with trying, Mare."

"I'm not blaming you," Mary said, though Judy knew that already. They'd been through fire together and not everything needed saying.

Judy's chair slowed to a stop facing the large window dotted with snowflakes. "Look at that!" she exclaimed, bounding to the window. The downtown office buildings, The Gallery, and the United States Courthouse looked like they'd been dumped with confectioner's sugar. "Isn't it beautiful?"

Mary blinked sleepily on the correspondence pillow. "They say it'll go to four feet. What a mess."

"It's so white!"

"Last year I couldn't get out of my house. They didn't plow the side streets."

"The flakes are so big. They look like Wheaties!"

"They'll close the courthouse and the jury will never come back. The trial will never end and I'll kill myself. They won't find my body for days and the ground will be too cold to bury me."

"It's exciting." Judy pressed her large hands against the surface of the window. It chilled her palms, and her breath made a cloud at the center of the glass. "The first good snow we've had this year. Isn't it a neat feeling?"

"I have no feelings. I'm too tired to have feelings."

"Lighten up, Mare."

"I can't, I'm a Catholic. Who works for Marta Richter."

"You mean Marta Erect." Judy huffed another cloud onto the pane and examined it. "Cool."

"If you draw a happy face in that, I'm pushing you out the window."

Judy turned and laughed, silver hoops dangling from her earlobes. A peasant dress swirled around strong legs and she was wearing gray wool tights that ended in Dansko clogs. Judy always dressed artsy and not even Marta Richter could bully her out of it. "It was a long, hard trial, and it's over. Erect will fly away as soon as the jury comes back.

She'll phone in the post-trial motions. You don't have to take any more orders."

"No, she'll never leave. She'll never go. She's not from anywhere and she'll never go back."

Judy shook her head. "What are you talking about, Mare? She'll go back to her office in New York."

"She said L.A. Her main office is in L.A."

"The letterhead says New York. I think she's from New York."

"She's not from New York, she doesn't have an accent. You ever notice she doesn't have any accent at all? The secretaries think she went to diction school."

"I thought the dictions went to law school."

"Be serious." Mary lifted her weary head from the papers. "We don't know where she lives. She has houses in Boston, New York, and Florida, I think, but I don't know where she lives. She never talks about it."

"She doesn't live, she just works. So what?"

"So we don't know where she's from. Who her people are."

"Her people?"

"Her people," Mary repeated, without elaborating. Judy wouldn't understand, since she was one of those unfortunates not raised in the Italian neighborhood of South Philly. "We don't know her family, her religion, anything. She's Jay Gatsby, the girl version."

"Erect? You have her blown out of proportion. You're giving her too much power. Erect is a workaholic and a control freak. She screams without cause and laps up publicity like a dog. In other words, she's a lawyer."

"No, think about it. She hasn't mentioned a single friend. She works alone. We have no idea when her birthday is. Mark my words, she's not of woman born. It says 666 on her scalp, between her black roots."

"You're out of control. You have trial fever."

"Remember, I warned ye. Ye be warned."

"You're nuts."

Mary considered this and rejected it. "And why aren't you tired? We worked this case together. Why am I always tired and you never are?"

"Because I exercise, doofus. I told you, come with me. I'll teach you to rock climb."

"Forget it." Mary dropped her head back on the correspondence pillow and wondered when her life started to suck. Their law firm flopped, things with Ned didn't work out, and just when Mary thought it couldn't get any worse, Marta Richter hired Rosato & Associates as local counsel.

"Then come skiing with me." Judy abandoned the window and plopped back into her chair, swiveling back and forth. "We can go cross-country."

"No. Forget it."

"You'll have the time of your life. We'll go to Valley Forge. It's beautiful in winter."

"George Washington didn't think so."

"Come on, after the verdict's in. We'll have a blast."

"Shut up. Stop being so cheery." Mary closed her eyes, and Judy checked her black runner's watch.

"It's almost dinnertime. I'm hungry. You hungry?"

"No." Mary opened her eyes a crack, but it was still a law firm and not a bad dream. "I'm never hungry and you always are. I'm always tired and you never are. That's just the way it is. There's nothing you can do about it. Nothing anyone can do about it."

"We can send out for something."

"It's a blizzard, Jude." Mary looked at her sideways and paused. "What do you think they're doing now?"

"Who? Erect and our favorite millionaire? Enjoying the sexual tension. Call me crazy, but two months of foreplay would be enough for me."

"I meant the jury."

"They're deliberating, of course. Trying to decide when the defendant will screw his lawyer. It's a role reversal."

"Judy, stop."

"They'd be at it already if Steere hadn't been in jail. It's the only open question in this case. When will they fuck, and how? Is there a way they can *both* be on top?"

"Judy, the case." Mary blushed. She could curse with any trial lawyer, but she was uncomfortable with Judy's sex talk. To Mary, saying "fucking" had nothing to do with fucking.

"Oh, the case. The case is a winner. It's a good jury and the D.A. didn't prove their case. Steere gets aquitted."

Mary allowed herself to believe it then, on faith. Judy had won every graduation prize at Stanford Law, had published legal articles, and had even been offered a clerkship at the Solicitor General's office. Mary suspected Judy was the reason they got hired at Rosato & Associates. Judy had raw intelligence and legal talent, but Mary had to work hard to get results, and did. "Maybe we'll get a bonus," Mary said.

"From Rosato? *Bennie* Rosato?"

"It could happen."

"She just started the firm a year ago. She's not about to throw money around, even at Girls 'Я' Us." Judy meant that Rosato & Associates was the first all-woman law firm in Philadelphia; five women litigators worked for the new firm. The fact that they were all women had attracted publicity, but whether it attracted clients remained to be seen. Steere was the firm's first major case, which was undoubtedly why Bennie Rosato entered the conference room that minute.

"Hello, you two," Bennie said, knocking on the doorjamb. She was on her way out, with an overcoat on her arm and a packed canvas briefcase slung over one shoulder. Benedetta "Bennie" Rosato's reputation as a civil rights lawyer was larger than life, and at six feet tall she intimidated the shit out of Mary, whose head popped up from the correspondence.

"Uh, we were just . . . organizing the file," Mary stammered.

"Right," Judy said, with an easy smile. "We're not exhausted or anything. We work constantly, even when the jury's out." Her blue eyes met Bennie's with a grin, and Bennie smiled back in a way that was friendly if not warm.

"We gonna win, Carrier?"

"How could we lose, boss?"

"That's the spirit." Bennie smiled, satisfied. Loose sandy hair streamed to her shoulders, wavy and careless, and her un-made-up features were large and not unattractive. Bennie wore a pantsuit of black wool, selected without excessive attention to cut, fit, or style. Bennie Rosato looked every inch the sunny, nononsense jock who won the scholar-athlete award in high school, which was just what she was. An elite rower in college, she still sculled every day on the Schuylkill River, a narrow ribbon of blue that rippled through the city. "How'd the jury charge go in? Did you get what you wanted?"

"Yes. They looked like they even understood it."

"A first. How was Marta's closing? I wanted to hear it but I had a dep."

"She nailed it, except when she started quoting Sun-Tzu. Their eyes glazed over."

Bennie frowned. "Sun-Tzu, the philosopher? What did she quote him for?"

Judy rolled her eyes. "I have no idea. He's Steere's guru. If you spend any time with Elliot Steere, sooner or later he hauls out Sun-Tzu."

Sitting at the table, Mary marveled at Judy's ease with Bennie. From their start at the firm, Judy acted more like Bennie's partner than an associate. Mary guessed it was because Judy and Bennie were so much alike. Both lawyers, athletes, and monstrously tall, as if from some legal master race. It made Mary nervous. Her chest blotched under her blouse and she wondered if she was cut out for the law. She was too short, for starters.

"You okay, DiNunzio?" Bennie asked. "Don't let up now. You're almost at the finish line."

Mary nodded in a way she hoped was perky. "I'm fine. I'm okay. I'm great."

"She's exhausted," Judy translated.

"Hang in," Bennie said. "Listen, Marta just called from a pay phone. She's on the way back and wants to talk to you. Says it's important. You can stick around, right? You two live in town."

"Sure," Judy answered, and Mary sighed. The same thing used to happen when she was at Stalling & Webb. Mary's apartment was within walking distance, so she was expected to work no matter what the weather. It was so unfair. Mary made a mental note to burn down her building.

"Good. Thanks," Bennie said, and her eyes scanned the conference table. The Steere file was scattered across its surface and manila folders were jammed into the accordions crookedly. It had been all the associates could do to pack the file in the rental car, drive it here, and lug it upstairs. "Better clean this file up, guys. Get the exhibits in order. You know how picky Marta is."

"Tell me about it. Anal is just a first offer," Judy said, and as soon as Bennie closed the conference room door, the young lawyers began straightening up the conference room. In short order, the twenty-five red accordion files that represented the defense in *Commonwealth v. Steere* sat upright on the glossy walnut table, arranged from correspondence to pleadings, trial exhibits, and lawyers' notes. News clippings took up five accordions and over seventy foamcore exhibits rested against the wall under a mounted blueprint of an oar. The two associates finished just as Marta Richter flew into the conference room, when it became instantly apparent that she couldn't care less about the file.

Marta felt composed, glued together again. The endless, stuffy bus ride back to the office had given her a chance to think. She had a plan, but she would need DiNunzio and Carrier.

Marta slipped out of her wet coat as soon as she hit the conference room, sat the associates down, and told them what to do, without telling them the truth about Steere. They would run to Rosato if they knew they were gathering evidence against a client, and Rosato was an opponent Marta could do without. So Marta pitched it to DiNunzio and Carrier as one more impossible assignment after two months of impossible assignments. The associates looked stunned.

"You want this *when*?" Mary asked, vaguely aware that she was not the first employee in America to ask this question.

Marta checked her watch and felt an already

familiar tightening in the pit of her stomach. "It's almost four-thirty. I need your answer by seven o'clock."

"Seven?" Mary moaned. Her head was spinning, her shoulders drooped. "Less than three hours?"

"Stop complaining. You don't have to draft a complete brief. There're no cases to research. Read the file and search the newspapers. Take notes on what you find."

"But the kind of search you're talking about could take days. A week. I have to write the motion *in limine,* about the prints on the car."

"The motion can wait. It's not that important. It's a loser anyway."

"But the rest of the exhibits have to go to the jury first thing tomorrow. This morning you told me—"

"Mary," Marta interrupted, "this discussion is taking longer than the fucking search. Just do it."

"Fine." Mary suppressed the BURN IN HELL YOU BITCH rising in her gorge and began scribbling on her pad as if some legal inspiration had suddenly visited her, like the Holy Ghost. *Definitely not cut out for this profession,* Mary wrote. *Convent looking better and better.*

Marta turned to Judy. "Your assignment will take longer, so get going. I'll meet with you after Mary. Figure on having an answer for me by eight o'clock. That should be time enough."

"Time isn't the problem." Judy shook her head. "This is a wild-goose chase. I'm not going to find anything. The assignment doesn't make sense."

"I'll explain this one more time." Marta held her tongue, but it was hard to check her urgency. A time clock ticked in her mind. She didn't have time to fuck around. "The Commonwealth has come up with after-discovered evidence, something that proves that Steere didn't kill in self-defense."

"How do you know this?" Judy asked.

"I can't tell you. It's confidential."

Judy was more taken aback than angry. "From us? We're all on the same side."

"Just do it, Carrier. I don't have time to fight with you."

Mary wrote on her pad, *I could take Angie's old room in the cloister. It had that tasteful wooden crucifix. The view was over the cemetery, but I'm not fussy. Anything away from the ice machine will do.*

"I don't want to fight either," Judy said. The higher pitch to her voice evinced confusion, not defensiveness. "I'm just trying to understand your thinking."

"You don't have to understand my thinking. You have to do your job."

"How can I do my job if I don't understand it?"

"Your job is to do what I say when I say it!" Marta shouted suddenly. Her face reddened and a vein in her neck threatened to pop. "I told you what to do and where to go. That's all you have to know. That's what you get paid for."

I look good in black, it's slimming. I don't even need a double bed. Or cable.

Judy fell into a startled silence. Erect out of control? Something was wrong. Marta seemed almost panicky, but Judy couldn't imagine why; the woman had just kicked butt in a huge murder trial. The newspapers and Court TV were touting her as the best criminal lawyer in the country. Judy would have expected Erect to be gloating right now. Usually they had to applaud if she farted.

"I want that answer, Judy." Marta stood up and snatched her coat from the chair. "And I want it before the D.A. files their motion tomorrow morning."

"We can deal with it then," Judy said, struggling with her bewilderment. "The judge will give us time to respond to anything they file. He can't make any kind of ruling without hearing from the defense." Judy's arms opened, palms up in appeal.

Mary thought Judy looked just like the Blessed Mother with her arms like that. To Mary, all associates looked like the Blessed Mother at one time or another. Like supplicants, pleading for mercy and finding none. She wrote, *I'll take Judy with me to the convent. She'll have to give up ESPN and ESPN 2, though. Not to mention that vow-of-silence thing.*

Marta tugged her trench coat angrily over her shoulders. "Don't you get it? I'm not about to let those clowns blindside me. I didn't get where I am by letting a D.A. get it over on me. If they have something on Elliot Steere, I want to know it and I want to know it as soon as they do."

"We don't have the resources they do! They have thirty lawyers on this case, plus the cops."

"You have no choice!" Marta shouted, full bore. "You have a job, now do it and shut up!"

Judy's face smarted as if she'd been slapped. She stood up and squared off against Marta on the other side of the table. "What if I refuse?"

"Then you're off the case and you leave Mary to do your assignment *and* hers. By eight o'clock."

Holy Mary Mother of God. Shoot me now.

6

Marta steered her rental Taurus into the blizzard blowing down Locust Street. Flurries flew at the windshield, the wipers beat frantically, and the defroster whirred loud as a blow dryer. Still, the windows stayed foggy. Traffic lurched to a standstill, stuck. Exhaust fumes formed noxious plumes all the way down the street. Marta glanced at the car clock. 5:35. Her fingers gripped the wheel and she honked her horn at the Subaru in front of her. "Move it, asshole!" she shouted, her voice reverberating inside the car. "Move!"

Marta honked again, but nothing happened. It drove her crazy that she could do something and nothing would happen. Marta had grown accustomed to a reaction from opposing counsel and judges, from clients and the press. She could always make something happen in court and even in love, as infrequently as that appeared. Marta had fashioned herself into a human catalyst, but here she was honking like a madwoman and the traffic was ignoring her. Nobody honked back or even gave her the finger.

She beeped the horn, louder. Longer, for the reaction. But she got none.

Marta tried to relax in the driver's seat. She drummed her nails. She hummed tunelessly. She even tried rubbing the furrow from her forehead. That she understood her reaction annoyed her even more. She was reacting to years of stasis, of nothing happening no matter what she did, to two parents who sat and drank and wasted, whose lives trailed off like a sentence. And no matter how many times Marta had begged, yelled, or hid their bottles, nothing had changed. The Richters lived in the woods near Bath, Maine, and Marta's father worked at the air force base there. He lost his job when she was six because she couldn't keep his bottles hidden and he ended up drinking himself to death long after Marta had stopped playing hide-and-seek with his whiskey.

Marta's mother became the breadwinner then, tugging the ten-year-old to the roadside. *Hey, mister! Sir!* The cars would whiz by. *Stop! Please! Hey!* As soon as a car stopped and its passenger door cracked open, the scam would begin. Marta begged not to do it but it made no difference. Nothing changed, not until the blue station wagon. That ended it, at least for Marta.

By the time she turned thirteen, she was behind the wheel of their battered Valiant, driving into town for milk, cigarettes, and another fifth. The cops in their small town didn't stop her because they knew her mother and it was safer to let a child drive than a drunk, especially when the child was Marta Richter.

Four foot eleven and on her own. Not that Marta blamed her parents or felt sorry for herself. On the contrary, it made her what she was today.

HONK! She hit the horn. Because she couldn't not.

She needed to get to Steere's town house in Society Hill. Marta was playing a hunch, betting she'd find something in his house that would lead to a clue, or something she could use for leverage. Besides, there was something Marta just had to know. Because now that she realized Steere wasn't interested in her, there was a key question that remained unanswered. Who *was* he interested in?

Marta stared at the foggy windshield and told herself her interest was only partly jealousy. If she could find out who Steere was sleeping with, she could get to him. Marta didn't know exactly how yet, but she'd been around long enough to know just how valuable that piece of information was. Especially since Steere was evidently keeping it a secret, even from her. Especially from her. His lawyer, whom he had betrayed.

HONK! Marta punched the car horn. She'd tear his fucking house apart if she had to. Break in and search every drawer. Read every address book, charge account slip, and travel record. Steere had said he was going to St. Bart's. How had he managed to arrange that? Where were the tickets? Who was the travel agent? Who was he going with?

Marta would find out. The answers would be in the house. Something would be in the house. It had to be.

HONNNKK! The traffic had stopped dead. It was maddening. Marta craned her head to see what was holding it up, but couldn't see anything over the line of traffic. She twisted around to see if she could reverse out, but there was another car behind her. She was blocked in. She thought of abandoning the Taurus, but that would only put her back at square one. 5:45. Marta had to get moving. The jury would be deliberating right now, even before dinner. Fuck!

HONNK! HHHOOONNKK!

Three cars ahead of Marta, Bobby Bogosian sat slouched in the driver's seat of his black Corvette. He checked the rearview to see if the bitch was still there. He couldn't see because she was so far back and snow kept falling on the back window, but he could hear her honking every five minutes.

Bobby laughed. It wasn't his fault he was blocking traffic. He'd been driving down Locust when the car died on him. Of all the luck. He'd called the Triple-A like a citizen, and they told him to wait, maybe he just needed a jump. So he waited and waited. He couldn't help it if he blocked the bitch's car. He was a motorist in distress.

HONK!

Bobby read a magazine while he waited, the new issue of *Dog World*. He read magazines like they were going out of style, but he never bought them at the newsstand, he only subscribed. It skeeved Bobby to think somebody touched his magazine before him.

He liked the subscriptions that came in a plastic bag, but not many did. The new *Dog World* had come today in the mail, and Bobby had taken it with him. He loved dogs.

HONK! HONK!

Bobby thumbed to the puppy ads in the back. He'd buy himself a dog, a pedigreed dog, as soon as he could move out of his shithole apartment and get his own house. He wanted a place in Delaware County that he could make into a kennel. He could become whatever you called it when you had a dog kennel. A *breeder*.

Bobby knew all about dogs. He knew the names of all the breeds, even hard ones like vizsla, and he could draw a pretty good picture of a rottweiler. Bobby went to the dog show every year when he wasn't in the joint and he would spend all day there, drinking strawberry smoothies, eating soft pretzels, and petting the pooches. It was a good show because you could hang with the breeders. They always had big spreads of food in the aisles of cages, and they were like a group.

HONK!

Bobby knew he would make a good dog breeder. It would be hard to sell the puppies, but he'd have to be professional, not get too attached. He turned the page. There was a picture of a little brown and white dog sitting on a plaid dog bed. It looked like the dog from *Frasier*. Bobby was pretty sure the *Frasier* dog was a Jack Russell terrier and bet the dog in the photo was one, too. To test himself, he covered the caption with his thumb. "A Jack Russell terrier," he said aloud, to lock in his guess.

HONK! HONK!

Bobby lifted up his thumb and squinted at the caption. He was nearsighted, but he didn't care if he went blind as a bat, he wasn't wearing glasses. Bobby held the magazine closer and the little letters came into focus. Jack Russell terrier!

HONK!

1

Judy Carrier stood outside the office building that housed Rosato & Associates on Locust Street, shaking her head in disgust. Erect was such a pill. She knew Judy would never leave Mary in the lurch. What kind of rock climber would leave a friend dangling by a rope? Judy sighed. Score another one for the forces of evil. It probably took that level of ruthlessness to be successful, but Judy wasn't willing to pay the price.

She pulled her ski cap down to her eyebrows against the blowing snow. The sky was an opaque gray that poured snowflakes. The weather report said the snow was falling at ten inches an hour. Judy loved it. Winter was one of the things she liked best about the East, especially a snowstorm this huge. It was Nature after assertiveness training. Reminding everybody that the natural hierarchy was greater than partners, associates, and secretaries.

But Judy had to get somewhere, and fast. She scanned the street. A caterpillar of traffic inched past her. How would she get there? Her car was parked on the street near her apartment and undoubtedly a snowcap by now. It would take too long to dig it out, much less drive it anywhere. Judy didn't have time to wait for a bus and a cab was an impossibility. Erect had taken the rental car, and it was too far to walk. The city was emptying out; soon the cars would be gone. Only the snow would be left, piling up on the street. Light, dry, flaky.

Perfect.

Judy planted her right pole until she hit asphalt, then skied forward on her left leg, gliding into powder so deep it buried her ski. She torqued her trunk easily and skied forward with her right leg, slipping into the natural swinging rhythm of cross-country skiing. Side to side, skating forward, in a yellow Patagonia parka and snow pants. It was less than an hour later and Judy was on her way, skiing through the inner city. It was fun. Just like Valley Forge, except for the crack vials.

She exhaled in deep lungfuls that puffed in front of her like a toy locomotive. Judy was sweating in no time despite the wind chill and blizzard conditions. It was growing dark and snow muffled the last of the workaday noises. Judy heard only her own panting, the *sssshhing* of her skis, and the cruel whip of the wind as her skis flew under the snow. She skied southwest, taking as many side streets as possible. Only a few cars braved the streets, their headlights piercing the flurries. Traffic got scarcer the farther out Judy skied and soon she was the only sign of life on the snow-covered street.

Judy enjoyed the growing sensation of solitude; it was the way she felt climbing, where it was only her and the rock. She dug her poles in and kept pushing. By the time she reached Grays Ferry, she felt completely relaxed. Her heart pumped happily and her muscles were warm and limber. It wasn't so wacky, skiing to get somewhere. At least no wackier than this assignment.

Going back to the scene of the crime, almost a year later. It made absolutely no sense. If the Commonwealth had found evidence incriminating Steere, it hadn't come from the murder scene. All the conditions had changed. The carjacking happened in late spring, not winter, and at midnight, not in the daytime. The assignment was absurd. Still, Judy popped out of her skis, left them and her poles by the curb, and walked, suddenly light-footed, to the spot under the Twenty-fifth Street Bridge where the carjacking had occurred.

Grays Ferry, the city's old slaughterhouse district, was a neighborhood marred by abandoned homes, deserted warehouses, and racial strife. The Twenty-fifth Street Bridge, which used to carry an elevated railroad through the neighborhood to points west, now cut a rotting swath to nowhere. The massive concrete pillars that buttressed it had eroded, their rusted reinforcement rods protruding like exposed ribs, and the underside of the bridge had crumbled off in chunks. Icicles spiked from

wide, jagged cracks rent in its bed, where its joints
had expanded and finally split open. The bridge
platform made a long roof over Twenty-fifth Street,
but it was low. A grimy sign on a pillar read WARN-
ING—MINIMUM CLEARANCE 13 FEET, 2 INCHES.

Dopey assignment. Judy stood in the street
directly under the bridge, where the double center
line disappeared under a dusting of snow. Two lanes
under the bridge ran in opposite directions, and
there was almost no traffic because of the blizzard.
The bridge sheltered Judy from the snow, but a brac-
ing wind snapped between the pillars and she felt her
eyes tear in the frigid air. The carjacking of their
client had taken place in the right lane, westbound.
Judy's wet gaze fell on the spot.

The first time she'd visited the crime scene,
blood had stained the gritty asphalt in a lethal pool.
Judy had never seen a crime scene before and had
stared at the blood for a long time, trying to appear
professional, which was code for emotionless. The
police had taped a cliched outline of the body in the
street and had set tiny cards, folded and numbered,
next to a bloodstain and a bullet casing, like grisly
place cards. Now the bloodstain was covered by
snow, as any leftover evidence would be. Boy, was
this dopey. Creepy and dopey.

Judy's muscles tightened in the cold and she
walked stiffly under the bridge to the cross street
where the killing occurred. She couldn't imagine
what evidence the D.A. could have on Steere. He
might have overreacted, but who could question

someone in that position? Judy mentally recon-
structed the crime. Steere had been driving home
after a fund-raising dinner at the University
Museum. The businessman had no date, even though
he was Philly's most eligible bachelor. He'd been
heading to his town house in Society Hill, but he'd
drunk a little too much and took a wrong turn from
Penn. It could have happened to anybody; Judy had
gotten lost in the University Avenue area herself
when she first moved to Philadelphia from Palo Alto.

Judy blinked against the snowflakes that strayed
under the bridge. To her left was a round concrete
pillar, one of the line bordering both sides of the
street. The pillars were thick, about four feet in
diameter, easily wide enough for a man to hide
behind. That was what had happened to Steere. It
was past midnight, and he had stopped at the cross
street under the bridge for the traffic light to turn
red. Steere had been driving with the car radio
cranked up. Judy liked that. It was the only thing she
liked about Elliot Steere.

There'd been no other traffic that night and no
one on the street. It had been warm and muggy, a
preview of a typical Philadelphia summer, so Steere
had put the top down on his convertible, a pearl-
white Mercedes two-seater. The car was new at the
time of the carjacking, and when Judy had inspected
it in the police impound lot, its pristine enamel was
sullied by a spray of dried blood. Judy had to exam-
ine the splatter pattern, standing behind Erect and
her blood expert. The expert found the pattern con-

sistent with Steere's account. Erect would have fired him if he hadn't.

Judy imagined Steere at the stoplight in the dead of night, sleepy and slightly buzzed behind the wheel of an expensive convertible. Suddenly, a large man jumps from behind a pillar. Steere thinks about hitting the gas, but the man yanks open the convertible door, sticks a knife at Steere's neck, and demands the Mercedes. Steere gets out of the car in fear, intending to surrender. He takes his gun with him just in case. But the carjacker slashes Steere's cheek, and Steere sees his own blood arc into the air, feels its warm rain on his face. He fights for his life. The gun fires while the two men struggle. The carjacker crumples to his knees and becomes the taped outline.

Judy shuddered as she stared at the white snow sprinkled on the street like so much baby powder and imagined the rich, red blood that was spilled. She even knew its composition: tests showed the carjacker's blood was Type O, and Steere's was AB. It had been Judy's job on the Steere case to maintain the trial exhibits, but nothing in them was helping her now. She squatted and brushed snow away from the spot with her hand, but found herself distracted by the snow's fine texture. Judy had been painting since she broke up with Kurt, who had left some of his art supplies behind. She was enjoying it and thought it made her more observant than she used to be.

Judy straightened and brushed off her knee. Everywhere was whiteness, the only splotch of color the traffic light at the cross street as it blinked from yellow to red, as it did the night Steere was attacked. Judy watched the traffic lights under the bridge changing and twinkling, their rich hues set in vivid relief against the snow. The red light glowed the brightest, tinging the icicles on its metal hood a crimson hue. The green registered cartoony, like green Dots candy. The yellow burned a hot circle like the sun; a dense chrome yellow, a Van Gogh color. Judy thought of haystacks and sunflowers and the rich gold of the artist's straw hat in a self-portrait. Judy could never get the yellows right in her own work.

Funny. Yellow, red, then green. Judy hadn't noticed it before and she wouldn't have noticed it at all but for the contrast between the snow and the colors. Under the bridge, where Steere had been attacked, the traffic lights were mounted sideways. Horizontally. They were bolted to metal frames under the buttressed ceiling of the bridge, maybe because of the low clearance. Thick covered wires snaked to the metal panel where the traffic lights sat in a row. Red was the leftmost circle, the yellow was in the middle, and the green light was at the right.

Odd. Judy couldn't recall seeing a traffic light set up this way elsewhere in the city, or at least it was uncommon. Nor did she remember it from her initial visit, when she'd been focused on the blood and the horror of the crime. Judy blinked at the traffic light, which blinked back. Colors shining bright against the white backdrop. The whiteness was just a blank sheet to her, without color of its own. Try as she might, Judy couldn't appreciate white as a color, only absence of color, and she couldn't imagine a world without color.

Then she remembered Steere's medical records, a joint exhibit of a hospital report. Steere had been taken to the hospital after the carjacking and an ER surgeon had stitched the slash under his eye. Another doctor had given him an eye test and noted that his vision was blurry. But Judy was thinking of the note in the medical records, *Dichromatism*. Color blindness. She had asked Steere about it later, and he'd said he was color blind and couldn't distinguish between red and green. Judy had wondered how he drove a car, but figured he knew which light was on top. Everybody knew that. Red on the top.

Wait a minute. Judy watched the traffic light under the bridge blink from red to green, sideways. How did Steere know the traffic light had turned red if the panel was mounted horizontally? There was no reason or logic to red being on the left. It could just as easily have been the other way around. There was no way to know, if you were color blind. Even if Steere did know it, he hadn't mentioned it in any of his interviews and he had been questioned in depth about the details.

Judy's heartbeat quickened. If Steere couldn't tell whether the traffic light was red, why did he stop, especially in this rough neighborhood? If you weren't sure a light was red or green and there was no traffic, wouldn't you go anyway? Was there something fishy about Steere's story? Had he meant to kill the man? Was this what the D.A. had learned?

Judy turned and hurried back to her skis. She wanted to talk to Mary about it before Erect got back. She pressed her boots into her ski bindings, slipped her hands into her pole straps, and took off for the office. It was almost dark and the snow showed no signs of letting up.

Judy skiied through the snowstorm, her eyes drawn to every light on the route back. Flurries swirled around traffic lights in whorls of red and eddies of green. Flakes swooped in fanciful halos around the white streetlights, standing out like impastoed brushstrokes against the night sky. The scene reminded Judy of *The Starry Night*, then of Van Gogh himself, and she found herself wondering how someone who appeared completely normal could, in reality, be utterly, truly, insane.

8

Mary DiNunzio slumped in front of the computer in her office and stared guiltily out the window at the falling snow. It was dark, and her best friend was out in a blizzard in the worst part of town because of her. The radio on Mary's desk reported that the temperature had dipped to five degrees, which felt like minus thirty with the wind chill. She snapped off the radio and pressed Judy to the back of her mind, but still couldn't concentrate.

Where was Marta? How much time was left? She glanced at her clock, a fake Waterford her parents had given her. 6:05. Shit. She had to keep working to have an answer on time. Marta had assigned Mary to read all the statements Steere made to the police and the press to see if there were any inconsistencies in his story. It was a stupid assignment, and Mary was having predictably lousy luck so far. She'd already read through the file, but it was completely consistent. Discouraged, Mary took a gulp of coffee from a mug that read FEMINAZI. At Rosato & Associates, even the dishware was political.

1955 of 2014 articles, said the computer.

Mary's brain buzzed with the caffeine. She used to drink a lot of coffee at Stalling, but at Rosato, coffee was a cult thing, with Bennie as Our Lady of the Natural Filters. Bennie's latest crusade was that the coffee wasn't hot enough, so she was actually perking the stuff on the electric stove in old-fashioned tin pots, like Mary's parents did. Mary sipped the scorching brew, winced in pain, and hit the ENTER key.

ELLIOT STEERE CHARGED WITH MURDER, read the headline, reduced to computer-byte size rather than tabloid screamer. Mary skimmed the first paragraph. The Philly newspapers, online at their own snazzy web site, had bitched about Elliot Steere since his rise in real estate development. Mary scrolled backward in time.

TRIUMPH BUILDING A LOSS, said a subhead, and the reporter detailed how Steere had bought the 100,000-square-foot building in 1975, a year after it was designated historic, with the stated intention of restoring it for condos. But the renovations never happened and Steere fell behind on the maintenance. Every year, Licenses & Inspections fired off a packet of citations for code violations, like a volley of blanks. Steere defended with lawsuits that tied the property up in litigation. In the meantime, the historic building crumbled. The story was repeated throughout the blocks of the city.

Mary sipped scalding coffee as she read. The article contained a litany of complaints against

Steere. The preservationists and Chamber of Commerce vilified him. Nobody was more vocal than the mayor of Philadelphia, Peter Montgomery Walker.

> "Elliot Steere is bringing down this city to his level," said Mayor Pete Walker in an exclusive interview with this reporter. "Frankly, by that I mean the gutter."
>
> According to the mayor's chief of staff, Jennifer Pressman, Mr. Steere presently owns 150 parcels in Center City, 82 of which have current fire and building code violations. In addition to his Center City properties, Mr. Steere is reputed to own hundreds of rowhomes in the city's outlying neighborhoods, with deeds recorded through a complex series of holding companies. Ms. Pressman said that the Mayor's Office is currently spearheading a review of these holdings.

Mary's conscience nagged at her. She was born and raised in Philly and was a huge fan of the mayor's. He'd managed to turn the city around and had plans to go further. The newspapers called it the "Philadelphia Renaissance," and it included a huge advertising budget to attract tourists, an Avenue of the Arts project that would build museums, a concert hall, theaters, and an entertainment complex on the Delaware River. The jewel in the crown was to be the newly developed historic district:

The city has launched a campaign to enliven the mile-square historic district, including a $20 million Visitors Center called Independence National Historical Park, to be built adjacent to Independence Hall and the Liberty Bell, as well as the nearby Colonial-era neighborhoods of Old City and Society Hill. Plans include the building of a Constitution Center on the mall adjacent to the United States Courthouse, unifying the area, according to Ms. Pressman.

All of these plans depended on the appearance of downtown Philly, which was unfortunately influenced to a large degree by Elliot Steere, who refused to repair his vast number of buildings. Why? Steere would waste his properties until the city paid his price to reclaim and restore them. He knew how critical his holdings were to the mayor's plans and he wouldn't sell until the price peaked.

Mary felt a second wave of guilt. Her hometown was trying to make a comeback and Steere was blackmailing it. Almost single-handedly obstructing the city's turnaround and, as a result, torpedoing the mayor's reelection. Mary bit her lip. She'd hoped she'd be working for the good guys when she joined Rosato. Hellfire licked at her pumps.

But Mary had to get to Steere's quotes if she was going to have an answer for Marta. She scrolled backward, going deeper into the online archives. She was praying Steere had said something to the media in the early stages of the investigation. God knows, he gave tons of interviews. She sighed and returned to the zillionth article.

> "I am absolutely innocent of any and all crimes charged," Steere told reporters. "It's a sad day when a man can't defend his own life without being harassed for it. This is a political prosecution. You know it and I know it."
>
> "Mr. Steere has no further comment," interrupted his attorney, nationally known criminal defense lawyer Marta Richter. "That's all for now, everybody."
>
> Members of the National Rifle Association protested Mr. Steere's arraignment by picketing in front of the Criminal Justice Center. Their spokesman Jim Alonso said, "We represent every decent American's right to defend his life and property."

A photo under the story showed Marta standing in front of twenty-odd microphones with a determined group of NRA types arranged decoratively in white T-shirts behind her. Each T-shirt had a red bull's-eye on the front and read PROTECTED BY SMITH & WESSON. Marta had orchestrated the demonstration but she couldn't convince the NRA guys to lose the T-shirts. Mary sipped her coffee, finally cooling. When would she work for the good guys? Or at least Democrats.

Mary hit a key for the next article, read more

quotes by Steere, then kept at it, article after article. She checked the clock. 6:15. Mary kept scrolling and reading, her heart sinking. She wasn't finding anything and it was getting later. Her head began to thud, a caffeine hangover. Still she kept reading, skimming each article until the boldfaced **Steere**.

6:31. Almost 7:00, and Mary still had no answer. She paused, rethinking the problem. Maybe she was using the wrong search. She'd been researching articles that contained the name Steere and was getting a civics lesson. Maybe she needed to approach it from a different direction. She tried to formulate a new search request, her eyes scanning her office for inspiration.

The office was small, tidy, and efficient. An antique quilt hung on the wall next to framed diplomas from Penn undergrad and law school and some honors certificates. There were two simple chairs opposite a pine farm table she used as a desk; her law books stood upright as altar boys on wall-mounted wooden shelves. Mary had decorated her office to inspire confidence in her clients while not offending corporate sensibilities. It was designed to make no statement but "HIRE ME PLEASE, YOU COULD DO A LOT WORSE." Which was precisely what Mary thought of her legal abilities.

Mary's gaze fell on her desk, atypically cluttered with papers from the Steere case, which had taken over her office the way it had taken over her life. She hated the case. A carjacking ending in death. Knives. Guns. Awful. Mary remembered the police photos with nausea and it hurt to look at the autopsy photos. Mary had seen too much death; her husband, and later. The Steere case wasn't helping to leave those memories behind. The next person who said "healing process" to her was getting a fat lip.

She stared at the Steere file and flashed on the photo of the dead homeless man, crumpled on the street in the fetal position. His eyes were open in death, his mouth an agonized black hole in a dense beard. Wild cords of his hair were soaked with blood. He wore baggy pants and no shirt. He'd had no ID or last known address, no friends or relations. The police had learned his name from the neighbors who lived near the Twenty-fifth Street Bridge.

His name was Heb Darnton. Mary had done the factual investigation on him and had interviewed the neighbors. They'd told her Darnton lived under the bridge, drunk most of the time. He used to shout at the passing cars but nobody thought he'd do any harm. The black community rose up at Steere's killing him. They demanded that Steere be charged with murder and demonstrated at the Criminal Justice Center, an inner-city counterpoint to the white suburban NRA members. Police with riot gear and German shepherds had to be called to keep order; for the cops and the press, the victim's identity became a detail as man morphed into symbol. Heb Darnton was forgotten in the fracas, but Mary never forgot a victim and never would. Because once upon a time the victim had been someone she loved.

The victim. Maybe that was it. Mary deleted the old search, typed in DARNTON, and hit GO.

Your search has found 2238 articles, reported the computer.

Ugh, no. She read the first couple, skimming for information about Darnton. The homeless man was mentioned only as Steere's victim. She read the next five articles. Nothing. She narrowed the search and put in Heb Darnton.

Your search has found 1981 articles, it said.

Mary skimmed the first few. They were the same as in the earlier search, but included Darnton's first name. Her brain was too tired to think and she drained her mug. She'd run out of gas. Christ. What kind of a name was Heb anyway? A nickname? She took a flyer, typed in HEB, and waited while the hard disk ground away. Then she caught the typo in the search request.

EB.

Damn it! Mary never could type. She'd tried to teach herself on that Mavis Beacon program, with no luck. She bought the software because she liked the pretty, entrepreneurial Mavis on the box cover and wanted to support her efforts. But Mary couldn't find the time to cyberpractice and then she found out Mavis wasn't even a real businesswoman, just a model. It was disillusioning.

Your search has found 23 articles.

Mary was about to delete the search request when her gaze slipped to the first article, about a farmer in Lancaster County outside of Philly, an

Amish man named Eb Stoltzfus. Eb and his friends were reportedly having problems with corn borers. Real helpful. Mary thought a minute. Eb. Ebenezer. She clicked to the next article. Sure enough.

> "'Ebenezer Squeezer' was my favorite song," said Jillian Cohen, a second grader at Glad-wyne Elementary School. "I liked it the best in the whole recital."

Mary jolted to alertness. Eb, not Heb? Ebenezer Darnton. Maybe that was the real name of the homeless man. The only way anyone knew his name was that he had told it to the neighbors. Maybe the neighbors were hearing Heb but he was saying Eb. The cops had followed their procedures for identifying him, but Mary had been more thorough herself in her neighborhood survey. She searched EBENEZER DARNTON and pressed GO!

Your search has found no articles.

Shit. It was 6:50. Maybe Marta would be late. Maybe Marta would die. Think, girl. If the search is too narrow, broaden the time. Mary hit a key to search all archives from 1950 to present.

Your search has found no articles.

What to do? Last try. She typed in EBENEZER and punched GO!

Your search has found 3 articles.

Yes! Mary punched up the first article. It was the police blotter from February 7, 1965. Her heart leapt with hope until she read:

A brown 1964 Oldsmobile was reported to be stolen from a parking lot on Joshua Road in Plymouth Meeting. Ebenezer Sherry of the Plymouth Meeting Police reported that this was the twelfth automobile stolen from township residents this year and feared that auto theft was on the rise, even in the suburbs of Philadelphia.

News flash. Crime spreads to suburbs. Mary sighed and hit a key for the second article. Maybe this was a bonehead idea after all.

Ebenezer Yoachim, 68, died today at Sinai Gardens Convalescent Home. Mr. Yoachim owned the Yoyo Dry Cleaners on Cottman Avenue and until his illness was a baritone in the barbershop quartet called the Troubadours. Mr. Yoachim is survived by his wife, Rachel Newman Yoachim, and his son, Samuel.

Mary felt let down. An obit. Couldn't be Darnton. One story left. She hit the key without enthusiasm. It was from April 12, 1965, and appeared in the business section.

Ebenezer Darning, of Greene Street in Center City, was promoted to teller at the main branch of Girard Bank.

Mary blinked, surprised at the similarity of the names. Darning/Darnton. She sat up straighter and scrolled down the page. Underneath the blurb was a thumbnail photo of a young man with a confident smile and a smooth chin. EBENEZER DARNING, said the caption. The man in the news photo was black, like Darnton. It was surprising. A black man promoted in that era? That was around the time of the Civil Rights Act. Racial discrimination was rampant then. Darning must have had brains and guts.

Mary leaned closer to the computer screen to see the bank teller's face. She couldn't tell what he looked like from the tiny photo, so she moved the computer mouse and clicked the cyber-magnifying glass over the man's face. The photo blossomed into pixelated squares but was still too small. The man's eyes looked closed, as if the shutter had been snapped at just the wrong moment. Mary clicked the mouse button again.

My God. She stared at the enlarged photo on the screen. The sight pressed her back into her desk chair. It was a photo of a young Eb Darning, but she could have been looking at an autopsy photo of Heb Darnton, his eyes sealed in death. Without the beard, there was a clear resemblance around the eyes, a protruding of the brow and a largish nose. It looked like the same man, over thirty years younger. Was Eb Darning the same man as Heb Darnton?

To be sure Mary needed to compare the computer image to the photos of autopsy photos in the file. Had she discovered something significant? Was this related to the evidence the D.A. had uncovered? Could everybody in the world type better than she did? Mary leapt from her desk chair and ran down the hall to the glass conference room.

9

The blizzard intensified as night fell outside the jury room in the Criminal Justice Center, but Ralph Merry was pleased. The jurors were going the right way, which was finding Steere innocent. Ralph believed 100 percent in the Fourth Amendment and argued that Steere was justified in defending himself when he got carjacked. Plus it would made a more upbeat ending for Ralph's book.

The jurors weren't allowed to sign any deals yet, but Ralph's wife, Hilda, had gotten calls from two literary agents in New York, who said several publishing houses were interested in the inside story of the Steere case. That's what publishing companies called themselves—*houses*—and Ralph thought they could call themselves whatever they wanted if they came through with six figures. Still, he wasn't going to make any deals with any *houses* until he made sure they would put his picture on the cover like they did with General Schwarzkopf's book. Ralph's book deal was this close, except that Kenny Manning was putting up quite a fight to convict.

"The man's guilty!" Kenny was saying. He had lifted himself from his seat and leaned halfway over the table on his strong arms, almost in Christopher Graham's startled face. "The brother walks up to the car, all the man had to do was drive away. That's it. He didn't have to *do* him!"

"Damn right," added Lucky Seven.

Christopher regained his composure and squared his broad shoulders as he stood behind his chair. He hadn't had much contact with black people, but he wasn't about to be intimidated by anything weighing less than a ton. "You can't look at it that way, Kenny. You have to put yourself in Steere's shoes."

"Fuck that, man. Steere had a SL600. Twelve cylinders! Car like that'll climb trees."

"Thas' right." Lucky Seven nodded, though Kenny ignored him.

"If I had a car like that and some crazy old dude come up to me, I'd take off and leave him spinnin'."

"If *I* had a car like that," Lucky Seven added, "I wouldn't be *here*."

Megan would have laughed if she weren't so anxious. She'd voted to acquit Steere, but didn't want to say so with this going on. The fighting was getting worse. She really wanted this trial over with. Her e-mail had already been deleted by AOL. Megan wondered if that guy she met in the chat room had written back. He even had his own webpage. Megan liked that in a man.

Christopher remained focused on Kenny. "But Steere was scared. He panicked."

"Ain't no call to panic!" Kenny shouted. "Dude was just drunk, is all. He wasn't gonna hurt nobody! He was jus' an old man talkin' out his mouth!"

Megan flinched at the decibel level, and Nick grew even more nervous. He couldn't believe this was happening. The voting, the hollering. He never decided anything without Antoinetta. His stomach was killing him.

"Gentlemen," said Mrs. Wahlbaum, who stood up at the middle of the table, a matronly fulcrum between Christopher and Kenny. Her form was stocky in a knit dress that flattened her generous bosom, and she raised her arms as if to separate the men. "Gentlemen, please. There are two sides to every story. We have to discuss this like civilized people, sitting down at the table, not shouting across it. You're calmer if you're sitting, you just are. It's your body language. I think it's a shame that that homeless man was killed, but I can't blame—"

"I wasn't talkin' to you, teacher," Kenny said, his smooth head snapping toward Mrs. Wahlbaum. "Back off."

"Just one minute, Kenny," Ralph said.

"I'm fine, Ralph." Mrs. Wahlbaum silenced him with a wrinkled hand. She knew the way to deal with bullies was to stand them down. "Why don't you both sit down, Christopher? Kenny? Just sit right down, both of you." She waved her arms at them, so hard she could feel the fat wiggle underneath. *Hadassah arms*, her sister-in-law called them, but that Yetta could go straight to hell.

Nick was getting more worried by the minute. He ate some Tums but his stomach was still on fire. He didn't like being here without his wife. Forty-two years he'd been married, and Antoinetta had made all the decisions. Paid the bills, cooked the meals, raised the girls. Nick wished he had something to relax him. He wished he had some milk. Milk was supposed to be good for ulcers. Or maybe some nice, cold anisette in a little glass.

Christopher folded his large frame into the hard chair, but Kenny didn't budge. "What?" Kenny said, with an incredulous laugh in Mrs. Wahlbaum's direction. "Teacher, you gonna tell Kenny Manning what to do, you got a lesson to learn."

"Kenny, I have forty years on you. You'd better show me some respect."

"Respect?" Kenny said, menacing her with a smile. "Show *you* respect?"

"The expert again," muttered Mr. Fogel. "The expert in sitting. She knows all about sitting. Ask her anything." He leaned over to Wanthida. "It's Iraq and Iran in here, and she thinks if they sit down, they'll make nice. Like it's automatic."

"I'm ignoring you, Mr. Fogel," Mrs. Wahlbaum snapped. Troublemakers hated being ignored. "Now, Kenny, you sit down. Sit, sit, *sit*!"

"Lady, you out your fuckin' mind?" Kenny spat out, his smile vanishing. "Who you think you are, be orderin' *me*?"

Ralph figured if he didn't step in Mrs. Wahlbaum would be dead. "Kenny," he said, "tell us why you think Steere is guilty. You can stand or sit, whatever you like. Make the case, like the lawyers. We'll listen. This is supposed to be a legal-type discussion."

"Hey, Ralph Mouth, back off my man," Lucky Seven said, and laughed nervously.

Isaiah Fellers sat off to the side, silent. He had voted not guilty the first time even though Kenny would be pissed off. The way Isaiah saw it, Steere was just protecting himself and his property. Didn't matter who was black and who was white. Steere had a right as a man.

"It wasn't an order, Kenny, it was a request," Mrs. Wahlbaum soothed. "Please. We have to reason together, all of us. Discuss it. Sitting down." Her knees were shaking slightly and she figured it was a good time to sit down. "See?"

Kenny stood alone, still braced on his arms at the other end of the table. Damned if he would sit down just because some Jew teacher told him to. She was dissing him but his arms were getting tired. The room fell quiet, waiting. Watching.

Nick wished he could cover his eyes. When the fighting stopped they'd have to vote again and he'd have to decide all alone. On his last visit with Antoinetta, she told him he should vote to convict. She said Mr. Steere was a crook and the Trolios had sold him their house for a song. But if Nick voted guilty he'd have to go up against all the other white people. He didn't know how to vote. When the paper came to him, could he write I STILL DON'T KNOW?

In the meantime Kenny had made a decision and

was pointing at Mrs. Wahlbaum. "Don't be tellin' me what to do, teacher. You understand what I'm sayin'?" His bicep knotted and nobody, including Nick, missed the small tattoo on his arm. It was a Chinese symbol that Nick couldn't read, which only scared him more.

"She understands," Ralph said, quickly.

Mr. Fogel shrugged his skinny shoulders. "Of course she understands. She understands everything. I bet she can predict the future."

"Fine, Kenny," Mrs. Wahlbaum said, knowing Kenny had to save face. "I understand."

"Just so you understand," Kenny said, a warning in his voice.

"I do. I understand."

"Good." Kenny slid into his chair almost as an afterthought. Lucky Seven didn't meet his eye.

Megan Gerrity glanced at her Swatch watch. Babies' heads tumbled around the circle. The watch was barely readable, but it was so cute. "It's almost seven o'clock. How late can we deliberate tonight? Does anybody know? Maybe we can fit in a final vote."

Kenny folded his arms like a musclebound child, but Christopher nodded, pleased. "We can deliberate as late as we want," he said. "We're supposed to call the judge and let the bailiff know when we want dinner."

They all wanted to vote again, except for Nick, who thought he was going to catch on fire. He sipped his water but it didn't put out the burning in his stomach. There was like a fireball racing up his throat. Nick couldn't keep it down. He blurted out, "I think I'm gonna be sick."

"What?" Christopher said, and around the table, eleven mouths dropped open.

10

Marta didn't reach Steere's Society Hill neighborhood until the Taurus's clock ticked to 7:01, but she was lucky to get there at all. The traffic jam on Locust had lasted forever, and she'd finally escaped it by driving up on the pavement for half a block and slipping down a side street. A frigid night had fallen and the snow blew harder. The windshield wipers pumped and the defroster had finally succeeded.

Marta looked for a parking space on the street near Steere's house. The cars parked at the curb were expensive lumps of snow. Society Hill was the most fashionable residential district in the city but apparently tough to park in. Marta drove around the block looking for a space. Her eyes kept straying to the clock's glowing digits. 7:04, 7:05, 7:06.

Fuck. It was getting late. She didn't have time to screw around with the goddamn car. The space didn't have to be legal, it just had to be open. There. Marta plowed through the snow and pulled up in front of the bus stop. She twisted off the ignition and climbed out of the car.

A cold blast hit her like a shock. Wind tore through her suit and raincoat. Snow chilled her shins and soaked her best pumps. Marta would have worn boots but she hadn't owned any since she was a kid. She spent her adult life going from airport limo to hotel, from cab to courthouse. She hurried down the street in a rut from a car tire.

The street was narrow, lined with costly colonial brick rowhouses, their restored shutters piled high with picturesque snow. Each house bore a historic cast-iron fire sign, but Marta cared little for history. Her own history would have damned her. One therapist had called her "self-realized" and she'd fired him for it.

Hey, mister! It's snowing hard again. *Please, mister, stop!* A blue station wagon stops. It looks big as a house. The front door opens wide and the man at the wheel wears black glasses and a tie. Marta doesn't want to get in, even though it's warm in the station wagon. She has a bad feeling about the driver. Something in his smile. Her mother is too drunk to notice. *Praise the Lord,* her mother says, and it begins again.

Marta pushed those memories away. Why were they surfacing now? Was it the snow? Didn't matter, she had no time for it. When she reached the corner, she squeezed between the parked cars, dumping snow on her legs, and climbed onto the sidewalk. The streets were deserted but lights were ablaze in the rowhouses along the street. Everybody was inside, hunkered down and riding out the storm.

Marta hurried down the sidewalk, passing first-floor windows. Warm yellow lights glowed through the slats of the wooden shutters. One living room had a fire in the fireplace and its flames flickered on the high ceiling. Marta imagined the families, snug and self-satisfied in·their homes; prosperous families, with cabinets full of food. Books lining every room and stacked on every coffee table. Mozart playing softly on the CD player. It was sheer fantasy, and it wasn't hers. Not anymore.

Marta shivered and churned ahead. She ducked to avoid the stinging snow and hide her face. Reporters could be waiting at the house, or the cops. She didn't want to be seen or recognized. Front Street, where Steere lived, was just around the corner. Steere's street overlooked the expressway and the Delaware River, and as soon as Marta turned onto Front, she caught a snootful of damp, snowy wind.

She clutched her collar closed and got a bead on Steere's house, sitting squarely in the middle of the street among other million-dollar houses. Marta slowed her step. She didn't see anyone in front of the house. A car traveled down the road slowly, and Marta sunk behind her wool collar and turned her face away. When the car had passed and the snowy street was silent again, she headed to Steere's town house.

It was a restored colonial of faded brick with

bubbly mullioned windows; four stories tall and the grandest on the block, too pretentious for Marta's taste. Marta adored houses and owned four if you included one condo; Steere's reminded her of her house in Beacon Hill, which was always cold, dark, and medievally drafty. Steere's town house was illuminated by a working gaslight next to its paneled front door, which sat off the street behind a six-foot brick wall. A skinny pile of snow lined the top of the wall, and in the middle was a locked gate of iron bars.

Marta hurried down Front Street to the house, wondering if the live-in maid was home. How else would she get in? The first- and second-floor lights were on, so Marta was hopeful. She reached the front gate, but it was too tall to scale even if she were desperate enough to try. Marta pressed the buzzer mounted next to an intercom in the brick wall. No response. She pressed the buzzer again, harder.

There was a crackling through the intercom, then the maid's voice. "Who is there?" she said, distinctly enough to be at Marta's ear.

"This is Ms. Richter, Mr. Steere's lawyer. I have to come in. Open the gate." There was a pause, then a metallic click at the gate's latch. The gate didn't budge, the mechanism evidently sluggish in the cold. "Try again," Marta said and gave the gate a solid push. It opened far enough for her to slip through and she climbed the few steps to the front door, which opened slightly.

The maid stood at the threshold, wrapping a

cardigan tightly over her uniform and squinting against the snow. Cold light from the entrance hall silhouetted her thin, short frame. Marta had met her once but had forgotten her name. "Missa Richter," the maid said. She was an older woman, and Marta vaguely remembered she was Polish or something.

Marta reached the top step and stamped her feet to defrost her shins. "And you're—"

"I go home now. My daughter, she need me. Snow day tomorrow from school," she chattered as she led Marta into the marble-tiled hall and closed and locked the front door. "I take your coat?"

"No, I'll keep it. I need you to help me. I have to find something for Mr. Steere. He asked me to bring it to him."

"Okay, okay, whatever you say," the maid said. Her face was lined with age and wear and her head of fuzzy gray pincurls bobbed. She seemed nervous, but Marta had grown accustomed to making people nervous and used it to good effect.

"Mr. Steere needs some special papers for his case. He said his girlfriend might have them. Do you know her phone number?"

"Girlfrien'?" The maid frowned.

"Yes. I know about his girlfriend. Do you have her number?"

"I don't, I have to go now. My daughter, she pick me up." The maid drew her sweater closer around her bony shoulders.

"What is his girlfriend's name? I have to reach her."

The maid shook her head, jittery. She glanced behind her and edged into a marble hallway. "I go now." She turned and hurried away, and Marta went down the hallway after her.

"Wait! Stop!" Marta hustled past a small elevator and a powder room. "Don't you want to help Mr. Steere? He'll be angry if you don't."

Marta found herself at the hall's end in a cavernous, book-lined library with cherrywood bookshelves extending to the ceiling. Rolling wooden ladders leaned against the shelves and leather wing chairs sat in front of a cold hearth. The library was empty. The maid had vanished. Across the room, double mahogany doors opened onto a spacious formal dining room with white marble floors. A set of modern, high-backed chairs sat around a long glass table dominated by a spiky crystal centerpiece, like a snowflake sculpted of glass. A frosted crystal chandelier cast shards of light around the room.

Where was the maid? Marta was spooked. She sensed the attack the split second before a pair of powerful hands seized her by the throat, choking the air out of her and lifting her bodily off the ground.

Bobby Bogosian squeezed the bitch's throat from behind and lifted her up by the neck. He held her there while she thrashed and grunted, running in the air like a fucking Road Runner cartoon. It wasn't like Bobby enjoyed the sight, because he didn't. He knew guys who got off on this shit all right, but to him it was a job. He was a professional. So when he thought the lawyer was gonna suffocate he threw her across the floor and she crashed into the dining room table.

"No!" she screamed, and Bobby thought it was funny how people always said "no." Like that would do anything. Like he could be persuaded. Just say no. He went after her.

Bobby covered the room in three bounds and shoved the bitch forward onto the table. Her head hit the glass thing in the middle and sent it crashing to the marble floor in a million pieces. Fuck! Now Bobby was mad. Professionals didn't make a mess. The fucking thing probably cost a thousand bucks. Fucking bitch.

She was howling and trying to kick and wiggle away, so he grabbed her hair and turned her around. He yanked her by the front of her blouse and slammed her head back onto the table. One shot, then another. Her eyes rolled around but she wasn't out yet. Stubborn bitch. Fine. He'd play it that way. Play it as it lays.

"What the fuck's the matter with you?" Bobby shouted in her face. "You broke that, you bitch!"

Marta tried to scream but couldn't. She gasped for air. Her throat closed. Her head exploded in pain. Tears of fright sprang to her eyes.

"What do you think you're doin'? Breakin' things! Trespassin'! You're a fucking bitch, you know that! You're a fuckin' cunt!"

Marta tried to catch her breath. Who was this man? What was going on? He was tearing the hair right out of her head.

"What the fuck do you think you're doin'?" Bobby slammed her head against the table again and shoved himself between her legs. He'd pin her to the table with his dick. Let the bitch feel it. See how she liked that.

Marta felt her legs wrenched open. Her skirt at her waist. No. Not that. She thrashed in his grip. Tried to push him away. Kick him, kill him. He banged her head harder against the table. Marta cried out in agony and terror. She fought with her hands. Clawed the air with her nails.

"You want to get in my good graces?" Bobby was screaming.

Marta was groggy from the blows. Her scalp was on fire. Warmth gushed from the back of her head. Blood. Hers. Her fear grew so intense it became remote. It was happening to someone else. She watched the violence as if from above and struggled to get her bearings. Think. Save herself. The man had been waiting in Steere's house. The man must know Steere. The maid had set her up.

"You want to get in my good graces? Answer me!" Bobby raged, spitting.

Above Marta the man's face was red with fury and hate. Her mind reeled. The man worked for Steere. Steere had sent him to stop her. Then he couldn't kill her and he couldn't rape her. She'd have to go on TV when the jury came back. Marta told herself she had the upper hand even though she was getting the shit beat out of her. Power was a state of mind.

"You want to get in my good graces? Answer me, you cunt!"

"You have graces?" Marta managed to say.

Bobby couldn't believe this whore! When it came time to do her, he might start enjoying his work. He pulled her head forward by her hair and rammed it back against the glass table again and again until she finally went out. It took two more shots than he thought it would.

Marta gasped as she bent over the sink in her hotel bathroom. Even the slightest movement sent pain arc-ing though her body. She must have bruised her ribs, and her back was killing her. Her head throbbed and her hands shook as she splashed warm water on her face and let it course down her cheeks. Marta was alive, but she was a prisoner. The thug was sitting in the living room of her hotel suite. He wasn't leaving until the jury came back.

Marta splashed more water on her face and tried to collect her thoughts. She'd regained consciousness in the man's Corvette, and he'd taken her to her hotel and walked her up to her room, pressing a Magnum between her battered ribs. How would she get free of him?

Marta twisted off the faucet and patted her face dry. Wincing, she reached around the back of her head, where a dozen goose eggs had hatched, and fingered the lumps to see if the bleeding had stopped. She came away with blood on her fingertips, her scalp swollen and tender. All her bruises were in back, hidden; a very professional goon. She opened the medicine cabinet stiffly and gulped three more Advil. Then she caught sight of herself in the bathroom's large, spotless mirror.

Marta's hair was disheveled, her makeup worn off. Her clothes were wrinkled and her gaze vacant. She hadn't eaten or drunk anything since lunch and her skin had a pinched, unhealthy pallor. Marta knew that face. She looked exactly like her mother after a binge. It was the last person in the world she wanted to be.

Praise God you picked us up! Our car broke

down back a ways. Me and the child here. Her mother pushes Marta into the front seat next to the driver of the blue station wagon. Gets in after her. Marta is thinking, No, that's not how we do it. You go in first, not me. But her mother is too drunk to remember. She closes them inside. Marta stares at the tall, silver stem of the door lock to make it stay up. The driver's knee bumps against hers as they drive off in the station wagon.

Marta shook off the echoes. She had to get going. She checked her watch. 8:30. Time was running out. What could she do? How could she shake him? Would there be more beatings? Something told her no. Steere wanted her paralyzed, not pulverized.

Marta unlocked the bathroom door and opened it quietly. She peeked through the crack and looked past her bedroom into the living room. She tensed at the sight of the thug even at a distance; her body remembered his blows even as her mind willed them to vanish. He was sitting on the plush sofa, his black cowboy boots crossed on the polished coffee table. He must have been six foot three, with a heavy brow, curly dark hair, and coarse features. He scratched his chest through a beige silk shirt as he read a magazine. He could have been somebody's lug of a husband but for the leather shoulder holster and Magnum.

Marta turned out the light and left the bathroom. The thug didn't look up from his magazine, and she eased onto her bed in front of the TV. A special news report was on. The mayor was holding a press conference, and she only half watched as a woman reporter shouted a question at him. Marta recognized the reporter from the Steere trial, a prom-pretty brunette named Alix Locke. Alix had dogged Marta for an exclusive interview, but Marta never gave exclusives, it was like making someone else the star. She feigned interest in the press conference while she tried to come up with her next move.

"Mr. Mayor," Alix said into a tall microphone in the aisle, "it's a yes-or-no question. Is there room in the budget to plow the side streets after this blizzard?"

If Mayor Walker was annoyed, it didn't show. He stood lanky, fit, and relaxed as a talk-show host. In the rep tie and rolled-up shirtsleeves he wore most of the time, the mayor was neither a handsome man nor an ugly one, with bright blue eyes, thick dark hair, and an electable smile. More persona than person, the image Mayor Walker projected was of a hard-working overgrown kid, just crazy enough to try and reverse the fortunes of a major American city. "Yes," the mayor answered, "there's ample room in the budget to plow the side streets, Alix. Didn't you read my budget? It's almost as good as Tom Clancy."

The reporters laughed and wrote it down. The press loved Mayor Walker, who, as far as Marta could tell, was a whiz at public relations. He kept his sentences short and grinned for every photo. He ate cannoli from an Italian bakery and fresh peaches from a Korean fruit stand; he was the first to check out a book from a new branch of the Free Library and the last to pet the anaconda at the Philadelphia Zoo. Most important, the mayor knew the secret to dealing with reporters: make their job easy, so they can go drink.

But Alix Locke wasn't smiling. "With all due respect, those residents who are snowed in may not find that funny when November rolls around."

The mayor's smile faded. "The residents of this city know it's not an issue of money. The issue is whether we can get the plows down the narrow streets. As you know, there are countless streets in this historic city which are barely one lane wide. It doesn't leave much room for a plow. With those streets, all we can do is our best."

"What exactly does that mean, Mr. Mayor?"

"It means that conventional snowplows won't fit down the street. They're too wide. We have to use the narrow plows and we're arranging now to buy them."

The reporters nodded and scribbled. Alix Locke pursed her lips and fumbled for a follow-up question. Marta leaned sideways and checked on the thug. He was still reading his magazine. *Dog World?* The man beat her to a pulp but he was kind to animals? Somebody explain this.

On TV, Alix Locke was doing her best Brenda Starr. "Mr. Mayor, you knew this problem would arise because it did last year. So the city had a year to order those snowplows. Why weren't they ordered and delivered by this storm?"

Marta stared at the TV images without seeing them. How would she get out of here? Then she had an idea.

12

Marta zapped the reporter into silence with the remote control and walked with discomfort to the living room. The thug looked up from his magazine, squinting slightly, and Marta stood at a distance, the nervousness in her smile genuine. She leaned on a large, paneled entertainment center near the telephone for support. "I have to call the office," she said. "You said no phone calls. What's a girl to do?"

"No calls."

"It's about the Steere case. It's important, and if I don't check in my associates will start to wonder. I said I'd be back at seven o'clock. I'm pretty punctual, and they know that."

"Tough shit."

"If I don't show up, they'll think something happened in the blizzard. Maybe they'll call 911."

The thug peered over the glossy magazine and his flat brown eyes registered skepticism. "So?"

"So they know this is my hotel. They may come

here looking for me, maybe send someone. You want to explain who you are? Why I'm here?"

"Shut the fuck up already." The goon set down the magazine. "What's the phone number?" Marta told him the number and watched as he plunked them into a Trimline phone on the end table, looking remarkably like a gorilla at a miniature piano. "Get on the extension and talk," he said, gesturing. "Keep it short. I'll be listening. Anything funny and it's over."

"Got it." In fact, Marta had counted on it. She picked up the receiver from the telephone on the entertainment center. "Hello?"

"Mary DiNunzio," the associate said when she picked up.

"Are you finished that motion *in limine*?" Marta asked, staccato.

"Uh, no. I mean, it's started, but it's not finished. I was doing the computer search. I found out that—"

"I didn't mean you should stop work on the motion!" Marta checked the thug's expression, and he seemed to be listening. In front of him on the coffee table lay the discarded dog magazine. It bore a battered subscription label, and Marta squinted discreetly to read the name. BOGOSIAN. "What happened to the motion? We have to file it tomorrow!"

"We do? We are?" Mary stammered. "Well, uh, I have the research, but I didn't write—"

"The research? Am I supposed to hand your research to the judge? Get started on it right now. I want it done by the time I get there." From the other end of the line came the sound of an associate sucking wind. Good. All according to plan. Marta hung up the phone, crossed her arms, and frowned at Bogosian. "Houston, we have a problem," she said.

"Huh?" He let his receiver clatter onto the hook.

Marta decided against explaining popular culture to a primate, especially one with felonies on the brain. "I have to go in. You heard her. She fucked up. I have to write that brief."

"I don't give a fuck."

"It's an important brief," Marta lied. "It has to be filed. I have to get to the office."

"You're not goin' nowhere."

"If I don't file a response, Steere's fingerprints will go to the jury. That evidence shows the placement of his fingerprints. It could put him in jail forever, maybe get him the death penalty. You want to tell him that or shall I?"

"You playin' games with me?" Bogosian's eyes flickered with malice, sending an undeniable tremor down Marta's spine.

"No. I'm just trying to do what your boss pays me to do."

"I don't have a boss, I'm self-employed."

"Fine. Steere, then. Whatever. This is no game."

"Oh yeah? Should I call Steere and find out if you're bluffin'?"

Marta laughed. "Steere's in a holding cell. You can't call him."

Bogosian smirked as he lifted the receiver, his

pinky finger extended absurdly. "Oh yeah? Why do you think they call it a cell phone?"

Elliot Steere was dozing in his cell when the flip phone in his breast pocket began to vibrate. His eyes flew open in alarm and he snapped his head to the corner of the cell, deftly slipping the phone from his pocket. "Don't call me," he whispered into the phone.

"Sorry, but I'm at the hotel babysittin' your lawyer. She wants to go to the office. Says she has to work on some motion. What do you want me to do?"

Steere glanced over his shoulder, where a black guard sat reading a paperback at his desk near the door. He was one of the night crew and never said two words to Steere. Steere's guard, Frank Devine, was on the day shift, and Steere hadn't gotten to any of the other guards. It was risky to deal with too many, and Steere hadn't anticipated the snowstorm, so he didn't know he'd need somebody at night. Another mistake. How annoying. "What motion?"

"Something about fingerprints. It's 'in somethin'.' Sounded like a foreign language."

Steere realized Bobby meant the motion *in limine*. The defendant's response had to be filed, they'd talked about it. But why did Marta want to work on it now? Why wouldn't she let it pass and fuck him up? It wasn't that important, was it? Steere paused, wary. "A motion, you're sure?"

"Sounds like the real deal. She talked to the other lawyer, a girl. On the telephone."

Steere thought a minute. What was Marta up to? He wanted to find out. "Let her go, Bobby, but go with her. Don't let her out of your sight. Do it." He hit the END button and returned the phone to his pocket just as the guard peeked in, his attention drawn by the movement in the cell. His scowling face loomed close to the bulletproof window.

"You say something?" the guard asked, rapping the window with a thick knuckle.

"Just talking to myself," Steere said. The guard turned his back, and Steere closed his eyes and rested his head against the unforgiving cinderblock. The wall was hard and scratchy, but in time Steere didn't feel it; he was weightless. The fluorescent lights were harsh and bright, but soon Steere didn't see them; it was pitch black. Steere sat very still, relaxed. Slipped back inside.

What could Marta be up to? It didn't matter. Even if she wasn't going to the office to prepare his motion, she wouldn't get away with anything. Bogosian would have her in control. She was way out of her depth with him; the man was a killer. Steere felt confident he'd made the right decision to let her go. Sun-Tzu would have said, *Make the enemy take a chance;* Elliot Steere would have said, Give Marta the rope to hang herself.

Steere considered the jury. He wondered if they were still deliberating and was satisfied that everything was in order there, too. He had specified that they not take long to acquit, and Steere's juror would obey him. After all, he had paid a substantial sum for a verdict of innocence. Justice didn't come cheap. Freedom can't be bought without foresight. It was a matter of taking the ceiling off your thinking, a vision thing, and all great leaders had it. As Sun-Tzu had said:

The victor first achieves victory, then conducts battle.

13

"AARRGHHH!" Mary DiNunzio had finally lost it. "AAARGH!" She buried her fingers in her hair and considered ripping it all out. She would perish from the endless work, and when they found her body, dirty-blond strands would be scattered around her like hay in a manger. The coroner wouldn't be able to explain the phenomenon, but any associate could. "WHY CAN'T PARTNERS EVER MAKE UP THEIR MINDS?" Mary shouted.

"Maybe she was kidding," Judy said, mystified. She sat in one of the chairs facing Mary's desk, bundled in a drippy yellow parka. Judy was still too cold to take it off, and snow from her boots melted onto the rug. The tip of her nose had thawed but she had a bad case of hat head.

"Kidding? Kidding?! Have you ever known Marta Richter to *kid* about anything?"

"It is odd," Judy said. She was thinking, something was fishy. Something didn't square. She couldn't put her finger on it. The blizzard was blowing outside and snow blasted past the window of Mary's office.

The temperature had dipped, and the police had warned everybody off the street. Why would Marta come out on a night like this to check a motion she knew wasn't written? Especially after she had put it on the back burner. "It really is odd."

"*Odd?* You think it's *odd*?" Mary began to laugh, a little crazily. "First she tells me to write the motion. Then she tells me to stop writing the motion. Then she screams at me for not writing the motion. You think that's *odd*?"

Judy nodded.

"*Odd* is not a word I'd use. *Odd* is a cakewalk compared to this. *Odd* is chump change."

"Well, it is—"

"SCHIZOPHRENIC! *Schizophrenic* is the word I'd use! Schizophrenic is what comes immediately to mind."

"Mary—"

"She's splitting, I'm telling you."

"Mare—"

"We got a bona fide multiple here, billing time."

"Wait. Relax. Chill. You sure Marta just said to do the motion?"

"I have ears, don't I? I heard her! Right on the phone, that's what she said!" Mary couldn't stop shouting even though she was giving herself a headache. "Look at my neck. Look at these blotches!" She opened her blouse at the neckline so Judy could see. "My head is going to explode! Warning, warning! Step away from the associate! Step away from the associate!"

"Maybe it's menopause," Judy said thoughtfully.

"I'm too young for menopause!"

"Not you, doof." Judy rolled her eyes. "Erect. Maybe Erect is going through the change."

"Not possible. Erect has no estrogen. Nobody with estrogen could do this to another human being." Mary deflated into her chair. Her head fell into her hands and she raked her hair back again and again. "Oh, God, why am I a lawyer? Why couldn't I have been a cowboy?"

Judy watched her with a twinge of regret. She'd gotten Mary into this mess. Made her leave Stalling & Webb to start their own firm, which never got off the ground. Still, something very odd was going on, and Mary wasn't getting it. "Listen, Mare. Marta Richter is a world-class trial lawyer. She's not stupid. And she may be compulsive, but she's not crazy. There must be a reason for what she's doing."

"No, there isn't. She's still a partner and they're all alike. I don't care if she's a woman and I'm supposed to like her. She should burn in hell. I should find another job."

"Think about it. Maybe Marta is seeing something we can't. Something we don't. It's like Van Gogh, seeing the colors we don't."

Mary kept shaking her head. "I have other skills, don't I? What color is my parachute?"

"Yellow."

Mary blinked, pained. "Yellow?"

"The yellows of Van Gogh. He can see them, but we can't." Judy shifted forward in her parka. "This is the same thing. Marta can see something we can't. We have to figure out what she's seeing, what she's doing. She's like Napoleon."

"Napoleon?" Mary was getting dizzy. Sometimes she thought Judy was just too smart for them to be friends. She needed a dumber friend. "I thought we were talking about Van Gogh."

"You know that story about Napoleon? That famous battle he was in?"

"No idea."

"You know it."

"No, I don't."

"I know you know it, Mare."

"I don't know it!" Mary wondered if Judy, Marta, everyone around her was going crackers. Maybe it was the snowstorm. Cabin fever, early onset. "Judy, what are you talking about?"

"Napoleon was in a battle, I forget which, and there was so much smoke and dust he couldn't see what was going on." Judy unzipped her parka. "Nobody could see what was going on because of the smoke. The sides who were fighting couldn't even see each other to shoot."

"Okay." Crackers. Losing it. Too much coffee. Not enough coffee.

"Napoleon told his lieutenants where to move his men anyway, in response to what he knew the other side would be doing. No one understood what he was doing, but he could direct the battle without seeing anything. All his soldiers thought he was nuts. But when the dust settled, who do you think won?"

"The lawyers?"

Judy laughed. "That's not funny."

"Yes, it is. You laughed."

"You're missing the point."

"No, you are. I have a motion to write and Napoleon will be here any minute."

"Is that all you're worried about?"

"No, but we'll talk about it on the way." Mary stood up and headed for the conference room, with Judy dripping behind.

Fueled by a pot of blistering Hawaiian Kona, Judy and Mary started to draft the motion, but they kept getting distracted talking about whether Heb Darnton was Eb Darning and Steere's color blindness. The more Judy thought about it, the fishier it got, and her suspicions solidified into theory. "Is it really possible that Steere intended to kill Darning?" Judy asked.

"Why? What's his motive?" Mary couldn't ignore the draft of the motion on her laptop and wondered how much time they had before Marta got back. "Where do you think Marta called from?"

"I don't know, you talked to her."

"I think she was at the hotel." Mary hit a key on the laptop and read the beginning of the last paragraph: **Traul courts aroudn the country have long held such evidence inadmisssable.** Goddamn Mavis Beacon. Betty Crocker wannabe. Mary rolled the trackball to the icon for Spellcheck. "So how long until Marta gets here and starts screaming?"

"A half hour if she takes a cab."

"Think that's enough time to finish the brief?"

"No."

"Okay, so what's his motive?" It was intriguing, but it wasn't work. Mary hit the SAVE key on the computer, to save her job. Maybe that's why they called it SAVE.

"I'm not exactly sure about motive, but think what we know about Steere. He's an egotist. Arrogant. Ruthless. A heartless asshole."

"Don't mince words now. And plenty of people are assholes. They don't commit murder because of it. It's not enough for motive." Mary noticed her laptop screen turn blank and her brief drift into power-saving sleep.

"Yes it is, in a way. It's a power thing. When some poor black guy tries to carjack Steere, he knows he can kill him and get away with it."

"That's quite a stretch, isn't it?" Mary reached into the center of the table and picked up the printout of Darnton/Darning's photo from the computer archives.

"It's consistent with Steere's personality."

"True, but it's not enough. If Steere killed intentionally, it has something to do with Darnton, if he is Darnton. Because he's Darnton, not because he's homeless." Mary scrutinized the photo for the umpteenth time and mentally compared it with the gruesome autopsy photos. "I bet Heb Darnton is the same man as Eb Darning. He'd be the right age, about fifty-one, fifty-two. Does it look like the same man to you, only older?" She slid the photo across the table to Judy, who caught it midway.

"He didn't age well, did he?" Judy asked, studying the photo. "You got a theory? Go with it."

"Let's say Darnton—Darning—is the man in the photo," Mary said tentatively. "He used to be a guy with a job, but now he's homeless. It happens every day. We know he was alcoholic, the neighbors told us that. Let's say he started drinking after he left the bank teller job and went downhill from there. Lost his job, his girl. Grew a beard."

Judy set down the photo, thinking aloud. "So you think this has to do with Darning?"

"Maybe. Maybe it wasn't a chance meeting between Darning and Steere. Maybe they knew each other."

"That's even dopier than what I said." Judy screwed up her large features, and Mary raised her hand like the Pope.

"Hear me out. Put together what we learned. Let's say Steere didn't know the traffic light was red. If he didn't, his actions don't make any sense, right?"

"Right. Unless he was really blitzed, which he wasn't, according to his blood tests."

"Besides, Steere's a big guy. He can absorb a lot of booze." Mary sipped coffee from her mug, more for courage than caffeine. "Steere's stopping under the bridge doesn't make sense unless you assume he wanted to meet Darning. They could have arranged to meet under the bridge. Assume Steere was stopping regardless of the light, to kill Darning. Then he made up the whole carjacking story."

"The carjacking was a lie?"

Mary shook her head. "Not a lie, a *setup*. Work with me. Remember, it's not a chance meeting." Although Mary was only thinking aloud, she felt her pulse quicken. "Steere was driving a new Mercedes. Two weeks old, right?"

"Let me double-check." Judy rose and went to the third accordion file. She flipped through the manila folders until she found the right one, yanked it out, and opened it up. "Here we go. The bill of sale for Steere's new car. It was three weeks old. $120,000! Wow!"

"What did he trade in? Bet it didn't look like the Snotmobile." By that Mary meant her ancient BMW 2002, the only chartreuse car ever sold.

"Look at all this stuff." Judy was agog. "'Airbags, leather-covered steering wheel and gear lever, speaker blanking plates integrated on the left and right side of the dashboard—'"

"Jude, what did he trade in?"

"I wonder what a blanking plate is. How could I graduate from law school and not know what a blanking plate is?"

"Judy! The trade-in."

Judy flipped to a series of long white documents and screwed up her face in triplicate. "Oh, here. Jeez. He traded in a Mercedes sedan. An S500. V-8. It says 'Five-Sitzer, four Turen.'"

"How old was the trade-in?" Mary craned her neck to read the document. "How many miles on it?"

"Half a year old. It had fifteen hundred miles on it." Judy looked up and the two associates locked eyes.

"It's not as if Steere needed a new car, is it?" Mary felt an ominous churning in the pit of her stomach and it wasn't the coffee. Suddenly the brief didn't matter and neither did her job. "What if Steere planned this whole thing? What if he bought the car to make the carjacking more plausible? What if Steere arranged to meet Darnton—Darning—to kill him? That's murder. Premeditated murder."

Judy cocked her head, skeptical now that Mary's expression was turning so grave. "You mean Steere used the new Mercedes as bait?"

"No. I mean Steere intended to kill Darning for some reason and bought the car in advance of that— to make the carjacking more plausible."

"Wait, wait, slow up. You're serious about this?"

Mary nodded. "It fits, doesn't it? It's consistent with what we found. Maybe Steere is a murderer." It made Mary sick to say it. "And we defended him. We probably got him off."

"Mary, wait." Judy shook her head. "Just because Steere bought a new car doesn't mean he's a murderer. Rich people do stuff like that all the time. An impulse purchase."

"A convertible? A white Mercedes that cost as much as a house?"

"So he's a show-off, and it was almost summer."

"Judy, he bought the most conspicuous car in history and drove it through the worst neighborhood in history. In the middle of the night. Isn't that suspicious? I mean, if you wanted people to believe you'd been carjacked, you'd go out and buy a car that was flashy enough to steal. Steere was making it look like random street crime when it was really murder."

Judy flopped back in her swivel chair with a sigh. Her lower lip puckered with concern. She was sorry she'd started all this, with the color blindness. She worried Mary was seeing murder mysteries because of her past. "But how could the D.A. prove this?"

"I don't know, they're a good office. Maybe they found some sort of after-discovered evidence. Your tax dollars."

Judy's eyes narrowed. "You still have a motive problem, Mare. Why would Steere want to kill Darning?"

"I don't know." Mary paused, then brightened. "Maybe there's a motive and we just don't know it yet. We don't have enough information. If we find the connection between the two men, we find the motive."

"What connection? There is no connection. One is at the bottom of the food chain and the other is at the top."

Mary blinked as the answer struck her. "What is the connection between a rich man and a bank employee? Get a clue. It rhymes with money."

Judy considered it. Maybe it wasn't completely nuts, or paranoid. "Wait a minute." She got up and searched the Steere file again, checking each accordion. "What bank did Darning work in?"

"PSFS. The Philadelphia Savings Fund Society. They're out of business now, but they still have the neon sign on top of their old building. You know the sign."

"PSFS? Sign? No."

"It's on the building, on the east side of town. It's huge, you can't miss it. It's a historic landmark now. You know it."

"Didn't we just have this conversation?"

"Forget it." Mary's headache returned. It was too late to be working. What a job. Mary remembered the plastic PSFS passbook she had as a child, in trademark tartan. It had an inky little S that stood for Student Account. Where was that frigging passbook now? Maybe she was rich and didn't know it. Then she could quit.

"Here it is." Judy had flipped to the back of a thick document and handed it to Mary. "Steere's most recent tax return. It shows all his bank accounts, even under his corporate names. None of them are at PSFS." Judy flipped through the other returns in the folder. "Even as long ago as five years, nothing says PSFS."

Mary read down the list on the tax form. Her heart stopped midway. "Steere has two accounts at Mellon Bank, for $100,000 combined. Now why would he leave that much money in an account that earns almost nothing?"

"What's the difference? Mellon Bank isn't the one Darning worked in."

"Yes, it is. Mellon bought PSFS about five years ago."

Judy blinked. "For real?"

"Mellon came out of Pittsburgh in the eighties and started buying up all the Philly banks, including Girard, which was a real Philadelphia thing. My mother won't bank at Mellon because they had the nerve to buy Girard."

"Odd."

"My mother?"

"No. I love your mother. I like your mother better than you do."

But Mary was thinking. "Maybe Darning rose up in the ranks at the bank, and there was some finagling with Steere's accounts or something. Bribes. Embezzlement."

"You're guessing."

"Can you blame me?" Mary asked, but that was all she said or needed to. She didn't want to talk about the past, she didn't even want to think about it. And she certainly didn't want to relive it.

Suddenly there was a commotion outside the conference room. The lawyers heard Marta talking to someone and sprang into action like Pavlov's associates. "Yikes!" Judy yelped, snatching the papers and photos from the table and stuffing them in the nearest accordion. "How'd Erect get here so fast?"

Mary punched a key to wake the laptop. "She took the broom."

14

Judge Harry Calvin Rudolph brooded at his heavy, polished desk in his modern chambers at the Criminal Justice Center, fingering the handwritten note that threatened to put the kibosh on his judicial career. The promotion of a lifetime was in striking distance, and Judge Rudolph wasn't about to let it slip away, not at his age. His hands had only recently begun to sprout liver spots and the strands of hair sneaking from under his French cuffs were just silvering to gray. Judge Rudolph was in his prime as a jurist. A scholar, a leader. He could make history.

Before he presided over the Steere case, Judge Rudolph had spent fifteen years on the Common Pleas Court of Philadelphia County. He'd wanted to be a judge so much in the beginning, he'd left private practice when it was beginning to prosper. Money wasn't everything, and young Harry was drawn to the scholarship, trappings, and prestige inherent in a judge's station. A robe, a gavel, a dais. He imagined what his Bucknell classmates would think. The frats who ignored him at rush week. Now Harry Rudolph was not only in the frat, he *was* the frat.

Judge Rudolph twisted the piece of yellow legal paper in his hands, remembering his idealism in the beginning. Leave it to others to fight for money; let his colleagues battle for the ephemeral power of partnership. Judge Rudolph's power was real, lasting, reinforced by judicial might. In his tenure on the bench he caused fortunes to change hands, ordered criminals to jail, and even locked up a couple of reporters. Judge Rudolph administered justice. When you had that, who needed money?

Fifteen years later, Judge Rudolph did. Fifteen years later, money was all he needed. The income of his peers had skyrocketed past his, even though he was making a hundred grand a year. He'd heard that Blumenfeld was taking home $450,000 at Dechert Price & Rhodes and Simonsburger was raking it in at Morgan, Lewis. Hell, *everybody* was raking it in at Morgan, Lewis. Judge Rudolph couldn't stand to look at their faces at reunions, law review banquets, or those rare occasions when his classmates appeared before him in court. He knew they were having the last laugh on the way home. In the Jag.

Judge Rudolph set the note down. If he held it in his hands any longer he'd tear it in two. He stared at it in contempt, there on his soft green blotter in the middle of his glistening desk. Just last week, Dave DeCaro came to court defending a CEO at Witmark. DeCaro was tanned from a vacation on Grand Cayman. A winter vacation to the *Caymans*, for God's sake, with all six kids and his wife. Judge Rudolph couldn't have done that in a pig's eye and he was ten times the lawyer DeCaro was.

The judge laced his fingers in front of him, studying the note. Christ Almighty. Not now. There was an opening coming up on the state Supreme Court, and Judge Rudolph was a shoo-in for the nomination. Justice Harry C. Rudolph. Chief Justice H. C. Rudolph. *Superchief.* He wasn't about to let this note ruin everything. Not his last chance.

The Steere case had gone so well and the judge had done everything right so far. No cameras in the courtroom; a gag order as soon as the lawyers started yapping. Only fifty spectators at a time; all press conferences after business hours. Two side-bars a day; arguments limited to five minutes a side. He'd even seen to it that the Steere jury could deliberate through the snowstorm · and bound Steere over at the courthouse. They didn't call him "Rocket Docket" Rudolph for nothing, and that was exactly the kind of thing that got the attention of the big boys. Keep the cases moving and don't fuck up the felonies. Steere was the case that would make him a Supreme Court justice. If this note didn't queer it.

Judge Rudolph fumbled beside his blotter for his reading glasses. Maybe he had misread it, in anger. Then again, maybe not:

*YOUR HONOR, ONE OF THE JURORS HAS A MEDICAL
EMERGENCY AND WANTS TO TALK TO YOU.*

*SINCERELY,
CHRISTOPHER GRAHAM, YOUR FOREPERSON*

The judge snapped off his glasses and barked,
"Send him in!"

"You were a tailor, Mr. Tullio?" Judge Rudolph
glared over his glasses at the juror, who couldn't have
been more than five feet tall. He wore a brown suit
with a hand-stitched lapel, worn thin.

"Yes, Your Honor. Until I retired. Your Honor.
Sir."

"You live in South Philadelphia, near Second
Street. Is that right?"

"Yes, sir. Your Honor. Near the museum."

"But the art museum's on the parkway."

"The Mummers' museum, I mean." Nick nodded with jittery vigor. "Got the Mummers costumes
and all. In glass."

Judge Rudolph cleared his throat. "Mr. Tullio, I
understand you have a medical emergency. Do you?"

"Yes. No. Your Honor. Not an emergency. I'm
not bleedin' or nothin'."

"I can see that."

"I just heaved, is all."

Judge Rudolph sighed deeply. "Is that your medical problem, Mr. Tullio? You—"

"Heaved." Nick slipped in the red cushion in the chair across from the judge's big desk. The seat was too wide and slippery for his heinie. He had to hold on to the armrests just to stay up. Nick kept looking around but not so it was obvious. It was just him against the judge and the clerk and the lady with the machine. Nick had never been in such an important place as a judge's chambers, with the papers and books and paintings. Thank God he was wearing his good suit. It paid for a man to be well dressed.

"Mr. Tullio? Your medical problem is that you . . . vomited?"

"It's my ulcer."

"You have an ulcer?" asked Judge Rudolph, correcting the man, who'd pronounced it "elcer."

"Yes, an elcer," Nick said anyway. "In my stomach. I want to go home."

Judge Rudolph would be damned if he'd lose a juror now. He'd sent the alternates home already, and it would take hours to get one back in the snow. The judge skimmed his voir dire notes, then the juror's questionnaire in front of him. "You didn't mention an ulcer in voir dire, Mr. Tullio. You didn't say anything about an ulcer."

Nick slipped sideways in his chair. "I wasn't sure I had one then. I mean, my doc said I don't have one, but I know I do. It's acting up from my nerves. It's burning."

"Your doctor examined you and he said you don't have an ulcer, is that right?"

"Well, yeah. But my stomach has a hole in it, I

can tell. And I heaved, which is like, proof. Your Honor. Sir."

"Do you need to see a doctor now?" the judge asked, as his stenographer tapped away. He was asking only for the record. A doctor wouldn't work on a night like this, doctors made too much money. Only judges had to work on a night like this. Trial judges.

"No, I don't need no doctor. I ate six Tums. Tropical flavor."

"Fine. You don't need a doctor."

"But my stomach hurts. From my nerves."

"You have an upset stomach, is that what your problem is?"

"Yeah."

Judge Rudolph leaned back in his chair and snapped off his glasses. He examined their tiny hinges while he thought about his record. He had handled this issue. Kept it from the press and anyone outside his chambers. Blocked the lawyers out of the action with the promise of a next-day transcript. Downgraded an ulcer to an upset tummy. Time to get the tailor back to the jury room. "Perhaps if you had something to drink, you'd feel better."

Nick's throat caught with hope. "You got anisette?"

"For an upset stomach?" Judge Rudolph pursed his lips. All my trials, Lord. No pun intended.

"It relaxes me. My stomach."

"Forget it," the judge said flatly. "You're in deliberations. You can have any nonalcoholic beverage you want. Soda or hot tea, a beverage like that."

"Maybe a nice glass of milk?"

Judge Rudolph waved at his law clerk. "Joey, go get Mr. Tullio some milk."

"Milk?" repeated the clerk. "We don't have any milk." He was a short kid who didn't look Italian to Nick, even though his name was Joey.

The judge frowned. "What do you mean, we don't have any milk?"

"There's no milk in chambers, Your Honor."

"Not even in the fridge?"

"No, Your Honor."

"You put milk in my tea, don't you?"

"No. I put cream."

"Christ, Joey. Get the cream then."

Nick raised his hand weakly. "Uh, I can't drink cream. It's too heavy."

"This is *light* cream," the clerk countered.

"It has to be milk," Nick said, but the judge and the clerk stared at him together. Nick wondered if they could sue him. Maybe he shouldn't have said anything. So what if he heaved? He wouldn't die. Nick felt himself slipping deeper into the big chair. He felt like he was drowning, like the only thing keeping him above water was the armrests. "Listen, I don't need no milk. You can forget I said anything about milk, Your Honor. Joey, forget it."

"Not at all, Mr. Tullio," said Judge Rudolph. He was protecting a record, not a stomach lining. "If you need milk, we'll get you milk."

"That's okay. That's all right." Nick shook his head nervously. "I don't even like milk. I hate milk.

Never liked it from when I was a little kid. I only drink it 'cause Antoinetta says to. If I never saw no more milk, I'd die happy. You can't die from heaving, can you? It was like, dry heaving."

Judge Rudolph slapped his glasses back on. "Mr. Tullio, if we had milk, would you drink it?"

Nick blinked. He wasn't sure if you could lie to a judge and if you did, would you go to jail. Maybe it was like being under oath when you came into a judge's room. Maybe it was like you swore on a Bible. Nick was sorry he said anything about his stomach. He shoulda just voted innocent like the other white people. He wished Antoinetta was here.

"Get Mr. Tullio his milk, Joey," ordered Judge Rudolph.

The clerk blanched. "Your Honor, I don't know how I'd get milk in a snowstorm. I'm sure all the stores are—"

"I don't care which tit you have to squeeze, Joey. Just get him the goddamn milk."

"Yes, sir," the clerk said and took off.

Judge Rudolph's gaze stayed pinned to the tailor. This conversation should have been over ten minutes ago. The juror should be deliberating, not sitting in chambers complaining about his tummy. For God's sake. Judge Rudolph hated the trial level. He belonged in the appellate tier, where the talk was about the law, not elcers.

"I hope Joey's okay out there," Nick said, just to make conversation because the judge looked so mad at him.

"I'm sure he's fine."

"Prolly."

"Probably," the judge corrected him.

"Okay. Good. He prolly is," Nick said, just to agree, but Judge Rudolph only looked madder.

"I'm not worried about my clerk, Mr. Tullio, I'm worried about you," Judge Rudolph said, though he didn't mean a word of it. He was worried about how that "tit" would play in the newspapers if it came out. Would women's groups oppose his nomination? "Remember, Carol," he said to the stenographer, "this transcript is sealed until I say further."

Carol nodded, understanding. She'd worked for Judge Rudolph since her divorce. If he went up to the Court, he'd take care of her. She'd skip a couple grade levels and the benefits were out of this world. "Yes, Your Honor."

"Thank you." The judge turned to the tailor and tried to look sympathetic. "Mr. Tullio, if you have no other problems and you're not in need of medical care, you can return to the jury and resume your deliberations."

"Uh, what? You mean, uh, go back?"

"Yes, of course. I'll send the milk in as soon as it arrives. The jury has a job to do right now, a very important job. Dinner tonight is scheduled for seven-thirty, under extended hours. You can get some sub-stantive deliberation in before then, I'm sure."

"I don't know. My nerves. The stress."

Judge Rudolph leaned farther over his desk, almost in the tailor's face. He'd be damned if he'd let this pipsqueak screw him over. "You're not telling me you're too sick to deliberate, are you?"

"Well, no. I mean, yeah. Yes. In a way. Your Honor."

"But you don't need a doctor."

"No, Your Honor."

"All you need is milk."

"Yes, Your Honor. Sir."

"So why can't you go back and discuss the case?"

Carol cleared her throat noisily, warning the judge off. Judge Rudolph knew he was treading on dangerous ground, especially since he hadn't called the lawyers in. How close was he to reversible error? Where was that goddamn law clerk? Damn!

"I can't go back because my nerves . . ." Panic seized Nick and strangled the life from his sentence. He felt too scared to talk and too scared not to. He couldn't go back to the jury and he couldn't stay here with the judge. It was like he was caught in the middle and something was squeezing him in a fist. "I just wish Antoinetta was here," Nick croaked, near tears.

Judge Rudolph scrutinized the tailor, scanning his working-class features and searching his wet and rheumy eyes. Suddenly, the judge felt as if he could see into the man's shopworn little soul. He understood what was happening, comprehended it with a crystalline clarity he hadn't experienced since his law review comment. "I know just what you need, Mr. Tullio," the judge said.

"You do?" Nick asked.

"Yes." Judge Rudolph breathed in deeply and his chest inflated. When he ascended to the bench of the Pennsylvania Supreme Court, he would do great things for the citizens of the Commonwealth. But right now he wanted them out of his chambers.

15

"I'm comin' into the conference room with you," Bogosian said as he faced Marta in the hallway at Rosato & Associates.

"No." As threatened as she felt inside, Marta had to stand her ground.

"I gotta hear what you're sayin'."

"You can't." Marta watched him eye the two young associates through the glass wall of the conference room. They were cleaning up the file, and Marta didn't want Bogosian anywhere near them. She felt bad enough leading him to them. She wouldn't jeopardize them further. "You can't come in. It's a privileged conversation."

"Big fuckin' deal," Bogosian said, though he had only the vaguest idea what she meant. So many fuckin' words. He hated lawyers. He never had an honest one in his life, and they couldn't keep him out of jail.

"How am I going to explain who you are?"

"I don't give a fuck. You're not leaving my sight."

Marta pointed a short distance down the hallway. "Look, there's another conference room directly across from the one I'll be working in. It has glass walls like the one I'll be in. You can see everything I'm doing. I won't make any phone calls, and if one comes in, you can listen in on your phone."

"You think I'm stupid? You could tell the other two lawyers."

"And put them in danger? Never."

"Fuck that. I'm comin' in with you," Bogosian said, and stepped so close Marta almost freaked. The last time he had been this close he'd beaten her unconscious. She suppressed the fear rising in her throat and walked neatly around him to the elevator bank, punching the DOWN button with authority.

"Then I'm not working on the motion," Marta said, struggling to keep her voice strong. "Take me back to the hotel right now. You can call Steere and tell him his fingerprints are coming into evidence."

"Fuck you."

"Fine. I'll call him as soon as we get back."

"You're bluffin'."

"Am I?" Marta turned and forced a smile. The beauty shot. "Want to find out?"

Bogosian thought a minute. What a bitch. Steere would go ballistic if Bobby called him on the cell phone again. And Steere did say he wanted the motion done. Bogosian figured it would be okay if he could watch her. Besides, what could she do? She was just a broad.

❖   ❖   ❖

"What have you got for me, ladies?" Marta barked at the associates. She closed the conference room door behind her and pulled out the seat at the head of the table. She was trying to hide her anxiety, but she wasn't fooling Judy, who appraised her with a critical eye. Her blouse was wrinkled, a first for Erect, and her eyes drooped as if she were in pain. Something odd was definitely going on. Judy would have asked Marta if she were okay, but Erect didn't invite that sort of inquiry. And Mary had an agenda.

"Marta, I have something to tell you," Mary said. She stood up nervously, her neck blotchy under her blouse. Mary had decided to show some balls for a change. Be a FEMINAZI. "Something important."

"Make it fast."

"I didn't finish the motion *in limine*. You can tell Bennie if you want to. You can fire me if you want to. The motion's not done."

"I don't care about the motion," Marta shot back. "Did you figure out what the D.A. has on Steere?"

Mary's eyes widened in surprise, and Judy found herself thinking: schizophrenic, even for Napoleon.

Marta rose to her feet as the associates told her about Steere's color blindness and the traffic light. Her instinct told her they were onto something. Steere had lied to her again, even when he supposedly confessed. Why hadn't she seen it? Steere had admitted he was a liar, yet Marta had swallowed his shit about killing a homeless man. What, did she need a fucking sign? She'd nail him to the wall.

"The only problem is motive," Mary said. "Maybe you know something that can fill in the blank."

Marta's thoughts raced ahead. First she'd have to shake Bogosian, who was waiting in the conference room across the hall. She could see him through the glass, a slick leather mountain, sitting at an identical conference table. He was reading his dog magazine and glancing over at them from time to time. Marta had told the associates he was her driver, but hadn't introduced him.

"This is the picture from Darnton's autopsy." Mary handed an 8 x 10 photo across the table to Marta. "We both think his real name is Eb Darning."

Marta picked up the photo. A corpse on a slab. A face in a morgue. She flashed on the Magnum that had bored into her ribs and realized something she should have realized before. If Marta uncovered the truth about this murder, it would cost her her life. Steere would send Bogosian after her and he wouldn't stop pounding until she was the corpse on the slab. The face in the autopsy picture. Marta had to put Steere behind bars for the rest of his life or she'd be dead. Her head thundered. Her wounds throbbed. Blood pulsed in her ears. The conference room seemed suddenly distant. The photo slipped from her fingers.

"Marta, are you okay? Marta?" It was Mary. Her expression was anxious, but Marta couldn't hear her clearly. It sounded like she was underwater.

Marta felt suddenly warm. Perspiration appeared under her blouse and on her palms. The conference room whirled around her. Papers and briefs and files circled like a tornado. She'd had spells like this as a kid, after the station wagon. She couldn't give in to it now or it would bring Bogosian down on them all. Marta forced a smile that even to her felt like a horrid grimace.

"Marta?" Judy asked, rising to her feet. Marta looked so pale Judy thought it was a heart attack.

"I'm fine," Marta said quickly. "Fine. Don't worry about it." She wiped back her hair with a shaking hand. The room came back into focus and the associates' voices came up. Whatever the spell was, it was ebbing away. She could see Bogosian out of the corner of her eye, his head cocked. He was standing up beside his chair, watching her. She gave him a dismissive wave and held the back of a chair for support.

"Are you having chest pain?" Judy was asking.

"Take a deep breath," Mary said.

"I'm fine." Marta braced herself against a chair as the merry-go-round of a room slowed to a complete stop. Across the hall, Bogosian eased back into his seat with the magazine. Marta breathed freer and she looked at DiNunzio and Carrier hovering around her. She realized they were concerned about her, which was confusing. She had toyed with the notion of slipping them a message about Bogosian, but now she knew she couldn't do that. It had to end here, at least for them. She'd work them like dogs, but she wouldn't get them killed. "Listen, you two, go home. Go home now."

Judy and Mary exchanged looks. "What are you talking about?" Judy asked.

"Go home. Now. That's an order. This case is over. Steere doesn't matter, forget about Steere. Go home."

"I don't understand," Carrier said. "What about the D.A.?"

"Forget about the D.A. We'll deal with him later."

"But Mary could be right. If we knew more about Darning—"

"Forget Darning. Go home."

Judy plucked Steere's tax returns from the table. "You didn't get to see these. They show a connection with the bank—"

Marta grabbed the packet and tossed it back on the table. "Forget the bank. Forget Steere. Go home, Carrier. Both of you, go home."

Judy stood stock-still. "Marta, are you on some kind of medication?"

"Do you need us to get you a . . . professional?" Mary asked.

Marta looked from one to the other and burst into laughter. They were like puppies, these two: dogged in their determination and loyal without reason. They reminded Marta of herself when she was young, protecting two drunks who didn't deserve it from bill collectors and school principals. Instead of making her feel closer to them, the insight distanced her further. "I said, go home."

"You can tell us," Judy said softly. "There's a lot of stress, and it's okay if you are. The pressure. The media. It would get to anybody."

"I'm not having a breakdown," Marta said firmly. "Go home. You've done very good work, and I . . . appreciate it. Thank you."

Thank you? From Erect? With that, Judy realized that Marta wanted them out of the picture for some reason. She was clearly upset about something, maybe even sick. She seemed to be protecting them, but that would be totally out of character. What was going on? Who was that "driver," anyway? The guy looked like The Hulk. Judy glanced at Mary, who she knew was thinking the same thing.

But Mary wasn't. Mary was thinking there'd been a miracle. That there really was a God and he'd spoken to Marta Richter. Taken her aside, thrown one white-robed arm around her padded shoulders, and had a Dutch-uncle talk with her in the sky. Warned her that if she didn't stop torturing associates, she'd end up a wealthy but crispy critter. That she'd be cast down to that level of lawyer hell where she'd have to listen to Alan Dershowitz whine for eternity. But even though the boss had apparently converted to a human being, Mary still wanted to stay with the Steere case. She hadn't come this far to get a killer off scot-free. Not with her history. "Maybe we should go home," Mary said lightly. She picked her jacket off the back of the chair. "I'm exhausted. Aren't you?"

"What?" Judy said, wheeling around to stare at her friend. "Aren't you interested in following up?"

"Nope." Mary slipped into her blazer. "Why would I be?"

Judy finally came up to speed. "Maybe you're right. We can deal with the D.A. when they file, right?"

Marta relaxed inwardly. "Walk her out, Carrier. That's an order." She liked the idea of the associates leaving together and she'd make sure Bogosian wouldn't bother them. She opened the conference room door. "Go!"

"Yes, sir," Judy said, and saluted.

"It's about time you learned to do that," Marta said, smiling. Across the hall, Bogosian looked up from his magazine and returned to it when Marta nodded. "You know, you both have to learn to take orders better."

Judy grinned, gap-toothed. "Don't bet on it." Erect. "Can we borrow the car to get home?"

Marta paused. The car was still at Steere's town house. She glanced anxiously across the hall at Bogosian, who sat near the doorway. "I left the rental at the hotel. The driver brought me over."

"We can walk home," Mary said as she strolled out the conference room door. "It's a good thing we live right in town."

Judy followed Mary into the hall. "See you, Marta. Call us if you hear from the jury."

"Don't worry," Marta said. She stood in the door and watched them walk down the hall to their offices, feeling a tug in her chest which stopped mercifully short of full-blown maternal feelings. It persisted until she noticed Carrier's ski boots making wet footprints on the new carpet.

The associates waited for the elevator when Judy spotted Erect watching them through the glass wall of the conference room. Judy waved at her, and Erect waved back. "Say good-bye to Erect, Mare," Judy said to Mary. "We have to show her we're leaving."

Mary waved. "Good-bye, schizo."

"She's not a schizo. Something's up." Judy faced the elevator and shook her head. "Something happened to Marta."

"A visitation. Angels and saints. Harps and trumpets."

Judy was trying to put the pieces together. "She looked scared."

"Fear of God. He took long enough. I hate it when he's late."

They both heard the rattle of the elevator as it zoomed up the shaft. Judy zipped up her parka and gathered her poles and cross-country skis. "Well, here we go. We have work to do."

"Agreed."

"And great snow to do it in."

"I know what you're thinking—"

"White. Fresh. Virgin."

"—and you can just forget it." Mary was swaddled in a heavy coat and Totes boots. She yanked her knit cap on. "No way, Fay Wray."

"Yes, way. Oh, yes." Judy lined up her skis and

snapped a bungee cord around them. "You will be mine."

"It's not happening, girlfriend."

"No time like the present."

Mary shook her head. "No. I'm smarter than I look."

"No you're not. And it *is* happening. Here and now. Coming to a snowdrift near you."

"I'm not doing the ski thing."

"Yes, you are."

Mary pursed her lips. "I don't have skis."

"I have an extra pair at home. There's no other way."

"We can walk."

"That'll take three hours."

"You want me to *ski* to the Twenty-fifth Street Bridge?" Mary said, raising her voice.

Judy shot her a warning glance and her blue eyes slid meaningfully toward The Hulk sitting in the conference room. He was a distance away but he was sitting right near the open door, flipping through a magazine. Judy couldn't tell if he was within earshot and she didn't want to take a chance. She was even beginning to feel funny about leaving Marta alone with him. She resolved to call the office and check on her when they got home. "You follow?"

Mary glanced over her shoulder at the man, critically now. He didn't look like a cabdriver and he had no uniform like a limo driver. Who was he, anyway? Mary felt dumb for not wondering about him before. "Maybe I'm not smarter than I look."

"Told you," Judy said as the elevator went *ding*!

Down the hall, Bogosian lifted his thumb off the caption under a bearded collie. Right again! He watched the lawyers get into the elevator and the doors close slowly behind them. So they were going to the Twenty-fifth Street Bridge, huh? Bitches. He'd have to follow up on that, too.

16

After the associates left, Marta returned to her seat at the conference table and pretended to work, scribbling nonsense on a legal pad. She considered leaving a note of some kind, but that wouldn't help her right now. She felt Bogosian's gaze on her. What if he decided he wanted to sit in the room while she worked? She had to hurry.

Marta reached for Steere's tax returns. She was intrigued by the Mellon Bank connection and flipped through to the back of the tax return packet, prepared by an expensive accounting firm. Marta felt a twinge as she opened the slick plastic cover. Predators like Elliot Steere couldn't exist without professionals to keep him rich and free. Professionals like her. She hadn't realized it until she became the prey.

On the third page of the packet was a listing of Steere's mortgage deductions. He owned a couple of investment properties in his name and apparently had three residences under mortgage; homes in Society Hill, Vail, and Long Beach Island, New Jersey. It was the New Jersey house that caught Marta's eye. An address in a town called Barnegat Light.

The beach house. Marta remembered what Steere had said in the interview room at the courthouse: that he was going to St. Bart's on a jet leaving from Atlantic City, if the Philly airport closed. She looked out the windows of the conference room. Snow flurries swirled around the building, blown in all directions by confused currents. No small plane would fly in this storm. Steere had lied again. Marta clenched her teeth.

Then she thought a minute, pushing her emotions aside. Why did Steere say that? Why say anything at all? He'd been thinking about the beach. Maybe he'd been thinking about his beach house. He used to say he missed going there, when he was in jail over the summer, and Marta had the impression he considered it more a home than his city town house. Maybe it was his hideaway with his girlfriend. Maybe there'd be a clue there. Something, anything. Marta felt desperate. Her life was on the line.

The telephone rang on the sleek credenza behind her, and Marta jumped. Who was calling? The court? Had the jury come back already? No! She leapt from the chair and grabbed for the phone. Across the hall, Bogosian did the same thing, picking up the phone in his conference room. The lighted button would have told him which line to use. "Yes?" Marta answered, anxious.

"Ms. Richter?" said a young man's voice. "This is Judge Rudolph's law clerk."

"Are they back?"

"No. Judge Rudolph asked me to inform the parties that he's granting the jury a conjugal visit. It was requested by one of the jurors. A transcript regarding the request will be available tomorrow to the parties."

"A conjugal visit, tonight?" Marta asked, relieved. She'd gain some time before the verdict. "It wasn't scheduled."

"It is now."

"Have they stopped deliberating for the night?"

"Yes, they'll resume at eight in the morning. Because of the snow, Judge Rudolph has ordered the deliberations be moved to the sequestration hotel."

"Thanks," Marta said, and hung up. Thinking.

Across the hall, Bogosian hung up, too. Watching.

Marta swiveled around and immediately got back to fake work. She kept her head down and wrote. She had to get rid of Bogosian, fast. By the time she'd filled a page with legal buzzwords, she had a plan. There was only one way to do it. Her heart beat faster. She checked her watch. 8:40. There was no time to lose. She'd have to execute it right under Bogosian's nose. Marta steeled herself. It was her only chance.

Now.

She got up, walked casually to one of the Steere files, and pulled out a manila folder at random. It flopped open, and as Marta paced with it she pretended to read. Out of the corner of her eye, she could see Bogosian reading and occasionally looking up, apparently satisfied she was hard at work. Each time Marta paced, she walked closer and closer to the telephone on the credenza, watching Bogosian and waiting for the right moment. She wouldn't get a second chance. He could shoot her through the glass if he wanted. In the next instant, Bogosian lowered his head and squinted at the magazine. It was Marta's moment and she seized it.

She plucked the telephone receiver off the hook and set it on the credenza beside the phone, then turned on her heel without breaking stride. If Marta could dial three digits—514—she'd have building security on the line. She couldn't risk calling 911 because the cops would want to take her in. There'd be questions asked and time wasted. Just three digits.

Bogosian was reading in his conference room. His back was to the phone so he couldn't see the button lit on the open line. Marta paced away from the phone and back again. She kept her face down to the file. She paced to the phone, quickly punched a 5 on the keypad, spun on her heel, and walked away from the phone.

Across the hall, Bogosian had set down his magazine. He stood up and shook his jeans down over his cowboy boots.

Marta paced back to the phone and hit 1.

Bogosian stretched his muscles and yawned. His leather duster popped open to reveal the Magnum.

Marta paced away and struggled to stay calm. Only one more digit to go.

Bogosian left his conference room and was crossing the hall.

Marta's heart leapt into her throat. She walked toward the phone and hit the 4. The call should connect to the security office. Come *on. Pick up.*

Marta heard a jiggling at the glass door. Bogosian was trying the knob, but it was locked. Marta pretended she didn't hear him and was engrossed in her reading. Fear returned and her heart fluttered. Her head throbbed. The words melted before her eyes. *Connect, goddamnit!*

"Hey!" Bogosian shouted. He pounded on the door. In a split second he'd draw the gun, but a split second was all Marta needed. She heard the faint click of the phone call connecting and a guard answering, "Security."

Bingo! In one deft movement, Marta blocked Bogosian's view of the phone with her body and hung up the receiver. "Coming!" she said, appearing to notice him for the first time. She hurried to the door and opened it with a sweaty palm.

"What the fuck are you doin'?" Bogosian shouted, bursting through the door. He shoved Marta out of the way, and she staggered back against the table, clutching a swivel chair to break her fall. Pain knifed through her ribs.

"I'm working on the motion," Marta said. She willed herself to stay calm. The call had connected. Security would come up and check it out. There was at least one guard on duty, he'd been there when she signed them in. How long would he take to get here?

Bogosian pushed past her and scanned the room in suspicion. His bulk seemed to fill the space. His movements were swift and powerful. He smelled of cold leather and adrenaline. "You done that motion?"

"Not yet. Half an hour, that's all."

"You got five minutes, then we go back."

Marta had to stall him. "It'll take longer than that."

"Too fuckin' bad." Bogosian had taken enough of her shit and he had nothin' to do. He'd guessed all the dog breeds and he couldn't test himself again. Besides, he wanted this bitch back on the reservation. He had the feeling she was jerking him off. Her, and the other two. What the fuck were they doing, goin' to the bridge? Bogosian motioned to the folder. "What are you doin' with that?"

"Reading it. For the brief."

"Yeah, right." He yanked the folder out of the bitch's hand and looked at the top page. It was typed and there were case names underlined. Bogosian remembered the legal papers from his own case. Bullshit. More lawyer bullshit. All they did was make paper. He threw the folder on the table and it skidded into the papers, messing them up. He wanted to mess them all up. Turn the whole table upside down. But then he couldn't find out what she'd been up to. "You haven't been following my directions here."

"What do you mean?"

"You know what I mean."

"No, I was just researching." Marta watched

with anxiety as Bogosian lumbered around the circular conference table, squinting slightly at the documents and photos. She realized he was nearsighted. He touched the papers scattered around the table's perimeter, moving deliberately as the minute hand of a clock. Where was security? Would they come? Bogosian flipped through the legal pad Marta had written on, and she was glad she hadn't left any notes.

"This what you were writin'?"

"Yes. You want to read it?"

"No, I don't want to read it," Bogosian said, mimicking her.

Marta's throat was a hard, dry knot. Where the fuck was security? They'd check even a false alarm, wouldn't they? If she got out of this alive she'd have them all fired. She lingered near the open doorway as Bogosian inched around the table. He was in the perfect position on the other side. Every muscle in her body wanted to run, but she told herself to wait for help. She remembered with a shiver how fast Bogosian covered ground.

"Why's the computer all black?" Bogosian asked, frowning over the laptop. "I don't like the looks of this."

"If you hit a key, it comes on again." Marta pulled out a chair near the laptop and grabbed her purse from it as if she were making room for him. No telling if she'd need it later. "Here, sit down," she said. "If you don't trust me, stay here while I work."

"Fuck you."

Suddenly Marta heard a noise behind her. The rattle of the elevators. The *ding* of the bell as the doors opened. Two security guards came off the elevator, laughing. One was the young man who had signed her in. This was it.

"HELP!" Marta screamed as she bolted from the conference room. "HE HAS A GUN!" She dashed past the shocked faces of the guards toward the exit stairway. Her heart raced. Her head pounded. Her ribs hurt so much it brought tears to her eyes. She flew down the hall and behind her heard the crack of gunfire. One, two, three shots. An anguished moan. Oh God. Marta hoped it wasn't the guards.

"HELP!" she screamed again as she pushed open the door to the stairway. She pitched down a set of concrete stairs, then another. Her pumps clattered on the steel edge of the steps. She panted from exertion and terror. No sound came from the top of the stair. There was no pursuit. Could Bogosian be dead? An alarm went off in the building and clamored in the concrete stairwell. Thank God. More guards would come. "HELP!"

Marta kept running. She hurtled down the stairs, leaping, nearly falling from landing to landing. A painted 10 on the wall told her there were ten floors to street level. She got dizzy as the tight stair twisted around. The alarm bell clanged in her ears. Her screams joined the cacophony. Six floors to the bottom. Go! Faster and faster, pitching forward. Flying down the stairs despite the pain and fear. Four floors left.

Bogosian wasn't chasing her. Maybe the guards killed him. Maybe she was free. Marta reached the bottom floor and threw herself against the exit door. It banged open into the lobby just as the elevator doors opened across the white marble floor.

It was a horrible sight. The elevator was an abattoir. Blood dripped from a huge splotch down its white walls. The two guards lay dead, crumpled in seeping heaps on the elevator floor. One had his face blown completely away. Between their bodies stood Bogosian.

Taking aim at Marta.

17

M arta ran, breathless, for her life. She streaked for the building's entrance, skidding on the slick marble floor, and burst through the glass double doors. She hit the street. Frigid air blasted her face and chest.

"HELP! PLEASE, SOMEBODY!" she screamed, though the snow-covered street was deserted. There were no cops around and no help. The security alarm was muffled outside the building. The guards were dead. The poor men. Bogosian was a killer.

"HELP!" Marta tore down the sidewalk in the deep snow, her purse flying from her shoulder. Icy flakes stung her face and lashed through her wool suit. She stumbled and her hand went elbow high into a snowdrift.

CRRACKK! Marta heard a gunshot behind her, echoing in the silence.

Oh God. Bogosian was going to shoot her down. Terror jolted her senses alive. She heard herself cry out as she half stumbled, half sprinted through the freezing snow. She dashed past darkened stores and swerved around the corner so he couldn't get a clear shot. Her legs were soaked and her feet numb, but she kept running. She couldn't hide because she'd leave footprints in the snow. Tears streamed down her face. "HELP!" she screamed futilely.

CRRAACCKK! Another gunshot.

Marta ducked, panic-stricken. Bogosian was going to kill her. His aim was off, but not for long. One of those bullets would find its target. Her spine. Her heart. Her head. She was going to die. She spotted the lights of Chestnut Street and raced across the street to them. There'd be people there.

"HELP!" Her leg muscles were tiring. Her chest felt like it would explode. She could feel blood running warm down the back of her neck; her wounds must have reopened. She didn't know how much longer she could run. Bogosian was strong. He would catch her and kill her like a dog. She couldn't let him.

Marta dashed around the corner onto Chestnut Street. A huge white pickup truck with a plow mounted on its front bumper churned down the street, pushing a heap of snow and ice in its path. Gargantuan tires jacked it up obscenely and ground snow into deep ruts in its wake. The pickup looked like it belonged at a monster truck rally. Its vanity plate read ELVIS.

Marta sped up, almost hysterical with relief. She would be safe. Alive. She had to get the driver's attention. She scissored her arms frantically, but the truck didn't stop. The cab was too high and dark to see in.

"HELP!" she screamed, but the plow still didn't stop. She couldn't hear herself over the roar of its engine. She had to get in front of the truck. Get the driver to see her.

Marta ran faster to catch up with the snowplow. Clouds of hot exhaust burned her eyes. Soot flew into her mouth. The truck's gigantic wheels powered through the snow, spraying splinters of ice. She had to stop the plow. She didn't have enough energy to keep running forever. She kept waving and it took almost all her wind. She ran as hard as she could, then harder. A few more steps and she'd be there.

One, two, three. Yes! Marta caught up with the plow and ran parallel to it. She waved her arms, frantic this time, but the plow still didn't stop. Fuck! Marta glanced wild-eyed over her shoulder.

Bogosian was running after her, closing in. A deadly figure charging into the storm. His gun was drawn.

Oh, God. Marta was out of choices. Only one way to go. She hoped it wasn't suicide. She darted in front of the massive snowplow. The driver honked loudly but he didn't stop rolling. What? Was he crazy? He'd run her over.

Marta bolted ahead to the middle of the street and ran down the street between the truck's headlights, waving, screaming. The driver honked again and kept coming. Why didn't he stop? Maybe he thought she was a nut or a drunk. The plow was moving so fast Marta didn't risk turning around or slowing down. A mountain of packed snow rolled at her heels, threatening to engulf her.

She burst forward in fear. Her breath came in ragged bursts that tore at her ribs. Her head felt light. Her legs buckled as she ran. Her pumps skidded with each stride. She raced into the snow and dark, momentum hurling her forward.

Marta checked behind her. A giant wall of snow chased her up the street, so close she could feel its chill. But she couldn't see anything behind the snowplow. If she couldn't see Bogosian, he couldn't see her. Marta had lost him.

She couldn't run another step. She jumped out of the snowplow's path, threw herself into a snowdrift at the curb, and dolphined under the surface of the cold powder.

"Fuck!" Bogosian shouted from the sidewalk. He watched the snowplow roll down the street toward the center of the city. The bitch was nowhere in sight, even if he could see that far. He couldn't go after her. There'd be people there for sure, emergency crews, and he had blood all over his shirt from the guards. Bobby wasn't about to risk his ass.

"Fuck!" he yelled into the storm. He spun around on his heels. He broke a sweat even though it was zero fuckin' degrees. Bogosian felt like he was all closed in, like he was back in the joint. He couldn't move, he couldn't breathe. The fuckin' noise from the radios. The fuckin' niggers with the do-rags. The stink.

"Fuck!" he shouted louder, but it only made him madder. He was all tensed up. He felt like a big giant coil ready to come unsprung. Like a cork that needed to pop. He wanted to scream. He wanted to kill. He wanted to come. Blood filled up his muscles, his dick. He heard himself yelling again and rammed his fist into the thick concrete wall of a bank.

Once, then again. He didn't even feel the pain. He hit it again and again until the skin on his knuckles split open and blood gushed out. Then he felt everything. Pain exploded in his hand. Heat came out of his own blood. Skin crawled all over his body.

Bogosian could take pain. He could take any pain. He drew his hand back and stared at his bloody fist like it belonged to somebody else. He remembered how his sister would cut herself. A straight-edge razor that made little baby slices on her thighs and arms. All in a row, like lines of coke. Dumb bitch. They were all dumb bitches. The one up the street and the other two. The young ones from the law office, going to the Twenty-fifth Street Bridge. Bobby knew what that meant. Grays Ferry, where Steere had popped that nigger.

He slumped against the building, suddenly exhausted. The snowplow and the other trucks were gone. The street was quiet. Bobby hid his face against the building. The concrete scratched his forehead. Snowflakes collected on his shoulders and fell in his collar. He didn't want to tell Steere he fucked up. He never fucked up before. He had to make it right, then he'd call.

Bobby stood up and tried to button his jacket to cover the blood, but his beat-up hand wasn't working. He was a stupid fuck to mess it up like that. He'd have to score a new shirt. Now where the fuck was he gonna get that? Motherfuck! Everything was fucked up! It was all that bitch's fault. She'd pay for it.

Bobby had to get it going again. He'd find her and the other ones, too. He might have to call Gyro, but that was okay. Gyro could help out, he was a meat-eater. Gyro would cut big time into his profit margin, but Bobby had to get the job done. That's what it meant to be a professional. Bobby closed his jacket and lurched into the snow.

18

Marta yanked the ratty curtain closed and flopped onto the plastic seat of the photo booth. Woolworth's was the only open store on Chestnut Street and it smelled simultaneously of disinfectant and dirt. Her pulse thudded, her chest heaved. Each breath was agonizing, and Marta inhaled to slow her breathing and ease the pain. She slumped in the booth like a boxer in his corner.

There was no noise outside the booth, and Marta suspected she was the only person in the store except for the salesclerks in their red smocks, two of whom she'd run into as she was coming in. The store would be closing in ten minutes, they told her, wide-eyed at her bedraggled appearance. She'd explained by saying she'd gotten caught in the storm. In a way, she had.

Marta's breathing returned to normal and the rib pain subsided slightly. She sat up and rested her back against the wall of the booth. PHOTO ILLUSIONS, read the sign in front of her. Underneath the sign was a TV monitor, and across the screen flickered a sampling of the photos offered with hokey cutouts: YOU with the President! YOU on a dollar bill! YOU wanted by the FBI!

Marta's gaze fell on a mirror framed with a fake wood. YOU with ELVIS THE SNOWPLOW! She looked away, purposefully avoiding her reflection. She didn't need a mirror to know what she looked like. Her hair stuck to her face in soaked strands and her skin was mottled with exertion, every wrinkle boldface with anxiety. Her suit was wet and hung in rags, but at least she was alive. She had escaped Bogosian. It was a miracle. Then she thought about the security guards, who hadn't been so lucky. They had families, unlike Marta. Who would have missed her if she'd been killed?

It caught her up short. The answer was clear. Nobody. Marta had no family left and wasn't seeing anyone who mattered. She loved no one; she supported no one. Not a soul depended on her except maybe her office personnel, who would find other jobs in a blink. They weren't exactly well paid. And they certainly wouldn't miss her. Once she'd overheard her secretary wishing her dead.

Marta squirmed on the hard seat. She bucked up as she always did, by calling on her inner resume. After all, she was one of the country's premier criminal defense attorneys. Past chair of the Criminal Justice Committee of the ABA, member of Trial Lawyers of America, guest lecturer and legal commentator. In other words, a highly retained pain in the ass. A bitch with a tax bracket that just wouldn't quit. Suddenly it didn't seem like much to have accomplished.

Marta used to think she had come so far. Escaped the Maine woods, gotten herself to law school and beyond. Put a country between herself and a woman who for years took her into car after strange car with the same dangerous lie. *Can you lend me twenty dollars, sir, to take the train? Our car quit on us, and we were on our way to the hospital to see the child's father. The next train station is right down the road.*

Marta knows the men don't believe the lie even as they give her mother the money and drop them at the train station, where mother and daughter wait five minutes and go right back out to the highway. Marta knows that the men give the money because of her; she's the prop, the token. An exhibit, even then. The only time there's trouble is the blue station wagon and after that, it stops. After that her mother goes out alone to the highway. And after a time, is gone longer.

Marta shook it off. It was past. It was over. Why did it keep coming back up? Why now? Her thoughts were mixed up, her world out of kilter. She wiped the bangs off her damp brow. She should be in the present, happy to be among the living. How many dead had there been, and why? Would she be the next one? No time to feel sorry for herself. She had to keep moving. Bogosian could still be after her. She still had the jury to beat and Woolworth's would be closing any minute. Marta stood up, brushed snow from her wet suit, and peeked out of the photo booth's curtain.

No Bogosian and no customers. The store was well lit and empty. Steel bins overflowed with cosmetics, hairbrushes, and rubber boots. Potato chips, spiral notebooks, and discounted videos stocked the shelves. Hot dogs rolled on a greasy rotisserie next to racks of women's shoes and winter coats. Marta hoisted her sopping purse to her shoulder and stepped cautiously out of the booth. She had some power shopping to do.

There was one good thing about selling your soul.

You got money for it.

The two associates skied south on Broad Street. Judy Carrier was in the lead and Mary DiNunzio followed in her tracks, two skinny ruts that refilled quickly with new-fallen snow. The blizzard had shifted into high gear and there was no traffic even though Broad usually served as the city's major traffic artery.

Mary could barely move in Judy's blue down parka and puffy bib overalls. Freezing snow blew into her mouth and stung her cheeks. She pulled Judy's scarf up to her nose, which was wet and drippy. So attractive. "I can't ski, I'm Italian," Mary shouted, shaky on the skis. Her toes were pinned to wood and her arms were stretched out at her sides. She felt like the Pillsbury Doughboy, crucified. In a freezer.

"What does being Italian have to do with it?" Judy called over her shoulder as she skied forward smoothly.

"Italians aren't made to do certain things." Mary pushed her skis forward in an imitation of Judy's lunging slip-slide, but the most she could manage was a penguin's waddle.

"What things?" Judy shouted, and the wind carried her words backward.

"Things nobody should do in the first place. Climb mountains. Ride horses. Everything you do."

"That's ridiculous!"

"Not everybody can do everything, Jude."

"The exact opposite is true. Everybody *can* do everything!"

Mary gave up. Empowerment wasn't for everybody. Not Catholics, anyway. Mary struggled to slide her left ski forward, but there was an icy patch on the track and she fell over. "Yiiiiii!"

"Use your poles!" Judy twisted around in time to see her friend flop sideways in slow motion. Mary had fallen three times in as many blocks. At this rate it would take them a week to get to the Twenty-fifth Street Bridge. It was hard going, harder than it had been when Judy was out before. The snow had gotten so deep it swallowed her thighs at points. If it weren't such a light, dry powder, it would have been like skiing in pea soup. "You okay?"

"Fine. Great. Never better!" Mary was struggling to get up, but couldn't get her bearings. She was a bright cobalt lump, like one of the new blue M&M's,

in the middle of the wide white boulevard. Snow drifted in mounds where the wind had whisked it and glistened in the streetlights like vanilla frosting on a birthday cake. Presiding over Broad Street was the lighted yellow clock tower on City Hall, a birthday candle burning gold. It read 9:30.

"Climb back up using your poles," Judy called out. "One-potato, two-potato."

Mary got a death grip on her ski pole and hoisted herself upright, only tentatively vertical. She brushed off her ski pants and shoved her gloves into the loops on her poles. She felt cold and cranky. Snow flew in her teeth like gnats. She was miserable every minute and it was still better than being a lawyer.

"Westward ho!" Judy faced forward, planted the tips of her poles until they hit asphalt, and pushed off, covering several feet in the next few minutes. Mary bridged the gap between them halfway up the block, as they approached Washington Avenue and the bright neon lights of the University of the Arts.

"You think Marta's okay?" Mary called out.

"Hope so!" Judy had telephoned the office but there'd been no answer, so she'd left a message at the hotel. Maybe Marta had been in the bathroom or not answering the phone. Maybe the jury had come back with a question and Marta had been called to court. Or maybe something had happened with The Hulk. Judy worried that whatever Marta was involved in might be dangerous, but Judy wanted to get to the bottom of it, too. She hadn't represented a criminal defendant before and she hoped she hadn't started with one who was guilty. Judy had to know, for herself, whether Steere was a murderer. She speared the snow with her poles and pushed ahead into the storm.

"Hey," said a voice Penny Jones recognized right off as Bobby Bogosian. Penny was so excited he popped forward in his recliner with a *thump* that felt like whiplash. Penny used to hang with Bogosian before Bogosian moved on to the big time. He was happy Bogosian was calling him after so many years, but he knew enough not to act it.

"Bobby," Penny said, like they just hung up yesterday. He pinched out his joint and dropped it in the ashtray. An old TV flickered in the background, showing scene after scene of the blizzard. Penny had the volume on mute.

"Still boostin' cars?" Bobby asked.

"Yeh, sure. You know me." Penny picked up nine cars a day and specialized in Jeeps. The money was okay except this winter. Hard to pop a Jeep under three feet of snow. On TV, the weatherman was sticking a yardstick in the shit and grinning like a moron. Friggin' snow. Every day, Penny was losing money. "I got a new business, too."

"Yeah, right."

"A new business, for real."

"You had a new business last time we talked. Those fuckin' machines, with the crane picks out the stuffed animals for a quarter."

"That's over. This is a *new* new business. An expansion, like."

Bogosian, at the other end of the line, shook his head. Couldn't believe he had had to call a little turd like Penny. Bobby couldn't raise Gyro, and Eddie was snowed in in the friggin' suburbs. He ended up with Penny only because he lived in the city and would have the right wheels. If he could see over the console. Fuckin' midget.

"Bobby, you there?"

"I'm here."

"You need somethin', Bobby?"

"From you? Only if you got a four-wheel drive. Like a Jeep."

"Hey, no problem." Penny looked past the clutter in his cramped apartment to a piece of plywood with keys hanging on it, like a valet parking board. Actually, it *was* a valet parking board. Penny brought it home from work, telling his manager it got stolen. Well, it did. Penny needed the board to keep track of the cars he was rebuilding in his new business. He'd boost the car, strip it, and sell the skeleton. Then he'd buy the skeleton back at auction, rebuild the car, and sell it with the title. Having good title jacked up the sale price. Made it nice and legal. "I got a coupla Jeeps. A real nice one'll be ready tomorrow. My inventory's a little low because of the snow—"

"I need a Jeep now. In stock."

Penny's bloodshot eyes scanned the keys on the board. "I got a nice new Grand Cherokee, just rebuilt. Title and all. I'd give you a great price, Bobby. Next to nothin'."

Bogosian snorted. "I don't want to buy a fuckin' car, you dick. You need it for the job."

"A job?" Penny couldn't believe his ears. "You got a job for me? What kinda—"

"Will you shut the fuck up?"

Penny told himself to shut the fuck up. Reminded himself if he don't have a good thing to say, don't say nothing. "Yeh," Penny said, and hoped it sounded like nothing.

"It's in Grays Ferry. The Twenty-fifth Street Bridge. You know where that is, jizzbag?"

"Yeh," Penny said. Fuckin' A! If he could do some jobs for Bogosian, he could make himself some real dough. Bogosian was the *man*! Bogosian was the bomb! Bogosian was *money*! Penny couldn't help jumping out of his chair and wiggling his ass like a little faggot. "When I gotta go?" he asked as his skinny butt swayed.

"Now," Bogosian said. "Right now."

"You got it." Penny boogied over to the bedroom for his gun. "I'm all ears, Bobby."

19

Bennie Rosato stepped off the elevator into a
nightmare. There had been killings again, at a
law firm she owned. Security guards were
dead, one Bennie had known well, an older man
named Pete Santis. Pete lived alone like Bennie and
they used to trade dog stories. Both owned the only
two golden retrievers in the world who were allowed
to jump on people. "Allowed, hell," Pete used to say.
"We're talkin' encouraged."

Bennie couldn't believe Pete was dead, but it was
his body she'd just seen loaded into the medical
examiner's van in a black zipper bag. It was his blood
she'd seen in the elevator cab downstairs. Pete died
defending what Bennie owned, maybe protecting her
people. She felt heartsick, stunned. The elevator
doors slid closed, stranding Bennie in the middle of
the hallway, where the news got even worse.

Nobody appeared to care. The hallway at Rosato
& Associates was empty except for a single uniformed cop who stood at the entrance to one of the
glass conference rooms. No yellow tape had been

strung up. No forensic photographers snapped photos of the crime scene. No police techs hustled through the halls vacuuming fibers or sampling dirt from the rug. Bennie had made a career prosecuting police misconduct cases and knew police procedure almost as second nature. None of it was being followed here.

Bennie had learned about the guards' murders from TV. No one from the department had called her and no detective came by for a statement. As soon as she heard, she'd thrown a Gore-Tex jacket over her jeans and workshirt and run the short distance to the office, only to find it quiet as a law library.

Two men had been murdered, two associates had vanished, Marta Richter was gone—and nobody was investigating. Bennie resisted leaping to the conclusion that it was payback. What was going on? She walked over to the uniformed cop, who had bright reddish hair and a coarse rust-colored mustache, and introduced herself.

"I know who you are," the cop said. He wore his cap low on his forehead, his arms were linked behind his back, and he stared pointedly past Bennie, like a Beefeater in blue.

"A fan, huh?"

"Not hardly."

Bennie stopped short of giving the cop the finger. "Should I take it personally that nobody's investigating these murders? Two security guards down, my God. I would think Homicide would be all over this. Half the guards in the city are former cops."

"Don't have nothin' to do with you, Ms. Rosato," the uniform said. "It's snowin' out there, if you haven't noticed. Most of us couldn't report in. The ones that got in can't get around the city. It's a blizzard. We're doing the best we can."

"What about the detectives? The day shift would have stayed in, wouldn't they?"

"Only one is left at Two Squad. It'll be his case. Every homicide tonight will be his case. He'll be here as soon as he can make it in the snow."

"Who is it? Which detective?"

"Don't know. That's confidential anyway. As you know."

"Why isn't he here? The Roundhouse is only half an hour away, even in the blizzard."

The cop looked at Bennie for the first time, with a slack expression that barely masked his hostility. "The detective isn't at headquarters. He's stuck on a double in West Philly. He'll get here when he gets here."

"So nobody can get to the scene? Not even a crime tech? A photographer? The department gonna just sit on its hands?"

"No," the cop said, "we already have an APB out on the shooter. I called it in, okay? That good enough for you?"

"You got the *shooter*?" Bennie asked, heartened. "So soon? How? You have an eyewitness?"

"I can't say. It's against regulations."

"That fast, it would have to be fingerprints." She looked around. The scene was clean, untouched. "But nobody dusted for prints yet. How'd you do it?"

"It's a confidential investigation. You know the rules."

"I hate the rules." Bennie was mystified. She opted for thinking aloud; it either worked or drove cops crazy. A win-win situation. "Let's see now, you can't have him on film, there's no video cameras in the building. And blood wouldn't come back so quick, or DNA. There's no crime tech here to sample it anyway."

"It's confidential, Ms. Rosato." The uniform shook his head. His paunch protruded slightly over his thick belt and he wore a black nylon jacket over his blue shirt, with a sobering black ribbon over his chrome badge. His nameplate said TORREGROSSA, Bennie noticed.

"You Italian, too?" she asked, and the cop burst into laughter.

"You think I'm that easy?"

"Can't blame me for trying, can you? This is my law firm. My people. I'll suck up if I have to. Wouldn't you? Where's your loyalty, *paesan*?"

The cop shook his head. "You sound like my mother."

"I sound like everybody's mother. You know why? Because I care. Now who's the shooter and how'd you find him?"

"Forget it."

"Fine, table the shooter for the time being. I don't care about the shooter, I care about the lawyers. You got any leads on the lawyers? DiNunzio and Carrier? Richter? They all signed in at the desk."

Bennie tugged a slip of paper from her parka and skimmed her notes. "DiNunzio and Carrier signed in at three thirty-five and signed out at eight forty-five. Marta Richter and guest, whoever that was, signed in at eight thirty-five and never signed out. You know that, right? You checked the log downstairs."

The cop nodded. "I saw the log downstairs. I know all that. Why do *you* know all that?"

"Those women matter to me, the security guards matter to me. The only difference is the women may still be alive. They have to be. I'm not trying to interfere with your investigation. I want you to do all you can. I want to do all I can, too. For once we're on the same side. Help me, would you?"

The cop's eyes flickered, and Bennie detected the slightest official softening. "You want my take on the way it went down?"

"Please."

"This is talkin' out of school, but the only blood around is in the elevator where the guards got shot. There's no signs of struggle in the office, so the lawyer who signed in later, Richter, wasn't taken by force. The office equipment looks fine. Everything is in place. I did a walk-through. You double-check and tell me if I'm wrong."

"Sure." Bennie felt relieved. "And the other two lawyers, the ones who signed out, are where?"

"No idea."

"Where could they be? I called their apartments, their homes. I can't find them." Bennie had even called DiNunzio's parents, who had already heard from TV that their daughter was missing. She had tried to calm Mary's mother, but her Italian wasn't up to it.

"I called Missing Persons, I put out an APB, but we got no personnel tonight. The storm is a bitch. We're doing everything we can to find them. You gotta cooperate with us. This is the worst possible night to investigate a homicide."

"Who is the shooter? How did you find him?"

"Ms. Rosato—"

"Please. Maybe I can help. Maybe I know something. It's a blizzard, a crisis. We have to work together, don't we? Cooperate. That's what you're telling me."

The cop sighed. "You didn't hear it from me, right?"

"No."

"His name is Bobby Bogosian. We know him. All we have to do is pick him up."

"Bogosian, I don't know that name. How did you find him?"

The cop cracked a smile, in spite of himself. "He left his magazine. I found it in the other conference room."

"How'd you know it was his, without prints?"

"It has a subscription label. Name and address right on it."

Bennie would have laughed if it hadn't been Pete Santis that got killed. "Smooth," she said.

"They get dumber every year, you ask me."

Bennie looked past his shoulder to the glass conference room. "You mind if I look around in there? I can help."

"No way are you going in there. That's a crime scene. You'll contaminate it."

"I won't touch anything. If I see something, I'll mention it to you. Maybe give you a leg up."

"No."

"I won't—"

"No!" he said, and his sharpness told Bennie she had crossed the line again. It wasn't intentional, this habit of hers, treading on authority's toes. She'd stop crossing the line if somebody would just tell her where it was.

"Fine, fine, fine. You win, Torregrossa. I'll just stand here in front of the door and look in. I can look, can't I? I have a First Amendment right to look."

"Look all you want. Knock yourself out."

"Thank you," Bennie said, like she needed the cop's permission to look in her own conference room. It was the best part of being the boss; she didn't need anybody's permission but her own. She walked to the threshold of the conference room and scrutinized it. Her Eakins print dangled askew on the wall, as if it had been knocked over when someone ran or walked by. A swivel chair had been upended and its feet stuck in the air like a crab on its back. The Steere file and exhibits were lying on the conference table. Photos sat on top of the heap, as if they had been examined recently. Bennie leaned closer to see them.

"Not another inch," the cop said.

"Gotcha." Bennie squinted to see the photos. They were grisly autopsy photos of the man Elliot Steere had killed, then a newspaper-type photo. It was Steere's victim. Next to the photos was a legal pad that read, *Heb Darnton/Eb Darning.* Hmmm. Bennie made a mental note of it, then tried to identify the handwriting. Detached capital letters, good-girl curlicues. Catholic school writing. DiNunzio's notes. Bennie gestured to the notes. "Looks like DiNunzio was researching something about the man Steere killed. Could that be tied in?"

"I'll point it out to the detective when he gets here."

"You want to call and see if he's on his way?"

"No."

"Maybe I should call."

A set of cold cop eyes slipped sideways. "Let the detectives handle this investigation. They know what they're doing."

Bennie didn't point out that she'd had some personal experience to the contrary. She'd lost one law firm because of police incompetence and she wasn't about to lose another. Her gut twisted at the memory. Bennie had been the prime suspect in a murder she hadn't committed, but innuendo had proved as damaging as indictment. There were phone calls from anxious clients, police leaks, and bad press, and Bennie had found herself watching the slow-motion crash of her first law firm.

But this time it had to be different. This time Bennie would protect her firm and prevent anyone else from getting killed. Marta Richter was her biggest client. The two were hardly friends, but Bennie didn't take any of her clients lightly. It was a fiduciary relationship, one of trust as well as finances. Bennie had told Marta as much in their initial meeting, making it clear that Rosato & Associates would partner with her, not just serve as a local mail drop. The two litigators had talked trial strategy, business development, and the possibility of future pairings. Bennie had even lent Marta her two best lawyers.

Bennie's thoughts turned to DiNunzio and Carrier. She had hand-picked the two lawyers and trained them. How were they involved with the guards' killings? Where were they, for God's sake, and what did it have to do with the Steere case, if anything? Could they be in jeopardy themselves?

Bennie's firm was under attack. There was blood on her walls. Her reputation, her name. If anybody was going to get to her firm it would have to be *through* her. This time she had to fight back. Adrenaline pumped in her bloodstream. She couldn't wait for the thaw to begin an investigation. She would begin now. Herself. Nobody knew police procedure better. Nobody had as much at stake. Bennie looked again at DiNunzio's notes. *Heb Darnton/Eb Darning.*

It was a starting point.

20

Mayor Peter Montgomery Walker paced the length of his huge, cherry-paneled office, in front of a remarkably bare mahogany desk. It was his show desk. The desk he used was in his private office behind the secret paneled door. It was where he kept his confidential papers, basketball hoop, and soda fountain. "We gotta get ahead of this, people! Steere's lawyers are missing and two men are dead!" he fumed. "We got a murder case and a blizzard here! We're not handling either of them!"

Large windows flanking the desk reflected the mayor's rolled-up white shirtsleeves and flying rep tie. He had the stamina to rant for twenty minutes; he jogged three miles a day by the Schuylkill River. His aides thought he ran to keep fit, but he ran because he liked the sun on his face and he loved the river drives. The mayor thought no city in the country had a nicer entrance than Philly's. It was prettier than Chicago's, even. "I will not lose this election because of the goddamn *weather*!" he shouted as he paced. "Or because of Elliot Steere!"

The deputy mayors shriveled in their club chairs against the wall. An aged secretary edged toward the mahogany door out of the office. Only the mayor's chief of staff, Jennifer Pressman, looked relaxed, leaning against a cherrywood credenza that held softball trophies and photos of the mayor's family and friends. One of the photos showed Jen with the mayor when he was the district attorney and she was his assistant. A tall, thin beauty with long dark hair and a slim-fitting matte gray suit, Jen watched the mayor from behind glasses with lenses round as quarters. She knew how to handle him from way back; let him bitch.

"Where's the crime lab reports? Where's the coroner's report? I want answers, sports fans! Why do I have to beg? Don't I look familiar?"

Jen didn't reply or even react. She had ridden the mayor's coattails to this job and as chief of staff had the managing director reporting to her, as well as the heads of all major departments. She had hired most of the top administrative employees, managed the high-profile literacy campaign, and continued the blood and organ donor drive she'd started at the D.A.'s office. Jen checked her watch. Almost midnight. Her cool hid the tension she felt inside. She had to go, but getting out of the office soon was out of the question. Stress, coffee, and no dinner. Ingredients for a migraine.

"And who're the detectives on the Steere case? Where the hell is Michael?" The mayor raked back his hair with an angry swipe and reflexively checked his hand to see if any had fallen out. His wife thought his bald spot was getting bigger, but his mistress disagreed. "Jen, do we know where Michael is?"

"The chief of police is at an FOP dinner with the inspector," Jen answered.

"Wonderful. Where's Sam?"

"He's at the Doral at a meeting. All the managing directors of major cities are there. He's the keynote speaker."

"The Doral? He *went*? He knew the Steere case was going to the jury!"

"He had a command appearance." Someday Jen would tell the mayor that his aides made themselves scarce in a crisis because of hissy fits like this one. The phone jangled in the scheduling office. The fax machine beeped in the secretary's area. Jen was beginning to see little pinpoints of light in the distance. Oh, no. It was her early-warning sign.

"Where's Tom Moran? He should know what's going on with Steere! Do the murders affect the court case? Can Steere move for a mistrial?"

"Moran's trying to get here, but the plows haven't gotten to East Falls yet." Jen pushed up her glasses, as if that would stop the lights in her mind. The mayor didn't know about her migraines, none of them did. It wasn't the kind of information you publicized if you wanted to get ahead in politics. "He's in touch with City Hall Communications. We can get him on the phone if you want."

"I don't want him on the phone, I want him here! Goddamn it, why does he have to live in *East*

Falls? From now on, everybody rents apartments in town! Get the same goddamn apartment if you have to!" The mayor stormed back and forth. "What's Moran doing at home anyway?"

"They had the new babies, remember?" Jen tried to ignore the telephones and faxes. A light began to flicker behind her left eyeball, frantic as a candle in a hurricane. "They're twins, and you're the godfather," Jen added, and one of the junior aides, Jack O'Rourke, started to giggle. *Idiot,* Jen thought. She didn't mind that he was stupid, only that he didn't know how stupid he was. The flickering behind her eye intensified.

"I can't be the godfather, I'm the mayor! I'm up for reelection in November and I'm further behind in the polls than last election! The writing's on the wall, people! Can you read silently while I read aloud?" The mayor charged across the red patterned Oriental. He only wanted to fix the city he loved and he couldn't catch a break. He hadn't gotten the Philadelphia Renaissance off the ground because of Steere. He wanted that prick in jail forever. It was the only way to shake loose those properties and win the election.

"I have a thought, sir," O'Rourke chirped up. "What if Steere's lawyers killed the security guards? What if they killed the guards and ran away with the suspect? Like a conspiracy."

"What?" The mayor bit his tongue not to tear the kid a new asshole. The kid never said anything worth hearing, but he was Frank O'Rourke's son and

the mayor wasn't above a little patronage if it got the job done. He was trying to keep this city afloat, and assholes like Elliot Steere were boring holes in the boat. Suddenly he whirled around on his wingtips and folded his arms with his back to his staff.

The aides exchanged glances behind the mayor's back. They tried not to laugh out loud as the mayor went into The Cone of Silence. It was their nickname for Mayor Walker's little quirk, and Jen usually found it funny. Not tonight. There was too much to do and the pinpoints in her head were spreading into large blotches of white light, like holes burning in a paper lantern. She needed to get her Imitrex injector from her desk. Her office was just across the hall. It would take her three minutes.

The mayor finally turned around, looking calmer. Redness ebbed from his face, and he stood still. "We should talk to the press, Jen," he said, his voice almost back to normal. "Take the high road on Steere. Two men are dead. Say we're doing everything we can. We'll make sure the Steere case goes forward and justice is served. Write that up for me. Got it?"

"Yes," she said, but she didn't know how she could possibly whip up a speech. The nausea was starting, and after that would come the pain. Unbelievable, immobilizing pain. She'd have to lie down in a dark room. She'd be totally and completely fucked.

"The headline is the new snowplows, Jen. Announce the snowplows right up front. Say that we were responsive. All the streets will be plowed, no matter how narrow. Is the press outside?"

"In the hall," Jen managed to say.

"Is Alix Locke still out there? I want her in on this. She's the one who made the stink about the goddamn plows."

Jen nodded, but even that hurt her head. "She's been out there since the murder story broke. She wouldn't go away. She's bitching that we're not releasing the police report."

"Why? She knows we don't release until the investigation's over. What is it with Locke? Why is she always in my face? I thought she was a Democrat."

"She's a reporter. Doing her job. Being a bitch." Jen's brain flooded with light. She was sick to her stomach. The pain was starting.

The mayor's secretary reappeared at the door. "Mr. Mayor," she said, her lined face alarmed. "Alix Locke is insisting on speaking with you. She won't take no for an answer, sir."

"Tell her to wait until the press conference like everybody else!" the mayor boomed, and his voice reverberated like a rifle shot through Jennifer's brain. Then the phone started ringing again.

"When it snows it pours," O'Rourke said, but none of the staff laughed. Least of all Jennifer, who bolted for her office and her Imitrex injector.

"I'll announce the conference," she said.

21

Christopher Graham wedged his powerful frame into the tiny chair in his hotel room and set his green bottle of Rolling Rock on his leg. Christopher hated conjugal visits. Like Mr. Fogel had said while they were playing cards on the last visit: "Neither of us has anybody to conjugate." Tonight Mr. Fogel wasn't up for cards, so Christopher sat alone and took another swig of Rolling Rock. The jurors were allowed one alcoholic beverage a night.

"This one's for you," Christopher said, hoisting the bottle in the silent hotel room. His gaze wandered listlessly over snow flying outside the window, the double bed with the polyester comforter, and the TV on its swivel stand. The hotel would pipe in a cable movie for free during the conjugal visits—tonight's was *Jurassic Park*—but Christopher kept the TV turned off. Beside him on the steel cart sat the remains of his dinner: fried chicken and Spanish rice, with ice cream for dessert. Christopher had come to hate fried chicken on this jury. Not as much as he hated chairs that were too small, though, and not half as much as he hated conjugal visits.

Christopher took another sip of beer. He found the whole notion of a conjugal visit distasteful, like the jurors were animals. Like the wives were mares in season, being brought to a stallion, coaxed into trailers for the trip to be covered. And the male jurors acted like animals all day the day of a conjugal visit. They didn't pay attention in court, shifting in their chairs and checking their watches. They reminded Christopher of stallions restless at the first hint of spring; throwing their heads back, prancing around the pasture. Even geldings got frisky come April and wouldn't stand still for shoeing.

Christopher rested the beer bottle on his thigh, making a wet ring on his heavyweight jeans. The TV came on in the next room, and a woman's laughter floated through the thin walls. Oh, man. Here we go again. It was Isaiah Fellers and his fiancée. Every conjugal visit for two months, Christopher would hear them talking and giggling, then the TV would blast and the headboard bang against the wall. The ruckus would rattle the flower picture over his bed, and Christopher would retreat to the bathroom to hide from the noise.

"Don't move!" a man in the dinosaur movie said through the wall. Then came the moaning of Isaiah's fiancée.

Christopher took another swig of beer and closed his eyes to the sounds. He thought love was better than that. He liked horses and their ways, but he wasn't an animal. Lainie never understood that. She used to whisper things in bed she thought would arouse him, but he wanted her to be above that. She was his wife. Then six months ago, Lainie had found another man and left the house. Didn't take anything, not even the curling iron she used on her bangs every day. He knew she'd come back someday, at least for the curling iron. She was real picky about her bangs.

"REEEAAAHHH!" somebody bellowed on the other side of the wall, and Christopher wasn't sure if it was the dinosaur or the woman until it ended in "BBAAABBBEEE." Christopher shook his head in wonder. No woman had ever made a sound like that with him. Either he hadn't been with enough women, or none had loved him that much.

Christopher thought of Mrs. Wahlbaum. She always smelled nice on visit day and seemed more alert. He'd met her husband, Abe, a tall, thin man with gray hair. Mrs. Wahlbaum held her husband's hand when she introduced him to Christopher; she was happy just to stand next to him. Christopher wondered if a woman would ever feel that way about him.

"RRRREEEHHHHHOOOO!" somebody shouted, and Christopher gave up trying to screen it out. He got up with his Rolling Rock, went into the bathroom, and flicked on the fan to mask the noise. The fan whirred to life, and Christopher sat on the tub's edge in the dark. He closed his eyes and soon Marta's face floated up to him out of the darkness. She was standing at his side, and Christopher imagined himself introducing her to someone, like Mrs. Wahl-baum did her husband. Marta's face would light up when she looked at him. Even her blue eyes would smile. It was plain to see that she adored him.

"RRRIING!" came a sound, barely audible over the whirring of the fan. Must be the movie. Christopher shook it off. "RRRIIIINNNG!" it sounded again, and he realized it was the telephone. Who could be calling? He left the bathroom and hurried to the phone. "Yup," Christopher said into the pink receiver.

"This is the sheriff downstairs. Your wife is here to see you."

Christopher was struck dumb. Lainie? Why had she come? She'd never come before. Only one of two things Lainie could have wanted from him, since he didn't have the curling iron. Either she wanted to get back together or she wanted to get a divorce.

"Should I send her up?"

"No. I mean, sure. Thanks."

Christopher hung up the phone and caught sight of himself in the mirror over the dresser. He didn't look surprised at all, he was good at not showing his feelings. Lainie used to complain about it, but there was nothing he could do. It was just the way Christopher was. It was his nature.

Christopher finger-combed his thick, dark hair with his fingers and checked his beard for crumbs. He smoothed down his flannel shirt and tucked it into his jeans. He didn't look half bad. He'd noticed one of the jurors, Megan, looking at him from time to time. He patted his stomach, still trim. Take it or leave it, Lainie. There was a knock at the door and he hustled to open it.

"Special delivery for Mr. Graham," said the uniformed sheriff. He grinned as he stepped aside.

"Hi, honey," said the woman standing there, who looked a lot like Lainie. She had hair like Lainie and clothes like Lainie, but she wasn't Lainie. "It's been a while, Christopher," the woman said softly.

Christopher looked at her eyes. They were clear blue and smiled up at him from the doorway. He'd know those eyes anywhere. "It sure has," he replied without hesitation.

"And away we go," said the sheriff, who did a Jackie Gleason out the door and left Christopher alone.

With Marta.

22

The blizzard blew, but Judy stood on the snowy stoop and knocked on the door of a rundown brick rowhouse catty-corner to the Twenty-fifth Street Bridge. Judy knew somebody was home because she could hear voices inside, and light shone through a ripped paper shade. She craned her neck to peek though the tear and almost fell off the stoop. She knocked again. No answer.

Standing on the sidewalk, Mary spotted a moving shadow on the paper shade. "Somebody's in there," she said, from a snowdrift on the sidewalk.

"Hello?" Judy knocked again. "Hello?"

The associates waited but nothing happened. Snow fell in gusts. The neighborhood was dark and quiet. Three houses so far, and no one was answering. The wind whistled down the street, buffeting Mary's face and sending frosty tendrils twirling toward her. Her cheeks were frozen and her nose leaked like a preschooler's. Her fingers were so numb she couldn't keep the poles and skis together.

Judy pounded on the door again. "Hello? Please

come to the door. It'll just take a minute." Still no answer. She turned away and tramped down the steps. "What do you think, Mare?"

"I think we keep at it."

"Why won't they answer?"

"Because it's a snowstorm? Because it's late? Because you're a lawyer? I don't know for sure."

"Am I scary-looking?"

Mary appraised her. A yellow knit ski hat, fringe of wet blond bangs, canary parka, and snowpants. "No, you look like a banana."

"Maybe I need a new rap. Begging isn't working. You got any ideas?"

"How about 'Prize Patrol!'"

"You're no help." Judy turned and lumbered through the snow to the next house. Mary followed, hoisting the slippery skis and poles up. A ski slid down into the snow, and Mary bent over to retrieve it. It was maddening trying to keep the skis in order. They were the wire hangers of sports equipment.

Judy climbed the stoop of the next house, 412. The two front windows had a brown curtain in them. She knocked on the front door, and a kid's face popped up under the hem of the curtain. A small, black boy with a smooth head. Judy waved at him, and he waved back.

Mary watched from the sidewalk as Judy waved at the boy again and he waved back again. It was cute, but it wasn't progress. "Jude, you know sign language for 'open the door'?"

"Can you open the door a minute?" Judy called out, knocking, but the curtain dropped and the boy vanished.

Damn, Mary thought, and wiped her nose on the sleeve of her borrowed parka. Suddenly the door opened a crack and a woman stood there in jeans and a sweatshirt, with her hand shielding her face against the blowing snow. The little boy hugged her knee and buried his face in her thigh.

"Excuse me," Judy said, "I hate to bother you. Did you know Heb Darnton or Eb Darning, the homeless man who was killed here last spring, under the bridge?"

"No, I didn't know him," said the woman irritably, from behind her hand.

"Well, maybe you can help me anyway. My name is Judy Carrier and I'm trying to find out about Heb. Did anybody around here know him? This is where he hung out. This corner, this street."

Mary remained eye level with the boy, who smiled at her shyly. She waved at him, and he waved back, his palm half hidden behind his mother's leg. "Momma, I want to go out and play," he said in a robust voice, but his mother found his shoulder with her hand and patted him.

"I don't know the man," the mother answered.

"Do you know anybody who did?" Judy asked.

The woman shook her head. "Listen, it's cold. I got to go now, I'm losin' heat with the door open."

"Momma?" shouted the boy, but the front door shut quickly and was locked, then bolted.

Judy sighed and trudged back down the stairs. "Well, it wasn't a total waste of time."

"Yes it was," Mary said. She picked up the skis from the snow, where they had fallen like pickup sticks.

"No, it wasn't. That little boy liked you. You made a friend."

"Kids hate me, and I don't need a friend. I need to know who Eb Darning is."

"You can always use a friend, Mare."

"Oh, please. Help with the goddamn skis, would you, California?"

Judy helped gather the skis, and the two women went from house to house in the blizzard, down the streets they thought the homeless man had frequented, checking the neighborhood around the crumbling bridge. Only a handful of people answered their doors, and none of them said they knew Heb Darnton or Eb Darning. The lawyers circled the block and ended up, discouraged, in the middle of the street they had started on. The storm had worsened and Judy's foot had grown cold even in the insulated ski boots. Her ankles were soaked because there'd been only one pair of gaiters and she'd lent them to Mary. "Even I have to admit this is not going well," Judy said.

"We can't just give up."

"We won't, but maybe there's another lead we can follow."

"I don't know any, do you?"

Judy thought a minute. "Maybe we could go to

Green Street, where Darning used to live. Try to find some people who knew him before he became homeless. Green Street is right in town, in Fairmount, on the other side of the Free Library."

Mary's mouth dropped open and snow blew inside. "That's on the other side of town. You want me to ski *back* across town, *past* your apartment, *all* the way to Green Street?"

"We can stop at my apartment. Get some hot chocolate."

"Who are you channeling? My face is about to fall off. My contacts are frozen. The only part of me that's dry are my ankles and that's because of those plastic things you gave me."

"The gaiters."

"Whatever. We can't do it, Judy. We'll be Popsicles. Twin pops. The kind that are supposed to break down the middle and never do."

"What?"

"Forget it." Mary squinted against the snow. "It wasn't a bad idea, though. Why didn't you say something before?"

"I didn't think of it."

Mary's heart sank. She scanned the rowhouses facing the storm like a stone wall. Some of the neighbors had talked to her in the spring, but that was then. Now they were a lot less friendly, maybe because the whole city thought Steere was about to walk. Still, she couldn't bring herself to let it go. Her role in letting a murderer go free weighed too heavily, and she didn't need more guilt.

Mary's gaze moved down the street, where some kids played in the pool of brightness cast by the streetlight. One kid flapped his arms to make a snow angel and two others wrestled in the snow, dark figures tumbling over one another like fairies in the night. They'd made a hill by packing the snow on one of the stoops and were sledding down the makeshift mountain on a piece of cardboard. One of the kids, the smallest, wasn't playing. He was standing off to the side, facing them. Facing Mary. It was dark, but his tiny shadow fit the little boy from the house.

"Judy, it's the kid!" Mary said, her heart leaping up. She dropped the skis with a clatter and hurried down the street, her legs churning in the deep snow. She slowed as she reached the boy, then stopped and waved. He waved back. He couldn't have been four years old. "My name is Mary," she told him. "What's your name?"

He didn't answer. He held his arms stiff at his sides in a hand-me-down parka and black gloves. His knit Eagles cap was stretched out of shape and floppy at its peak.

"Do you have a name?"

Still no answer.

Mary tried to think of what to say next. She was never good with kids, but her husband had been. He'd taught school and wanted a passel. She tried to think of what Mike would have done, but it had been so long since she'd heard his voice in her head. Judy caught up with her, lugging their skis and poles.

"What *she* got?" the boy asked loudly, pointing to the skis. He had a big voice for such a little kid.

"They're skis," Mary answered.

"Skis?" he said, testing the word.

"Right, skis. You can play with them in the snow." Mary saw interest sparkle in his large, round eyes and wanted to get through to him. But she needed help from somebody who was better with kids. "Judy, skis are fun, right? A lot of fun. They're like toys."

"No, they're not." Judy frowned under her hat. "They're serious equipment. They're not toys."

Mary wanted to throttle her. "Don't be so technical." She grabbed a maroon ski from Judy's hand and held it in front of the boy. "See? You want to touch it?"

Startled, the boy edged away.

"There's nothing to be afraid of," Judy said. She wrenched the ski from Mary's hand. "Skis are cool. Watch this." The boy's dark eyes followed her as she turned the ski over, set it down on the snow, and gave it a push. It glided to the boy like a model sailboat in a fountain, and he looked down at it and grinned. "Cool, huh?" Judy said, and looked back over her shoulder. "Why am I doing this, Mare?"

"Because I think our friend likes to play outside," Mary said, her gaze on the boy. "I bet he plays outside all the time and I bet he makes lots of friends."

Judy smiled, catching on. "I bet you're right, Mare." She eased slowly onto her haunches, eye level with the boy, and Mary stood behind her, watching his reaction. They were concentrating so intently on the child that they didn't notice the white Grand Cherokee coming slowly around the corner and rumbling toward them in the snow. The driver of the Cherokee was Penny Jones and he was heading straight for the women, his hunting rifle under the front seat.

23

Jen Pressman fled the mayor's office and hustled down the marble corridor in City Hall. This migraine was going to be a whopper. She needed that Imitrex. A flock of TV and print reporters dogged her, headed by Alix Locke.

"Jen!" Alix yelled in her ear. "Jen Pressman! What will the mayor say tonight at the conference? Come on, Jen, tell me."

"You'll see in an hour," Jen said, wishing Alix would stop shouting. She was supersensitive to all the sounds in the corridor. The clacking of her own heels. The snapping of camera shutters, the whir of the motor drives. Jen wanted to cover her ears.

"Where's a copy of the mayor's speech?" "Do you have a copy of the speech?" "Will he get the plows?" "Did the deal go through with the Canadians?" "Can you confirm or deny?"

"Press conference in one hour, in the conference room down the hall," Jen said, elbowing her way ahead. No one would have guessed spots were popping and jumping behind her eyes.

"What's the deal on the security guard murders?" "Any suspects?" "Any leads on Richter or the others?" "What do the police have to say?"

Jen didn't bother answering. She had lost the ability to distinguish whose questions they were. It was all a cacophony. She felt seasick but couldn't let it show. She waved them all off, pushing through the gauntlet until she finally reached the mahogany door across the hall. CHIEF OF STAFF, said the pullout plaque. Jen yanked the heavy door open, and a white-hot light blasted her eyes. Seared through the shutter of her pupils. Cut like a laser right through to her brain. "Ah!" she cried out, putting up a protective hand.

"Turn off that light!" shouted her secretary. "I told you! No TV cameras in here. Turn it off!"

"Turn that fucking thing off!" Jen screamed. The TV light sputtered to darkness, but she was reeling, seeing exploding lights everywhere. She pressed into the wedge of reporters to get past the reception area to her office.

"Are we getting the new plows, Jen?" Alix Locke shouted, among others. "Is it true we paid a fortune for them?" "When will they get to the streets in the Northeast?" "Why don't they plow the streets off Vare Avenue, Jen?"

Jen barreled ahead, leaving the reporters behind. She heard her secretary shouting for them to leave, but she couldn't bear any more shouting. Not one more minute of it or she would scream and her cover would be blown.

Jen flew down the short corridor to her office, ran inside, and shut and locked the door. Her large office was unrecognizable. The furniture had melted into shapeless forms. She couldn't focus on her diplomas. Her poster for the City Hall blood drive was a crimson blur and a banner for the organ donor drive read GIVE A LIVER, SAVE A LIFE GIVEALIVERSAVEALIFE.

Jen ran to her cluttered desk against the window. It faced north over the ornate Masonic temple and ordinarily she loved the view. Tonight she couldn't see it. She tore open the right-hand drawer and felt for her purse. It wasn't there, where she always put it. Oh, no. The injector was inside it. Where was her purse? Jen rifled through pencils, pens, and paper clips for the brown Coach bag. It wasn't there. Had she put it here? Where was it last?

Jen ripped through her personal bills. Nothing but paper. She threw them up in the air, frantic. She had put it here, hadn't she? Had she locked the drawer? There'd been thefts even in her office. Jen tried to think through the pain clenching like a fist behind her eyes. Of course she hadn't locked the drawer. It was unlocked when she came in.

Nausea bubbled in her stomach. She almost burst into tears. The snow and all, and the murders. She'd forgotten to lock the drawer. Now she didn't have the Imitrex. Fucking what was she going to do? She had only minutes before she'd collapse completely. Jen flung open the second drawer and ransacked it for her purse, then searched the third. Memos and other papers flew everywhere, floating to the carpet. Please don't be lost. Please be here. But it wasn't.

Jen leaned on the desk for support. Think. Yes! She had a spare injector in the ladies' room. She ran for the office door and flung it open, trying not to cry. Trying not to scream, not to puke. She took the hallway corner full speed and dashed flat out to the ladies' room. She wrenched the door open, slammed it behind her, and ripped open the mirrored medicine cabinet. Her vision was almost gone; she had to find the injector by feel. It was hidden in an empty Tampax cylinder and marked JEN ONLY OR DIE. Her whole world was dissolving. Dematerializing. Breaking up into a jagged kaleidoscope of light and pain.

Jen fumbled with shaking hands through the skinny glass shelves, knocking everything out. She heard the thunder of a toothbrush as it crashed to the basin. The din of a plastic cup as it smashed to the floor and rolled around the porcelain tile. Where was the goddamn syringe?

There! Jen grabbed the Tampax with the syringe and fell onto the toilet seat. She bit off the cap, spit it out, and jammed the needle through her panty hose and into the muscle of her thigh. In three minutes she would be human again. She closed her eyes and tears slipped from beneath her eyelids. Relief was on the way, except there were the sounds of a scuffle outside the bathroom door and then someone started pounding on the door.

"Jen, it's Alix! Alix Locke. I need a copy of that speech!"

24

Marta stood in the hotel room of one of her jurors, about to engage in conduct that would constitute jury tampering and obstruction of justice, as well as violate several key ethical and disciplinary rules. She didn't want to think about what would happen if she were discovered. Humiliation, loss of license and livelihood. As much as she needed to be here, Marta felt slightly stunned that she actually was. She scared herself at times.

Christopher was even more stunned than Marta. He couldn't say anything, and *she* wasn't saying anything, so they stared at each other for a minute. It was unreal. She was Marta Richter, everything he ever wanted in a woman, and she was dressed up like the woman he'd married, Lainie. Christopher couldn't deny his feelings. He wanted Marta, and here she was. She'd come to him, dressed as his wife, on a conjugal visit. He didn't know if it was luck or Providence.

"Do you mind if I sit down?" Marta asked, finding her voice.

"Yes. No. Sure. Suit yourself," Christopher said. He gestured awkwardly toward the bed, then caught himself. What was the matter with him? Just because he thought about an affair with her didn't mean it was going to happen. Christopher was supposed to be a gentleman. He pushed his room service cart out of the way and patted the chair. "Uh, here. Here, in this chair. I mean. Would be better."

"Thanks." Marta took off her knit hat and perched on the edge of the chair. She had to get to the point and fast. Maybe it was the beard that hid most of his features, but Christopher was so impassive Marta wasn't sure he knew she wasn't Lainie. "Do you know who I am, Christopher?"

"Marta."

"Right." He'd called her by her first name, and Marta wasn't entirely surprised. "I bet you think this is a little strange. Not to mention illegal."

Christopher laughed, and it came out like a gulp. Of what? Fear? Hope? Love? His own laughter was a sound he didn't hear often, and it sounded odd. It made him aware that the ruckus from next door had finally stopped. They'd even turned off the TV. "Well, yes," he said, his voice low, out of caution. "I was, well, wondering."

"It's a surprise, I know."

"Huh? Sure. Well, yeah. You look good," he blurted out, and as soon as the words left his mouth he winced. He was a grown man with his own business and he was acting like a teenager. It was all because Marta was so beautiful, and dressed in casual clothes, she looked more friendly. Softer. Christopher could actually see them together. Married. Maybe because she was wearing clothes like his wife's. "I mean, you look a lot like Lainie. You did a real good job. How did you know what Lainie looks like?"

"I have her picture in the file. It's from the newspaper. The photo of the two of you, above your engagement announcement."

"How did you get ahold of that?" Christopher asked in surprise. "It was only in our local paper."

"One of the jury consultants got it from the computer. If it's published, it's on the computer. Local or not."

Christopher wasn't sure he liked them spying on him like that, but he couldn't be mad at Marta. She looked so good, different. Her hair was all changed. The stiff blond cut was gone, replaced by a looser brown hairdo. Lainie used to call her haircut a "shag," but it didn't look shaggy on Marta. "What did you do to your hair? Did you cut it? Dye it?"

"Not exactly. I didn't have much time." Marta reached up and yanked the wig off her head. The shock of it brought another surprised laugh from Christopher.

"Oh, man," he said, sinking onto the dresser in front of the bed. "Man, oh, man."

"I got the whole outfit at Woolworth's." Marta scratched her scalp, relieved to have the itchy wig off even though it had kept her head warm. "I remembered what your wife wore in the photo and the way she kept her hair."

Jesus. The resemblance was eerie. Christopher had so many questions. Why was Marta here? Was it because she had feelings for him, like he did for her? "Uh, how did you get past the guards downstairs?"

"I told them I was Elaine, Lainie. I remembered we looked alike. The sheriffs didn't recognize me. In fact, one of them told me he'd seen my picture. I mean, Lainie's picture."

Christopher nodded. He'd shown the guards his wedding picture once, but he didn't tell them Lainie had run off. Not even Mr. Fogel knew why Lainie didn't visit, because Christopher didn't like to talk about it. One day he'd take the damn picture out of his wallet and throw it away.

"You're wondering why I'm here," Marta said, suddenly uncomfortable in his gaze. He was looking down at her from his perch on the dresser, his strong legs spread slightly. Christopher's body language was as subtle as an express train, though his expression was still unreadable. "I have a problem," she began, and told him the whole story.

Christopher listened intently, resting on the edge of the dresser. His face betrayed no emotion even when she told him about the killings of the security guards, but inside he was horrified. He had never heard anything like it, and the more Marta talked, the more worried he became. She was in danger. "How can I help?" Christopher asked when she was finished.

"Get the jury to convict. I'll work on finding out why Steere killed Darnton, but I need you to work it from the inside. The jury has to find Steere guilty of murder."

"*Guilty?*" Christopher asked, astounded. "They're about to find him innocent. They're going to acquit."

"They can't."

"We voted twice. It's nine to two, with one juror abstaining. We think it's self-defense, just like you said. It's going your way."

"Not anymore." Marta had never been so unhappy she was kicking ass. "Who's voting to convict? Kenny Manning and one of the other black men, right?"

"Not all the black people are voting to convict. Kenny Manning is, I think, but not Gussella Williams." Christopher heard himself lecturing, but he figured he was entitled. The jury deliberations had made him think a lot about race. Skin color didn't make a difference to Gussella, but it made a difference to Kenny. Just like it made a difference to Ralph Merry. Christopher didn't understand people sometimes. Horses didn't group together by color, and people were supposed to be smarter than horses.

"Okay, fine. Whatever," Marta said. She had picked an almost all-white jury, figuring they'd favor a white businessman against a black homeless man, and she'd been right. Race wasn't everything, but Marta had to be realistic. Now she was working against herself. Against time. "What about Mrs. Wahlbaum, the schoolteacher? She wants to acquit, right? Will she stay with it?"

Christopher nodded. He didn't think anything could move Mrs. Wahlbaum when she'd made up her mind, not even Mr. Wahlbaum.

"And the young girl, the computer programmer? Megan Gerrity? Will she hang tough?"

"I don't know. Probably."

"She'll acquit." Marta shook her head. Fucking liberals. Any other time she would have kissed their asses, now they could cost her her life. "You have to hold out. Tell them you're voting to convict and stand your ground."

"I can't do that." Christopher crossed his arms in his flannel shirt. "Today I voted to acquit. I almost convinced them. They want to go home. They're tired of living in a hotel."

"Tell them you changed your mind," Marta said. "You thought about it. You've been wondering why Steere didn't testify and tell his side of the story."

"Judge Rudolph said that wasn't supposed to matter."

"Say it matters to you, you can't help it. Juries always wonder why the defendant didn't take the stand. If Steere was defending himself when he shot that man, why didn't he just come forward and explain what happened? Elliot Steere is not a shy man, he's a killer. Announce your vote and stick to your guns."

"Wouldn't that make it a hung jury?"

"You have to convince them all. I don't want it hung. I don't want a mistrial. Either one of those, Steere is free and I'm dead. It has to be a conviction, nothing less will do. And take your time. I need all the time you can give me."

Christopher tried to think of what he'd say tomorrow. He pictured the other jurors sitting around the table, looking at him like a crazy man when he told them he'd changed his mind. He'd been so adamant today. Christopher liked to think he was a man of his word, but Marta was in real trouble. Two men had already been killed.

Marta rubbed her forehead with anxiety, and it throbbed in response. "Who's the foreman? Ralph Merry?"

"No. I am."

"Wonderful!" Marta took heart. What a break. Maybe her plan would work. Maybe Christopher could make this happen. "Then you *can* persuade them. Jurors look up to the foreman. They look for a leader. That's why they picked you in the first place."

"No."

"You're being modest."

"No, really," he said, but Christopher would die before he'd explain what happened. It was hard enough to talk with Marta here in his room, right across from him. In his bedroom. Christopher felt as if she knew how often he thought about her. So many nights he had pictured her here, and now she was. He had to know. "Why did you come to me, Marta?"

"I needed to get to the jury."

"But why me? Why did you pick me? You didn't know I was the foreman. You were surprised."

"I came to you because you were most likely to help."

"Why did you think that?"

Marta paused, then let it rip. "Because I think you're attracted to me."

The hotel room seemed suddenly very still to Christopher. The silence sounded loud. He didn't know what to say. He could keep his feelings inside, but he'd let so many feelings go in his life, seizing none of them. This feeling, it seemed, should not pass. This feeling had the strength of a runaway horse. It was time to take it in hand. Grab hold and hang on. Cowboy it. "Do you have feelings for me, Marta?" Christopher asked, and his heart felt like it was stuck on his Adam's apple. "Tell me, yes or no. Because I do have feelings for you."

This was not a conversation Marta wanted to have right now. Every instinct told her to lead him on, lie to him, even take him to bed if it got her what she wanted. Marta couldn't imagine telling the truth with the stakes this high. Then she looked at Christopher's rugged, open face and couldn't imagine not. He was a decent, kind man, and she was asking him to do something that could get him thrown in prison. He deserved a straight answer. "No. None at all," she answered. "I don't even know you."

"I see," Christopher said quickly.

Marta swallowed hard, sensing his hurt. Funny how she hurt a little, too. For him. But she had to go forward. "Will you help me anyway?"

25

The white Grand Cherokee stopped in the middle of the street and parked with the engine running. Its white enamel paint camouflaged it in the blowing snow, blurring its boxy outline in the storm. Exhaust snaked in a ghostly cloud from its tailpipe and trailed off in a gust of wind. Its windshield wipers flapped slowly in the snow.

At the end of the block, Judy was kneeling down, pushing the flat end of the cross-country ski to make it go back and forth. The snow came up to the very edge of the little boy's coat. "Now it's your turn," she said to him. "Slide it back to me."

Without a word, the boy bent over and sent the ski back to Judy. Then she slid it back to him, and he repeated the game with a growing smile. "Did you know my friend Heb?" Judy asked, sailing the ski to him.

The boy nodded and kept his eyes glued to the maroon ski. Mary felt her heartbeat quicken, but she stayed behind Judy and kept her mouth shut. The ski reached the boy, and he caught it in his hand-me-down black glove.

"Heb got hurt, didn't he?" Judy asked.

"He got shot." The boy's eyes moved with the ski. Back and forth. "He dead."

"Did you see him get shot?"

"No. I didn't see, I heard. Bang, bang, bang, BANG!" the boy shouted, summoning all the strength in his small body. He shoved the ski hard.

Judy stopped the ski like a shortstop and glanced up at the boy, then at his rowhouse. It faced the bridge, catty-corner to the spot where Darning was killed. She eyeballed the distance from the house to the bridge. About fifty yards. The child could have seen something. "You sure you didn't see him get shot, now?"

"I was sleepin'. The BANG woke me UP. I heard it out the window."

Judy gathered from the shout that he felt strongly about it. "Was Heb your friend, too?"

"Yes." The boy nodded. "He give me street money."

"He gave you money?"

"He was rich."

Mary blinked. "What?"

Judy asked, "He was?" She sent the ski across the snow.

"Dennell!" shouted one of the older kids, who was standing in the middle of the street. They had stopped playing and were going inside, abandoning the cardboard sled and snow angels. "Dennell!"

Suddenly, the boy turned around and ran off, kicking up a tiny wake of snow in his path.

"Wait!" Judy called after him, but he didn't turn back. The lawyers watched the boy run to the older kid and climb the stoop into his house. Their front door slammed closed, echoing in the street, which fell abruptly silent. The wind had picked up and was tossing the flurries this way and that. Down the street sat the Grand Cherokee, parked with its engine rumbling. Lost in the snowy backdrop, its windshield wipers moved back and forth.

Judy straightened up and brushed caked snow from her knees. "Did you hear that? How can a homeless man be rich? Panhandling?"

"Not in this neighborhood, and this was the only place he lived. He slept under the bridge."

"Welfare would barely support him, much less leave him money to pass out to a kid. Maybe Darning saved the money from his job with the bank."

"Saved it, from the sixties?" Mary asked. "A bank teller's salary? Why do you always look for the best in people? What kind of lawyer are you?"

Judy smiled and shook snow from the ski bindings and poles. "Okay, maybe he stole it from the bank when he worked there. Embezzlement, skimming the accounts. Taking bribes to shift the money around."

"Now you're talkin'. But what would that have to do with Elliot Steere?"

"Maybe Darning stole it from Steere's account a long time ago, and when Steere found out he killed him." Judy bent over and laid the skis on the snow in pairs, but Mary didn't seem to be taking the hint. Down the street, the white Grand Cherokee waited, undetected. Silent.

"Why wouldn't Steere report it to the cops?" Mary asked.

"Maybe he wanted to handle things on his own. Maybe he went to talk to Darning about it and things got out of hand."

"No. It doesn't sound right. The kid said Darning was rich."

"You can't take a little kid's word on what rich is, Mare. Five dollars is rich to a kid that young." Judy pressed her boot into her ski clip, leaning on Mary's shoulder for balance. "Let's go, girlfriend. Time to roll."

"The kid said *street money*. Do you know the phrase *street money*?"

"What phrase? He didn't mean it as a phrase. The kid lives on the same street as Darning, literally. Street money. Get it?" Judy popped the other ski on and slipped her hands into the pole straps. "Come on. Put your skis on."

"I think the kid was repeating something he heard. Something Darning said. There is a term *street money*."

"There is? What's it mean?"

Mary smiled. "You're so totally, like, Californian. It's what you pay for votes. You give somebody street money so they can buy votes in their district."

"Fascinating."

"Welcome to Philadelphia."

"Thank you very much." The wind was gusting hard, and Judy's ankles were wet and chilled. "Put your skis on, Mare. We'll discuss it at my apartment."

Mary tried to find her ski clip with her boot, but the ski kept slipping away. "You know, a lot of those articles I got from my computer search were about Steere and Mayor Walker. How much they hate each other."

"Yeah, so?" Judy knelt down and steadied Mary's ski until her boot finally clicked in.

"So maybe it's a political thing. The election is coming up. Maybe street money was paid or will be. Maybe there's some political angle to this."

"Next ski," Judy said, squinting against the spray of ice particles blowing into her face from the ground. "Let's go, Mare." With her eyes half closed, Judy couldn't see the smoked glass window of the Grand Cherokee sliding down to the halfway point, even if she had been looking.

"Are you listening, Jude? It could be political."

"Put your fucking boot in the fucking clip."

"Jeez Louise. Touchy, aren't we? I'm trying to solve a murder here. It's not easy." Mary nosed her other boot down, finally found the clip with her toe, and locked it in.

"Hallelujah." Judy straightened up, telemarked to turn around, and skied a few feet down the sidewalk to take the lead. "Follow me," she called back.

"Maybe Darning gets the money from somewhere," Mary called after her, hobbling through the snow. It was so damn cold. The air was too frigid to breathe. "Someone gave him street money."

Across the street, the Grand Cherokee's window edged down past the halfway point. Its tinted glass was mottled with powdery snow. It was too dark to see the driver. The engine idled and exhaust wafted from its tailpipe. The windshield wipers beat harder.

"Let's get into the street, where it's easier," Judy yelled to Mary. She looked for an opening between the cars parked at the curb. Covered with snow, the cars looked like an Almond Joy bar. Judy spotted a space and headed for it, skiing into the street. "Come on, Mare. Try and keep up."

"Show-off," Mary muttered.

Judy took off into the middle of the street and skied away from the ruts made by passing cars. The snow was knee-deep in some spots. It had been hours since Judy heard a weather report.

Mary made her way into the street with difficulty. She heard a loud hydraulic cranking and saw a snowplow in the distance, with a yellow caution light flashing on its cab. Maybe they were plowing the streets on the way to Judy's apartment. It would help. Mary couldn't believe anybody went cross-country skiing for fun. It was brutal, endless work. For that she could go to the office.

"Mare!" Judy called to her. "You okay?"

Mary tried to answer, but her words were swallowed by the cold wind and the noise from the snowplow. She struggled against the storm and tried to keep up. It was a lost cause. Snowflakes flew into her eyes. Her hands were wet in her gloves. The blizzard didn't seem to be letting up. Mary fell behind Judy a few feet, then half a block.

Behind Mary, the tinted window of the white Cherokee slid all the way down. A hand in a leather glove appeared from inside the car and brushed snow from the door frame. A second later, the barrel of a hunting rifle nosed out and pointed down the street.

26

It's a great truck, Christopher had told Marta. *Don't judge it by the way it looks. The tires are new this year. Bridgestones.*

Marta identified Christopher's ancient truck instantly because it was the most disgusting wreck in the hotel garage: a faded blue pickup with a dented white cover over its long bed. Its back fender and body were marred by dings, its doors rusted with cancerous edges, and it cowered in a far corner of the underground garage like a leper. The only bright spot on the truck was its cherry-red bumper sticker: FARRIERS SHOE IT BETTER.

The bumper sticker was Lainie's idea, Christopher had said, though Marta could have guessed as much.

She lingered near the garage wall and glanced nervously around for Bogosian. Had she lost him for good? She didn't think he'd followed her to the hotel because she'd kept checking behind her. Still, she couldn't be sure. Maybe he was lying in wait like he'd been at Steere's town house. He knew there was a conjugal visit scheduled, maybe he'd anticipated she'd try to reach the jury. Or maybe Steere had. Still, she had to go.

Marta hurried to the truck, slipped the key in the lock, and climbed inside when the door creaked open. She tossed her purse onto the beat-up passenger seat. The truck was cold and smelled oddly of singed hair. The front seat was littered with empty coffee cups, waxed paper from Dunkin' Donuts, and cellophane bags of withered carrots. A flashlight rolled on the floor and a large green rubber ball was wedged at the end of the seat. HORSEBALL, it said. Huh?

Marta inserted the key, pumped the gas, and twisted on the ignition. The engine made the tiniest click, but didn't turn over. Christopher had warned her this would happen.

Be patient, he'd said, *the car hasn't been driven in two months. And don't flood the engine.*

Marta checked her watch. 10:15. She had to get going. She turned the ignition key again, but no luck.

Give her a minute or two. Talk to her. She likes when you talk to her.

Fuck that. Talk to a truck? Christopher had way too much time on his hands. Marta forced herself to wait and scanned the garage again for Bogosian. The damn windshield was too dirty to see through and she wiped it with a cold fist. A few cars were parked on this level. Bogosian could be behind any one of them, waiting to grab her. She remembered the vise of his hands around her throat, choking the breath from her. Panicky, Marta twisted the ignition key again. The engine didn't respond.

Stay calm. Give her time.

But Marta didn't have time. She had to get this truck moving. She had to get away. She looked around. Bogosian could be anywhere. Marta forced herself to wait and tried to imagine what had happened since he'd killed the security guards. The cops had to be swarming all over Rosato & Associates. They'd see Marta's signature on the log. They'd be looking for her. The press would follow.

She just needs to warm up. Wait, then give it another try.

Marta tried the ignition again, but the engine only coughed. Fuck! Marta had to hit the road. There was no other way. If it would have gotten her anywhere, she would have surfaced and told everything she knew about the guards' murder, but she couldn't prove Bogosian was linked to Steere. She couldn't even prove Bogosian existed. Rocket Docket Rudolph was pushing the Steere case through on greased skids; Marta doubted even a murder in the office would slow him down. Steere would never permit a continuance anyway, and Marta couldn't run the risk.

Keep trying. Don't give up.

Words to live by. She twisted the key and the engine finally turned over, rheumatic but alive. Marta slammed the truck into reverse and it stalled while she was backing out. Twice. She finally got it rolling and steered it out of the garage, paying the parking bill with cash.

The truck nosed into the blizzard, which threatened to overwhelm its worn windshield wipers. She was heading north to Steere's house in New Jersey, following up on her hunch that the beach house was special to Steere and that she'd find some clue there. Some piece of evidence. Something incriminating. She was going to Long Beach Island, wherever that was. Marta needed a map.

She flipped open a messy glove compartment and searched for the maps. They fell onto the seat beside her and she rifled through them as she navigated the storm. There were wrinkled maps of Maryland and Pennsylvania. Then Bucks County, Chester County, Delaware County. Finally, New Jersey.

Marta almost drove into a telephone pole trying to open the New Jersey map and smooth it out. It was too dark to read the map. With fingertips on the wheel, she felt on the floor for a flashlight and shined it on the map. It was impossible to read in the jittery pool of light, but Marta got the general idea—over the river and through the woods. At least a three-hour trip in the snow. She had no time to spare.

She checked the rearview mirror again. There was no rear window defroster, and the scratchy plastic window was completely dark. No headlights shone through, so Marta felt reasonably sure she wasn't being followed. The roads had been plowed, but were barely passable. At least the gas tank was full. Marta accelerated and the truck hiccuped three times, then responded.

The temperature was as frigid as Maine in winter and Marta shivered in the chilly truck. She hit the button for the heat and blue smoke leaked from the vents. Marta shook her head at the sight; she'd owned a Corvair Monza that used to do that, too. Things came full circle if you lived long enough and Marta wanted to live long enough. She switched the smoke off and zipped up her coat instead. Marta had gotten the outfit at Woolworth's: a cap, a pair of long johns, a fake down coat in brown plaid, and matching plaid snowpants. She was toasty even though she looked like furniture.

Marta found the radio and turned it on. Nothing. She spun the dial. Silence. So the radio didn't work, either. Fuck. Marta wanted to find out what was happening with the cops. She checked the rearview again. No one was following her. Still she felt vulnerable. She needed protection.

Look in the tool chest, Christopher had said. *There's tools you can use as weapons.*

Marta glanced behind her. Where was the tool chest? It was a pigsty back there; racks of horseshoes straddled a workbench and clanged together as the truck plowed through the snow. A small forge was tucked in the back with tanks of propane sitting next to it. A leather apron lay crumpled in a heap over a blackened anvil. Then Marta saw it. In front of the anvil were two tool chests, and the larger one was full of old chisels, hammers, and files.

Look in the big tool chest. Take the pritchel.
What's a pritchel?

It looks like a big spike, ten inches long. You can use it as a knife, for protection.

Marta smiled to herself. Two months ago, she didn't know what a farrier was. Now she was tampering with one. She stretched behind the seat and yanked the chest closer, then rummaged through the tools and found a small hammer with a pointed tip.

If it has a pointy head, it's a nail set. Don't take the nail set. It's too light.

Okay, fine. No nail set. It wasn't anything Marta had learned in law school. She shoved her hand to the bottom of the toolbox. The tools clinked as they tumbled together and she came up with a knife that had a long, oddly curved blade, like a miniature scythe.

A hoof knife looks like that thing that the Grim Reaper carries. Forget about the hoof knife. You'll stab yourself. Find the forge hammer, too. That'll help.

Marta tossed back the hoof knife. Never take a hoof knife when a forge hammer will do. She thrust her hand back into the tool chest. There were several hammers, but one was especially large and heavy with rounded ends and a bowed wooden handle. The forge hammer! One down, one to go. Marta put it in her lap, but couldn't find the pritchel and gave up before she crashed the truck.

The traffic was sparse as Marta headed out of the city and reached a blue bridge that spanned the Delaware River. It was being plowed, and she drove behind a Port Authority snowplow like she belonged there. Marta didn't need a radio to tell her it was illegal for a civilian to be driving in these conditions, but once she'd tampered with a jury, the rest was downhill. She zoomed over the bridge a safe distance behind the snowplow and churned through the toll bridge into New Jersey.

She motored by a sign for Cherry Hill, then a series of strip joints; a seamy place called The Admiral Lounge, which she'd bet had never been patronized by an admiral, and the Liquor Ranch. Yee-hah. The truck rattled along, giving Marta time to consider her next move. She was hoping she'd find something in the beach house, but what if she didn't? She'd have wasted half the night. How much time did she have before Bogosian found her, or the cops did? The jury would reconvene first thing in the morning.

Marta kept an eye on the rearview mirror. Still no one behind her, but there were a few cars ahead. She drove for over an hour on Route 70 to 72 east and went round and round a rotary at Olga's Diner, which had a crowd despite the storm. Marta was relieved to see that the blizzard was lessening and the accumulation less in Jersey than it had been in Philly. The bare windshield wipers had a fighting chance. Marta sped up and passed a sign that said MEDFORD, then fields covered with only a thin blanket of snow.

Suddenly a green minivan appeared out of nowhere, and cut her off. Marta shouted in alarm. A loud *thud* rocked the truck. It skidded out of control and spun crazily around. Marta squeezed the steering wheel and wrenched the wheel against the skid, struggling to stay upright. Her purse was thrown against the door. The truck pinwheeled and stopped in a snowdrift like a bumper car. Marta's head snapped backward, then forward. The engine stalled. The truck fell still. The accident was over as abruptly as it had begun.

Marta felt dazed, dizzy. Her ribs ached again and soreness returned to her head. She unclenched the wheel and regained focus in time to see the minivan reversing in front of her. She caught a flash of the minivan's driver, a woman. The woman steered the minivan away and raced down the highway. Affixed to the back window was a sticker: WORKING PRESS. Fuck! It was a hit-and-run. The driver didn't even stop. A reporter, it figured.

Marta sat still and waited for the pain to subside. When it didn't, she suppressed it and assessed the damage to the truck. The minivan had hit her on the driver's side, but the windshield was still intact. The hood looked okay, even if the front was crunchier than before. Marta hoped that the engine still worked. She had no time to spare. Her watch said 12:35. She brushed the hair from her eyes and twisted on the ignition.

"Start, goddamn you," she ordered, and it did. Like a charm. On a dime. It was improved, if anything. About time she got a break. She threw the truck into reverse, spun the wheels futilely, then rocked the fucking thing back and forth until she'd worked her way out of the snowdrift and was heading the right way, down the same road the minivan had taken. Its red taillights glowed in the distance as Marta rattled behind. She passed strip malls and fast-food joints, and stopped for traffic lights at regular intervals. The minivan didn't stop for a single red light.

"You after the big story, you jerk?" Marta called after the minivan, though it hurt her jaw to shout. "It's snowing, is that the story? It's white? It's cold? It falls out of the sky?"

Another traffic light turned red, but the minivan tore past it. If Marta had time, she'd stop the van and take the reporter's name. She flashed on the face behind the wheel. A face framed by dark hair, with conventionally pretty features. Large eyes, upturned nose. Who did she think she was? Then Marta realized she knew the woman.

It was Alix Locke, the reporter who'd covered the Steere trial. Alix had been all over Marta and reported about her every day in the newspaper. Alix was the one giving the mayor a hard time at his press conference. Why would Alix be rushing to the Jersey shore? She covered only the major news stories, like Elliot Steere and City Hall. Was there news that important at a beach resort? In winter?

Marta turned the knob on the car radio again, but it was still dead. Maybe there was major flooding or a boardwalk washed away in the storm. But that wasn't Alix's type of story. She didn't do weather or features, only hard news. What was going on?

Marta ignored the traffic light and kept the minivan in sight. A rotary was coming up fast. The minivan chose the first exit without slowing down, even though snow covered the sign. Marta had to check the map but it was dark. She didn't want to lose the minivan, but she didn't want to take the wrong turn. She fumbled for the flashlight as the truck approached the rotary and groped a cylinder rolling back and forth in the seat. She held it up. A stick of Old Spice deodorant. She threw it down. The rotary was coming up.

Marta went fishing again and came up with the flashlight. By then, the minivan had disappeared into the snow flurries. Marta couldn't read the sign even up close and was forced to come to a full stop to see the damn map. She rested the map on her lap and aimed the flashlight's beam on the coastline to Long Beach Island. Surrounding it were the Pine Barrens, acres of them. The road Alix had taken led to Long Beach Island.

Marta flicked off the flashlight, hit the gas, and followed down the highway. There was no one on the dark snowy road until Marta spotted Alix way ahead. Marta thought as quickly as whiplash allowed. Why was Alix going to Long Beach Island? Why had she been so certain of where she was going, even with the sign obscured? Alix had evidently been to Long Beach Island many times before.

Marta accelerated, hoping to catch the minivan. What did she know about Alix? That she was young, sexy, and pretty. That she was single, because she'd mentioned that to Marta once, trying to find some common ground to get the exclusive. No doubt about it, Alix was an aggressive reporter. A star.

Marta tested her theory. Alix Locke and Elliot Steere; the two were a perfect match. Good-looking, driven, and successful. And Alix appeared to be heading for Long Beach Island, where Steere owned a beach house. It couldn't be just a coincidence, could it? Was Alix Locke Elliot Steere's lover?

Marta hit the gas. It was certainly consistent. Alix had featured Steere's defense in her articles and had even been criticized for favoring the defense. Marta had assumed the good press was because of her, but maybe it was because of Steere. He was the main beneficiary.

It was a trial lawyer's hunch, but Marta sensed her theory was right. Alix was a thorn in the mayor's side, and the mayor was Steere's nemesis. Marta remembered the press conference on TV, at which Alix had badgered the mayor. Maybe that was to further Steere's goals. And Alix and Steere would have to keep their affair a secret for fear of compromising Alix's job and jeopardizing her reporting on Steere.

Marta sputtered past sugar-frosted maple, pine, and scrub oak trees. She felt certain she was heading in the right direction. Alix was going to lead her to Steere's beach house and maybe to the clues she was looking for. At the very least, Marta could confront Alix. Demand the truth. Demand justice.

Marta's spirit surged. She felt energized. Justice! She hadn't known that was what she was searching for, but since the murder of the guards, something had changed. If it had been jealousy in the beginning, it was different now. Now she wanted the truth about the murder Steere had committed and she had defended. Now she wanted to bring Steere to justice. Working his mistress over would be icing on the cake. Marta could still have fun, couldn't she?

The truck barreled ahead. Beside the highway, white birch trees dipped their heads, their branches laden with wet snow. Marta used to love birch trees. She grew up among them in the woods. Slender and warmly white, their bark etched with lines as inky and precise as a fountain pen's. Marta tried to remember the last time she'd been in the woods or, for that matter, anyplace that didn't have valet parking. Her life had changed so much and she'd left so much behind, the good with the bad. It took the birches to remind her of what was good.

The truck plowed forward under a starless black dome of sky. In time, there seemed to be more sky than before. Marta knew why: she used to enjoy studying nature until she realized it wasn't billable. The trees were getting shorter, the scrub pines punier by the mile. It meant the amount of sand in the soil must be increasing. She was getting closer to the beach.

Marta kept her eye on Alix's minivan and trailed her through the Pine Barrens, then past hospitals, gas stations, and marinas, and finally over a concrete causeway to Long Beach Island. Unless Marta missed her guess, Alix Locke would lead her to the front door of Elliot Steere's beach house. The only thing Marta didn't know was:

Why?

27

Penny Jones was trying to aim his hunting rifle out the white Grand Cherokee, but his hand was shaking too much. The dope he'd smoked had worn off and he wasn't totally into this job. Shit, he'd hunted since he was a kid. Deer, pheasant, all kinds of shit, but not a person. Penny never killed nobody before. This time he had to. He had to prove himself to get back with Bogosian. It was once in a lifetime.

Penny rested his rifle in the crook of his arm, steadied his elbow on the door, and squinted down the sight. There was a shitload of snow and his eyes kept watering on account of the cold. He told himself not to think. Just cap her and not think. The snow was coming down but Penny thought he could get a clean shot. He'd only get one shot with the noise this motherfucker would make.

Penny blinked his eyes clear. There were two lawyers in the street, skiing. The lawyer in the front was tall and the one in the back was short. The big lawyer was already out of range because Penny had dicked around. He targeted the short one in the back, closer to him. She couldn't ski anyway. Survival of the fittest, right? If Penny took one out, it would keep the other busy. Two birds with one bullet, right?

Penny waited for his shot. He told himself it was no big deal to whack this broad. Fuck, she was a lawyer. They should give him a medal. Penny got a bead on the blue coat at the end of the barrel. He aimed through the snowflurries at the middle of her coat, directly at her heart.

Fuck. Wait. He wasn't ready. He needed the Jeep in a better position to make a fast getaway. Plus it was too fuckin' quiet. He set the rifle on his lap, pulled nearer the side street, then braked, leaving the car in drive. He took aim with the .30-.30 stuck in the crook of his arm, feeling the weight. Bearing down. Watching the target through the snow. The short lawyer was still in range, skiing into the light of a streetlight. Good. The blue coat reminded him of a bull's-eye. A nice, easy target.

Penny pulled the trigger partway back. His hand was still shaking. Pussy. He should just shoot. Nothing to be jittery about. No reason to stall. It wasn't like he'd get caught or nothin'. He'd have plenty of time to get away. Penny's eyes darted around to make sure, his finger cold on the trigger. There was nobody on the street. It would take the cops forever to get here. It was fish in a barrel. Except for how quiet it was.

Then Penny heard it. A racket from a couple streets over, like a snowplow creaking. The noise would cover the gunshot. The snowplow driver would think he'd popped a chain or hit a manhole cover. Everything was going Penny's way. There was no one around. He would be a hero. An asshole buddy of Bobby Bogosian's, rich as shit. All Penny had to do was pull the trigger. He was an excellent hunter.

And it was lawyer season.

Judy planted the tips of her poles in the snow and turned around. Mary had fallen again. That was twice she'd fallen so far and they hadn't even gotten off Twenty-fifth Street. Poor thing.

"Mare!" Judy called out, but she knew Mary wouldn't be able to hear her. She was too far away and the snowplow was noisy.

"Mary!" she called again anyway. Judy didn't want to ski all the way back to her if she didn't have to. They'd never get home if she had to backtrack, and her ankles were wet. Judy squinted down the dark street into the driving snow. Mary was taking a long time to get up. Time for the cavalry.

"Up and at 'em, Atom Ant!" Judy turned her skis around, telemarking, and started to ski back. What was she doing, lying there in the snow? Clowning around. Typical DiNunzio.

"Come on, lazy. Get up!" Judy shouted as she skied. The snow hadn't let up, and the wind was a killer, lashing Judy's cheeks. The wind chill must be a record. Mary shouldn't be lying in the snow like that.

She'd only soak her snowpants and feel clammy the whole trip back. A rookie's mistake.

"Mary, get up!" Judy yelled, but her friend didn't move. Snowflakes collected where Mary's legs lay on the ground, scissored in her skis. Her poles were still looped around her wrists. She wasn't making any effort to get up, and the snow from the ground had to be blowing right into her face. What the hell?

Judy skied harder. Her throat tightened. Instinct told her what her brain wanted to deny. Something was wrong. Judy skied so fast she almost tripped forward, then threw down her poles, popped her ski bindings, and ran the last few feet to Mary. She fell to her knees beside her. "Mary? Are you okay?"

"Yes." Mary's eyes were open but unfocused. She seemed dazed. She lay on her side in the snow. Her poles were still strapped to her hands. "Sure."

"Why are you lying here?"

"I'm skiing." Mary's eyelids fluttered. She breathed heavily. "Here I come. I'll catch up."

"What?" It made no sense. Judy bent over her friend, who appeared not to react to her closeness. She touched Mary's cheek. It felt clammy, and cold.

"I'm thirsty. Got milk?" Mary giggled, and Judy bent closer and caught sight of her friend's back. A circle of crimson oozed in the middle of her parka. Blood dripped onto the snow. It was the reddest red Judy had ever seen against the whitest white. She tore the hat from her head without knowing why.

"HELP!" she screamed. Judy looked wildly around.

"HELP, SOMEBODY, PLEASE!" she screamed again at the top of her lungs.

Sirens screamed as two paramedics exploded from the back of a fire rescue truck and set upon Mary. Red emergency lights bathed the falling snow in crimson. Snow like drops of blood showered Judy, who stood shivering with cold and fear. She held fast to Mary's skis, just for something to hold.

The rescue driver leapt from the front seat, raced to the back of the chunky red truck, and yanked a stretcher out. Its wheels bounced off the patterned steel of the vehicle's floor and vanished in the deep snow.

"She was shot in the back," Judy called to the paramedics, her eyes blurry with tears. Mary had lost consciousness waiting for the ambulance and looked lifeless even though she was still breathing. Her eyes were closed and her face was pale in the lurid red light. Her head rocked to the side as the paramedics checked the wound on her back and covered her with a thin green blanket. They lifted her onto the gurney on a hurried three-count.

Judy couldn't bear to see it. She couldn't bear not to. She dropped the skis and hustled after the paramedics as they hoisted the front of the stretcher into the truck. One of the paramedics scrambled in beside the stretcher and the other paramedic rolled it in from behind. The driver dashed back to his seat and tore open the door. They were leaving. "I'm coming," Judy shouted.

"No riders," the paramedic barked. He wasn't wearing a jacket and his short-sleeved uniform showed a knot of biceps as he tried to close the truck's thick door. "This is a snatch and grab. We got rules."

"She's my best friend!"

"I don't make the rules."

"I have to go with her!" Before the paramedic could stop her, Judy jammed her arm inside the doors and climbed into the truck. "I'm not moving," she said, and crouched against the inside wall of the truck. "Sorry."

"Have it your way," the paramedic snapped, "only because I can't leave you in the friggin' snow," He slammed the doors closed and twisted the lock. "Rock and roll!" he yelled over his shoulder, and the rescue truck lurched off with its siren screeching.

Inside the lighted truck, the paramedics set to work instantly, a feverish team. The muscular one cut the sleeve of Mary's parka and sweater, felt with knowing fingertips for a vein, and stuck an IV into the crook of her elbow. "Possible gunshot wound to the left lung," he shouted to the driver over Mary's still, bundled form. "Grade Two shock. She's losing one thousand to two thousand cc's. She'll need two, maybe three units when we get to the dance."

The other paramedic checked Mary's vital signs. "Respiratory rate, thirty. Blood pressure, ninety over fifty. Heart rate, one-thirty."

The driver palmed a crackling radio and repeated everything into it. Judy couldn't make out the crackled response. She couldn't tear her eyes from Mary as the paramedics moved around her. The skin on her face looked rubbery. Whiter than snow. Bloodless.

Judy's teeth began to chatter and she folded her arms against her chest. She huddled in the corner of the speeding truck. It was heated inside, but Judy had never felt so cold in her life.

28

Long Beach Island looked like a witch's index finger on Marta's map and sheltered a stretch of New Jersey coastline from the Atlantic Ocean. The map's scale showed that the island was about twenty miles long and only half a mile wide at some points. Smaller and skinnier than Marta expected.

She followed the green minivan down a wide, snowy street that seemed to run the length of the island, north to south. The street was empty, though the storm had been lighter here, too. A blackish-gray sky shed only a dusting of snow. Marta guessed the island was deserted because of the winter, not the storm.

Marta's truck rattled down the street, trembling in the strong gusts from the Atlantic on the right and the bay on the left. The street must have been the main drag in summertime because it was lined with darkened stores advertising boogie boards, bathing suits, and suntan oils. Marta drove past shell shops, Laundromats, and restaurants. The signs were evidence of more food than any human could consume: BURGERS FRIES RIBS SHAKES PIZZA and the no-frills, BREAKFAST. A placard on a toy store simply said BUY IT, and Marta gave it points for honesty if not specificity. She kept the minivan in sight and drove through a town actually named Surf City.

The minivan and truck traveled up the island, due north. Steere's beach house was in Barnegat Light, and Marta checked the map with her flashlight. The town was at the northernmost tip of the island, where the minivan was heading so fast.

Marta accelerated to keep up. The traffic lights had been turned off. She passed easily through a commercial district and into an area that looked residential. Scrub pines reappeared by the roadside, their needles lined with snow. Evergreens lined the road like Christmas trees on display. Junky beach shops were replaced by houses of different shapes and sizes; saltboxes with weathered siding sat next to spacious modern homes on stilts, with multiple decks and large glass windows. Wooden signs in a snowy divider told Marta the towns she was passing through: NORTH BEACH, HARVEY CEDARS, LOVELADIES.

Marta traveled behind the minivan for ten minutes, then twenty. The truck was freezing without a working heater and she wiggled her fingers in her gloves to keep her blood circulating. The windshield wipers had finally met a snow they could handle and pumped madly in pride. Marta stretched her neck, aching from the accident, and felt her goose eggs, sore from Bogosian. She was as beat up as the pickup but somehow her senses felt alive. Urgent.

Marta watched the homes pass on either side of the street, illuminated only by the truck's headlights. They cast little light, and Marta figured she'd crunched a headlight in the accident. The houses loomed large in the darkness and almost all were empty. They were about four and five deep to the beach and fewer than that to the bay. The farther out Marta drove, the larger and emptier the houses.

In ten blocks the houses became mansions and more modern. There were showplaces with whimsical paint jobs, their pinks and yellows bright even in the dark. Stark white contemporary homes sat far from the road, directly on the beachfront. The construction looked new and the homes custom-built. One white one reminded Marta of her glass beach house on Cape Cod, except the lots were bigger here and dotted with snowy vegetation. She sensed she was getting closer. If Steere had a house on the island, it would be in the most exclusive location.

Marta followed the minivan another five blocks, where it turned right onto a cross street and headed toward the ocean. Marta followed it to the street and stopped at the corner. She shined the flashlight up at the street sign. Steere's street; it was the address she remembered from his tax form. Marta had been right. She switched off her headlights so Alix wouldn't see the truck and turned right.

Marta coasted down the street, looking for the minivan. She was almost at the end of the street when red taillights flared on the right, near a snowy curb. Then they went dark. Marta waited in the pickup, slumping low in the beaded seat. A figure got out of the van, black raincoat flapping and dark hair blowing in the light snow. Her face was clearly visible in the light from the open van door. It was Alix Locke for sure.

Marta sank lower in her seat. In the distance stood Steere's house, which was unexpectedly different from the modern houses on the way. The back of the mansion faced the street, but Marta could see it was old and graceful, with Victorian buttresses and cantilevered towers. Three stories tall and covered with dark gray shakes, it sat farther from the main road than any of the other houses. Marta guessed it had been built on a bulge in the island. Pine trees, beach grass, and snow-covered dunes surrounded the mansion, partially concealing it. Marta could understand why Steere loved the house—and why he might use it to hide something important.

She watched Alix climb a dune and head toward the house. When Alix was out of sight, Marta parked the truck a distance from the minivan and cut the ignition. What was Alix up to? Marta grabbed her forge hammer and flashlight and was about to get out of the truck when she remembered the pritchel. She might need more protection than the hammer.

Marta flicked on the flashlight and turned around to root through Christopher's tool chest for the pritchel. After some digging, she pulled out a long pointed spike with a tip as sharp as a dagger.

The pritchel, just as Christopher had described it. A crude tool of heavy black iron. "Do you have this in navy?" she said to no salesperson in particular, then pocketed both tools, tugged on her gloves, and climbed out of the pickup.

Marta caught a faceful of snow whipping hard off the ocean and ducked her head. She was unprepared for the wind's force and the depth of the darkness around her. It was pitch black and the stormy sky permitted only the faintest moonglow. She cast the flashlight's beam to the glittery surface of the snow and walked toward the minivan, boot-deep in powder. Marta reached the minivan and shone the flashlight inside to make sure it was empty. It was, so she followed Alix's footsteps to the dune, the snow groaning underfoot.

Marta came to the dune and clambered up it. Her ribs ached with each step, and snow and ice bit her cheeks. The wind blew stronger the higher she went. The sea air smelled of brine and storm. Marta climbed to the pearly crest of the dune and when she reached it ducked to brace herself against the wind buffeting her face and drumming in her ears. She stuck the flashlight in her pocket and peeked over the dune.

Dunes coated with snow rolled in sensuous, milky mounds to Steere's Victorian mansion and to the gray-black sky, horizonless in the storm. Between the dunes dipped a valley of alabaster, crossed by the windswept shadow of a woman. Alix, her hair flying sideways, hurrying to the dark mansion.

Marta crouched on the summit of the dune and her bruised ribs screamed in protest. She waited and forced the pain from her mind. She couldn't risk going yet. She'd be exposed on the open dunes, and if Alix saw her, it would be over. Marta hunkered down in the snow like a soldier in a foxhole. Not that she knew anything about foxholes, but she had a vivid imagination. You had to, in criminal defense.

She watched Alix climb the next dune. As soon as Alix disappeared over the far side, Marta stood up and sprinted down the dune, half tumbling and half sliding. She reached the bottom of the white bowl between the dunes and ran ahead to the next, climbing up, up, up the side, running as fast as she could in Alix's footsteps, spraying snow behind her. When Marta scuttled to the crest, she threw herself down on the elbows until her chest stopped hurting.

Steere's mansion in the dunes stood stately and graceful, especially close up. It had stature, style, and class; qualities Steere could only buy. A vast expanse of incandescent snow encircled it like a warm cloak, and beyond the mansion churned the black Atlantic. Snow sprinkled from the sky like superfine sugar from a spoon and dissolved on contact with the dark, angry ocean. A light snapped on at the back entrance to the mansion, drawing Marta's attention. There was a security light mounted at the house's back entrance and one over a three-car garage. The lights must have been motion-sensitive and they illuminated the entire back of the house.

Marta watched as Alix fumbled with a key chain and let herself in the back door. The back door slammed closed with a sound lost in the roar of wind and surf. Marta stood up and ran toward the beach house, the wind drumming in her ears.

29

Mayor Walker's staff called his private bathroom the Frank L. Rizzo Memorial Can, but not in public. The bathroom had been built with donations from friends of the former mayor, who evidently wanted their hero to dump in style. The walls were covered in white marble veined with gold and the toilet was elevated on a matching pedestal. The counter surrounding the sink was marble, too, and all the fixtures were gold-plated. The total effect was Rome under Nero, a good analogy for Philly under Rizzo.

Mayor Walker hated the bathroom, but detonating the Rizzo head would cost him every vote in South Philly. He closed his eyes to the white marble and washed his face with cold water, trying to stay alert even though it was well past midnight. "Talk to me, Jen," he said between splashes. "What's the latest?"

"Steere's lawyer, DiNunzio, is in the hospital." Jen stood in the doorway and rested on the marble jamb for support. She'd barely taken her Imitrex in time and her head hurt worse than a hangover. Jen had so much to do, but all she wanted was to lie down.

"DiNunzio gonna live?"

"Doubtful. I drafted an obit and put it in the podium with your speech. It's Insert A. If she's dead by showtime, put it in."

The mayor paused. Jen could be so cold. "It's too bad. Local boy?"

"Local girl."

"Oh, right. Where was she from?"

"South Philly. Went to Penn Law, yadda yadda yadda, friend to all, yadda yadda yadda, sorely missed. It's in the bio, on the podium. DiNunzio was the one with that stalking thing a while ago."

"She was? I won't mention it." The mayor let cold water run down his cheeks. "Did you double-space the speech?"

"Of course."

"You used the font I like, the big one?"

"Humanist."

"Thank you."

"No, Humanist is the font."

The mayor colored. "Good. Now what else?"

"Richter is still missing, and they haven't picked up the suspect in the security guards' murder. The other lawyer is fine."

"Judy Carrier, right?"

"Right."

The mayor grinned. When you're hot, you're hot. "So Carrier can proceed with the Steere case."

"Yes."

"Excellent." He rinsed his face and slurped water from cupped hands. He didn't know why everybody hated Philadelphia tap water. They called it Schuylkill Punch, but it tasted great to the mayor. "Carrier a Philadelphian, too?"

"Not native."

"Then she doesn't count, not with these voters." He straightened up, snapped off the gold faucets, and snatched a fluffy white hand towel from the marble rack. He felt better already. If Steere still had a lawyer, his chances of a mistrial were low, considering that the case had already been submitted to the jury. Maybe he'd be convicted after all.

The mayor toweled off, deep in thought. Steere's lenders must be getting nervous. When would they call his notes? If Steere's properties went at auction, the city could buy them back at bargain prices. Or maybe the banks would sell them to reasonable businessmen; thieves he could deal with, not a prick like Elliot Steere. "Steere's a prick, you know that?" the mayor said.

"I know." Jen nodded. She'd listened to variations on this theme for years. The mayor was obsessed with Elliot Steere. He'd insisted the D.A. charge Steere with murder and ask the death penalty. The mayor always let his emotions get the best of him. That was why Jen was hedging her bets.

"Take the Simmons Building, for example. A

hundred-fifty-year-old building, one of the most beautiful in this city. Historic building, all sorts of history. Important history, *Philadelphia* history, you know? Nice white arches, like the old Lit Brothers. Steere buys the building for two mil, watches it fall apart, then sells it to Temple for ten mil."

"Sounds like a good deal to me," Jen said, but she knew the mayor wouldn't agree. Not that she cared. She had to get out.

"Maybe so. Maybe it was a good deal. But you know what? The man didn't love the building," the mayor said, wagging a wet finger. "The man did not love the building. If you're gonna own a building like that, you gotta love it. It's not like toilet paper. That's a prick for you. You understand? Only a prick would do that."

"Yes."

The mayor wondered if Jen were really listening. "Can you put that in a speech?"

"That Elliot Steere is a prick? I don't think so."

The mayor shook his head. That wasn't what he meant and she knew it. Sometimes he didn't like Jen very much at all. She did good things for the city, though. The literacy program, the blood drive, the organ donor thing. All on her own initiative, back when they were at the D.A.'s office.

"Are we done yet?" Jen asked. "The press is out there waiting."

The mayor rubbed his face red. "Where's our friend Alix Locke?"

"Gone, thank God."

"She has a hard-on for me, Jen. She won't quit until I'm a civilian again. She's trying to screw up my chances for reelection, single-handed. What did I ever do to her?" The mayor dropped his towel on the edge of the marble sink, and Jen picked it up and hung it on the marble towel rack.

"Don't start with this, okay?" Jen ran her manicured nails through her dark hair. She was drained. She had to go. It was getting later and later. "The reporters are waiting. There's more of them since the DiNunzio shooting. Let's feed the animals and go home."

"Any national press, or just local?" The mayor leaned close to the mirror and fingered the stubble on his chin, trying to decide whether he had to shave.

"Local so far. CNN is on the way, but they're having trouble in the snow. You should shave."

"Again? I shaved twice today. My face is killing me. I get those little red bumps." The mayor shuddered, but Jen plucked a disposable razor off the shelf and handed it to him.

"Shave. We have company. Come on. We have to go. They're waiting."

"If CNN shows up, I'll shave. How's that for a deal?"

Jen sighed. "Listen, we have to go. I have to go."

The mayor was appraising his reflection. He saw a strong, vibrant man, full of energy and passion. A figure of commitment, intelligence, and integrity in the prime of his political life. Courtney called him a total stud, but his wife didn't use words like that. Maybe because she was a different generation. "Jen, I have to ask you something."

"What?"

The mayor tilted his head down slightly. "Am I going bald?"

30

Judy slumped in a chair in the hospital waiting room and stared at the stale blood on her palms. She felt sick to her stomach. She couldn't get all the blood off when she'd washed. It had dried to black and caked in the lines and creases of her palms, limning each wrinkle with a line as fine as a sable brush's. Her lifeline was painted with the blood of her best friend.

Judy stuck her hands between her legs so she wouldn't look at them anymore. It didn't help. Mary's blood stained her snowpants, from where she had cradled her in the snow. Judy looked around the room for distraction. A TV was on, mounted high in a corner of the empty waiting room, which was reserved for surgeries. The volume was turned off on the TV, but Judy could see it was a never-ending update on the blizzard. The snow fell on the TV screen just as it fell outside. A reporter interviewed a bureaucrat in a tie and a ski hat. Then the screen showed a picture of huge dump trucks salting the highway.

Judy couldn't focus on the screen. Her thoughts kept returning to Mary. Lying on the ground, bleeding. She was in surgery now. They were doing everything they could, a doctor had told her, as had one of the nurses, an older woman. Everybody was doing everything they could, Judy kept telling herself over and over, like a mantra. She would repeat it to Mary's parents and her twin when they came. But the DiNunzios were old, and Judy worried they couldn't take a shock like this.

Judy tried to settle down. She'd have to have it together if she was going to see the DiNunzios. She eased back into the chair and crossed her legs, avoiding the stain on her pants. She laced her fingers together, then folded her arms. She would have called her parents but they were traveling again. Judy looked around the room. Her gaze had nowhere to rest.

Judy caught sight of the TV and sat bolt upright in disbelief. The screen said SPECIAL REPORT above a photo of Marta, superimposed against the offices of Rosato & Associates. There was a photo of blood smeared on the elevator at the office, then two quick photos of the security guards in the building. What? What was happening? Judy couldn't believe what she was seeing.

A TV anchorwoman came back on. Her lipsticked mouth was moving but no words came out. The TV was on mute. Judy leapt from her chair and hurried to the TV. She was tall enough to reach it but she couldn't find the buttons. Where was the volume control? She yanked a chair under the TV and clambered up on it.

Up close, the anchorwoman's face was flat and large, the colors the ersatz hues of television. Her eyes were the blue of sapphires, her lips a supersaturated pink. She kept talking silently, opening and closing her mouth. Judy looked everywhere on the TV console. Where was the volume?

Film of Marta came on, talking in front of the Criminal Justice Center. Behind her was its modern stained glass. It must be file footage from the Steere trial. Judy was panic-stricken. Had something happened to Marta? Was she shot, too, like Mary? What about the security guards? Judy searched frantically for the TV buttons. No controls. She groped the console. Cool, seamless plastic. Fuck! Where was it?

"Where's the volume?" Judy shouted, though she knew the floor was empty. There hadn't even been a receptionist at the desk when she came up to the floor. "HEY!" she shouted. No one came running but she didn't want to leave the TV. Maybe it was remote-controlled. Judy twisted on the chair and scanned the room for the remote. The coffee tables, the end tables, and the seats were bare.

On the TV screen, Mayor Walker was giving some sort of press conference. His face looked grave behind the microphones and a podium with the city seal. To his left stood his chief of staff, looking equally somber. At the top of the screen it said LIVE. What were they saying? Did it have to do with Marta? With Mary?

Judy spotted a small plastic panel under the screen and hit it to see if it would pop open. It didn't. She hit it again but the panel still wouldn't open. She hit it harder, pounding with her fist until the lid came up. Tiny dials protruded from a recessed compartment, and Judy twisted them back and forth with bloodstained fingers. The fake colors on the TV switched from flesh tones to hot orange, from royal blue to black. Judy still couldn't hear the TV. Where was the fucking volume?

On the screen, the police inspector was being interviewed, standing in front of the Roundhouse in the snow. What was going on? A commercial came on. The news report was over. No! Was someone shooting them all? Who was behind this? Steere? Judy couldn't let him. She'd fight back. She needed to hear. She hit the TV panel until the lid broke off, then pounded it harder, cracking it into sharp plastic shards, straight through the fucking panel. Smashing it, destroying it, obliterating it. Killing all the phony colors with the force of her might and her will and her pain. Raging until her hand was covered with blood and finally it was her own.

Judy sat in her chair with her hand packed and bandaged with gauze. She'd taken three stitches and refused a sedative. She'd scrubbed her snowpants and washed her face and hands. A nurse had brought her an antibacterial soap and it had taken off most of the blood on her good hand. She felt drained, her emotions spent. She watched the scene around her with an odd detachment.

Bennie Rosato had arrived, in jeans and a sweater, her large face un-madeup and drawn. She made sure Judy was okay, then sat trying to comfort Mary's mother, an elderly, birdlike woman with teased hair. The mother sobbed as she sat with Mary's father, a short, bald man whose laborer's body had gone soft. His eyes were red-rimmed, but he was comforting his wife.

With them sat Mary's sister, Angie. Angie was Mary's identical twin. Her hair, though shorter, was the same dirty blond, and her eyes were as brown and large as Mary's. Her mouth was a perfect match, full and broad. Judy liked looking at Angie. It was as if Mary were in the waiting room, whole and healthy again.

Angie was speaking in low tones to her parents and to Bennie. The four of them sat huddled close together, a nervous, weepy circle. Judy couldn't hear from where she was sitting, but she watched Angie's lips move like the anchorwoman's on TV. The DiNunzios were on mute, in two dimensions. Everything around Judy seemed distant. She wanted to keep it that way. Let Bennie comfort Mary's parents, she would know what to say. Judy had to figure out what to *do*.

31

Marta dashed down the snowy dune behind Steere's house and ran toward the left side of the house. The security lights blasted her with light as soon as she reached their invisible ambit. She picked up the pace, sprinting beside her leaping shadow, spraying snow with each bound past the house's back entrance. As tempted as she was to follow Alix into the mansion, it was too risky. Lights were going on inside, and Marta needed to see what was happening.

She made it to the shadow of the side wall and turned the corner. The security lights blinked off. It was dark again. Marta leaned against the house, breathing hard. Her ribs speared her insides. She hadn't exercised this much all last year. Wind and snow gusted off the ocean and whipped through Marta's hair. Her eyes stung with snow and salt and she clung to the rough shakes of the wall, blinking. Snow buried her gloved fingers and stuck to the wooden shakes in splotches. Snowdrifts reached to her knees.

She had to keep moving. Marta inhaled deeply, steeling herself for the familiar rib pain, and ran through the snowdrifts alongside the house, sliding a hand along the wall so she wouldn't fall. The windows were high and light poured over Marta's head from the house. She hurried along the wall, reached the front of the mansion, and peeked around the corner. The facade of the house was even grander than the back and its frontispiece was an immense wraparound porch. A bank of arched windows dominated the front wall and light shone through them, illuminating a living room.

Bookshelves filled the room, showcasing fussy leather volumes of red and brown. Victorian couches and antique chairs surrounded a carved mahogany coffee table. There wasn't a TV in sight; it wasn't Steere's taste, maybe it was a decorator's or Alix's. On the other side of the fireplace was a darkened dining room and a kitchen presumably beyond; Marta had shopped for enough old houses to know. Alix was nowhere in sight, at least from a parallax view. Marta would have to move center to get a better look. Small dunes nestled in front of the house, and Marta spotted one that sat about thirty feet from her. Wind off the ocean roared at the dune and blew snow from its crest in a frosty fan.

Marta scrambled for the dune and was in front of the porch when she was jerked back suddenly. Her coat was caught on a wooden fence. She pulled but it wouldn't come free. Marta was in plain view of the living room, standing in a square of light. She tugged her coat and looked at the window, then froze.

Inside the house, entering the living room from another entrance, was Bogosian. Marta almost screamed. Bogosian was right across the porch on the other side of the glass. He could see her if he looked out to sea. His head was swiveling left and right. He was looking for something. Someone.

Marta panicked. She yanked her coat with all her might, but it was still caught on the post. She was totally exposed, struggling with the fucking fence. If Bogosian spotted her she'd be dead. She tore at the coat and was about to slip it off when the fence shuddered violently and the coat came free. Marta fell backward into a chilly snowdrift and lay still as a dead snow angel, her thoughts feverish.

Where had Bogosian come from? Had he driven here? Where was his car, the garage? Marta hadn't bothered to look for tracks in the snow, she'd been too distracted by Alix. She hadn't seen Bogosian following Alix, so he must have been here already. Waiting. Maybe he'd figured Marta would try to search Steere's beach house. Or maybe he'd arranged to meet Alix here.

Marta was too frightened to answer the questions. Snow froze her neck and fell behind her ears. She lay perfectly still so she wouldn't draw Bogosian's attention. Still, she had to find out where he was. She gathered her courage and peered over her boots at the house. The living room was empty. Where was Bogosian? Was he coming after her? She could make a run for the truck.

She started to go, then stopped. Bogosian stood on the stairway to the second floor. Marta shivered with fear and cold. She flashed on the bloodied security guards. She had to get a grip. What was Bogosian doing? She had to see.

Marta flopped over, chin in the snow, and crawled the few feet to the small dune. She crouched behind it, wind pummeling her back. Her hair lashed her cheeks and she shoved it away with a snowy glove. The surf crashed on the beach, a deafening white noise. Bogosian was motionless in the middle of the staircase. He seemed to be squinting up the stairs.

Marta looked up to the second floor of the mansion. A light blinked on in a far window, where a bedroom would be. It was too high for Marta to see inside. On the stair, Bogosian cocked his head like a pit bull, his large hand resting on the banister. Whatever was going on, it didn't look like Bogosian and Alix had arranged to meet here. An ominous feeling rumbled in Marta's gut.

The light in the second-floor bedroom snapped off. A split second later, a light appeared in the window next to it. Alix must have been going from one room to the next. Marta craned her neck but still couldn't see anything. What was going on? She had to move back if she wanted to see upstairs.

Marta edged from the dune toward the ocean, low as a snow crab. She backed against another dune and ducked behind it. From her new perspective, she could see Alix's head and shoulders in a room on the second floor. Alix appeared to be searching for something in an exercise room, with a Stairmaster and a Lifecycle. Marta watched as Alix opened a cabinet in the room and rifled its contents. White towels and Evian bottles fell to the floor. What was Alix looking for?

On the stairs, Bogosian took a step up, running his gloved hand on the banister.

Marta looked up again. The exercise room went dark. In the next minute a light went on in the middle of the second floor, where a set of French doors opened onto a wooden deck. The French doors gave Marta a full view and she could see Alix was in a home office. She was tearing open file drawers and ransacking them. Papers sailed to the carpet. Alix kept searching. What was she looking for?

A sudden movement on the stairs caught Marta's eye. Bogosian eased his Magnum from his shoulder holster.

My God. Marta looked up at Alix. She was still searching the files, on her knees in front of the file cabinet.

Bogosian started up the stairs with his gun drawn. Did he know Alix was up there? Did he mean to kill her? Why? Marta didn't know what to do. Panic constricted her chest.

Alix was tearing at a cardboard box with her nails. She kept clawing at it, then grabbed a scissors from a desk and slit it with the scissor blade.

Bogosian reached the top of the stairs. Marta

felt her heart thundering though her thick coat. What could she do? She had to do something. She couldn't let Bogosian kill Alix. No one was around. It was the middle of a blizzard. Marta couldn't make it inside the house in time if she tried. She rose to her feet, unsteady in the fierce wind.

Alix was kneeling in front of the cardboard box, reading its contents. Bogosian appeared in the office doorway and aimed his gun point-blank at her forehead. A wave crashed loud as a thunderclap, and Marta heard herself screaming even over its roar.

32

Snow swirled around the steel skyscraper that served as a platinum setting for the city's largest and most expensive law firm, Cable & Bess. Light sparkled from its emerald-cut windows like a diamond choker strung around the building's neck. A sterling-haired attorney sat in a corner diamond talking on the telephone. A trim sixty-two, John LeFort remained composed and professional, even though it was past midnight and on the phone was the fifth unhappy banker he'd spoken with. All of them were lenders of LeFort's client Elliot Steere.

"I assure you, the Steere debts are under control," LeFort was saying. He ran a forefinger over one of his dark eyebrows, which sheltered his light eyes and fine features like a sturdy roof. A Harvard graduate, LeFort was the consummate banking lawyer, so he didn't judge his clients. Some became rich, some failed, and all tried again.

"The debts are not under control, to my mind," the banker responded. This time the banker was Morris Barrie at First Federal. LeFort had dealt with

Mo Barrie many times over the years and knew him well. The men spoke the same language, so this conversation, which could otherwise be ugly or profane, would be quite civilized.

"We'll need another waiver, Mo," LeFort said evenly. He always used the term "we" when referring to his clients, to encourage their creditors to think of them as a team. A team they couldn't quit.

"I'm not so sure, John," said Mo, who at this point was showing worrisome signs not only of quitting the team, but of selling the franchise.

"Another month on the principal payments would do it."

"We've rolled over the one-month waiver six times. How long can we keep waiving? Steere owes both past and current principal payments on his outstanding loans."

"It's a temporary situation," LeFort soothed. His gaze wandered over his desk, which was stacked with squared-off correspondence and legal pads. A Waterford pen and pencil set and black-and-white photographs were the only personal touches; LeFort much preferred black-and-white portraits to color. "We're meeting the interest payments. We'll resume principal payments as soon as the acquittal is in, any day now. The bank retains the properties as collateral. The debt is secured."

"I'm at a loss to see how. I reviewed the leases, and those properties can't generate the cash to resume principal payments, with the interest and taxes. The purpose of the investment was the resale of the properties. Steere's legal position makes that untenable, perhaps impossible."

"Our legal position is sound."

"Sound, you say? His defense lawyers are dropping like flies. One vanished and one shot. It's been on every broadcast. My wife thinks they jumped ship, for God's sake!"

LeFort laughed, not so loudly as to be impolite. Bunny was a hysteric, everybody knew it. "Remember that the jury is deliberating. They have the case. I sat in the courtroom, I saw the closing, and I can tell you that in my judgment they will acquit by the end of business tomorrow."

"So you say, but Steere's refinancing brings the debt above conservative appraisals—above anybody's appraisal—of the liquidation value of the property. On paper, these nine buildings are valued at ninety-three million. They're probably not worth sixty million, and our exposure is growing."

"We're almost out of the woods, Mo."

"John, the committee is concerned. Deeply concerned. Every hour the jury takes to reach its decision decreases the salability of the properties. If the jury is hung, this could go on for another year. Then we can't wait for the best offer. We'll have to liquidate."

"You won't have to liquidate."

"I don't mind telling you, I'm out on a limb at this point. Personally, I mean." Mo sighed, and there was the musical *chink-clink* of ice cubes against crystal. LeFort knew what that meant. Glenfiddich, the elixir of downside analysis.

"I wouldn't worry overmuch, Mo."

"How can I not? I've lent you more than the properties are worth in a fire sale. No, more than they're worth, period. The committee will have my head for this one." Another *clink*, then the sound of a discreet sip. "John, if Steere has any hidden resources, hidden assets, he should bring them into play. Anything in Switzerland, the Isle of Man, the Caymans. God, man, now is the time. Concealing them is no longer—"

"There's no concealment," LeFort assured him. There was nothing to hide. Steere's net worth was by any measure negative, he was so extraordinarily leveraged, but no one with whom Steere did business could admit as much. In other words, if Steere weren't so in debt, he'd be broke. LeFort no longer found it ironic that massive debt was as potent as massive wealth.

"I know we're not the only lender," the banker said. "Not the only note. We certainly don't want to be the last one to call."

LeFort flinched when he heard the C word. Some thought *cancer* was the ugliest C-word, but banking lawyers knew better. "Calling the notes is a lose-lose proposition; you know that, Mo. You don't want to send us all into bankruptcy court for the next three years. The bank would have to settle for an embarrassing fraction. Stay the course and you'll come out in clover."

"John, my back is to the wall this time." There was another *clink*, then ice rattling hollowly. The bottom of the tumbler. LeFort guessed Mo would pour another, and he did. So what John had been hearing around the club was true.

"Don't forget," LeFort added, "you have Steere's personal guarantee on the refinancing."

A laugh, and a gulp. "What's the personal guarantee of a convicted felon worth?"

LeFort stiffened. This conversation was growing tiresome, and he'd already had four others like it. It was time for hardball. "Are you calling the notes, Mo?"

"I didn't say that."

"Good. Then we'll need thirty more days."

"I can't do that, John."

"If you can't, then call the notes."

"I can't do that either," the banker said, frustration clear in his voice. "If Steere's intention is to sell the properties to the city, I would urge him to entertain reduced offers now. We had two calls today from the mayor's office. They want those properties, John. They said fifty million was the starting point."

"We're not ready to sell yet. We expect the price to rise as the election gets closer."

"More money from the city, John? It's blood from a stone."

"Not from the city. We understand a group may be getting together to buy the buildings. Leonard Corbin and his group."

"We can't wait for that. The committee won't stand for it. One of those properties should be under an agreement of sale by the end of the week."

LeFort squared his padded shoulders. "The properties will sell for a fair price when we see fit."

A heavy sigh, then silence. "This is killing me, John."

"We've done business together for years. The bank stands to profit handsomely from these loans. It has in the past, it will in the future."

"But this news with the lawyers, it's shocking."

"Eye on the ball, Mo. The jury doesn't know about that. Let's keep our wits, shall we?"

"Okay, John. Eye on the ball." The banker heaved a final, liquored sigh and hung up.

Elliot Steere sat in his cell with his eyes lightly closed, resting his head against the cinderblock wall. The pockmarked guard had told him about the dead security guards and about the associate, DiNunzio. The battle had been joined. His forces were prevailing, but there had been a problem. Steere had to assess the latest situation, then take action. He had many options. Room to move. He only looked like a man in prison.

Steere rested his hands beside him, relaxed his body, and let his thoughts run free. The first thing he did was consider his forces: a woman and a man. The woman had been instructed to destroy the file. She would do it because Steere had ordered her to and because it incriminated her. Steere assumed she was retrieving the file and destroying it, unless he heard to the contrary. So far he hadn't, so all was well.

Steere considered the man, Bogosian. He had

been instructed to stay with Marta, but something had evidently gone wrong. But Bogosian would still have her in his control. He wouldn't let her go. He would stay with it until he finished the job or finished Marta.

Steere's face remained a mask. His eyes moved under his closed lids. There was no alternative now but for Marta to die. She had outlived her usefulness. The case was already at the jury. If she vanished and turned up dead later, Bogosian could make it look like a suicide or robbery-murder. Bogosian would get the details right. He had done it before.

Steere breathed deeply, into a greater state of meditation. Bogosian had evidently gotten to DiNunzio at the railroad bridge. It was unexpected, but he had done it to salvage the operation. It was a smart tactic and it had shown initiative. Steere would reward Bogosian for it. It was as Sun-Tzu had said: *Never overindulge subordinates, because they will be like spoiled children; view them as infants and be able to lead them into battle.* Steere was feeling that way about Bobby now. Almost fatherly. Then it passed.

What action could Steere take now to achieve victory? He had to be flexible, stay relaxed. His enemies were in disarray. Scattered, wounded. Steere had the superior position and he had to stay fluid to capitalize on the circumstances. *Be like water in battle; water conforms to the terrain in determining its movement, and forces conform to the enemy to determine victory.*

Steere's thoughts became clear as spring water

and flowed like a stream. The damage he had done to his lawyers could provoke a mistrial. That was the last thing he wanted. He had ensured the jury's verdict and he knew his juror would be successful. A mistrial would cost Steere his juror, keep him in jail, and disquiet his lenders. No. He wanted his case moving ahead, his verdict inevitable as the tides. Steere must be found not guilty, and soon. Nothing less would do.

Steere considered his business position. His lenders would need the verdict, too, as soon as possible. They'd be threatening to call the notes. He had instructed LeFort to play hardball and he knew they'd toe the line. The banks didn't want to call on him. They loathed confrontation and conflict, even conflict as contained as litigation. Steere smiled inside. The bankers knew nothing of war, either. Once everybody had the bomb, nobody had the balls to use it.

Steere breathed deeply. *Be like water in battle.* Consider if one of the lenders called a note. An electrical fire in one of the buildings would raise the capital. Steere would assign the bank the right to collect the insurance, and it would allow him time on the other notes. In no event would Steere permit the mayor to get the properties. Steere had a strategy to ensure the mayor's defeat, and the properties were integral to it. *Both sides stalk each other over several years to contend for victory in a single day.*

Suddenly there was a knock at the window of his cell, jarring Steere from his meditation. It was the guard, leaning near the thick plastic window. "Mr. Steere," he said, "your lawyer is here to see you."

33

Bennie sat in front of her computer in the spare bedroom she only euphemistically called a home office. Books and papers stuck out of the bookshelves over her computer monitor. Old coffee cups and dirty spoons threatened to engulf the ergonomic keyboard. A reddish golden retriever named Bear rested at Bennie's feet among wet Sorel boots, old faxes, and dog hair tumbleweeds. To Bennie, you could clean or you could enjoy life, and these things were mutually exclusive. Wasn't it Justice Brandeis who said sunshine was the best disinfectant? Bennie took it as a housekeeping philosophy.

She clicked the computer mouse and stared at the enlarged picture of the black man on the screen. Eb Darning, a bank employee; clean-shaven and well-groomed. Bennie clicked again and displayed a photo of Heb Darnton she'd clipped from the online newspaper. It must have been a file photo. Heb had a thick beard, wild hair, and a deranged expression.

Bennie tilted the photos so they were side by side

on the screen. *Eb Darning/Heb Darnton.* She had plugged in both names in every website about Philadelphia she could find, including the local newspapers' sites. Bennie sat back in her chair and compared the two photos. It could have been before and after pictures of the same man.

Bennie was shocked. What had the associates stumbled onto? What was going on in her law firm? Was this what had gotten Mary shot? And how was Marta involved? There were too many questions, all of them threatening the existence of Rosato & Associates. Bennie couldn't lose everything she had worked for, not again, and not without a fight.

She stared at the man's picture. Eb Darning. He had the answers. The online article said he had lived on Green Street in the sixties. Bennie knew Green Street well, it was in the city's Fairmount section. Bennie had a client on Spring Garden Street, a barber who cut everybody's hair in the neighborhood. He would know Darning or he would know somebody who did.

Bennie reached for the phone.

BEAN'S PROCESS read white letters painted in a crumbling arc on the tiny storefront. The barbershop hadn't changed since the fifties. It was wedged flat as a jelly sandwich between a rib joint and a restored apartment building. Its fluorescent lights shone bright through the snowstorm.

Bean lived above the shop, but he met Bennie in

262 — LISA SCOTTOLINE

it, standing next to her as she sat in one of the old-fashioned chairs, of white porcelain with cracked red leather cushions and headrests. Bean was most at home in his shop, which Bennie understood perfectly. "Sorry to get you out of bed," she said.

"Don't think nothin' about it." Bean waved her off with a dark hand that was surprisingly small for someone of his girth. At sixty-seven, Washington "Bean" Baker was still large, with chubby cheeks and brown, wide-set eyes, but the most remarkable aspect of his appearance was the unusual shape of his bald head. His forehead bulged where his hairline used to be, his chin protruded, and his skin color was brown tinged with red. Growing up his mother had decided her baby's head looked just like a kidney bean, so she called him Bean. "I'd come down for you anytime, lady," he said.

"Even though I lost your case?"

"I tol' you nothin' would come of it. Nobody gonna stand up agains' the cops. They shake you down and get away with it."

"Now they wouldn't."

"Why?" he asked, with a slow smile. Bean did everything slowly. He thought carefully before he spoke and moved only with deliberation. It was a comforting trait in a man with a straight razor at the carotid. "You learn a few tricks since you were young?"

"Just a few. So have the juries. Today those cops would have been convicted."

"Should I be waitin' on a refund?"

"Hey, I took you on contingency, remember? I didn't stick you."

Bean smiled. "I know. I jus' said it to get you riled up."

"I feel bad enough already," Bennie grumbled. "I shoulda had 'em. They lied on the stand."

"They sure did." His voice was soft, his tone matter-of-fact. "They're cops."

"I owe you one."

"Forget it. I jus' like to see you get worked up."

Bennie edged forward on the barber chair. "Do you know anyone named Eb Darning, Bean?"

"Eb?" Bean rubbed his bald head with his fingertips, kneading his red-brown scalp like soft clay. "Eb? Long time ago. Eb. I remember Eb."

"What do you remember about him?"

"Only one thing to know about Eb. He drank too much. Had a problem with the bottle. Went to the state store every day. I used to see him. Eb was there soon as they opened. He'd be waitin' on the sidewalk. Tol' me he only bought one bottle a day. If he got more than one, he'd try to drink 'em both down."

"Any drugs?"

"Just the bottle."

"When was the last time you saw him?"

"Ten years, maybe twelve."

"Take a look at this." Bennie pulled the computer photo of the clean-shaven Eb Darning from her coat pocket and handed to Bean. "Is this him?"

"Sure. That's Eb."

"Now I want to show you another photo." She passed Bean the photo with the beard. "Take a look at it and tell me if you think it's Eb, too."

"This him?" he asked after a minute.

"You tell me."

Bean walked with the photo to the cushioned benches against the shop wall and eased his bulk into one of them. The benches had been scavenged from various restaurant booths and were stuck together in mismatched banks of red, blue, and brown. They made a vinyl rainbow against the white porcelain tile on the wall. A black pay phone with a rotary dial was mounted next to the tile, and yellowed political posters were taped to the back wall, with faded pictures of black ward leaders. Bennie let her eyes linger on their bright, ambitious faces because Bean would be looking at the photo for the foreseeable future. "Well?" she said when she couldn't wait any longer.

Bean looked up, blinking. "Doesn't look like the Eb I knew, but it could be him. The eyes, it could be him. He didn't have no beard when I knew him. That I know for sure. He came in for a shave, time to time."

"If the beard were gone, would that be Eb?"

"Could be. Could be." Bean handed back the photos. "Got old fast, he did. I wouldn'ta recognized him if you hadn'ta said somethin'."

Bennie took it as a tentative yes and slipped the photos back in her pocket. "What kind of man was Eb, do you remember?"

"A drunk."

"I mean his personality."

"To me, he was a drunk. Thas' all. All drunks the same." Bean shrugged a heavy set of shoulders. He wore a loose-fitting blue barber smock with baggy pants even though the shop was closed. Bean always said he slept in his smock, but Bennie hadn't believed him until now. "Eb was quiet in the chair, when he was sober. Rest of the time he jabbered."

"Did he talk about work?"

"Work. Yeah."

"He worked at the bank, right? PSFS."

"Bank?"

"Yes. PSFS."

Bean's focus fell on a clean linoleum floor with black-and-white tiles. "That was only for a while. A year maybe. I know 'cause Eb started wearin' a tie. Then he quit and he stopped wearin' the tie. Wore that tie for about, say, a year."

"Why did he quit, do you know?"

"The bottle. Eb never kept work for too long. Always lookin' for the angles, you know? I offered him a job once, sweepin'. Eb said no thanks." Bean frowned so deeply his forehead wrinkled like an old bulldog. "Said, 'I don't do that work.' I didn't like that, I sure didn't."

Bennie smiled. "Who wouldn't work for you, Bean? I'd work for you in a minute."

"You? You a slob. I seen your office."

"We're talking about Eb now, not me, so tell me about Eb. Everything you know."

Bean settled deeper into the cushioned bench.

"Eb. Eb. Let me see. Eb was the type of man, he didn't want no real job. Wanted the easy money. Lookin' for the angles. All the time, lookin'. You know what I mean?"

"Yes."

"Eb liked the jobs at City Hall."

"City Hall?"

"Thas' what I remember."

"What did he do there?"

"Jobs."

"Who did he work for? What department?"

Bean smiled, this time without warmth. "Woman, what kind of jobs you think a man like that does for City Hall?"

"I don't know."

"Don't be silly."

"Educate me. What jobs?"

"L and I, for a while."

"Licenses and Inspections?"

"What department don't matter, call it what you like. Building permits, the fleet. Parking Authority, what have you. Eb worked for City Hall. Eb did what he had to do. He got paid in cash money."

"Did he have any friends?"

"Not that I know."

"Wife? Girlfriend?"

"No wife. Maybe a girl, for a while."

"Anyone special?"

"No. Coupla girls."

"Damn."

"Wait." Bean held up a hand. "You're rushin' me

now. I said 'no' too fast. There mighta been a kid."

"A *child*?" Bennie hadn't read anything in the newspapers about a child. No one had come forward.

"Little girl." Bean nodded. "I saw it, in a picture in his wallet. A school picture of a girl. Real cute."

"What was her name?"

"Don't know. Never talked about her. I axed when I saw the picture and Eb just shook his head. Didn't say nothin', just shook his head. He had a long look on his face, a bad look. I figured somethin' bad happened to that little girl. Like she passed and Eb didn't want to speak about it."

Bennie paused, trusting Bean's instincts. "Eb had no one else except the daughter?"

"No."

"No friends from work?"

"No. Sat in the chair, didn't say much 'cept to answer. Sometimes he got a shave, like I said. When he was goin' for errands. For the city."

"What errands?"

Bean cocked his head and frowned. "Now how do I know what errands?"

"Maybe he said. Give me a break here. I'm trying to figure this out. What did he say about the errands? Can you remember?"

Bean closed his eyes as he thought. His eyelids fluttered, slightly greasy.

"Didn't you ask him, 'Why you need a shave today, Eb?' 'Why are you all dressed up today, Eb?'"

"Hush now and let me think. You an impatient, impatient woman."

Bennie clammed up.

"Eb used to say somethin' 'bout 'inspection,'" Bean said slowly, and opened his eyes.

"Building inspections?"

"Maybe that was it."

Bennie was thinking of Steere's city properties. They would have to be inspected every year. Steere's violations were notorious. Somebody had to be looking the other way. Somebody who was working the angles and got paid in cash. "That was when?"

"You're takin' me back now."

"Twenty, thirty years?"

"Maybe. I don't remember."

"When was the last time you saw Eb?"

"Don't know. I los' track of him. Heard he los' his place, moved away. Drinkin' all the time. Don't know where he is now. Ain't seen him."

Bennie paused, debating whether to tell Bean what had become of Darning. She couldn't tell him that Eb was the homeless man Steere killed. The information was privileged, and Rosato & Associates was in unethically deep shit as it was. But she couldn't just leave him in the dark. "Bean, I'm sorry, but I think Eb may have been murdered."

"Thas' too bad," he said, but Bean's expression didn't change. It was strange to Bennie because the man had a huge heart.

"You don't seem that upset."

"I ain't upset. I ain't surprised neither."

"Why?"

"It happens."

"Murder?"

Bean nodded, and Bennie did feel silly. "The killer won't get away with it."

Bean just smiled.

"He won't. Not if I can help it," she said, then caught herself. What was she saying? Steere was her client, a Rosato client. Bennie's firm was being paid to get him off. Wait a minute. Was that what had happened? Was that why Mary had been shot? Why Marta disappeared? Were they working to get to the bottom of Darning's murder, with a mind to hanging Steere? Their *own client*?

Bennie couldn't let that happen. Not to her firm, not to her practice. It could ruin them all. If Steere was a killer, it wasn't the job of his own lawyers to bring him to justice. That would be a betrayal, a violation of the ethical duty that made the most sense to her. Loyalty.

Bennie had to put a stop to it. She stood up, grabbed her coat, and slipped it on. "I gotta go, Bean. Thanks a lot for the information."

"It's still snowin' out there. Why don't you set until it slows up?"

"No thanks."

"I could trim that mop on your head."

"Gotta run," Bennie said as she hit the cold air.

34

Judge Rudolph pondered the bad news propped up on his elbow next to his snoring wife, reluctant to leave the warmth of his king-size four-poster. The judge had been fast asleep when he got a call from his law clerk telling him that two of Steere's lawyers were missing or shot and security guards had been murdered. Christ, if it wasn't one thing it was another. Judge Rudolph knew he had a terrible night ahead and it would begin as soon as his bare toes hit the cold hardwood floor. He had some concern for the lawyers, but he had to keep his focus clear. What about his elevation to the Court?

"How long, Lord?" Judge Rudolph muttered to himself as he swung his skinny legs out from under the white baffle comforter. His feet chilled on contact with the hardwood floor that Enid refused to cover with anything as plebeian as a rug. He scurried to the bathroom in his boxer shorts and stood shivering on the rag bath mat. It was too cold in this damn house. Enid kept the thermostat at 68 degrees, and his toes were blue half the time. The judge hugged himself to get warm and wiggled his feet on the bath mat. He wasn't moving off that rug. The tile floor would be ice.

The judge inched the bath mat over to the toilet with his toes. He'd have to get to chambers and deal with this mess. The snowstorm howled outside the bathroom window. He'd call the sheriff to drive him in. Not even a blizzard would stop him. It would take more than an act of God to keep Harry Calvin Rudolph from the Supreme Court of Pennsylvania.

The judge lifted the seat up. It would take a minute since that go-round with his prostate. But he was okay, he was fine, he still had a long career ahead. Breathe in, breathe out. Reeeee-lax, like the doctor said. Say it slow, "Reeeee-lax." Then it came, with his thoughts.

One lawyer was left: the big blond, Carrier. Legally, the case could go forward as long as one lawyer was alive, assuming the defendant didn't object. But if Steere filed for a mistrial or a continuance, that would make for a different result. Judge Rudolph didn't know the law on this point exactly because there was no law on it. How often did the lawyers get knocked off while a jury was out? The judge had told his law clerk to get his ass into chambers and come up with the right answer. Joey, who couldn't even buy milk.

Judge Rudolph jumped off the bath mat and scampered back across the chilly parquet to his dressing room, where he landed with both feet on the Oriental rug. His feet were so cold. He slipped into his socks first and was halfway into his suit pants when the telephone rang.

"Damn!" He hurried into the den to get the phone, holding his pants up with one hand. The last thing the judge needed was Enid awake and bitching. She hated the Steere case. She'd missed their winter vacation to Sanibel because of it, and when Enid didn't get to play golf she became unbearable. Judge Rudolph scooted down the hall into his den just as the phone rang again. He snatched it from the hook and his suit pants dropped to his ankles when he realized who the caller was. "Mayor Walker," the judge said, surprised.

"Cold enough for you, Harry?" the mayor asked. His voice sounded casual, as if he called the judge in the middle of the night all the time.

"Sure as hell is." Judge Rudolph wasn't having any of it. The mayor was a Democrat and the judge a Republican, so the mayor would never back him for the Court. Pennsylvania was one of the few states that still voted for its judiciary, like prize heifers in a county fair, and for that the judge thanked his lucky stars. Except for the Democratic enclave that was Philadelphia, most of the state was conservative and Republican. "Quite a storm."

"Blizzard of the century."

"At least of the reelection."

Both men laughed unpleasantly. Judge Rudolph, standing in a wool pool of suit pants, knew Mayor Walker had pushed Steere's prosecution. The mayor would like nothing better than a mistrial, which would keep Steere in jail and release his properties. The judge would like nothing better than a verdict, which would ensure him a new robe.

"I'll get to the point," the mayor said. "I gather you've heard the news. Someone is killing Elliot Steere's lawyers."

"I wouldn't go that far." The judge hoisted his pants up by their waistband. He'd be damned if he'd discuss the Steere case with the mayor. How would it play out later?

"I would. Murder, kidnapping. A tragedy, and a catastrophe for the case."

"It's a tragedy for the guards' families, but it shouldn't affect this case." The judge was choosing his words carefully. It was risky to even entertain the call. Judge Rudolph knew only one way to protect himself. He pressed a button beside his phone and the audiotape hidden in his desk drawer clicked noiselessly into operation. "I have no intention of discussing the merits of the Steere case with you," the judge said as distinctly as possible.

"I'm not calling to discuss the merits," the mayor said, equally distinctly. Peter Walker didn't get to be mayor by being completely obtuse. His own tape recorder had been rolling from the outset. "I called to touch base with you on the procedure with the blizzard. Iron out the logistics. I've declared a snow emergency, but I can get the jurors escorted to their homes. When do you anticipate you'll be dismissing the jury?"

"There will be no dismissal. The jurors will remain in sequestration and continue their deliberations."

"What? I can't imagine it would be lawful to go forward in these circumstances. One of the associates on the defense team, Mary DiNunzio, is in intensive care and not likely to pull through."

"The defendant has a lawyer, a bright young woman," the judge said. Maybe this was his chance to redeem himself for that "tit" comment. "She's very competent to handle the trial, as are many of the women who come before me. She works in an all-woman law firm, you know, Rosato and Associates. I have a great respect for that firm. I have no doubt they'll do everything in their power to protect the defendant's right to counsel and due process."

On the other end of the line, the mayor rolled his eyes. Who was up for election here, the judge or him? Oh. Both. "Lead counsel is missing, too. Marta Richter. How can you proceed without her?"

"Ms. Richter isn't missing. My law clerk spoke with her this evening and she was fine."

"She may have been kidnapped!"

"That's speculation. Ms. Richter's whereabouts when court is not in session are not my concern. I have no facts which lead me to believe—"

"You don't have all the facts, Harry."

The judge paused. The mayor could have useful information. "Have the police found evidence of kidnapping?"

The mayor paused. The judge could have useful information. "Has the defendant filed for a mistrial?"

Both men went mute while their tape recorders whirred away. A Philadelphia standoff.

Judge Rudolph cleared his throat after a minute. "I'm extremely uncomfortable with this conversation."

"I don't see why. I'm not asking you anything confidential. Whether a motion for a mistrial has been filed is a matter of public record. The roads are unsafe in this blizzard, and if you're continuing the deliberations, you'll need extra police personnel to transport the jurors to the Criminal Justice Center. Advance notice of that will help the city accommodate your needs during this state of emergency."

"The case is going forward," the judge said firmly. Judicially. "If the defendant wants a mistrial he may file a motion through Ms. Carrier or on his own. He may even telephone me if he wishes. My law clerk knows where to reach me at all times. That's where you got this number, isn't it?" The judge shook his head. He'd ream Joey out when he got to chambers. Strike two for that boy. "Also, I've ordered the jurors to continue their deliberations at their hotel, so I won't need to transport them to the Criminal Justice Center. I expect this will be our last conversation on this matter." The judge hung up the phone and buckled his suit pants with satisfaction.

His toes wiggled happily, suddenly warm.

❖   ❖   ❖

Across town at City Hall, the mayor threw his telephone at the paneled wall. It fell to the red Oriental carpet in a tangled heap.

Jen watched it tumble with a grim look on her face. "Told you you should have let me call," she said.

35

Standing on the windswept dune, Marta saw Bogosian's head snap toward her at the sound of her scream. He must have heard her. He'd come after her.

She took off, running flat out down the snowy beach. It was pitch black. Marta couldn't see a thing. Snow blew everywhere and became ocean. Ocean churned everywhere and became sky. Wind pummeled her face and buffeted her ears. Run. Run *away*. Into the darkness and noise and cold. *Run away*. Fast as she could. Fast as she had from the station wagon, her mother calling after her. *Run away*.

Marta tore down the beach. Her cap flew off. She glanced back and caught sight of the lighted house. Alix was pounding at the French doors. Bogosian must have locked her in. He was coming. Oh God. In a minute he'd be on the beach. He'd shoot at her like before. Only now there'd be no monster snowplow to rescue her. *Run away*.

Marta veered toward the water's edge where the snow was thin. Wind caught her full in the face and chest. She streaked down the beach, splashing in the surf. The waves crashed, the spray frigid at her shoulder. Icy water drenched her coat. Marta couldn't see where the beach ended and the water began, so she kept running in a straight line away from Steere's beach house.

Her breath came in panicked bursts. Her legs ached from running in heavy boots. Her shoulders felt weak under the soggy coat. Marta couldn't keep up the pace much longer. She spotted a white modern house in the distance. A place to hide.

She angled away from the water and bolted through the snow for the house. The wind blew off the ocean, propelling her forward. As Marta got closer to the house she scanned it for hiding places. It was too dark to see and she just kept going. Her heart felt like it was about to explode.

Crack! Crack! Gunshots.

Marta felt a jolt of terror. Bogosian. The Magnum. Where was he? Marta couldn't tell where the shots came from. The storm and the sea swallowed the sound. How close was he?

She was almost at the white house. It was tall, built on stilts. Where could she hide? There was a wraparound deck, but it was too exposed. She ran under the deck, looking wildly around. It was dark under the house. No snow to show her tracks. A wooden door banged in the wind toward the back. An outdoor shower.

Crack! Another gunshot. Louder. Closer. No time to lose.

Marta ran to the shower stall and slipped inside. It was dark. She saw nothing. Her fingers fumbled to lock the bolt and she bumped into an inside shelf. She felt for the shelf with jittery fingertips and clambered onto it. What to do? Pray Bogosian didn't find her? No. She needed a weapon. Then she remembered.

Christopher's tools. She yanked the forge hammer out of her pocket. A hammer against a gun? She shook with terror. Her panting was too loud. Her ribs seared with pain. Her pulse wouldn't quit. She raised the heavy hammer and peeked over the top of the stall in the dark.

There. Bogosian. A large shadow against the snow, white shirt flapping, lurching down the beach. His gun was drawn. His head was down. He was looking for footprints in the snow. He turned toward the house.

God, no. Marta's stomach torqued. He was walking toward the house. Following her tracks. She could see the glint of his gun as he got closer.

Marta ducked and tried to silence her panting. She found a skinny crack between the boards of the stall and pressed her eye to it. She could see Bogosian, but he couldn't see her. She told herself she had the advantage and willed herself to believe it. She would surprise him.

Bogosian lumbered toward the house. He stopped, crouching to touch the snow. Tracing the footprints. He straightened up and followed them directly to the house.

Marta bit her lip so she wouldn't scream.

Bogosian kept coming. His gun was drawn, ready to fire. He was ten feet from the house, then five. Going straight up to the porch. Stopping right where Marta had, in front of the wraparound deck.

Marta didn't move, she didn't breathe. Then she remembered the pritchel. She reached into her pocket and grabbed the spike. What could she do with it? Marta forced herself to think despite her fear. In the movies, they threw things to create a distraction and run. That wouldn't work. Bogosian would shoot Marta down as she ran.

Bogosian cocked his head, reminding Marta again of an attack dog. This time it gave her an idea.

She scratched the pritchel against the wood and gave a soft whimper like a puppy. A little lost dog trapped in the shower stall. The thug was a dog lover, wasn't he? He'd practically memorized that magazine.

Bogosian swiveled toward the sound. He aimed his gun at the stall.

Marta's heart leapt into her throat. She scratched harder and whimpered more fearfully. It wasn't hard to fake.

Bogosian took a step under the house, then another. He was so tall, she could reach him if she could draw him near enough. He had the advantage at a distance. Guns will do that.

Marta scratched even harder. She whimpered as low as she could, as if she were wounded. Starving. Near death. Three more steps was all she needed to reach him.

Bogosian took one more step, then the second. Then the third. Striking distance.

Please, God, help me. Marta raised the forge hammer and brought it down on Bogosian's head with brute force, driving the iron ball through his crown. His skull cracked like a pavement. Blood gushed from the wound, hot and wet, splattering Marta's face. She screamed in horror.

Bogosian's eyes went round as the moon and they stared at her.

He was dead as he stood.

36

Elliot Steere sat behind the thick bulletproof window in the interview room and watched with masked amusement as Judy Carrier tried to interrogate him. She was a young woman, and her bowl haircut and oversized features made her look like an oversized rag doll. Carrier had been questioning him for almost fifteen minutes and had managed to keep her temper even as she got nowhere. Steere could see from her expression that she was growing angry and desperate. A potentially troublesome combination, even in toys.

"I want to know what the fuck is going on," Carrier was saying. She stood behind the chair on her side of the window and gripped the backrest. Steere noticed her right hand was bandaged but didn't mention it.

"I am on trial for murder and awaiting a verdict."

"You didn't tell us the truth."

"I didn't tell you anything. You're a junior associate on my defense. I deal with Marta."

"Where is Marta?"

"I don't know."

"Who shot Mary?"

"I don't know."

"What does street money have to do with Eb Darning? What do you have to do with Eb Darning?"

"What's street money?"

Judy's anger bubbled to the surface. "You don't know what happened to Mary, you don't know what happened to Marta. You don't know the 'driver' who took Marta to the office and you can't explain how you knew the traffic light was red. For a man who's supposed to have all the answers, you don't know jack shit."

Steere brushed smooth a wrinkle in his pants. "If this is what you interrupted me for, I'll go back to my cell."

"Someone's trying to kill your lawyers. Why do I get the feeling it's you?"

"Absurd."

"You know what I think? I think you're a murderer. I think you murdered Eb Darning and I think you hired somebody to kill my best friend."

"You're not talking like my lawyer, Ms. Carrier." Steere stood up and shook down his pant legs. "I'm going back to my cell. Do not call for me until the jury has returned."

"You expect me to go forward as your trial counsel?"

"Expect it? I insist on it."

"I knew you would." Judy folded her arms and

her blue eyes narrowed. "The last thing you want is a mistrial or a continuance, am I right?"

"Correct. The jury has the case. My name must be cleared."

"And if I don't want to clear it? If I withdraw from the case?"

"I'll oppose. My constitutional—"

"I figured as much. That's why I wrote this." Judy pulled a packet of papers from her inside pocket and pressed them through the slot in the bulletproof window. "It's handwritten. Not the prettiest motion in the world, but it'll do the trick."

Steere glanced at the papers without touching them. "What is this?"

"A motion for a mistrial. Considering what's happened to my co-counsel, I have reason to believe my life is in danger. It's an emergency motion."

Steere tried to suppress his smile. "Since when are your fears legal grounds for a mistrial?"

"Since now. I'm not too worried about precedent on this one. There's no law on what happens when someone uses the defense team for target practice. I'm not one for precedent anyway. When you're right, you'll win. Case law or no."

"Very interesting, but you can't file a motion without my approval. And I'm not giving my approval to any such motion."

"Too bad. I already filed it."

Steere paused momentarily. "You didn't."

"Yepper. I left it under the door of the clerk of the court's office downstairs, timed and dated." Judy checked her watch. "The motion is filed as of five minutes ago. I'll serve the D.A. and the judge as soon as I leave here. It'll be of record in the morning."

Steere appraised her anew as they stood tall on either side of the divider.

"Your only choice is to fire me. Either way, I'm no longer your lawyer and I get my mistrial." Judy grinned, and Steere noticed the gaps between her teeth.

How unattractive, he thought.

37

M arta couldn't stop shaking. Her left hand trembled around the pritchel and she forced the tool into her pocket. She crouched on the wooden bench in the shower stall and waited for her tremors to subside. She had killed a man, self-defense or not. The legal excuse didn't alter the moral question. The quivering in her muscles taught her that lesson, and she knew it was one she would never forget.

Marta was a killer now. The thought nauseated her. Frightened her. She thought back through the clients she had defended. Murderers, some of them rich. Most too high profile to do it again or not crazy enough. But they did it once, as Marta had. Did you get one free murder if you were a Richter client? Did she? Marta trembled on the bench, waiting to feel like herself again. Hoping the quaking would pass, and the questions.

She wiped her eyes on a clean part of her coat sleeve and rose stiffly. Her knees wobbled and she groped for the shower wall. She found the front door, felt for the bolt, and drew it back with fingers that were slick with warm blood. The door swung open. The sight was grotesque. Bizarre.

Bogosian was still standing, dead on his feet.

Marta gasped. She didn't know people could die standing up. Maybe there wasn't enough wind under the house to knock him over, or his feet were too big. It made her sick to think about it. Then she felt a momentary tingle of fear. He was dead, wasn't he?

Marta forced herself to step closer to check. Bogosian's dull brown eyes were rigid, fixed. His coarse features were frozen in agony. Blood streamed from his head in rivulets. Marta looked away, sickened. She'd seen enough autopsy photos to know Bogosian was dead. She wasn't about to feel his pulse.

She hurried by the corpse. The Magnum must have fallen in the snow, but she didn't see it. She didn't need it anyway. She didn't even want to touch it. She hustled under the deck to the beach, then turned into the wind.

Marta made a beeline for Steere's house, the only light on the beach. Wind filled her hair and briny snow pelted her face. This time the mist from the ocean felt cool and cleansing. She scooped a handful of snow and rinsed her cheeks and hands. It was freezing, but it heightened her senses. Her relief. She was alive. Safe.

She began to run to the house. Alix was locked in the office, and there was a lot Marta wanted to know. What had Alix been searching for? Did it have to do with why Steere killed Darning? Her stride lengthened as her plan took shape. She would get Alix to give a statement in return for immunity, then turn it over to the D.A. It would put Steere away forever. He might even get the death penalty.

And what about Marta? Steere would retaliate and send somebody else after her, but she would have hired security by then. She had the resources to protect herself. Money would do that. Insulate her behind anonymous walls. Pay for plane tickets to her different houses. Send her to deserted islands in the Caribbean. Get her lost. Marta didn't care if she didn't practice law again. She couldn't turn back now anyway.

She inhaled a lungful of cold, salty air, and it sped her like a spinnaker toward the house. Time to close this case. She would bring Steere to justice. The lights of the mansion house got closer, jittering with each hasty step, and soon Marta could see the French doors to Steere's office. Something was flapping there, fluttering.

She squinted against the driving snow. Sheer curtains flew from the doors in the wind, sucked from the room like an incubus. The French doors were slamming back against the house in the wind. Steere's office was empty.

Alix was gone.

Once inside Steere's office, Marta tried to shut the French doors against the storm. The wood around the doorknob had been broken and was too splin-

tered to close completely. Why hadn't Alix unlocked the door from the inside? It must have been
locked with a key, one she couldn't find in her
haste. Alix had apparently escaped off the second-
floor deck, taking her answers with her. And
Marta's hopes of learning the truth about Darning's
murder.

Marta spun around in frustration and surveyed
the ransacked office. Walnut file drawers hung open
and folders spilled onto the floor. Messy papers blanketed the glass top of the desk. A cushy leather desk
chair had rolled to the wall. The computer on the
desk had been disconnected and its fifteen-inch
monitor lay smashed beside the French doors,
gray wires dangling from its back. Alix must have
used the monitor to break the doors. It was the
heaviest thing in the office. But what had Alix been
looking for? She undoubtedly didn't find it. She
would have run from Bogosian without continuing
her search.

Marta's gaze fell on the cardboard box that Alix
had tried so frantically to open. She knelt before it
and yanked on the box top. Trifold brochures were
stacked inside, describing a resort development deal.
Was that what Alix wanted? Unlikely. Marta closed
the top, leaving a watery red print of her own palm.
This wouldn't do. She'd leave blood everywhere. It
gave her the creeps.

Marta got up and found a bathroom in the hall
that connected to the master bedroom. She flicked
on the light with her arm. The glistening white

counter was well stocked with cosmetics. Lipsticks plugged the holes in a plastic organizer; eye pencils rolled around a Lucite tumbler. It must be Alix's bathroom. A magnified makeup mirror extended over the sink, and Marta caught sight of her reflection.

She almost screamed. Her magnified face was red with watery blood. Her hair hung in thick ropes around monstrous blue eyes. Marta couldn't go around looking like this, especially if she went back to the city. She'd have to shower. On the bathroom sink was a white tube of facial cleanser. Clarin's Doux Nettoyant Moussant, it said. Alix's self-important face wash. Marta grabbed it and took it into the shower.

After a warm shower, Marta padded into the bedroom to find something to wear. Just as she'd suspected, a walk-in closet next to Steere's was stuffed with women's clothes. Marta scanned the perfumed clothes, and picked out a tan cashmere sweater and camel pants. What the well-dressed mistress will wear. She slipped into the clothes, then searched the closet for good measure. She went through the silk blouses on padded hangers and looked behind the dresses. No clues of any sort. She moved on to the night tables and storage bins under the bed. Nothing. Marta thought a minute. Alix had been searching office papers.

Marta hurried back to Steere's home office and

the drawers Alix had ransacked, hoping she'd find what Alix hadn't. Hair dripping wet, she yanked open a drawer and read through the labels of the accordions in it. A divider read BUSINESS PROPERTIES and contained manila folders for five different areas of Philadelphia. One folder read CENTER CITY, and Marta pulled it out and opened it up.

Steere's major buildings and the loan documents for each. He had more property than she thought and it was highly leveraged. There were lenders in and out of state and the notes were spread among a number of different banks. No single bank would know how much Steere owed, and from the looks of it, his debt was huge. Hundreds of millions of dollars. Marta closed the manila folder and reached for the next.

BUSINESS PROPERTIES—NORTHEAST. More properties, more loans. Even a criminal lawyer could see that Steere's business operations were precarious, the properties heavily leveraged. Each lease was held in a corporate name and Marta counted at least twenty different names. None of them appeared to have partnerships, since no partners had signed on any of the notes. Steere was the key man in every transaction. Marta closed the file folder and replaced it. It was intriguing, but it wasn't what Alix had been looking for. What had she wanted, and why now?

Marta paused. Why now? That could be the answer. It could be that the missing papers would implicate Steere in Eb Darning's murder.

Otherwise, why the frantic activity at this point? Assume Steere had sent Alix to get these papers after Marta had told him she'd find evidence against him. He did have a portable phone. Maybe Steere called Alix and told her to find the file and hide it elsewhere. Or shred it, keep it secret. If Steere wanted it secret, Marta wanted it all the more.

Marta stood at the file cabinet, thinking. Then she remembered that the police had searched Steere's city town house when he was first arrested. The D.A. tried to get a warrant to search Steere's beach house, but Marta had successfully opposed it for lack of probable cause. But Steere wouldn't have taken any chances. If there were any evidence here relating to the crime, he would have had it hidden, or disguised it. It could be something that looked innocent but wasn't. Like Steere himself.

Marta's gaze circled the home office. Across the room was a small credenza with two drawers left open. She hurried to it, opened the top drawer, and thumbed through it. Personal records. One manila folder read ANTIQUES and was filled with furniture receipts. English Interiors—One mahogany lowboy, $1550.00, read the one on top. Marta slipped it back.

She pulled the next file, labeled BOAT. Boat? Marta didn't know Steere had a boat. She flipped to the bill of sale. FOUR WINNS 258 Vista Cruiser, twenty-five feet long. It had cost $47,425 and had been bought almost four years ago. Also in the folder were insurance documents and docking bills from LBI Marina. *Piratical* was the boat's name. Perfect for Steere, but not helpful.

Fuck. What time was it? Marta checked her watch. 1:45 A.M. She tensed. The jury would resume deliberations in seven hours. Could Christopher turn them around? Where could those papers be? Maybe hidden elsewhere in the house. Somewhere she wouldn't expect. Marta abandoned the credenza in a hurry, then checked the other rooms for anything that seemed out of the ordinary. Nothing.

Marta hurried downstairs and searched the first floor. She rummaged through bookshelves and kitchen cabinets. Highboys and lowboys. Nothing. She didn't even know what she was looking for. It was an impossible task. She plopped on the living room rug. Her fatigue was catching up with her. She didn't know what else to do. On the living room wall hung a large framed blueprint of the mansion. BUILT IN *1888*, TODD HUNTER, ARCHITECT, read the architectural block lettering.

Marta blinked, distracted. She loved houses, even plans for houses. The blueprint was a deep marine color, and the architect had drawn in white. She could see the ruled lines describing the living room and dining room, then the dotted swinging lines for the double door between them. This was an old, old house. No wonder it wasn't up on stilts like the others she'd driven by. Marta knew from her beach house on Cape Cod that the newer houses would have bedrooms downstairs and living areas on the upper floor, to take advantage of the ocean view.

Marta frowned, the house hunter in her disapproving. It was a problem with Steere's house, for all its grace and elegance. No water view. She looked at the bank of windows that faced the beach. They were large, but dunes obscured the ocean view. Snowy mounds lay around the house like loose pearls.

Marta thought a minute. Why would Steere, who could afford any house on Long Beach Island, choose one that had no ocean view? Then she remembered something. What had Steere said? In the interview room at the courthouse? *I love the beach, but I hate the water.* The memory jerked Marta awake. Steere hated the ocean. He hated it so much he'd bought a house with no view of the water. So why did he own a boat?

Marta scrambled to her feet and sprinted back upstairs.

38

Judge Rudolph stood behind his desk in his chambers and frowned at the handwritten motion for a mistrial, which had been hand-delivered to his chambers. His law clerk sat across the desk, red-faced. Joey had been stupid enough to accept service of the motion papers. Strike three. Judge Rudolph wouldn't take him to the high court, if he ever got there, now. "You should have refused it!" the judge snapped, throwing the papers onto his desk in anger.

"I'm sorry, Your Honor."

"You should have told her to file it during business hours."

"I know, Your Honor."

"It doesn't have a clerk's time stamp. There's nothing official about it. You could have told her you didn't have permission to take it."

"Yes, Your Honor."

"You could have asked for her ID, for God's sake. How did you even know who she was? Why do you let strangers into my chambers like that?"

"She wasn't a stranger. It was Judy Carrier. I know her from court, Your Honor."

"Don't backtalk me! I have my personal things in here! This is my chambers, not yours!"

"Yes, Your Honor. I know." Joey sat on the chair opposite the judge's desk. His head hung over the legal pad and photocopied cases in his lap.

"The woman shows up to serve papers and you hold out your hand?"

"Carrier said she filed it, Judge."

"At one o'clock in the morning?" The judge was shouting now. "How could she file it, you idiot?"

"She said it was an emergency."

"It's *her* emergency, not *my* emergency. You know how many papers we get here that some lawyer calls emergency papers? How many, Joey? A million? Everything's an emergency to a lawyer!"

"Yes, Your Honor."

"Who runs this case anyway, the lawyers or me? It's not an emergency unless I say it's an emergency! Until then it's just more paper. Another lawyer with another pleading. Paper. Garbage. Trash. How many times do I have to tell you?" Judge Rudolph snatched off his tortoiseshell glasses and rubbed his eyes irritably. "My God. I hate this."

"Yes, Your Honor."

"Will you shut up? Will you just shut up?"

Joey nodded. He thought about saying "yes," but decided against it. It was a confusing question.

"Did you research the legal issue at least?"

"Yes. There's no case directly on point, but I

found a good law review article and researched analogous cases on the Manson trial, and—"

"Don't write me a book, Joey. This Carrier broad filed a motion for a mistrial. I want to deny it. Will I get reversed?"

"Not if the defendant opposes the motion, which he does in his letter."

Judge Rudolph stared at Joey in disbelief. "What did you say? The defendant wrote a letter, opposing?"

"Yes, sir."

"*Steere himself?*"

"Yes, sir."

"Christ! Why didn't you say so, you moron?"

"You were yelling—"

"Give me that letter! Christ! What's the matter with you?"

The judge snatched the paper from Joey's outstretched hand and slapped his reading glasses back on. The letter was handwritten and the judge read its contents aloud, his voice full of wonder. "'My lawyer filed a motion for mistrial in this matter without my knowledge or authorization. I oppose this motion for a mistrial . . . hereby ask the Court to consider it withdrawn . . . I expressly do not wish a mistrial . . . I wish to proceed as my own counsel . . . Signed, Elliot Steere.'" The judge pulled his chair out and eased into it in amazement. What luck! It was almost too good to be true. "How did we get this?"

"One of the sheriffs brought it up from the lockup."

"So it's really from Steere."

"Yes, Your Honor."

Judge Rudolph shook his head, his eyes glued to the letter. He'd never had a case like this one. Had never read a case like this one. It had a life of its own.

Joey cleared his throat. "I found cases saying that a defendant has the right to proceed *pro se* in a criminal case, even if he fires his lawyer in the middle."

"Of course he does." Judge Rudolph skimmed the letter over and over, incredulous as a lottery winner. "It's the defendant's right to counsel. It's a personal right. He can exercise it or waive it."

"Yes. True. I knew that. I found cases saying the rights in a criminal trial are personal to the defendant, analogous to those cases where the defendant wants the state to execute and the courts won't let the lawyers intervene."

"That's not on point."

"Well, in the Manson case—"

"Shut up, Joey."

"Yes, Your Honor."

"You're embarrassing yourself." Judge Rudolph looked up from the letter. "Has this letter been served on the D.A.?"

"I don't know. Ms. Carrier told me she served the motion on the D.A., but I don't know about the letter from Steere."

Judge Rudolph paused. He wasn't in the clear yet. "Get me the D.A. Think you can handle that?"

39

Judy had only one lead to follow and it brought her back to the Twenty-fifth Street Bridge. She had grabbed a lone cab at the courthouse and the ride took only a half hour through plowed streets. There was no traffic because nobody but Judy was crazy enough to brave the blizzard.

Grays Ferry was deserted and Judy felt uneasy as soon as the cab turned onto Twenty-fifth Street. The scene chilled her. Mary had been shot here only hours ago, yet no sawhorses or yellow tape marked the spot. Bennie had told her at the hospital that the cops were shorthanded, but what would become of whatever evidence was at the crime scene? Judy found herself staring at the spot where Mary had been shot. Fresh snow buried Mary's blood, concealing what had happened. Even Judy's skis were lost in the snow or long gone.

"Miss? The fare?" said the cabdriver.

"Sorry." Judy fumbled in her zipper pocket for a bill and handed it to him. "Keep it, okay?" She stepped out into the cold and walked up the street to the house.

Judy climbed the familiar, snowy stoop next to the brown living room curtains and knocked hard with her good hand. She didn't expect an instant answer, it was the middle of the night. Judy knocked until a light went on inside the house and kept knocking until she heard voices near the front door. Then she started shouting. There would be time for apologies later. Now she had to get in and get answers.

Judy sat across from the mother in her living room, telling her the whole story. The room was cramped and its furnishings old, but clean and simple. A worn couch, an old TV, and a radio-cassette player on a table with some cassette tapes beside it. Children's books and X-Men comics were stacked on metal tray tables that served as end tables. The thin-paneled walls were covered with children's photographs, all boys. Their front teeth vanished in one picture and reappeared in the next, playing photographic peekaboo. The focus of the living room was a large portrait that hung over the couch, a posed photograph of the mother and her three sons, with the small Dennell in her lap.

The mother was tired, awakened from sleep, but listened without comment, her neat head tilted at a dubious angle. Her features were large and not entirely pretty, but her round eyes showed intelligence. She had on a thin white robe and her short hair was cut natural. The only time she touched it was when Judy explained how Mary had been shot. "Why aren't you goin' to the police about this?" the woman asked warily. "Why you comin' to me?"

"I will, but all I have now is suspicion. They can't do anything about it tonight anyway. Besides, if your son knows something, wouldn't you rather have me talk to him than the police?"

"At this hour of the night? No."

"I'm sorry about that. I can't help it."

The woman wrapped her robe closer around her slim body. "My baby Dennell don't know this home-less man you're talkin' about. Dennell never said nothin' about somebody named Eb. Or Heb."

"I think Dennell did know him. He told us he did. Dennell plays outside a lot, doesn't he? He must have talked to Eb while you were at work."

"Dennell don't know him. He don't know people hangin' on the street. He don't talk to those people."

"How do you know that? You work at the store during the day."

The mother pursed her lips. "Look, I do what I can. I work, I don't take no handouts. Rasheed, he watches the baby when I'm away, or the neighbor lady. What do you know about it anyway? You don't know nothin' about it."

Judy reddened. "I'm just telling you what Dennell told me and Mary."

"Like I tol' you, Rasheed watches Dennell good. I told him not to let the baby talk to no strangers."

"Heb wouldn't be a stranger. Some of the neighbors knew him."

"I didn't. Not me."

"Dennell said Heb was rich."

The mother's brow knitted. "He said that? To you?"

"Yes, he told me Eb gave him money."

"Dennell don't have money."

"Isn't it possible that Heb gave Dennell money?"

"No. I never saw a dime of it."

"But Dennell told me about street money. Did you know about that?"

"Street money?" the mother scoffed. "You don't know if Dennell was for real or not."

"Does Dennell lie?"

The mother didn't reply.

"I didn't think so," Judy said, and the mother looked at her hard.

The window in the children's crowded bedroom was insulated with Saran Wrap and Scotch tape, and Dennell's skinny bed sat underneath the peeling windowsill. The little boy squinted sleepily against the sudden brightness from a ceiling fixture of old, frosted glass. "Momma?" the boy murmured without opening his eyes.

"Dennell, wake up and talk to me a minute, baby." The mother stroked his head as he lay against a pillow covered with Star Wars characters. "There's a lady here to ask you some questions."

"I'm the lady with the skis," Judy said softly, sitting at the foot of the bed. "Remember me, Dennell?"

The boy's eyes remained closed, and his mother shook him gently by the shoulder. He wore a thick Sesame Street sweatshirt; the bedroom was cold despite a space heater whose two squiggly coils glowed orange in the far corner, near a bookshelf cluttered with battered board games, paperback books, and cassette tapes. The two older sons shared a double bed and one son was wide awake as the other slept. It was the oldest one who was awake, and Judy judged him to be about fifteen. He wore a bright red T-shirt that said CHICAGO BULLS. "Whas' up, Ma?" he asked.

"None of your business, Rasheed. Go back to sleep."

Rasheed quieted but stayed propped up in bed next to his somnolent brother, watching the odd scene. His face was long and handsome with strong features and dark, smallish eyes. Tacked on the wall above the bed were posters of Michael Jordan, Scottie Pippen, and Dennis Rodman's hair.

"Dennell," said the mother, shaking the boy only reluctantly. Dennell dozed on.

Judy considered giving up, but it was too important. Somebody had tried to kill Mary and she had to get to the bottom of it. She had a rapport with this boy, and the police wouldn't. Something was telling her it had to be done tonight. Now. "Dennell," Judy called. "Remember we played with the skis?"

The child cracked an eye. "The skis?"

Judy inched up on the bed beside Dennell's mother. "I slid the ski to you. We played, remember?"

Both large eyes flew suddenly open. "You said it's not a toy!" he said in the loud voice Judy recalled.

"Well, it isn't."

"I fink it is!"

Rasheed snorted. "'Think.' You got to say 'think.'"

"Fink!" Dennell repeated.

Rasheed shook his smooth head. "He can't say 'th.'"

"Shhh," said their mother, waving Rasheed off and turning back to Dennell. "Baby, you know a man named Eb Darning?"

Dennell nodded. His round eyes rolled from his mother to Judy and back again. He had eyelashes so long they curled up at the end, like a baby camel's.

"He give you money?"

Dennell nodded again, and his mother groaned. "What you do with this money, boy?"

"Did I do bad?"

Rasheed propped himself up higher on his elbows, his expression as intent as Michael Jordan's. "Don't lie, D."

"I ain't lyin'!" Dennell shouted, and his mother patted his leg.

"Settle down now," she said. "Don't be shoutin'. How much money?"

"I don't know. Two. Ten." Dennell shrugged, his tiny shoulders lost in the sweatshirt. "Ten."

"Ten dollars?"

"Yes. Ten."

"Where's this money now?"

Dennell blinked but said nothing.

"He ain't got no money," Rasheed said, and Judy glanced over. Rasheed looked uneasy. You didn't have to be a mother to know what was going on, and the mother turned from her youngest to her oldest.

"Rasheed. You know something 'bout this money?" Rasheed shook his head, and his mother stood up and put her hands on her hips. "Young man, you look me right in the eye and tell me you don't know what this baby's talkin' about."

"Ma—"

"You heard me. You look at me and lie to me. Don't be a sneak."

Rasheed flopped backward on the bed, his eyes on the ceiling. "I ain't a sneak."

"Nothin' I hate worse than a sneak. A sneak's not goin' anywhere in this world. No how. No way. Now you tell me."

Rasheed sighed. "The man give him money and shit."

"Watch your language. Now, what money?"

"Dollar bills."

"How many? Ten?"

"More," Rasheed said to the ceiling.

The mother folded her arms. "Where's this money now?"

"I got it."

"Get it, boy."

Rasheed sighed theatrically, tore off the covers, and swung his large feet out of bed. He started explaining as soon as he hit the thin rug. "It's my money, straight up. Dennell give it to me."

"Get it," his mother said.

"He can have it, Momma," Dennell said helpfully, but was ignored.

Rasheed strode to his closet in his oversized T-shirt and Champion sweatshorts. He was tall and thin, with wiry calf muscles knotted in long legs. He slid the closet door aside on a broken runner and reached in the messy closet to the top shelf. "I was saving it."

"You were keepin' a secret."

"I was savin'. You're always sayin', 'Save, save, save.'" Rasheed shoved a shoe box aside, revealing another tucked way back. It said ADIDAS on the hidden box. "I was savin' in case I didn't get those sneakers for my birthday. The Air Jordans."

His mother looked pained and her body sagged with resignation. "You know I can't get you those sneakers, Rasheed. They're a hundred dollars. I don't have that kind of money, boy."

"I know it, that's why I'm savin'. To get 'em myself."

"You can't get 'em yourself!"

"Yes, I can. You're always sayin', 'Try, try, try.' 'Save, save, save.' Now I'm doin' both and you're rip-shit."

"Rasheed, that's enough. Why didn't you tell me about the money?"

He shrugged. "I don't know."

Judy watched in silence. She felt like an intruder, but was thrilled that her search was leading somewhere. She held her breath as Rasheed grabbed the shoe box from the shelf, plopped it on the bed, and lifed off the lid. Dennell sat up and tried to peek in the shoe box, and his mother peered inside. "God help me," she said in a hushed tone, and Judy looked in the box.

A thick roll of money nestled in the corner of the shoe box, coiled like a snake. There was a twenty-dollar bill on the outside, but Judy had no way of knowing how much was on the inside. Where had all that come from? Underneath the money was a bright white notebook, and it caught Judy's eye. She was dying to know what it was. "Rasheed," Judy asked, "is the white notebook yours or did that come from Darning, too?"

"He gave it to ME!" Dennell chirped up, sitting cross-legged on his bed. "He tol' me to keep it. So it don't get stole."

"Can I see it?" Judy asked, and Rasheed handed it to her. She opened the notebook. Its pages were filled with lists of numbers written in pencil. What did the numbers mean? Was the handwriting Darning's?

"There must be a hundred dollars here," the mother said, astonished as she plucked the money roll from the box and flipped through it.

"Only eighty-two," Rasheed corrected.

"*Only* eighty-two?" she repeated, shocked. "You took eighty-two dollars from a man on the street?"

"I didn't, Dennell did."

"He don't know better, *you* do," she shot back as her surprise turned to anger. "You don't take money from nobody on the street! You don't take money from nobody. You know what they want for their eighty-two dollars, boy?"

Rasheed looked down. "The man didn't want nothin'."

"I work for my money, son. So will you."

"I work. I was gonna shovel—"

"You're damn right you're gonna shovel! You'll shovel all winter, *for free.* I'll loan you out. Then you'll remember. You don't take money from *nobody.* And you don't keep secrets from *me.*"

"What was I supposed to do? Tell you?"

"Yes, tell me." Veins bulged in her slender neck. "Tell me, so we could give it right back."

"Give it back?" Rasheed started to laugh. "Are you crazy?"

"Yes, I am. Watch this!" Suddenly the mother peeled a twenty from the roll, ripped it in two, and threw the pieces into the air.

"Mom!" Rasheed shouted. "What are you doing?" He scrambled for the money as the pieces sailed to the bed and landed on his brother, who, incredibly, remained asleep. "Stop!" Rasheed pleaded, but his mother was already ripping up another bill, then another, and the one after that, throwing them into the air, setting the pieces flying around the shabby bedroom like snowflakes.

"You think I'm crazy?" she grunted to tear a

stack of ones. "This is what I'll do if I ever, *ever* catch you taking money again!"

Dennell clapped in delight at his mother's adventure while Rasheed scurried to fetch the money falling to the carpet. The mother kept tearing until all the bills were gone and the room a blizzard of cash. "Get the point, boy?" she shouted, her expression grim and satisfied.

"Wha?" asked the middle son, waking up. He rubbed his eyes in bewilderment as money floated around his bedroom. "Is this a dream?"

The mother laughed, and Judy did, too. But Judy's smile was because of what she had in her hand. Eb Darning's notebook.

40

Marta shined her flashlight through the snowy cyclone fence at the LBI Marina, where Steere's bills had showed he docked his boat. The marina was tucked in a harbor on the bay side of the island, ringed by shuttered summer homes and protected from the brunt of the snowstorm at sea. Next to the fence sat a flat-topped wooden building, apparently a small office. On its wall was a faded JET SKI RENTALS sign. A frayed basketball hoop fluttered in the breeze.

Marta poked her fingers through the fence and leaned closer to get a better look. Snow fell steadily, but the bay was calmer than the ocean and rippled with choppy whitecaps that washed onto the docks at the ends. There were no boats in the water, which looked frozen in spots. Wooden slips covered with snow jutted into the empty water. Next to them stood a tall boat lift with a canvas sling. The marina was vacant, deserted, and dark except for a boxy security light on the outside of the office. Where were the boats?

Marta cast the flashlight through the snow flurries to her right, behind a covered section of the fence. Boats stood on dry land, in racks. There were motorboats and sailboats, their decks and awnings blanketed with snow. Marta estimated thirty hulking white outlines in the boatyard but didn't know if any of them were the *Piratical*. She had no idea what Steere's boat looked like even when it wasn't covered with snow. She'd have to get inside the marina to read the names.

Marta tucked the flashlight into her pocket and squinted up at the fence in the snow. It was tall, about eight feet high, and she tried to remember the last time she had climbed anything. The memories came back only reluctantly, they had been so long buried. She'd climbed oak trees in the woods, and rail fences. Onto a pony, bareback; even into her father's lap. Marta used to be a tomboy before she became a lawyer, a grown-up version of a hellion anyway. If she had to climb, she could climb.

She hoisted herself up and tried to wedge the tip of her boot into the cyclone fencing. Her boot was too large. Marta kicked the fence, driving her toe in. The fence jingled and shook. Snow tumbled onto her head. She brushed it off, pulled up her hood, and began to scale the slippery fence. Her parka weighed her down; her snowpants felt clumsy. She almost lost a boot but she made it halfway up and kept plugging.

When Marta reached the top she was panting. She threw a puffy leg over the bar and stopped to catch her breath. Wind gusted through her hair, freezing her ears. She blinked against the snow as she looked around her. No alarm began clanging and the marina wasn't ritzy enough to have a silent alarm. Marta felt safe.

Then she fell off the fence. The flashlight slipped out of one pocket and the pritchel slipped out of the other.

Marta replaced both without comment and lay for a minute in a snowdrift beside the fence. The pile of snow wasn't as soft as advertised, and Marta's body ached. She wiggled her arms and legs, taking inventory. Her head hurt but she couldn't remember when it hadn't. So far she had survived a car accident, a killer, a fall, and psychotherapy. Marta was beginning to think she was invincible, if not entirely professional.

She got up and brushed herself off. The dock was slippery, covered with snow, as were the empty boat slips. They looked like five capital I's facing her. Marta grabbed the handrail because she wasn't sure where the dock ended and the water began. She tramped over to the large boatyard in the snow, flicked on her flashlight, and began reading the names of the boats on the racks.

Free 'n' Easy, Skipperdee, Weekend Folly. The names were legible in the blowing snow because the letters were so big. The wind whistled off the bay as she read. *My Girl, Showboat, Slip and Fall.* The boats were all out of New Jersey, but none of them was Steere's. Marta hurried to the next rack.

Our Keough. Molly's Deal. Semicolon, but no

Piratical. She bit her lip. Steere's boat had to be here; Marta had seen the docking bills. There'd been no other bill that showed Steere paid anybody to move his boat, or that he'd put in a claim for its loss. It was here and she would find it and whatever was hidden on it. Papers, a clue, whatever.

Rate's Bait. Huggybear. Amazing Paul. Some of the boats were registered in Maryland and a couple were from points north: Camden, Maine, and Marblehead, Massachusetts. Marta squatted on her haunches and read the last line of names. It was dark on the far side of the marina, less protected from the sea. Saltwater lashed the fiberglass hulls, and Marta turned her face to avoid a drenching. *Mandessa, Ebony,* and *Go Below.* She reached the end of the row of boats and stood up. Where was the *Piratical*? How could Steere hide a boat?

Marta looked around. Next to the marina's office, close to the water's edge, was a cinderblock building large enough to house boats. Maybe *Piratical* was inside. She hurried to the building. She reached it and shone the flashlight through its garage doors, pressing her nose against the cold glass like a kid at an aquarium.

It was dark in the building and there were no security lights. Marta squinted, her nose a refrigerated pancake. She could make out vague outlines of more boats on racks, but there was no way she could read the names from here. She had to get inside. She eyeballed the panes of glass. They were large enough. Marta drew back her rubber boot and with a technique only a lawyer could envy, drove her toe through the brittle glass. It cracked with a tinkling sound and she kicked until she had broken the pane completely, then squeezed through the jagged frame and scrambled onto the floor inside.

The floor was paved cement, dry except where pools of water had leaked under the door. Marta grabbed the flashlight and stood up among the glass shards. She dusted off quickly, leaving a tiny pile of snow behind *Pigpen*. It was quiet inside and it felt good to be out of the snowstorm, sheltered and protected. Just her and *Jail Bait*, *Bet Thrice*, and *Ain't Nobody's Business*. Where was *Piratical*?

Marta cast the flashlight around the warehouse. Its roof was of a corrugated metal and its steel reinforcing showed. The air smelled musty, and the building had the windless, still cold of a large, unheated space. It was full of boats, maybe owned by those with the money for indoor storage. She headed for the boat racks.

Marta hustled up the aisle, shining the flashlight on the boat names. *First Edition*, *No Nonsense*, *SSCP*. She rose on tiptoe, craning her neck to see the highest racks. *Philly Boy*, *Compuboat*, *Hi-De-Ho*. They sounded like a racing form, with name after stupid name. A grisly *Sucker Punch*. A boozy *Mai Tai Time*. The intellectual *Einstein's Dream* and its dinghy *Feinstein's Dream*.

Marta sloshed with dripping boots down row after row and read twenty more boat names, none worth repeating. She went down the aisles with the flashlight as fast as she could, left to right, bottom to top. The garage was silent except for the squeak of her boots as she turned. Finally the jumpy circle of light fell on *Piratical*. Marta almost dropped the flashlight.

The *Piratical* was a sleek motorboat and looked larger than its twenty-four feet because it was up on a rack. It was painted a bright white and made a huge wedge in the row, like a generous slice of birthday cake. It sat on the bottom rack, probably because it was the heaviest. There was a shiny gray outboard motor mounted next to the boat's stairs. Marta climbed aboard excitedly.

The boat's upper deck had a large sitting area shaped like a horseshoe, and elevated from the general seating was a padded driver's seat behind a steering wheel; the helm, Marta guessed it would be called, though she knew nothing about boats. She stood by the helm, taking it all in as it fell under the flashlight beam. She was learning fast.

In front of the helm was a compass with a clear plastic bubble over it. Marta could see through it to a floating red needle. Every surface on the *Piratical* was neat and clean everywhere she looked. There was something strange about it, though; Marta couldn't quite put her finger on it. She stood, puzzling, then checked her watch. Almost three o'clock in the morning. In a few hours the jury would reconvene. Marta had to hurry. She flicked the flashlight around the helm, but there was no place to hide anything.

Wait. There. On the left near the floor was a storage compartment. Marta squatted and opened the recessed cabinet. Papers! She pulled them out so she could see them better. A blue pamphlet that said THIS IS YOUR BOATING HANDBOOK and a packet of waterproof maps of New Jersey and the Chesapeake. A black *Boating Almanac.* Fuck! Maybe there was something stuck in its pages?

Marta flipped through the almanac, accidentally cracking its spine. Ouch. She loved books and never cracked their spines. But this time, it told her something. No one had read this book. She looked again at the maps. They were neat and unwrinkled in the flashlight's beam. None of these references had been consulted. The boat was clean. Marta wondered if the *Piratical* had ever been used.

She straightened up and scrutinized the boat next to *Piratical* for comparison, *Atta Boy*. Its cup holders were lined with dirt and its driver's seat was worn, with a worn pillow at the helm. The coiled yellow wire in *Atta Boy*'s storage was dirty, but in *Piratical* it was spotless.

Piratical had never been used. Sailed, driven, whatever. Had Steere bought the boat and never used it? Why? Did it mean anything?

Marta had to keep searching. She stepped over the maps and went down the couple of steps to the living quarters below. It was dark and she ran her fingers against the wall until she found a switch. The cabin was cleaner than a hotel room and smelled like a new car. A sink and microwave were to the left; a tiny refrigerator sat under a sparkling counter. Marta opened the refrigerator door, but it was empty and its racks hadn't been put in. Its vinyl odor confirmed her suspicions. Never used. Did it matter?

She crossed to the eating area, which had a blue-striped seat around an oval Formica table. Shipshape and untouched. It didn't make sense. Why buy a boat if you hate the sea? Why buy it and never use it? Marta sensed she was looking at a $40,000 file cabinet. Something was here. She would find it. She was getting close. She had to be.

She went into the living area and feverishly upended all the seat cushions. There was nothing. Behind the living area was a sleeping area in a matching fabric. She turned over all the cushions and clawed at the rug sections underneath to see if any would reveal some sort of hidden compartment. She found nothing.

Marta thought a minute. There had to be an engine, right? The boat didn't run on baking soda. She remembered the gray outboard Evinrude she'd seen and hurried to the top deck. If there was an engine, it had to be up there somewhere.

She aimed the flashlight at the deck. On the white floor in front of the seating area were two aluminum handles. She swept the maps aside with her hand and yanked on the handle. The deck of the seating area opened up and underneath was a square-cut hole. A light went on automatically inside the hole and Marta set the flashlight on the deck.

VOLVO PENTA was written on the black engine, which looked like a car engine. She knelt down and felt around. There was no grease anywhere and no glop built up on what looked like a battery. The *Piratical* had never even been turned on. Turned over, who cared. Marta felt around in the engine and the other black things there. God knew what they were, but it didn't matter. They weren't hiding the papers she wanted.

She let the lid slam closed, plopped onto the deck, and picked up her flashlight, flicking it around aimlessly. The circle of light jitterbugged over books, maps, and the spotless deck. Marta had to be missing something. She wasn't thinking clearly. Something had to be here, or all was lost.

She unzipped her jacket with a sigh and stretched out her legs like a stuffed teddy bear. Ice from her boot dripped onto one of the maps, and she watched the water drop. Drip. Drip. Wetting the map. Marta was suddenly too tired to figure or plan. To search or break in. She watched the water drip onto the map. It was a nice boat. *Piratical*. A pirate's boat. A map. *A map.*

Marta sat bolt upright.

A treasure map? Could it be? She leaned over and grabbed the wet map. FIGHT POLLUTION TO KEEP YOUR WATERWAYS CLEAN! proclaimed the top map. Marta unfolded it with excitement. Pirates. A map.

The treasure. The boat's never being used. It all made sense. The *Piratical* was a logical place to store a map. A hiding place under everybody's nose, yet almost impossible to find. The boat was in inside storage so the map wouldn't get wet.

LITTLE EGG HARBOR TO CAPE MAY. Marta squinted as she read the map. The Atlantic Ocean was at the top in white and there were numbers everywhere. 24, 27, 37. Marta had no experience with nautical maps and guessed they were depths of the sea floor. It was land she was interested in, on a hunch that a man who hated the sea wouldn't bury something under it, even if he could.

Marta's eyes traveled the shoreline on the map. How like Steere. He was in real estate. His true love was land. It had made him his fortune, now it kept his secrets. And judging from his boat's name, Steere thought of himself as a pirate. That meant the treasure would be buried on land, near the beach house Steere loved. Marta just sensed it.

She scanned the map left to right, looking for Long Beach Island. Ocean City, Sea Isle City, Seven Mile Beach. Where was Long Beach Island? She flipped the map over. There. At the left of the map it said Long Beach Island, over a tan length of land. The towns were Beach Haven and Holgate, then the island ended. It was the southern tip. Where was Barnegat Light? Marta wanted the north.

She threw the map aside and searched through the other maps. Maryland, Virginia, the Chesapeake. Nautical maps for waterways Steere would never

sail. Decoys for the real map. She picked up NAUTI-
CAL CHART 12324. SANDY HOOK TO LITTLE EGG HAR-
BOR. Marta unfolded it and spread it out on the deck
of the cruiser. It took up most of the floor.

On the map, two skinny strips of tan beach came
from either side to meet in the center, like the claws
of a hard-shell crab. At the center was the bulb that
was Barnegat Light, and Marta traced with her finger
where Steere's house must be. She saw the lighthouse she had spotted in the distance, then the
stretch of dunes, but there was no X for buried treasure. Was it too much to ask? A little help now and
then?

Marta peered at the map under the flashlight's
beam, looking around the Barnegat Light area for a
pen or pencil mark. Any kind of sign that would
show where Steere had buried something. She saw
nothing. She bent closer, her nose almost an inch
from the map. Still nothing. She even thought back
to what she knew the beachfront looked like. She
couldn't remember a marker or sign. It was a normal
beachfront.

Fuck. Marta sat back up on her haunches. It had
to be here. She was running out of time. Maybe it
was the way she was looking at the map. She held it
up close to her face and shined the light on it.

Suddenly something flashed in her peripheral
vision. A little lick of light. What was that? Marta
held the flashlight and looked over the top of map as
she shined it. A tiny dot of light appeared on the deck
of the boat. What? How?

She squinted behind the map. A minuscule tunnel of yellow pierced the map and came out the other side. It was right near Steere's house, on the shore. Marta followed the light beam back to the map. There was the smallest of pinholes in the map. The flashlight's beam shone through like a break in the clouds.

Marta flipped the map over and touched the pinhole gently. It felt softly ragged, a tiny pinprick. This was it. It couldn't have been a mistake or coincidence. Marta had found the X, at least as much of an X as Steere would give. Her heart thudded with anticipation.

She flipped the map over again. The pinhole was about a centimeter from the shoreline. She looked at the scale. 1:40,000 nautical miles. There was something called statute miles, and yards. Not much of an X, but it was all she had. Marta would have to calculate the spot's location. It was either that or dig up New Jersey.

41

Jen Pressman had managed to escape the mayor and was finally in a car. A municipal-issue Crown Victoria, it had no snow tires, and she had to drive slowly on the city streets. Broad Street and Philadelphia's other main arteries had been plowed once, but it was slow going once she left them. Jen couldn't drive fast anyway. The migraine was teasing her and she still felt sick to her stomach. Bright snow bombarded her eyes and her vision went in and out of focus. The Imitrex was keeping her migraine at bay, but intense pain lingered at the edges of her brain like a stage villain waiting in the wings.

Jen reached the expressway with difficulty. There was no traffic on the road because of the mayor's ban. If a cop tried to stop her, she'd flash her City Hall ID and he'd let her pass. The job had catapulted Jen's career into another zone entirely. If the mayor won reelection, she'd wait a decent interval to quit, then sell herself as a partner to the law firm with the highest bid. She'd hired most of the mayor's staff, which would come in handy when she came back to lobby on a client's behalf. The beauty part was that it worked even if the mayor lost the election. Either way, she was covered. Like Switzerland.

Jen fed the car more gas. Her headlights made two bright tunnels down the snowy highway. Streetlights and snow seared into her brain. The white spots at the back of her head burned whiter and brighter. Jen considered pulling over but she couldn't. It was so damn late. If she stopped now she'd fall asleep in the car and maybe freeze by the roadside.

The car floated sideways toward the cement median, so Jen backed off the gas. Snow flew at her windshield, each flake a dot that grew bigger as it got closer. It reminded Jen of a foul ball that hit her at a Phillies game, as she sat with the city solicitor's staff behind third base. Jen had seen the ball as it flew, spinning in an arc right toward her, its red stitching going round and round. She had put her hands up too late to catch it. The hard ball hit her finger and bent it back, fracturing it. She had to sign a release saying she wouldn't sue the stadium or the city. The city solicitor had laughed her ass off.

Jen stared out the windshield as she drove. It was getting harder and harder to see. The snow blew hard as balls being thrown at her. Hundreds of them, then thousands. Jen had been dodging them her whole life, in secret. Trying to drive between them, trying to get beyond them.

The car barreled ahead in the snow. Whiteness was everywhere, on the windshield and the road, covering buildings beside the expressway. There was no other car in sight or any form of life. It seemed so bright even though it was night. Jen fumbled for her sunglasses in the console but they weren't there. It wasn't her regular car since she hadn't been able to find her purse with her car keys. She'd had to borrow another car from the municipal car pool.

Suddenly there was hot white light at the back of her eyeballs. Behind her eyes, in the center of her brain. Her headache flared into brightness and flames. Jen blinked to clear her vision but all she saw was a hot, molten core. She hit the brakes but the car kept moving straight, then sideways. She couldn't see anything but white hot light. The car rolled over and over until it smashed into the concrete median. Jen felt nothing but agony, saw nothing but light. And in the split second before she died, she felt released.

42

Judy was trying to concentrate on Darning's white notebook, but anxiety kept getting the best of her. Would Mary be all right? She picked at the bandage on her hand. Who shot Mary and why? Would they be coming after her next?

Judy glanced around her empty apartment for the twentieth time. It was quiet except for the plastic clicking of her Kit-Kat clock as its round eyes darted this way and that. Snow fell steadily outside. There was no traffic noise or sirens. Judy felt like she was the only person awake in the city. Except for the killer.

She shifted on a stool at the kitchen counter and shivered despite her thick gray sweatsuit and sweat socks. Judy's apartment was three floors up and there was a buzzer system downstairs. It was a large apartment painted a soft ivory, with a galley kitchen off a large living room, where a foldout canvas futon sat against a wall in front of an Ikea coffee table. Pungent odors of turpentine and acrylics wafted from a bedroom converted to a painting studio. A red mountain bike and colorful loops of rock-climbing rope occupied the space under the two front windows. The articles reassured Judy that she was safe and at home. Secure.

She bent over Darning's white notebook and tucked a strand of stray blond hair into a wide black headband. The notebook had a spiral at the top and was a typical assignment book, like a student might keep. A math student, that is. The notebook contained only numbers, written in pencil. They were recorded single-spaced on the skinny lines in a double column:

39203930	38475400
10983485	49832625
24930491	98563423
21049382	86241221
29282019	66734202

Judy counted the numbers on the first page. About thirty-six. She flipped through the book and estimated it held about 110 pages. So how many numbers were there in the book? 36 x 110. Oh-oh. Judy's calculations fizzled as they traveled her brain's circuitry. An attack of math anxiety. Judy told herself it was all society's fault, but that didn't make her add, subtract, or multiply any better. Long division was out of the question and caused ovarian cramps.

She retrieved a pencil from a jar of paintbrushes and palette knives. She scribbled the problem on a piece of scrap paper, bit her lip, and stumbled to a solution. About 3,960 numbers. But what did they mean? Judy stared at the lists. It was a nightmare—a mathphobe analyzing a notebook of numbers. She forced herself to think despite the disability imposed upon her by sexists and Republicans.

39203930. The number was too long to be a house or phone number. It couldn't be a Social Security number because they were nine digits. Judy paused. Eb Darning had been a banker; maybe they were bank account numbers. She grabbed her purse from the counter, found her checkbook, and opened it. At the bottom of her Sierra Club checks were some blubby black symbols, then *289403726,* then more symbols, and after that *0 384 273.* The seven-digit number was her account number. Judy had to look at it every time she endorsed a check for deposit because she couldn't remember numbers. It didn't look like the eight-digit numbers in Darning's notebook.

She hovered in thought over the notebook. Different banks had different systems. Maybe Darning's bank had a different way of numbering accounts. But that would mean the white notebook dated from when he worked in the bank, in the sixties. Judy examined the notebook. Couldn't be. It didn't look that old. Its pages weren't curled or frayed at the edges. She guessed the notebook was three or four years old. Not carbon dating, but accurate enough.

So what did the numbers mean? They had to mean something, didn't they? Darning was comfortable with numbers. With money. Judy thought a second. Maybe they were serial numbers from bills. She went through her wallet and pulled out the cash inside. Three one-dollar bills with Kelly green serial numbers. *B12892443E. F40155765E. L34522346G.* She dug deeper and fished out a twenty. *B38-803945C.*

Judy was intrigued. The serial numbers on the bills were eight digits, like the numbers in the notebook. But the serial numbers had letters at either end and the numbers in Darning's notebook didn't. Damn. What could they be? What would a certain serial number mean anyway? Counterfeiting? Bribes? Judy had nothing to go on and didn't think they were serial numbers anyway.

She pushed the bills aside and picked up the notebook. Darning had written the numbers with a purposeful hand, not scribbled or messy. They almost looked as if they were copied from somewhere. Where? Darning had given the notebook to a little boy, Dennell. Why? Did Darning know Steere was going to kill him? Did Steere kill Darning *for* the notebook? Judy kept thinking of the eighty dollars in the shoe box. Where had Darning gotten it? Blackmail? Did the notebook have anything to do with it?

Judy had no answers so she went to the refrigerator. Her best ideas came to her while she stood in front of her Amana, and she believed it was the freon fumes. She breathed deeply. Still no answers. She grabbed the milk carton, popped the cardboard spout, and took a slug.

Judy closed the fridge and glanced at the black Kit-Kat clock. Usually it made her smile, but not tonight. Tonight it meant she was getting nowhere, struggling to multiply while her best friend was fighting for her life. Judy looked at the telephone and considered calling the hospital again. She'd called ten minutes ago and they'd told her Mary was in intensive care after surgery. There would be no new news.

Judy popped a chocolate chip cookie into her mouth from a crinkled Chips Ahoy bag on the counter. Her thoughts returned to Marta. The TV news had reported she'd been missing for hours. Judy felt a twinge. She considered telling the cops about the notebook, but they wouldn't do anything about it tonight in this weather. Besides, Judy sensed Marta was alive. She remembered the endless demands Marta had made during the Steere case. People like Marta survived. It was the people around them who succumbed.

Still, where was Marta? What had she learned about Steere? Judy stopped her munching and reflected how dopey she'd been to fall for that lie about the D.A. Marta must have learned that Steere killed Darning, but she couldn't figure out why either. Judy sensed they were working on answering the same questions right now. Where could Marta be? Could she make sense of these numbers?

Judy's confused gaze met those of the man in a glossy print thumbtacked to the wall over the kitchen counter, Cézanne's *Self-Portrait in a White Cap*. She had bought the print at the art museum because she liked the look in the painter's eyes. They were brown as chocolate-covered almonds, and Cézanne's short, layered brushstrokes projected assurance and solidity. When Judy had stood close to Cézanne's paintings at the show, she could see the thickness of the paint and how the artist had waited for one layer to dry before applying the next. Waiting and painting, reworking and recombining the pigments. So different from her favorite artist, Van Gogh. Cézanne knew what he wanted to do but unlike Van Gogh it came from his head, not his heart.

There was a lesson in it. Judy had to disengage her heart and start using her head. Forget about her math anxiety and Mary and Marta and figure this puzzle out. Solve it. She looked anew at the first page of the book just as the doorbell rang. Startled, she turned toward the sound, her pencil poised. Who could it be? Judy felt edgy again.

She dropped her pencil and eased off the kitchen stool, away from the apartment door. On the way she grabbed her portable phone from its cradle, ready to dial 911. Would the police answer on a night like this? Would anybody? She slid a carving knife from the butcher block.

The bell rang again from downstairs. Judy wasn't sure what to do. She wasn't buzzing anybody in blind. There was no intercom downstairs, her building being older. Judy tiptoed to the window and peered at the street from behind the snowy sill.

43

Assistant District Attorney Tom Moran's life had become a living hell. Torture without rest, suffering without relief. Constant screaming and crying pierced his eardrums. He hadn't slept all night and was sweating like a beer bottle in summer, so stifling was the tiny rowhouse in East Falls. His mother-in-law had cranked up the heat because it was the first night his daughters were home from the hospital. Ashley and Brittany Moran. *Twins.*

Holy Mary, Mother of God. His mother-in-law, in her quilted robe, held the newborn Brittany, whose agonized screams filled the living room. His mother, in her flannel nightgown, held the newborn Ashley, whose agonized screams filled the dining room. Wandering between the two rooms in pajamas, like lost souls in purgatory, were his tipsy father-in-law, who peaked as a high school quarterback for Cardinal Dougherty, and his angry father, who couldn't be in the same room with his mother since their divorce. Satan was present in the form of his sister-in-law, who allegedly came to "help" for the night and brought her three little devils. God only knew where his wife Marie was.

"Tom! Tom! We need two receiving blankets in the living room! They're in the nursery!"

Tom ran to fetch the receiving blankets, whatever they were. He didn't bother to figure out who was making the demand. There were so many demands for him to meet, their source was academic. His tie flying, Tom bolted upstairs to the nursery he hadn't finished painting. On the stairs he almost tripped on one of the devils, who was corkscrewing his index finger into his freckled nose. "Don't do that, Patrick," Tom said to his nephew.

"Shut up, dorkhead," the kid muttered.

Tom turned on the stair, but he didn't have time to go back. He hit the nursery at full speed and sidestepped the baby gifts and paint cans. Marie had been after him to get the cans out before the twins were born, but the Steere trial took all his time. Only two of the nursery walls were Blush Rose and only half the baseboards were Cotton Candy. Meantime Tom had probably lost the fucking Steere trial. He'd stood in front of enough juries to know they weren't with him and he was too tired to give a shit.

"Tom! Tom, bring two pacifiers when you come down!"

Tom tripped across the shaggy pink rug to the changing tables. Underneath were shelves full of disposable diapers, Desitin, and baby powder. He shoved it all around but didn't see any receiving blankets. Or what else? Pacifiers. Meanwhile, all hell was breaking loose on the Steere case. The security guards got dead, DiNunzio got shot, and Richter went AWOL. Where the fuck were the pacifiers?

He searched the soft toys and baby gifts on the floor. No receiving blankets and it was time to receive. Tom tore through the baby gifts. A pink rattle flew in the air, then a pink playsuit. Everything was a rosy blur. Marie wanted girls, so at least she should be happy. That used to make Tom happy, giving Marie what she wanted. Providing, fixing, *doing*. That was his job. But this twin thing went too far. Now the Steere case was exploding and he was snowed in. With the screaming twins. In Baby Hell.

"Tom! Tom, the blankets! And the pacifiers!"

Tom chucked a fluffy white bear to the side. He was an assistant district attorney of a major metropolitan area. He had attended St. Joe's University and Villanova Law. He had ambitions to be a Common Pleas Court judge. He had no room for a baby in his life, much less two. He drop-kicked a pink elephant.

And now Tom was going to lose Steere, he knew it. The indictment shouldn't have been brought in the first place. *The best thing I can do for you,* his boss had said, *is to give you a case nobody can win. Then you don't look bad when you lose. Try this case for me, Tom. I'll remember you did.* That's what his boss had said, but he failed to add that falling on your sword was vastly overrated as a career move. Plus you're the one that has to go to work the next day with your spleen in your hand.

"Tom! Tom! The blankets! And the pacifiers!"

Tom rummaged on a flowery chair until he found two pink blankets that were too light to keep even a doll warm. He ran downstairs with them and stopped when he saw the devil sitting on the stair, finger still embedded. "Hey, little dick," Tom said under his breath. "Find any diamonds?"

"Mom!" the kid wailed, and ran screaming.

Tom ran down to the living room where putrid, sulfurous smells arose from the screaming and crying. The air reeked of yellow baby shit, like mustard gas, and he detected a wheaty new stench, puked-up formula. The babies vomited like volcanoes—*gastric reflux,* according to his mother-in-law—and the lava on Tom's shoulder was already rancid. The house was so damn hot and his mother-in-law wouldn't let him open a window—*Are you crazy?*—because of the draft on the twins. Tom handed the battle-ax the blankets and fled on foot.

"You forgot the pacifiers. I said pacifiers!"

Tom veered left and hustled back to the stairway. He knew he was supposed to be happy but he wasn't. Everything had changed overnight. His wife had blown up like a balloon. His house was swollen with people. His career had been warped out of shape by the Steere case. He'd been working like a dog for a year now, unfortunately the same time as Marie got pregnant. He knew there would be some point when he would feel happy, but that time hadn't happened yet.

Tom raced across the nursery to the two pink dressers against the unpainted wall and tore open the first drawer by its bunny knob. Inside were itty-bitty undershirts and little hooded sleepers. He mushed them around. The twins wailed louder, shrill cries of the colicky floating up from the depths.

"Tom, the pacifiers!"

He dashed to the two Toys "Я" Us bags beside the two cribs. The white bags bulged like Santa's sack. A long receipt was stapled to the bag and Tom looked at the sticker in shock. Two hundred bucks!? He ripped into the bag. Two animal mobiles to make the babies calm. Two black-and-white cubes to make them smart. Two blue bunnies to make them sleepy. Two pacifiers to shut them up.

"Tom, hurry!"

Tom tore out of the room with the pacifiers and raced down the stairs. How would they afford two kids on his salary? Twice as many tuition bills. Double the doctor bills. Twice the clothing bills. Two weddings. Tom handed off the pacifiers, his wallet reeling.

"Tom! Get a water bottle!"

Tom ran to the kitchen where Marie sat at the table, engulfed by her sister and father. She winked at Tom from the center of their freckled circle. Everybody in Marie's family winked like they had Tourette's. Tom winked back and twisted on the tap. He had long ago stopped recognizing his wife, whose slim body vanished with their sex life. Marie had retained enough water to fill a swimming pool. Tom ran a shaking index finger under the tap.

"Tom! Tom! In here!"

Tom spun on his wingtips like a gyroscopic

father. He didn't know where the sound was coming from, which demand to meet, the twins or the Macy's-balloon wife's or the bitchy mother-in-law's. Tom! Tom! Tom!

"Tom! The phone! The office!"

"Shit." The office? The jury? The judge? The pacifiers? Tom left the water running and raced into his study, where the two other devils were drawing on his briefs with a crayon. SHIT FUCK PISS, they were writing. "Sean, Colin, stop that," Tom said. He took the crayon out of Sean's hand and gave him a scissors, then handed Colin a letter opener and shooed them both out of the room. Tom picked up the bottle, uh, the phone. "Hello?"

"TOM!" boomed a man's voice over a speaker-phone. It was Bill Masterson, district attorney of the City of Philadelphia. Masterson's basso profundo echoed like the Wizard of Oz. Tom went weak in the knees. Oh, no. The only time Masterson called his assistants was to fire them. "Tom, you're not here!" Masterson bellowed.

"I will be. I'm on my way."

"I'm in, but you're not. I don't get it. Where are you, Moran?"

"At home."

"Why are you there? Get your ass here!"

"Uh, they're still plowing me out." Tom squinted out the window. Two cops were directing a snowplow down his street. The blade had fallen off the first plow and they had to jerry-rig another. "I'll be right in."

"Why the fuck were you there in the first place?"

"My wife had twins, sir."

"I don't care. Get in here. Steve told me you'd be here an hour ago."

"They sent a car for me, but it couldn't get through—"

"I don't care. You shouldn't have left the office."

"I thought I had time. The jury was out."

"I don't care. Don't you get it? Why the fuck did you leave the office?"

"To check on my wife and babies."

"I don't care. Why do you think I care?"

Tom broke a sweat. The twins howled in the background. "Tom!" someone yelled. "TOM!"

"Tom!" Masterson barked. "You tried Steere, yes?"

"Yes."

"So why am I the one in the office? I don't get it. You tried the case, but I'm in the office. You work for me, yes?"

"Yes."

"You work for me, but I'm the one in the office. I don't get it, do you?"

"No," Tom said. "Sorry—"

"Look, I don't care. Steve took a call from Judge Rudolph's law clerk. There's an emergency hearing scheduled. Get your ass to the office. You hear?"

"Yes."

"You hear me, Tom?" Masterson said, and the speakerphone clicked off.

"TOM!" someone yelled, and he picked up his briefcase and ran.

44

M arta sat in the truck with her flashlight, the nautical map, and a skinny ruler she'd found in one of Christopher's tool chests. The ruler was double-edged and easy to read, even if it reeked of whatever comes off the bottom of horses' hooves. She checked the time. 4:15 in the morning. Oh no. She was running out of night. Would Christopher change the jury's vote? Could he turn the tide?

Marta squinted at the calculations she'd made in the map's margin. The numbers swam before her eyes. Her logic had gone fuzzy a half hour ago. She'd tried to calculate the yards from the coastline to the pinhole, then stopped when she realized how witless that was. She had no idea where the coastline was, with the tides and the storm and the spin of the earth's rotation and the moon in the seventh house. Her brain had melted to yogurt. Her head thundered from her wounds and the sheer effort of staying awake.

Hold on. There was another way. She could go back to Steere's home office and find the deed, which would describe the plot of land exactly. Using it, she'd be able to calculate the yards from the house to the pinhole. That could work. It had to. She set the stuff aside, twisted on the ignition, and turned the truck around toward Steere's house.

SSSHUNK! The shovel hit the first icy chunk of snow and Marta started digging. The storm had lessened but was still blowing off the sea. The surf crashed behind her. She could barely see the shovel in the light from the flashlight, stuck in the snow like a floor lamp. Digging for treasure may have been crazy, but Marta preferred to think of it as a long shot. She sensed something was under there and had to believe that her calculations, made from a reconciling of deed, blueprint, and nautical map, weren't that far off. So she'd dragged Christopher's horse manure shovel out to the middle of the beach, over dune and erosion fencing, and had begun to dig. There was no more time for geometry or numbers. There was no time for anything but action.

Marta pressed the shovel into the snow and drove it deeper with the bottom of her boot. Every muscle in her torso ached, but she had grown accustomed to the pain. She lifted the shovel, but she'd piled on too much snow in her haste and the snow slid off. Marta had shoveled snow in her childhood, but never in the dark before, or in a blizzard. By the ocean. With a man she'd killed down the beach.

Marta jabbed at the top layer of snow for a

lighter load and threw it to the side successfully. The wind blew it off the nascent pile and carried it away from her hole. She went in for another load. The snow grew wetter the deeper she dug and felt heavier on the shovel. No matter, she told herself. She'd dug out three shovels of snow. Only 398,280 more to go.

SSHUNK! Marta tried not think about it. Bogosian, up the beach. Darning, his face frozen in death. Steere, and how she'd been fooled, or her other cases and clients. How she'd come to be on a beach in the middle of nowhere, attempting the impossible. She tried to convince herself she wasn't dead tired, desperate, or a fool. At least she had done one thing right in this case; she made sure those girls were safe. Carrier and DiNunzio were probably home asleep in their beds.

Marta dug deeper, but was still into snow. When would she hit sand? A foot more, two? Then how far down would the treasure be? Two feet, three? She took another scoop. Her back was as sore as her ribs. She bent from the knee and took another heap of snow. Then another ten and another ten after that.

SHUNK! Sharp pains wracked her lower back and her arms felt like they were about to fall from their sockets. She was drenched with sweat under her coat. Her neck felt clammy where snow had melted under her collar. Wetness sluiced down her face and cheeks. Still she kept digging. Marta would dig all night if she had to. She might be wrong and she might be crazy, but she would not be denied.

◇　　　◇　　　◇

Marta stared at the empty hole in the purplish light of dawn. Her body sagged and her faint shadow drooped on the snow. Her hair was drenched and her face was soaked. Salt air stung her eyes, and she told herself that was why tears kept welling up in them. It was almost dawn, probably about six o'clock. Marta had run out of time. Out of luck. It had all come down, it was all coming apart.

The hole was empty. A good four feet of dark, soggy sand, with water in the bottom, like a pool for a child's sand castle. Marta had dug it out, then clawed it out. When her gloved hands slowed her, she stripped them off and used her bare hands until they were scraped raw and insensate. Nothing. There was nothing there. No treasure, no papers, no clue. No treasure chest full of incriminating evidence. It was all over. There was only emptiness.

The sky was bright now that the storm had passed. Soon the sun would climb the clouds and the world would wake up. Coffee machines would gurgle and toasters would ring. Fax machines would awaken convulsively. Computer screens would crackle to life, obeying encrypted instructions. Telephone lines were probably being repaired this very minute and roads plowed clean. The morning was a beginning to everybody else, but to Marta it seemed like the end.

The night had been dark and under its cover she had been free to move, to run. To search and dig. But dawn would bring police and questions. They would find Bogosian's body. They would want her to account for the security guards at the office. They would want answers. It was all over. Steere had won. Marta had lost. There would be no justice.

She let the shovel fall to the snow. The sky was dim, the atmosphere thin. A frigid wind whipped off the sea, a blast so cold and dry Marta imagined it could kill germs. Disinfect the world, eradicating virus, disease, pestilence. Hate, grime, blood. Murder. The surf crashed behind her like someone tapping her on the shoulder. Marta answered, turning.

The ocean glimmered, barely visible. The waves that had seemed black as india ink last night were jade green, and the sea foam was tinted ivory. Whitecaps broke on the shore, one after the other, and sea bubbles raced in all directions and vanished. In the distance Marta could see the lighthouse and a rocky jetty near Steere's beach. The sight was desolate and beautiful, and she felt like it had been scrubbed as clean and raw as she was. As if God had taken a stiff wire brush to the world.

Marta considered walking into the waves just then. Leaving the fucking shovel on the ground and strolling right in, as if she were walking into a courtroom. Taking over. Striding into the Atlantic like she owned it. Marta could do that. The waves would welcome her and take her in and suck her up, her soggy coat and her aching back and her numb fingers. She even knew the depths of the water by the shore, if indeed that was what those precisely etched numbers on the nautical map had meant.

Marta pictured herself walking in to three feet and starting to float at six feet and by fourteen feet she could tread water, just for show. By sixteen feet she'd begin to dip below the frigid waves and they'd knock her around a little, but by eighteen feet she'd have them licked like she licked everything else. After all, she was undefeated.

Marta turned for a last look at Steere's house, in the light of a new day. It was majestic and serene. She owned no house like that anywhere. Not New York, Boston, L.A., or Cape Cod. She was never home anyway. She was never anywhere. She was always in motion. Marta knew where the VIP waiting room was in any USAir hub. She could work the cruise control on a rental Taurus without asking. She kept the fax numbers of every Four Seasons Hotel in her bulky Filofax.

Marta's wet gaze lingered on Steere's house. What a thing a house was! To think that she could walk into the Atlantic without ever having owned a real, honest-to-God home! And Steere's was a nice one, worth every zero. She imagined herself as its buyer, waltzing through for the first time. The house was set so beautifully, nestled alone among the dunes. Location, location, location.

Now that the sky was brighter, Marta could see how high the dunes rose in front of the house, tall and bright white in the new sun. No wonder they had been so hard to run on, they were steep. The wooden erosion fences crisscrossing them had done their job. Marta could see the wooden fence that had caught her coat last night. It crossed the beachfront in two directions.

She blinked against the glare. Funny. One fence ran down the beach from the upper left of Steere's property, and one ran from the upper right. Only the tops of the wooden posts showed, and Marta could see them clearly as the sun rose and a warm golden blanket slipped over the snowy beach. The two wooden fences met at the side of the house, about forty feet from where Marta stood. The tops of the slats made two dotted lines. And where the two dotted lines met, smack dab in the center, was a rather distinct X.

Was she exhausted? Was she crazy? Was her mind playing tricks on her? Marta wiped her eyes with the back of her sleeve, but the X was for real. An X, right next to Steere's house. X marks the spot! The pinhole in the map must have been a backup, in case the fences shifted. Marta bent over and grabbed her shovel.

45

A large, chilly presence, Bennie Rosato stood just inside Judy's apartment door as the associate gushed an explanation, from color blindness to a handwritten motion for a mistrial to Darning's white notebook. Bennie remained unmoved, stiff in her Gore-Tex jacket, unwilling to set foot in the apartment. As the managing partner of the law firm that bore her name, Bennie needed to maintain a professional distance from her employees, precisely because of times like this. Times she dreaded. "So what I'm hearing," Bennie said slowly, "is that you have been gathering evidence to incriminate Elliot Steere."

Judy nodded so eagerly that hair slipped from her headband. "I'm working on it. The notebook means something; I just can't figure it out yet. It's full of numbers. I think it has something to do with street money."

"You're missing my point, you're gathering evidence against one of our clients."

"Well, against Elliot Steere." Judy stood behind

the canvas futon and leaned on its back. In her hand was the notebook.

"Run that by me again, Carrier. Are you making a distinction between Elliot Steere and our other clients?"

Judy blinked. "Yes. Of course. Elliot Steere is a killer. A murderer. He sent somebody to kill Mary and Marta."

"You have proof of this? Of any of it?"

"Not yet, but—"

"Not yet?" Bennie struggled to restrain herself. The associate seemed to have no idea how dangerous this game was. It was like watching a toddler play with an assault rifle. "Do you realize what you're doing? You're Steere's lawyer. Even if you had proof of his wrongdoing, the only ethical thing you could do is file a withdrawal from the case. You get to bow out, not sabotage his murder trial."

"The judge wouldn't have granted a withdrawal."

"You didn't even try. You should have come to me. I could have filed something with the court. We could have fought it together. Legally. Even if we couldn't, you still have no right to be gathering evidence against your own client. It's the D.A. who has to prove the case against Steere, and if he can't, Steere deserves to go free. Period."

"But he's a murderer!"

"What is this, Ethics 101? Elliot Steere is a client of our law firm, *my* law firm. Last time I saw one of his checks, it was made out to us, for a very large retainer."

Judy shook her head in disbelief. "So what? What does he buy for his money?"

"*Loyalty,* without apology or reservation. He buys all our efforts and skill, everything we know about the law and courtrooms. He paid for it, he's entitled to it. There is no shame in that, none at all. That's business. *My* business."

Judy felt sick inside as Bennie spoke. She could never agree with Bennie and regretted telling her about Darning's notebook. Time to correct the error. Judy didn't think Bennie had focused on the notebook, so she let it slip from her fingers. It fell to the rug behind the futon and Judy nudged it underneath its canvas skirt with her toe.

"Didn't you stop and think?" Bennie asked, her temper giving way. "Didn't you realize you have an ethical obligation here?"

"My loyalty to Steere ended when Mary got shot. My hands had her blood all over them, they still do." Judy held out her palms, but Bennie wouldn't even look.

"That makes no difference."

"It makes all the difference in the world! What's in *your* veins, Bennie? *Ice?*"

Bennie stood tall. "You're a lawyer in my employ, Carrier. I hired you to work on this case, handpicked you and DiNunzio. It was a choice assignment, the most significant case in our office. Steere was supposed to be our calling card."

"I understand that, but the case has gone wrong."

"Nothing was wrong with the case until you filed that motion for a mistrial—without the client's authority. Before that, it was outside the record that Mary is in the hospital. It was outside the record that Marta is missing and that you found some magical notebook. As far as the case was concerned, nothing outside the record even existed. "

"I can't divide my brain that way. Outside the record, inside the record."

"Bullshit!" Bennie shouted. "You're supposed to be a trial lawyer. You filed motion papers against a client's express orders. He gets to define the scope of his representation, not you. If Steere is as smart as I think, he's gone forward on his own or hired someone else. You got my firm fired, and for conduct so egregious we could all be disbarred."

"I was trying to find out who tried to kill Mary, and why."

"Are you insane? That's not your concern. That's not your job. You got me fired, you got us fired, and so I have only one recourse."

"Go ahead. Fire." Judy grinned crookedly even though she felt like crying.

"You're fired. I'll send you the termination forms as soon as possible. I'll also send you some forms to report this to the disciplinary board. If you don't file them yourself, I'll file against you. Don't make me do it."

"I'll think about the disciplinary board a little later, if you don't mind. I'm more worried about Mary than myself right now."

Bennie couldn't let that pass. "Don't think I'm not worried about Mary. I'm the one who sat there with her parents. But what you're doing—and what she was doing—was wrong. Ethically wrong."

"But not morally wrong."

"That's not your judgment to make. I took on Steere's representation, and you work for me. What happens to the legal system if each lawyer makes his own judgments about a client's morality?"

"Justice. Finally." Judy stared at Bennie, who returned her gaze with equal fury.

"No. Nobody will have a lawyer they can trust. And justice doesn't have a chance." Bennie yanked her jacket zipper up and turned to go. "Enough. Clean out your office as soon as possible. Don't talk to the press."

Judy held her head high. She didn't have anything to be ashamed of. Her only regret was hurting Bennie and the firm. "I'm sorry it turned out this way. I'll see you at the hospital, probably. Or around."

"Not so fast." Bennie held out her hand and was pleased to see it wasn't shaking. "You said you had a notebook. Give it to me and I'll turn it over to the police."

"No."

"What?"

"I'm not giving you the notebook."

"You can't refuse me."

"Why not?" Judy cleared her throat. "You're not my boss anymore. I'm single again."

Bennie didn't laugh. "Stop screwing around and give me that notebook."

"No."

"You're keeping it from the police, who might be able to figure out what it means."

"I'll figure it out myself. I know the case. I'm smarter than they are."

"You're not trained the way they are. They're professional. They have tools, resources at their disposal."

Judy's mouth dropped open in mock surprise. "I can't believe my ears. Bennie Rosato, destroyer of cops, *defending* them? They almost deep-sixed you last year."

Bennie pursed her lips. Shit. This kid was a whip. Too bad the firm was losing her. "The cops can handle it."

"Not tonight, in this weather. You said so yourself, they weren't even at the office. Did they find the notebook or did I?"

"It's not a competition, Carrier."

"Yes it is," Judy said, her voice suddenly urgent. "That's exactly what it is. It's a race. I didn't find out in time to save Mary, but I can still save myself."

Bennie paused. She should have realized it. Of course Carrier would have been scared. "You're in greater danger if you keep it. Did you ever think of that?"

"It's my judgment, not yours. Like you said."

Bennie didn't know what to say or do. She couldn't beat the notebook out of her, and Carrier was right about the attention the police would give it tonight. She opened the apartment door and walked out, torn. Conflicted.

"Good-bye," Judy called after her, but Bennie was too upset to answer.

Blinking against the flurries, Bennie stood in the snowstorm outside Judy's building and looked up at the associate's apartment. Warm light spilled out of the large, uncurtained window but Carrier wasn't in sight. Bennie's emotions wrenched her chest. She was tempted to go up and retract what she'd said but she couldn't. She couldn't sanction what Carrier was doing, it was dangerous and wrong, but she wouldn't thwart it, not yet anyway. Bennie looked up at the snowy sky, which was brightening. It had to be close to dawn, almost morning. The jury would be back in deliberations soon. Carrier didn't have time to stop the verdict even if she tried.

Snow fell on Bennie's face and thick knit hat. So Carrier had found a notebook of Eb Darning's with numbers in it, and had learned something about Eb and street money. And Bennie's old friend Bean had told her that Eb worked at City Hall for cash. Was it connected? Was Darning's notebook a record of cash payments? Money for votes? The answer would be at the heart of the city.

City Hall.

Bennie turned from the building, jammed her hands in her pockets, and began the trek. If she could figure out what was going on, maybe she could protect Carrier. She trudged down the street in deep drifts. Every step felt heavy but it wasn't the snow. Bennie was thinking about DiNunzio. *What's in your veins, ice?* It had hit home. Bennie had been feeling more responsible for Steere than for her two associates. Where was her loyalty to them?

Bennie tucked her head into her chest against the driving snow. She was responsible for the associates as well. She was the one who had accepted the Steere representation without a second thought; she'd seen financial viability and a dramatic opening for her law firm. Bennie had never dreamed it would turn out like this, with one associate terrified for her life and another near death.

She kept her head down and turned north into the storm. If there was a way out of this, Bennie had to find it. That was part of being the boss, too.

46

Marta dug through the sand like a terrier as soon as her shovel hit something. It was hard, whatever it was, and it wasn't a clamshell. It rang when the shovel struck it, a metallic *ding*. Marta shoveled in a fever. Sand flew until a tan spot appeared at the bottom of the hole. It was camouflaged, barely visible in the morning sunlight. Something was there. What was it?

Marta fell to her knees, dropping the shovel beside the deep hole and uprooted erosion fencing. She clawed with her gloves and shoved the wet sand to either side of the hole. The sun shone cold on her back but she still had time. It wasn't too late. It wasn't over. She had found it!

Marta's heart raced with excitement and exertion. She dug and dug, perspiring in her heavy coat. The patch of tan metal widened in the wet sand. She clawed faster. Her fingers raked the sand in five deep ridges. Underneath it was a metal box of some kind. It *existed*.

The hole began to widen. The circle of tan metal

grew. Five inches, then eight, then ten. Marta burrowed around the box. The top was smooth metal, like a strongbox. Sunlight winked on the water covering the box in a thin layer. Marta rooted in the sand until she exposed the thick lid of the box. She heard herself laughing, giddy with relief and delight. What was it? It was good. It was something. It was *it*! What Alix Locke had been looking for. What Eb Darning had died for. What Elliot Steere had killed for. It was almost hers!

Marta cleared the perimeter of the box and tried to wrench it out of the sand and snow, but it was stuck in the sand. She tore off her gloves and rammed her fingers between box and sand. Her fingers were bloody but she didn't care. She flattened her hand between the box and the sand and wedged her fingers straight down, deeper and deeper. Her fingertips drove to the bottom of the box and she yanked with all the strength she had left. The box came free in her hands.

Marta fell backward onto her butt and scrambled to sit upright. It was a locked strongbox about the size of a legal pad, six inches thick and apparently watertight. Marta sat on the frigid beach with the box on her snowpants, momentarily stumped by the large Master padlock, of heavy gray metal. She'd have to break it to get inside.

Marta struggled to her feet with the box and looked around. The beach was deserted and the storm had passed. The wind had died down and the snow had formed a thick, icy crust. But the sun was high. It was morning. How long before somebody found Bogosian's body? How long before they came after her? What was in this fucking box?

Marta shook it and something inside jostled. Not rattled, not clanged, just jostled. *Shifted*. It made almost no sound. Was it paper? Was it money? What was it? She had to get inside. She thought about looking for a key, but that would take too long. She didn't want to search Steere's office again or the *Piratical*. There had to be a better way.

Christopher's pickup truck. The back of the truck was full of evil tools. One would break the padlock. Marta tucked the box under her arm and ran up the beach. She picked up her pace to a sprint like a star receiver, the box in the crook of her arm. She could bust the padlock with a hammer. Saw it off. *File* the fucking thing down.

Marta's heart lifted as she dashed across the snow, her boots crunching through the hardened top layer. An ocean breeze blew sweet and clear. A slight wind gusted at her back. So the box was locked. So what? She giggled as she ran. Her breath came easily as she scooted past Steere's house. Her coat was soaked but it felt light on her shoulders. She wasn't even tired. She'd blow the box wide open. She'd melt the thing in the forge. She'd *chew* her way in.

She hit the dune running, up, up, up and over the crest, then down again, almost falling. The box felt secure under her arms and she kept running, down the glistening white valley between the dunes. There were no footsteps in the snow except Marta's. She ran up the dune and caught sight of Christopher's pickup, parked by the snow-covered curb.

She half ran, half skidded into the truck, fumbled for the keys, and nestled inside the driver's seat with the strongbox on her lap. She twisted around and thrust her hand into one of the tool chests. Out came a hammer with a spike at the top. The nail set! Rock and roll!

Marta set the strongbox between her padded knees, held it steady, and brought the nail set down against the padlock. The box slipped. She tried it again and hit the padlock, but it remained intact. She hit it again and made solid contact. *Clang!* The padlock stayed locked. Fuck!

She tossed the nail set aside and went fishing again in the tool chest. She found a saw with a fine-tooth edge, held the box still on top of her leg, and applied the saw to the lock. Marta had never used a saw in her life and it showed. The saw went crazily left and right. She pushed too hard and it wouldn't move against the lock. She pushed too easy and it went too fast, barely scratching the metal. An emery board did more damage.

Marta flopped the box over on its back and sawed the latch with vigor. The padlock wiggled back and forth but the saw's teeth barely etched the surface of the metal. She sawed again and almost amputated her index finger, which was frostbitten anyway. Not a good idea. She threw the saw back in the truck and searched the chest again. An old iron horseshoe! Marta hooked the shoe through the lock and tried to wrench it off. No go. There had to be something in the truck that would open this god-damn padlock! The truck was a hardware store on wheels!

Marta got out of the truck with the strongbox and slammed the door behind her. She stormed to the back of the truck and yanked the back door open. The forge, a tiny oven without a door, was on the left. She could melt the strongbox down!

Marta tried to shove the box into the forge, pressing with her shoulder. The box was too wide. She grabbed the box and slammed the lock against the back edge of the forge, but succeeded only in denting the forge. The padlock stayed fast. What a product! What a company! Marta wondered momentarily if it were publicly traded, then grabbed the box and drop-kicked it across the snow. It landed in a snowdrift and disappeared. Uh-oh.

Marta ran after it, growling, and dug it out. Fucking padlock. They weren't kidding in those commercials where they shot the shit out of the thing. She set the box down out of the snowdrift and jumped on it over and over, like a trampoline. She climbed off and looked down at her handiwork. The lock survived, as did the frame of the box. This wasn't funny anymore. Marta snarled and whirled around. Her gaze fell on the pickup truck. Of course.

She left the box in the center of the street and sprinted back to the truck. She climbed into the driver's seat and slammed the door. The driver's clock said 7:01. She still had time. She could make this happen. Christopher would be working for her. Everything would be okay as soon as she cracked the box. She released the emergency brake and twisted on the ignition. The truck coughed twice and turned over.

Marta heard herself cackling softly as she gunned the engine. A padlock against a lawyer? No contest. She wrenched the steering wheel to the left and aimed straight for the box.

47

Bennie barreled in her wet parka down the marble corridor of City Hall, past the glass-etched sign that read ADMINISTRATION REPORTERS. The elegance of the sign belied what was beyond the next door. The City Hall press room was even filthier than a precinct house, which was why Bennie loved it.

She flung open the mahogany door and deftly avoided the newswire machine that obstructed an entrance hall choked with empty vending machines and a grimy shelf of mailboxes. The floor was a gritty brown tile strewn with crumpled memos, discarded gum wrappers, and curly faxes. A dusty dictionary with marbleized endpapers sat on a battered bookstand. An old wooden coatrack had fallen against the wall with the weight of reporters' coats. The air smelled vaguely electrical with a hint of body odor.

On either side of the entrance hall stood eye-level partitions covered with dirty burlap and wrinkled clippings. Beyond them were offices filled with cluttered wooden desks and dingy file cabinets. Bookshelves were packed with papers, plastic spiral notebooks, and superseded style manuals. Each newspaper had its own office in the press room and on the door of the *News* office hung an open shark jaw.

Bennie peeked over the left partition at the starchy back of an old friend, Emil Gorebian. Emil sat erect at his keyboard and tapped with an expert's skill. He had covered the City Hall beat for thirty-four years but had been demoted to the night shift when he declined to retire early. The city editor had told him the newspaper "wasn't downsizing, it was right-sizing," and Emil had politely allowed as how a human being wasn't a suit. But it didn't matter, the suits were in control. Which was why Bennie could never work for anybody else. "Emil!" she called over the partition.

"Bennie!" Emil said, the alarm in his voice tinged with a courtly Middle Eastern accent. "What am I hearing about you? Your office, murders. How terrible!"

"I know." Bennie dripped into the office, slipped out of her snowy hat and parka, and popped them on the back of an empty chair. She looked around. The other desks were empty. The dirty gray computers were on, their screen savers ever-changing, but the scuffed chairs sat vacant. "Where is everybody?"

"The young Turks? Most can't get in because of the snow, they are too tender. The others are hounding the innocent, like good reporters. Myself, I am waiting for my editor to call, to give me some very important instructions like I don't know what I'm doing. So tell me, what is going on?"

Bennie flopped into the ratty chair and shook the chill off. "I'll sue the paper for you, I told you. We don't have to go to court, it's a union paper. We can grieve it. It's easy."

"No." Emil pursed his lips, which were full and vividly pink under a frosty gray mustache. His eyebrows were shaped like thick commas over round eyes. His nose was a parrot's beak set against exotic olive skin. "They are not worth my anger, or yours."

"You've given over thirty years to this newspaper. You've won awards and your experience—"

"Please. Times have changed. It's a spot news operation now. They care nothing for history. Experience has no value. It's what happened today, not yesterday. Now tell me what is happening. Can I help?"

"I need information about someone who used to work here in the sixties."

"Who?" He cocked his head, his interest piqued. "I know everyone who worked here then."

"His name is Eb Darning."

"I don't know him," Emil said immediately.

"What? You sure?"

"Yes."

"Think about it. You know everybody here?"

"I do. If I don't know him, he wasn't here." Emil patted his tie, which he wore with a white oxford shirt, still pressed despite the lateness of the hour. Or the earliness.

"How can you be sure so fast?"

"I'm sure that fast. How slow do I have to be to make you feel confident of my answer? I told you, I don't know him, so he didn't work here."

Bennie smiled, remembering that one of the reasons she liked Emil was that he was the only person more hyper than she. One day she'd introduce him to Bean and they'd kill each other. "Darning may have worked for L and I or Fleets. Maybe the Parking Authority."

"Very specific."

"Work with me, Emil."

"Is this about those murders?"

"Yes."

"Fine." Emil's gray head, with its puffy side part, snapped to his computer. He hit a few keys and pressed ENTER. "Eb Darning, you say his name is. Eb is a name?"

"Yes."

Emil frowned at the screen. One neat wrinkle creased his forehead deeply, as if even his brow had been starched. "What kind of a name is that?"

"Not Armenian. He was black and a youngish man at the time. He might have had a daughter. He definitely had a drinking problem."

"In City Hall, it's a job qualification," Emil muttered as he focused on the screen. "These old 286 machines annoy me. They take too long. Here."

"What?" Bennie scooted her chair closer. On the computer screen was a list of names.

"Here are the L and I employees for 1960. No Darning is there."

"Let's try 1961."

Emil hit a key and drummed his fingers while the computer cranked away. "Why aren't you married, Bennie? You should be married."

"I'm dating a very nice man, who's unfortunately out of town."

"Dating isn't married." Emil frowned at the monitor. "I have someone I want you to meet."

"No. Your last fixup was a disaster."

"This one likes women who work."

"How enlightened."

"An Armenian, of course. A member of my church. His wife died and he wants to remarry."

"Forget it."

"Bennie," Emil said, his eyes focused. "I want to see you happy. I hope you will find a husband."

"I don't need a husband. I need Eb Darning."

Another list finally materialized on the flat matte monitor. Names in faint green letters floated in an inky background. Emil's sharp eyes ran down the list. "No Darning." He hit another key. "I'll try the next year."

"Thanks." Bennie struggled to keep up with Emil as he read. "Darning might have been a building inspector."

"Not here," Emil barked before he was off to the next list. He and Bennie checked employee lists for all the City Hall departments for the past thirty-odd years, but Eb Darning's name didn't appear on any of them. Then they checked variations on Eb Darning's name, including Heb Darnton, for the same time period. No variations appeared either. Confused, Bennie produced Eb's clean-shaven photo and showed it to Emil.

"Never saw the man," he said, handing it back.

Bennie returned it to her jeans pocket. She didn't tell Emil that Darning was the same man Elliott Steere had killed, for the same reason she hadn't told Bean. He didn't need to know it to help her. "Emil, I know Darning worked here and he might have gotten paid in cash. How is that possible?"

Emil smiled tightly. "I was afraid of this. Perhaps he was a party employee, not an employee of the city."

"So?"

"So he worked for the party. He performed jobs for the party. City Hall was a different place then. You know that. You're a hometown girl."

"So you're saying that Darning wouldn't show up in the employee lists. He was invisible, at least officially."

"Yes."

"Nobody would know him, and if they did, they wouldn't say."

"Yes. He may have been paid for odd jobs. For influence. Even for vote-getting. Does that jibe with your information?"

"Yes," Bennie said. Her thoughts hurried ahead. What was it that Carrier had let slip? "Like 'street money'?"

Emil nodded. "Payment for votes. It was commonplace then. Now, not so. Or so I choose to believe."

Bennie eased back in the chair and tried to process the information. So Eb Darning was a drunk on the party payroll, who was paid street money by someone for votes. Was Steere the someone? He had to be. Why else would Steere kill him? Steere hated the mayor because the city wasn't ponying up for his properties. Maybe Steere had paid Darning to fix votes against the mayor in the last election, and Darning had decided not to keep quiet about it any longer, so Steere killed him. Steere wouldn't take the risk otherwise, especially a personal risk.

It made perfect sense, and Bennie had been around enough official corruption to know it followed the same sleazy patterns. It wasn't Philly's first encounter with vote fraud, and no matter what Emil chose to believe, it wouldn't be the last. Something was rotten at City Hall and Bennie could smell the stink. She stood up and grabbed her wet jacket and hat. "Where's Jen Pressman's office?"

"The chief of staff? Down the hall next to the mayor's. Why?"

"I have to ask her some questions. How can I get a meeting with her? She hates my guts. Because of the police misconduct cases. Every time I sue the city, I put her in the chair."

"I know Jen Pressman. She likes me. I'd be happy to go with you." Emil's dark eyes flickered with the remembered thrill of the hunt.

"No, what I have to discuss with her is confidential."

"I won't go in with you, I'll merely introduce

you. Get you in. Pave the way. If it's something big, you'll give me the exclusive."

"You dog." Bennie smiled. "What about that phone call you were waiting for from your editor?"

Emil glanced up at the ancient black clock on the wall. "It's eight o'clock. My shift was over a long time ago. Let him call somebody who's the right size."

48

Marta stood over the metal strongbox in amazement. She had run the thing over in the pickup and it lay crushed in the deep rut of snow. Still, the Master padlock had stayed intact even after the hinges on the strongbox had popped. What were these padlocks, kryptonite? No matter, if Marta couldn't get past the fucking lock, she'd go in through the broken hinges.

She picked up the box, wrenched cruelly out of shape, and squinted through the hinges. She could see the edge of a manila envelope. Her heart beat quicker. She pried the hinges with her fingers but her gloves were clumsy. She tore them off and held them in her teeth while she tried to wrench the lid off the box. No luck. It was too badly smashed.

Marta ran back to the truck with the box and sat in the driver's seat while she searched the tool chest. Chisels, hammers, and about three hundred pritchels tumbled by. Why hadn't they been this easy to find last night? Her fingers groped the bottom of the chest and she came up with a thick Phillips head screwdriver. Good enough.

She grabbed the box and drove the screwdriver between the demolished lid and the box, trying to pry them apart with the screwdriver as a lever. She couldn't wedge the screwdriver in because she'd crushed the box too flat. She tried again and again, breaking a sweat even in the cold car. It was late. The sun was up. She had to hit the road before the cops found Bogosian's body.

Marta abandoned the screwdriver for a hammer, braced the box on her lap, and pounded the twisted metal hinges. The jarring hurt her legs and the pounding reverberated in her skull, but she hammered away. She was about to scream with frustration when the lid popped up. She tore it off and it flopped aside, hanging by the padlock.

Marta's mouth went dry. Inside the smashed box was a manila envelope, the kind her L.A. office used for mailers. The envelope was crumpled from being run over and there was no writing on the front. She ripped open the envelope with a nervous hand. Inside was a stack of paper, which she pulled out and set on her lap. They were printed pages that looked like computer entries:

>18 294 827
>03 04 95
>03 06 85
>03 31 99
>F

>5'7"
>BRN
>C
>–
>*/1
>Jamie Rodriquez
>110 Kenwall Avenue
>Philadelphia, PA 19103

Underneath the single-spaced grouping was a UPC code, a miniaturized signature, and a photograph of a young man with a fuzzy goatee and slacker's expression.

Marta reread the entries. They appeared to be some sort of identification. It was familiar, but Marta couldn't place it. She studied the next set of information, also grouped together:

>29 837 471
>11 10 95
>11 06 55
>11 30 99
>M
>6'2"
>BLU
>C
>–
>*/1
>Cliff Jay Martin
>3329 Dickinson Street
>Philadelphia, PA 19147

Again, underneath was the bar code, a miniaturized signature, and a photo. The photo showed a gaunt man with glasses; its harsh lighting made him look cadaverous. What photo could be so unflattering? Marta thought a minute. It was an ID with a photo. A photo ID that made everybody look their worst. A driver's license!

She skimmed the lines of information excitedly. BLU, for eye color, and the M, for gender identification. Birthdays at the top and expiration and renewal dates. It was the information entered for a driver's license, fields in a record, for computer use. Marta's office grouped information in records like this for form letters and fee agreements. She was looking at a computer file of driver's licenses. But what did it mean?

Marta flipped through the stack and estimated the page count. Just under a hundred pages in the stack and most pages had four fields, each with photos. Why would Steere hide this? What was incriminating about it? It appeared to be perfectly innocent, but nobody buried something innocent.

Marta flipped through the pages for a clue. The drivers all lived in Pennsylvania, so presumably they were issued Pennsylvania licenses. The ages, race, and sex of the drivers were different. Black women, white men, the old and the young, stared up at Marta from the sheets, revealing nothing.

Marta skimmed the addresses. Bustleton Pike. Wolf Street. Ninth Street. Baltimore Avenue. E Street. Apartments and houses, all around the city.

She looked again. All the addresses were in Philadelphia. Marta thumbed through the pages to double-check. None were from suburbs or towns outside the city. So? What did this file have to do with Darning's murder? Marta stared out the frosty windshield, thinking. A dusting of snow lay on the truck's hood, too thin to conceal its dings and dents.

Suddenly she heard an engine sound and a jingling in the distance. The sound got louder, coming from the main drag. Marta slouched low in the driver's seat and watched the street from the driver's side mirror. A new snowplow drove past the cross street with chains jangling on its tires.

Marta checked her watch. 8:30. Her gut tightened. She was late. The business day had started. People were moving around. Snow dripped off the trees like raindrops. She had to get going. Fast. She gathered the papers into a stack, shoved them back into the envelope, and stuck it in her purse. She'd have to do her thinking on the way back to Philly. She wondered what the jury was doing. Would Christopher be able to do the job?

Marta tossed the file aside and twisted on the ignition. It made a noise, then nothing. The truck wasn't turning over. No! Not now, for God's sake! It was working before! This wasn't fair. It couldn't be happening. Marta tried to stay calm and remember what Christopher had told her.

Be patient. She just needs to warm up. Don't flood the engine.

Fine. Marta fed the gas gently and turned the ignition key. It cranked, then died.

Talk to her. She likes when you talk to her.

"Start or I'll sue your fucking ass!" Marta shouted as she hit the ignition. The truck started right up.

A law degree was a good thing to have.

Marta twisted the pickup onto the island's main drag and headed south. The file jiggled on the duct-taped passenger seat. The street stretched in front of her like a landing strip of melting snow, and Marta drove past the house where Bogosian's body lay. No one was around and there were no cars in the driveway. The house looked shuttered and closed.

Marta's stomach felt queasy. She had killed a man and was leaving his body in the snow. Strangely primal feelings of respect for the dead welled up. She thought of her father's simple grave, then her mother's. Marta had paid for her headstone, but didn't even go to the funeral. She sped up, trying to leave her emotions behind.

A car drove by in the opposite direction and its driver negotiated carefully past her in the slippery snow. Marta tugged her hood up and pulled it low over her forehead. She couldn't afford to be recognized. The guards' murders and her vanishing act had to be all over the news. She wished she could find out what was going on. She tried the truck's radio again, twisting the black dial uselessly. No soap.

Marta pressed the gas pedal and the truck sputtered slightly before it picked up speed. Along the strip she could see one or two stores opening up, a bagel shop and a 7-Eleven. She steered the pickup off the island and onto the rotary that led to the causeway, following Route 72. Light traffic traveled the highway, the drivers driving with caution in the snow.

Marta kept her face low and checked the clock. 9:16. She wouldn't get to Philly for hours. The jury would have been in session all morning. She hoped Christopher was delaying the jurors' final vote. She would need the time to piece together the file. She didn't understand the significance of the driver's licenses, but she knew who did. Alix Locke. The newspaper offices were right in Philly. Marta would find Alix, tell her she had the file, and make a deal. A long prison sentence could be very persuasive to a woman accustomed to cashmere.

Marta drove the pickup as fast as road conditions allowed. The highway had been plowed and salted, and mounds of snow at the shoulder were dissolving to gray slush. Snow-covered scrub pines and reedy white birches reappeared, but Marta had no time for reminiscing now. The truck hiccuped slightly, so she kept the gas flowing. She checked the fuel gauge. Still a quarter-tank left.

The truck hiccuped again. What was happening? The truck lurched slightly, then coughed. Marta eased off the gas. The truck slowed down and its coughing turned to hacking. Was something wrong with the engine? The hacking sounded terrible. Marta thought the thing would vomit blood.

"Don't you dare!" she shouted, but this time the truck wouldn't be intimidated. The warning light on the dashboard flickered to red. The engine stalled and was silent. The truck coasted to a stop in the middle of the deserted highway, almost a hundred miles from Philadelphia.

49

Judge Harry Calvin Rudolph sat atop the mahogany dais and scanned his courtroom. Elliot Steere sat alone at the defense table, wearing yet another Italian suit, one that everybody but judges could afford. The assistant district attorney, Tom Moran, slumped in his chair at the prosecution table, his eyelids curiously at half-mast. The gallery was empty except for the trial junkies who inhaled the Steere case like hot pizza. Any reporters able to get to the Criminal Justice Center in five feet of snow were scattered in the designated area in the very back row. Siberia, where they belonged.

Judge Rudolph checked his watch with a discreet twist of the wrist. It was barely ten o'clock in the morning, but no law required him to wait for a studio audience. He banged the gavel. "I am convening this hearing in the matter of *Commonwealth v. Steere* to ascertain that the defendant Elliot Steere's waiver of his right to counsel is knowing, intelligent, and voluntary. Let's begin. Mr. Steere, please rise."

"Yes, sir." Steere stood up in front of his seat. He

had no lawyer but he hardly appeared powerless. On the contrary, with a rested, confident expression, he looked as in control as he felt.

"Mr. Steere, you sent me a letter in this matter, did you not?"

"I did, sir."

"Is this the letter you sent me, Mr. Steere? You may approach."

Steere walked to the bench like a seasoned litigator and examined the letter the judge handed him. "It is, Your Honor."

"You wrote this letter yourself?"

"Yes, Your Honor."

"You sent it to me last night at approximately one o'clock in the morning, is that correct?"

"Yes, Your Honor. I asked one of the guards to take it to you, since I had no lawyer."

At the back of the courtroom, two reporters scribbled notes into steno pads. A sketch artist sat next to them, drawing hastily. Steere looked even taller in her sketch.

"You may be seated, Mr. Steere."

"Thank you." Steere returned the letter to the judge and strode back to his chair at counsel table. He took his seat, crossed his legs, and brushed his pants leg into order.

Judge Rudolph turned to the assistant district attorney. "Mr. Moran, my law clerk has provided you with a copy of Mr. Steere's letter. Did you receive it?"

"Huh?" The assistant district attorney started in his seat, his eyes red-rimmed and bleary. The stiffness of his three-piece suit seemed to be the only thing holding him up, like a legal El Cid. His head was full of the colicky crying of the twins. On the legal pad in front of him were a set of scribbled calculations and each number was multiplied by two.

Judge Rudolph waved the letter like a white flag. "Did you get a copy of Mr. Steere's letter?"

"Yes, I got it, Your Honor." Tom cleared his throat and tried to stay awake.

"Does the Commonwealth have any objection to its being admitted into the supplemental record?"

"No, Your Honor."

"Fine," Judge Rudolph said. "Would the court reporter please mark this letter as the next exhibit?" The judge handed the letter across his desk to Carol the court reporter, who had to stretch to take it. Tom watched her skirt hike up her slim, muscled thighs. His wife Marie used to have great legs. Now they were puffy and red pimples dotted her calves. She smeared tubes of cortisone cream on them every night. Tom hoped the leg zits went away soon.

"Mr. Steere," Judge Rudolph said. "As you know, we are here because you state in your letter that you wish to represent yourself for the remainder of this trial. Is that still your wish?"

"It is, Your Honor."

"You are not represented by counsel at this hearing, is that correct?"

"It is," Steere answered. "I do not wish to be represented by counsel. I know my rights."

"You are aware that the Court has attempted to

contact your lead counsel, Marta Richter, and has been unsuccessful."

"I am aware of that, sir. I repeat, I wish to proceed as my own counsel. I do not wish any of my previous counsel contacted on my behalf."

"You can afford counsel, can you not?"

"Of course I can afford counsel. I simply don't need counsel. My case is before the jury and I rely on their judgment." Steere nodded toward the courtroom gallery, where a silver-haired John LeFort sat with another lawyer in the front row. "I have the Cable and Bess firm on retainer, Your Honor, and my attorneys are present in the courtroom this morning. They will act as my legal advisers if need be."

"And you are satisfied with their representation, Mr. Steere?"

"Completely."

Judge Rudolph nodded. "The expertise of the Cable and Bess firm is well-known. There is an outstanding motion *in limine,* however, filed by the prosecution. Your former counsel Ms. Richter mentioned she would be filing a response."

"She was mistaken. I have discussed the matter with my attorneys and we will not be filing a response. I do not want further delay in my trial."

"Fine." This would go in well. All the bases were covered. Steere was holding up like a champ. Time to wrap it up. "Mr. Steere, although you have made your wish to represent yourself more than clear, Pennsylvania law requires that I hold a formal, on-the-record colloquy to make the determination that

your waiver is knowing and voluntary. Do you understand?"

"Yes, Your Honor."

"Good. I will be asking you a series of questions intended to determine that you understand
that you have the right to be represented by counsel, that you understand the nature of the charges
against you and the elements of those charges, that
you are aware of the permissible range of sentences
for the offenses charged, and that if you waive your
right to counsel you will be bound by all the
normal rules of procedure. Am I making myself
clear?"

"Yes."

Tom Moran blinked to stay awake, but he kept
slipping into a dream. He couldn't find the pacifiers
and the twins were about to be married. No one
came to the wedding reception because he forgot the
reception blankets. The twins and their husbands
moved into the nursery, which remained unpainted
because he ran out of Powder Puff.

"This matter is somewhat unusual in that it has
already been submitted to the jury," the judge continued, "but I am holding this colloquy out of an
abundance of caution. As far as scheduling, your letter requests this matter to proceed with dispatch. I
will have the jury resume its deliberations as soon as
this colloquy is over."

"Thank you, Your Honor."

"Quite welcome." Judge Rudolph reached for
his colloquy notes. He would go down the list and

ask each question. By the last one, the Steere case would be back on track. It was finesse like this that destined Judge Rudolph for greatness. He eased his glasses back to the bridge of his nose and began with the first question.

B ennie and Emil walked down the wide hallway, past the huge mahogany door flanked by
display cases and an etched-glass sign that
read OFFICE OF THE MAYOR. Rose and gray marble
wainscoting covered the walls. The corridor was
empty and its marble floor lustrous as a casket.

Emil pointed left, down the hall. Double mahogany doors opened onto the middle of the corridor
and TV lights poured from them, casting a bright par-
allelogram on the shiny floor. Laughter echoed from
the room. "Another grip 'n' grin," Emil said. "Does
this man want to be reelected or what?"

"I gather. Won't Pressman be there?"

"She only goes to some. She's probably in her
office." Emil reached the door with a gold number
painted next to it. "Let me do the talking. The secretary is a friend of mine. You stay behind me."

"Emil, I'm a foot taller than you. You can't hide
a sequoia with an olive tree."

"Then we cover your face." Emil tugged Bennie's

hat down. "To the left of the door is a waiting room. Sit there until I get past the secretary. Understood?"

"Yes, Your Honor."

"Don't be such a joker. Men don't like that."

"Then I'll stop. Right away."

"Hmph." Emil straightened his tie and opened the door onto a sparsely furnished secretary's area with high ceilings. It was empty except for a secretary who was fast asleep, propped up by her elbow on a desk that faced the door. Emil flashed Bennie a thumbs-up sign and pointed to the waiting area, which held a couch and two chairs around a small coffee table. Bennie marched obediently to the couch and sat down. To the left was a water cooler and a shelf of slots for mail. Down the hall must have been Pressman's private office.

"Flossie," Emil whispered. "Flossie?" He touched the secretary's arm and she woke up with a start.

"Oh. My. What?" The secretary's sleepiness vanished when she recognized Emil. "Emil, my goodness! I must have been snoozing on the job. How embarrassing!" She laughed nervously and patted a gold chain around her neck.

"That's all right. I sometimes doze off myself now that I'm on the night shift."

"Now I know how you feel. I was here all last night." She straightened her navy sweater and finger-combed her short brown hair. She looked middle-aged, with soft jowls around the laugh lines in her face. Snapshots of lithe Bengal cats covered her desk. "I don't know how you do it."

"Not very well. Sometimes I feel like a mole. How did your stuffed grape leaves turn out, by the way?"

"They were wonderful! I've been meaning to thank you. My daughter-in-law ate three and you know how picky she is. She reminds me of you-know-who. Her nibs." The secretary jerked a resentful thumb toward Pressman's office.

"I'm so pleased the grape leaves turned out well. You didn't fry the leaves too long, I hope. That is the secret."

"No," the secretary said, "I followed the recipe exactly. It was so much easier than I thought."

"Now, tell me, why have you been here all night, Flossie?" Emil's voice was honeyed as baklava. Back on the couch, Bennie rolled her eyes, wondering when he was going to get to the point.

"The snowstorm, of course. The snowplows. What a mess. The cats must be so upset. Smoochie can't sleep without me, poor thing."

"I understand completely. On night shift, I hardly see my wife or the girls. It's hard to get used to."

"I'm so mad about what they did to you, Emil. I never buy the *News* anymore."

"Flossie, my fight is not yours. Anyway, I don't mean to keep you, I wanted to see Jennifer. Is she in?"

"No." The secretary's lip curled. "She left a while ago. Just cut out and left. I have to stay because I'm a 'subordinate.'"

"What?"

"Don't get me started."

"Where did she go? I would like to see her."

"Home, supposedly, but we can't reach her there. I don't know." The secretary shook her head. "She'll probably be in soon, and you're welcome to sit and wait."

"If we must, we must. Thank you," Emil said graciously, but back at the couch, Bennie just growled.

51

The jurors sat at the conference table in the hotel in the same positions as they had in the deliberations room at the courthouse. The hotel conference room was large, modern, and windowed, like the one at the Criminal Justice Center, the legal pads sat stacked in the middle of the table, and the ice water tasted the same. In fact, the only difference between yesterday and today was that Christopher Graham had, to the astonishment of all, changed his vote. And shaved off his beard.

"You changed your vote?" asked Ralph Merry, his soft jowls draped around a mouth open in surprise. "You think we should *convict* Steere?"

"Absolutely," Christopher answered, with as much certainty as he could muster. "I vote guilty as charged."

Megan was amazed at the change in Christopher, and she wasn't thinking about his vote. Without his beard, Christopher's chin was strong, with a rugged cleft in it. His lips were full and nicely formed. He looked ten years younger, and thinner. Megan edged forward in her chair. "You shaved your beard?" she asked.

Ralph ignored her. "But, Christopher, yesterday you said we should acquit Steere. You've said he was innocent from the beginning. Why did you change your mind?"

Megan couldn't get over it, over him. The difference in Christopher was so awesome. He looked way hunky. "I think you look better without your beard."

Christopher smiled and shrugged happily. He felt better without his beard, like a new man with a fresh start. Lainie didn't want him and neither did Marta. Well, he was starting over, but he couldn't tell Megan that. "I don't know why I shaved, but I know why I changed my mind. I couldn't sleep all night. My conscience got to me."

"Your conscience?" Ralph asked in disbelief.

Gussella Williams looked crestfallen. "Christopher? You're changin' your vote? You're not puttin' us on?" Her large features collapsed into a frown that broke Christopher's heart. He paused, uncertain, and scanned the jurors one by one. The pain on Gussella's face was reflected on almost every juror around the table. They were even wearing their Sunday best, dressed up to go home today. Christopher felt terrible keeping them from their families, especially Mrs. Wahlbaum, who looked at him last, her eyes hooded in disappointment.

"Do you mean this, Christopher?" she asked, uncomprehending. She couldn't have felt worse if her best student flunked a midterm. "Please explain this to me."

Christopher reminded himself of his purpose and bore down. He would tell the truth, in a way. "I'm sorry, Mrs. Wahlbaum. I'm sorry, all of you, but I think Steere belongs in jail. He's a dangerous man. A murderer."

Smack! Kenny Manning slapped a loud high five with Lucky Seven, but theirs was the only joyous reaction. The other jurors remained puzzled.

"For real?" Nick asked. He was surprised. He woke up this morning all calm. Now he was getting all nervous again. Last night he knew just how to vote. Antoinetta visited him and told him what to do. He should vote not guilty. It would be over sooner if he did and go better for him in the neighborhood. Now Nick was all confused.

"But why?" Mrs. Wahlbaum asked. "You have to have some sort of rationale. Please explain."

Christopher cleared his throat. He'd spent all night rehearsing. "I don't agree with what Steere did. I don't understand why he just didn't drive away. If a man came up to me and I was in my truck, I'd drive away."

"Damn right," Lucky Seven said.

Mrs. Wahlbaum frowned. "Mr. Steere was frightened. In fear of his life, as you said. I thought you showed a real understanding of the situation yesterday."

"I hadn't thought it out yesterday. I needed to sleep on it."

"But you were so perceptive. So sensitive."

Christopher looked as uncomfortable as he felt. "I guess my conscience got to me. Steere shouldn't have just shot the poor man in cold blood."

Mrs. Wahlbaum's penciled eyebrows drooped. "Mr. Steere panicked. He didn't know what to do. It was a biological reaction, for self-preservation."

Martin Fogel folded his skinny arms. "She's a biologist now," he said, but Christopher ignored him and stood up at the head of the conference table, in front of a large window. The snowstorm was still going strong. Snowflakes fell from the gray sky on an already whitened city. The room was quiet and the snow muffled what little noise there was outside.

"It doesn't make sense that Steere was that afraid," Christopher said, as he stood behind his chair. "Why was he so afraid? The poor man was obviously homeless. Drunk to boot."

Megan couldn't take her eyes from Christopher. His shoulders looked so broad in front of the hotel window. She had on her best Urban Decay makeup, thinking she'd get back on-line today. But when she looked at the new Christopher, Megan suddenly stopped missing her computer.

"I wonder if Steere was afraid of the knife," Ralph Merry answered dryly. "My guess is that the knife had something to do with it. Besides, the man was a carjacker, not a hobo or something."

"But the man was drunk," Christopher countered. "He couldn't have used a knife."

Ralph shook his head. "Christopher, the defense

proved the carjacker wasn't that drunk. Remember that expert? The carjacker's blood alcohol showed he wasn't dead drunk. He could still have done some damage with a knife like that."

"I disagree," Christopher said. "It was an empty threat, and Steere killed him for it."

Lucky Seven grinned, and Kenny Manning crossed his arms. "Man's goin' down," Kenny said, nodding.

Christopher's head bobbed in unison with his new allies. "Also, why didn't Steere take the stand? Why didn't he just get up there and testify? Tell his side of the story?"

"We aren't permitted to consider that," Mrs. Wahlbaum said. "Mr. Steere had a right not to take the stand. We're not supposed to hold it against him."

"I know, but I can't help wondering," Christopher said. "Think about it, Mrs. Wahlbaum. We took an oath. We have to find the truth. It's our responsibility to wonder why somebody has something to hide."

"We're supposed to deliberate using what the judge told us," she insisted. "We have to look at the law and the evidence."

"But at the end of the day, it's our conscience," Christopher said as firmly as possible. He pointed to his chest beneath his flannel shirt and it made him feel even more emphatic. "We have to make the decision and we have to live with it."

"Thas' right," Lucky Seven said. "Everybody

else, they go right on. The judge and lawyers go to the nex' case. We the ones, we got to live with it."

Christopher nodded. "Why did Steere shoot him? Why didn't he just hit him—clock him—and drive away? Or if he had to shoot him, why didn't he shoot him in the shoulder or someplace else that wouldn't kill the poor guy? Instead, he shot to kill."

"Coulda done a million things," said Lucky Seven, and Christopher nodded again.

The jurors' heads wheeled back and forth.

"Right," Christopher said. "Exactly. I know how you all feel and I felt the same way yesterday. But here's something all of us are forgetting. A homeless man is dead today because of Elliot Steere. A man is dead. Nobody can bring him back."

The room fell silent suddenly. Megan glanced at Mrs. Wahlbaum, who pursed her lips. Nick took a shaky sip of water. Wanthida looked down.

Only Gussella looked at her fellow jurors with undisguised scorn. She wasn't about to miss another week with her grandson. When babies were that young, they grew so fast, and Gussella wanted to hold that little boy in her arms. She could feel his softness against her skin, a warm bundle. Chubby arms to snuggle around her neck. Little fingers to coo over. A crinkly Pampers on that little butt. She couldn't wait a minute longer. "Are you all crazy? That man done wrong! He was tryin' to rob Steere's car! He held a knife to Steere's throat! We all saw how his lawyer showed it. He cut Steere right in his face!"

"Under his eye," Mrs. Wahlbaum added. "Mr. Steere could have lost his sight."

Mr. Fogel said, "Thank you, Dr. Wahlbaum. She's an eye doctor now."

Christopher faced them all. "Yes, that's all true. Everything you say is true about what that man did. But the question we have to answer is, did he deserve to *die* for it? Would *you* have killed him for it?"

"Damn," Lucky Seven said softly, and even Mrs. Wahlbaum looked like she was thinking twice.

Ralph Merry looked from face to face and worry crept over him. The jurors could go south on him. Christopher might be able to reach them in that down-home way he had. Christopher might be able to talk them into changing their votes, even though they were so close to acquitting. He might hold out and force a hung jury. He could wear them down.

Ralph considered his options and chose the one that made the most sense. He had to nip this sucker in the bud, before the worm started to turn. The jurors had gotten up expecting to go home and thought they were just an hour or two from a unanimous vote to acquit. Even Kenny Manning had acted less cocky than usual at breakfast. The brothers were breaking ranks. Ralph had the Big Mo, like George Bush used to say.

Ralph checked his watch. 11:10.

He'd have this sucker over with by lunchtime. The jurors wanted to acquit and he had to clinch the verdict. He'd blitz this battle like General

Schwarzkopf. Get in, kick ass, and get out. This was his own personal Desert Storm. After all, he had a deal to live up to. With a killer. "Anybody else need a bathroom break?" Ralph asked, trying to sound casual.

52

Marta stood on the sunny shoulder of Route 72 in front of a sooty, pitted mound of snow. Purse on shoulder, she was thumbing a ride. She wanted to suppress the déjà vu but it was inescapable: Marta was back beside a highway, surrounded by snowy woods. Waving, hoping, begging a ride. Familiarity and fear flooded her, undeniable. She was terrified to do this again.

Please, sir! Please stop!

An oil truck with a long silver tank headed down the highway. Marta held up her hand but couldn't bring herself to flag down the truck. It was as if she were paralyzed. Her muscles refused to respond. Her heart pounded in her chest. She felt dizzy and broke into a sweat.

Please, sir! Please!

The oil tanker rumbled closer. Its tank glistened like a bullet in the sun. Marta had to catch it. She tried to wave but her arm still wouldn't move.

Please, sir. Please stop!

Please stop. Please don't. The oil tanker roared

closer. The driver with the glasses was almost upon her. She could feel his hand on her knee. Sliding up her thigh. Fear rippled through her limbs. Her knee buckled. She wanted to panic and run. She was trapped in the station wagon. Open the door. Run out. Run away. *Run away.*

Then she blinked. The driver with the glasses had vanished, replaced by a trucker with a beefy face. He wore a white uniform, not a tie and jacket. He wasn't the man in the station wagon. Marta swallowed her anxiety and waved. Hard, then harder. Pumping away wildly.

"Please stop!" she heard herself shout. The voice was hers, not her mother's. The gesture was her own, too. Marta wasn't a liar or a drunk. Her car really had broken down. She really did need a ride. She jumped up and down, almost slipping in the slush. Yelling at the top of her lungs. She didn't care. She had to get him to stop. And she felt free, absolutely free.

"Please STOP!" she cried, but her shout was swallowed up in the Doppler effect of the huge rig as it roared past her. Marta jumped to avoid the fan of gray slush it sprayed in its wake. She stopped trembling as the truck rolled down the empty highway, shrank into a silver speck, and finally disappeared into thin, cold air.

Ten minutes later, Marta was in a blue Dodge Omni, inching down Route 72. An older woman was at the wheel, going to Philly to visit her divorced daughter. The ride should have been a lucky break, but less than a mile down the highway Marta regretted ever accepting it. It was 11:30, and she could have walked to Philly faster. "Are you *sure* I can't put the radio on?" Marta asked, trying again. She had to know what was going on. Was the jury still out? Were the cops after her?

"No radio," the woman replied flatly. She was about sixty-five years old, with a cap of straight gray hair yellowing in the front. She could barely see over the wheel, which she squeezed with arthritic knuckles. A skinny brown cigarette dangled from her lips, dusting her thin cloth coat with ashes.

"Not even for a minute or two?"

"No radio."

"Why not?"

"It's my car and I don't like radio. I don't like music."

"I didn't want to listen to music, either. I want to hear the news. I have to hear the news."

"No radio." The woman shook her head, her chin tilted up as the car crept along. "I don't like news. I never listen to news. If news comes on TV, I change the channel. At lunchtime I watch my stories. You know why? All the news is bad."

"Don't you want to hear the weather report? It's a snowstorm."

"I look out the window, that's my weather report." The woman sucked on the cigarette and her hollow cheeks got even hollower. "If it's raining I get my umbrella. If it's snowing I get my Totes. What's so hard?"

"But there's a blizzard in Philly," Marta said, about to explode. "You need a traffic report. Don't you want to know what routes to take to see your daughter?"

"I know how to get to my own daughter's."

"What if you can't get through because of the snow?"

"I'll get through. If my daughter needs me, I'll get through." The woman blew out a puff of smoke that rolled onto the dashboard like a wave. Acrid smoke filled the compact car, and Marta rolled down her window a crack. "Don't do that!" the woman snapped. "It's freezing out."

"Sorry." Marta rolled the window up. Her nose stung. Her eyes watered. She sweated inside her coat and snowpants. At this speed, they'd never get to Philly. If not for her motion sickness, Marta wouldn't know they were in motion.

"Keep that window shut! I'm older than you, not as strong." She flicked some ash into an ashtray crowded with crushed butts and looked over. Her brown eyes were reproachful behind her pink-framed bifocals. "I'll catch my death."

"It's so smoky in here."

"Oh, one of those, are you? Smokers have rights, too, you know. It's discrimination! In the Pancake House, the smokers have to sit by themselves. On the nonsmokers' side, they could have anybody there. They could have drug addicts there, or tuberculosis people. They don't have a sign saying NO DRUG ADDICTS, do they?"

Marta smiled, almost persuaded. Maybe it was the cigarette smoke, depriving her brain of oxygen. She peered out the window through the carbon monoxide. The trees dripped melting snow, and their car was so poky Marta had time to identify each tree. It took her until Pennsauken to persuade the woman to turn on the goddamn radio, and a few minutes into the news, Marta picked up a report on the trial:

"This is Howard Rattner reporting from the Criminal Justice Center in Philadelphia. The jury is expected to return this morning from deliberations in the murder trial of real estate developer Elliot Steere. The jury has been out only a matter of hours, and court observers expect it to return soon with a verdict of acquittal. Legal experts say the jury should know nothing of the murders last night of two security guards in the offices of Rosato and Associates, the all-woman law firm defending Mr. Steere."

Marta tried to stay calm. Good, the jury was still out. Christopher had delayed them successfully. Maybe he could persuade them to convict. She couldn't give up hope.

"In a related story," continued the reporter, "no developments in the status of two of the lawyers formerly defending this murder case. Elliot Steere's former lead counsel, Marta Richter, is still missing and her whereabouts are unknown. Another defense lawyer, Mary DiNunzio, remains in intensive care, fighting for her life. As we reported, Miss DiNunzio was shot in the early morning hours by an unknown assailant and spent the night in surgery."

Marta sat stricken, reeling as they went though a tollbooth.

"Told you, it's always bad news," said the old woman. "Murder. Killing. That's all they put on. That's all that matters to them." The woman moved to turn the radio off, but Marta grabbed her hand.

"No, stop. I need to hear this."

"All right, fine." The woman quickly withdrew her hand. "Don't get excited."

Marta turned up the volume. The reporter said, "The police have no suspects in connection with the shooting of attorney Mary DiNunzio. We'll keep you posted as events unfold both in and out of the courtroom. Back to you, Jane, for the latest on the blizzard that has buried the Delaware Valley."

Marta tried to get a grip. Mary, shot? What had happened? Had Bogosian done it? How? Marta didn't know what to do. She felt shaken, torn. She was drawn to see Mary, but she'd be recognized and taken in if she went to the hospital. The press would be everywhere. Everything would be lost. No, not the hospital. Not to Alix Locke, either. Suddenly Marta knew where she had to go.

53

Ralph Merry ducked into a stall in the men's room, unbuckled his pants, and dropped trou. His white boxers stretched between his knees, and the packet they'd sent to Ralph's wife was taped inside the waistband. He'd carried the damn thing every day like they told him to. He'd felt like a secret agent taping the packet to his skivvies in the morning, but now he was glad he had. He would never have guessed Christopher would pull a Benedict Arnold. The man turned out to be just plain weak.

The packet was tiny and plastic, no bigger than a thumbnail, and it contained white powder. Ralph didn't know what the powder was, but they told him it wouldn't kill anybody, just give him a stomachache for a day or two, long enough to get him off the jury. They told Ralph to use it if he got in a jam. Ralph figured this was a jam all right.

The urinals flushed as he peeled the packet off the waistband, leaving white threads stuck to the tape. Ralph threw the tape in the toilet and tucked the packet under his sleeve, like he practiced with his wife during the conjugal visit when she brought it. It was so easy to smuggle it in; of course it wasn't picked up by the metal detector. Ralph had realized what a cakewalk it would be to smuggle drugs into the country. The United States had to do a better job protecting its borders; it was a question of integrity, national integrity. Ralph double-checked the packet under his shirt cuff and pulled up his pants.

"Ralph, you fall in?" asked the sheriff, who was standing by the door.

"Nah, I'm good to go." Ralph flushed the toilet for show and opened the stall door.

54

Marta sat in Judy's apartment, sickened as the shaken associate told her the details of Mary's shooting. So Marta hadn't been able to keep the associates safe; they were both in it up to their eyeballs. And judging from the time Mary had been shot, it couldn't have been Bogosian that did it; he was in Long Beach Island around that time. Steere must have sent someone else. Someone who must be out there, waiting. Marta had set in motion something she couldn't control, jeopardizing them all. It had gone too far. She was spent after the long, exhausting night. It had to stop.

"Wait until you see Darning's notebook," Judy was saying, from the stool at the kitchen counter. A small TV sat on the counter on low volume; the news covered the snowstorm continuously. A blue bag of Chips Ahoy sat open-mouthed next to the TV.

"No, I don't want to see it. I don't care about the notebook. I care about you and Mary."

Judy blinked at the unexpected sentiment.

Erect? "The notebook could lead to why Steere killed Darning."

"Not our concern," Marta said. Her manner grew calm suddenly. She felt centered, more in control than when she was a control freak, ironically. "We'll take the notebook and file to the police. Tell them we want protection, too."

"Did you say 'file'?" Judy straightened up on the stool. "What file?"

"It doesn't matter." Marta hadn't told Judy anything about the buried treasure or Bogosian. It was safer if she didn't know. "This has gotten way out of hand. Trust me."

"Now you sound like Bennie."

"Rosato? She knows about the notebook?"

"She's concerned about my ethics. I'm out of a job."

Marta winced. She'd gotten one kid shot, and one ruined. "We'll take the notebook and the file to the police. Leave the whole thing to them."

"Is that the file you mean? That envelope there?" Judy eased off the stool and pointed to the manila envelope peeking from Marta's purse.

"People are dead. Mary's been shot. No file is worth that."

"Mary's the reason I want to see that file. She wanted justice, and so do I. Don't you? Isn't that why you went after Steere in the first place?"

Marta felt a twinge. "Not in the beginning, don't kid yourself. It was jealousy, not justice. My motives were impure."

"So you did the right thing for the wrong reason. It doesn't make any difference now. Steere killed Darning. We have a notebook that could prove it. Now could I see that file?"

"It's too late." Marta stood up, grabbed her purse, and zipped up her heavy coat. "Let's go. You're in danger as long as you have that notebook. We both are."

"We worked all night for this evidence. It's better than anything the cops have done. What's in the envelope? What kind of file?"

"Nothing. I don't even understand it. Maybe the cops will. Come on, pack up. Let's go."

Judy folded her arms and stood her ground. "Wait. I'll make a deal with you. Let me see that file. You look at the notebook. If we learn nothing in five minutes, we go straight to the cops. I promise."

"No."

"We've come this far. What have we got to lose? Five minutes?"

"I don't care. Get your coat. We're outta here." Marta headed for the door, but Judy stepped in front and blocked her path to the door. The two lawyers stood toe to toe.

Marta laughed abruptly. "You gonna hit me? Go ahead. I'm like a be-bop clown. I pop right up."

Judy paused, unwilling to resort to striking Marta, though she'd fantasized about it during the trial.

"Excellent choice." Marta sidestepped the associate and headed to the door. "Get your coat, kiddo."

"I don't think so," Judy called after her. "I won't go with you unless you give me the five minutes. If you go to the cops now, you go alone. Without me or the notebook."

Marta stopped in her tracks and turned around, incredulous. "Where did you learn shit like that?"

"From the master, of course," Judy answered, with a gap-toothed grin.

The sequestration hotel had plied the jurors with a breakfast tray of bagels, Danish, and coffee, set on a credenza in the conference room. Ralph Merry hovered over the leftover food and coffee. He'd eaten the same cherry Danish every day for two months and he couldn't wait to check out of this place. First thing he'd do was travel and stay in better hotels than this one. Maybe take a cruise, too, with the wife. But right now he had a mission to complete.

Ralph shook a Styrofoam cup from the upside-down stack next to a bronze plastic jug of coffee. He kept his back to the jurors, who were sitting around the table listening to Christopher yammer like a bleeding heart. Ralph couldn't tell how many of them were buying it. He had to assume a worst-case scenario. There was no margin for error. Zero tolerance. He couldn't cross a man like Elliot Steere.

"Who wants more coffee?" Ralph boomed. "Anybody else for fresh coffee while I'm buying? How about you, Mrs. Wahlbaum? Mrs. Williams?"

Ralph kept his voice cheery, like he was barbecuing with his wife and grandkids. Who wants hot dogs? Who wants hamburgers? Same thing.

"I'd love some coffee, Ralph," Mrs. Wahlbaum said.

Ralph grinned. "No problemo, young lady. How would you like it?"

"Extra cream and sugar."

"Roger dodger, my dear." Ralph poured Mrs. Wahlbaum a tall cup of coffee. Steam curled from the top. "Christopher? Want another cup of hot brew?"

Christopher looked at his Styrofoam cup. It was empty and he'd had enough coffee for the morning. "I guess not. Thanks anyway."

A miss. "Come on, Christopher. If you're gonna convince me to convict that rat bastard, you're gonna need some hair on your chest."

Megan laughed. "No way, Ralph. Christopher's trying to get rid of unwanted hair. Right, Christopher?"

"There you go," Christopher said with a smile. He liked the way Megan was looking at him. She was a pretty girl except for the blue-painted fingernails, but he supposed they were considered sophisticated in Philly.

"Christopher," Ralph said gruffly. He glanced from Christopher to Megan and didn't like what he saw. No time for tomfoolery like this. "Have some coffee. I'll pour one for you and Megan, too."

"Okay, I'm addicted to coffee," Megan said. "I

get the latte at Starbucks. Do you like Starbucks coffee, Christopher?"

"I never tried it," he answered. He had to get out more. "But I'll take a cup, too, Ralph."

KABOOM! A direct hit on the second shot. Cheered, Ralph picked up the plastic pitcher and began to pour. "How do you take it, soldier?"

"Cream and sugar."

Ralph filled Christopher's cup with hot coffee and slipped the packet of powder from under his cuff. He palmed the packet, grabbed two packs of sugar, and tore the end off all three together. Then he poured the sugar and the powder into the hot coffee, stirred with a plastic stick, and tucked the leftover plastic back under his cuff. His heart thudded as watched the powder dissolve, but he was no coward. His resolve didn't waver.

"Don't forget mine, extra sugar and cream," called Mrs. Wahlbaum.

"Got you covered, young lady," Ralph said. He set Christopher's coffee aside so he wouldn't get it confused with the others, and poured the other coffees.

"How about me, Ralph?" Wanthida asked. "I take mine black."

"Hold your horses, darlin'. Christopher asked first and he's the foreman. He's the one doin' all the work." Ralph picked up Christopher's coffee, walked over to the table, and handed it to him. "See if I put enough sugar in, Chris."

Christopher took a quick sip. "It tastes great. Thanks, Ralph. Appreciate it."

"Sure thing," Ralph said, and had to remind himself that Christopher wouldn't die. He'd just get a tummy ache and spend some time in sick bay. He'd be out in two days, after the verdict was in and Steere had walked. Ralph would hold up his end of the bargain. The payoff would be deposited in a special account. Ralph couldn't wait to call his literary agent. They damn well better put his picture on the cover. "Let me get those other coffees," he said, and hustled away.

56

Marta only reluctantly skimmed the list of handwritten numbers in Darning's note-book and half wondered if they represented money or account numbers. There were no patterns she could discern. The police would do better. "Three minutes left, kiddo," she said, testy at the associate sitting next to her on the futon.

"Four minutes." Judy hunched over the computer file spread on the coffee table. "You're right about this file. These are records used to make driver's licenses. It's a database, a computer file of driver's licenses."

"It doesn't tell us anything, and I have no idea what the notebook means. It's a bunch of eight-digit numbers. That's it. Two minutes and we roll."

"These numbers are eight digits, too."

"What numbers?"

"The numbers at the top of each field," Judy answered, pointing. "The operator's numbers, from the driver's licenses."

Marta looked over. The way the numbers were

spaced, she hadn't noticed. Hmm. "Probably just a coincidence. There are about four thousand records in the computer file. How many numbers are in the notebook?"

Judy looked at Marta in astonishment. "About four thousand. Holy shit," she said, but Marta tried not to jump to conclusions.

"So there are four thousand numbers in the notebook and four thousand driver's licenses in the file. We don't know if there's a connection."

"Connection? What connection could there be?"

Marta paused, thinking. "It's possible that the notebook is related to the file. If the notebook is a list of numbers and each computer record has an operator's number, then maybe the notebook is a list of the operator's numbers from the computer file."

Judy's eyes widened. "You think they match? Like a copy?"

"Possibly." Despite her better judgment, Marta felt a jolt of excitement. "If so, we should be able to find each of the operator's numbers in the notebook. Read me a number from one of the driver's licenses."

Judy picked up the top computer page. "*22 746 209.*"

Marta scanned the list of numbers on the first page of the notebook with Judy looking over her shoulder. Two sets of keen eyes raced down the page. "Too bad they're not listed in any order." Marta asked, "Do you see it on the first page?"

"Nope."

"On to the next." Marta turned the page and they both skimmed the list on the second page. Judy was obviously excited, though Marta was trying not to get carried away with her. It felt strange to work so closely with an associate, and not entirely unpleasant. "See it on page two?"

"Nope."

"Onward and upward." They read page three and continued, page after page, until they reached page ten. There, in the middle of the page, sandwiched in the middle of the list on the left, it said:

22746209

"Yes!" Judy shouted in delight. "We figured it out! We're geniuses."

Marta laughed. "Oh, yeah? Then what's it mean, whiz kid?"

"I have no idea. What do you think?"

Marta paused. She considered going to the cops. They were so close. "Give me that sheet. I want to see who number *22746209* is."

Judy showed her the computer sheet. There was a field of information and a photo of an older white man with a faint smile. "It's William Swenson. 708 Greentree Court, Philadelphia."

"Set Mr. Swenson aside and read me another number. Let's not go off half cocked. We only matched one of them."

"Okay. *92294593*," Judy read, then hung on

Marta's shoulder as she thumbed back to page one of the notebook. "Beginning at the beginning, huh?"

"I'm nothing if not methodical."

"That's one word for it."

Marta glanced over her shoulder. "Read, kiddo." They went down the lists on the first page and the second, and stopped at the list on the fifth page. There it was:

92294593

"Awesome!" Judy almost cheered.

"Totally."

Judy laughed. "I didn't know you had a sense of humor."

"I don't. Tell me who Mr. *92* is."

Judy looked at the second driver's license on the sheet. The face of a middle-aged woman squinted behind bifocals. "She's Helen Minton of Rhawn Street, in Philly."

"Set her aside. Check five more, then I'll believe the theory."

"I'm sure we're right."

"You're young and impetuous. Now read."

Judy read Marta another number, which the lawyers found in Darning's notebook, then four more after that. They found each number in the notebook and set aside each license when they matched it. "Now what?" Judy bubbled when they were finished.

"We call them up."

"What? Why?"

"To see what we can learn." Marta checked her watch. Almost one. No time to lose. She picked up the portable phone. "Hand me the first sheet, then get me a phone book. Hurry up."

"You like to give orders, don't you?"

"Love it. Get the book."

Judy reached under the end table for the phone book. "It makes you feel powerful."

"I am powerful."

"But people don't like to be bossed around."

"Your point is?" Marta asked slyly, and Judy threw the phone book at her.

"Is this the Swenson residence?" Marta asked, with the associate sitting close enough to hear the voice on the telephone receiver. She felt strangely silly, like they were schoolgirls making phony phone calls. In a way, they were.

"This is the Swensons'," said the woman on the other end of the line.

"May I speak to William Swenson, please?"

"That would be my husband."

"Is he in?"

"He's dead. My husband is dead."

"I'm sorry, I didn't know," Marta said, caught off-balance, and Judy deflated like a hot air balloon.

"He died in a car accident four years ago. A drunk driver crossed the median."

"I'm sorry to hear that."

"Thank you. Can I help you with something?"

"No, thank you," Marta said. "Thanks again for your time." She pressed down the plastic hook. "Read me the next phone number."

"Say please."

"Before the jury gets back."

"I hear you," Judy said quickly, and read off the number.

Marta punched in the phone number, albeit in a darker mood. She had to solve this thing and she had to solve it soon. She couldn't shake the thoughts of Bogosian or Mary. Was there a killer out there now? Waiting? "Is this the Minton residence?" she asked when a young woman picked up.

"Yes."

"May I speak with Helen Minton?"

"That's not very funny, you know. You're a real jerk, whoever you are."

"Excuse me? What? I have to speak with Helen Minton."

"No joke?"

"Yes. Absolutely."

"My mother was murdered," the woman said with the flatness of deep anger.

"Oh, I'm sorry," Marta said. What was going on here? "I'm very sorry."

"I thought everybody knew, at least around here. She was killed in the pharmacy during a holdup. The scum who shot her just got to court. Sitting there every day with his fancy lawyer, tryin' to beat the rap."

Marta couldn't ignore the pang she felt. "I'm sorry. Really sorry."

"Almost four years later, to the day. That animal had four more years than my mother."

"I'm sorry. I wish you the best. Thanks," Marta said and hung up quickly. Hadn't the other woman said four years, too? What did it mean? It seemed too coincidental. Marta was almost there, she could feel it. "Read me the next number. Quick."

Judy recited the number and Marta punched it in. "Is this the Jacobs residence?"

"Yes," said a young man's brusque voice.

Marta braced herself. "May I speak to Sherry Jacobs, please?"

"Nope. Sherry died about four years ago."

Marta stopped. Four years. Bingo. "I'm so sorry."

"Don't be sorry. Sherry wasn't the nicest person in the world. I'm her brother-in-law, take it from me. She used to torture my wife somethin' awful. 'You're too this, you're too that.' She could be a real bitch."

"I see."

"She left all her money to a dog, can you believe it? Put my wife through the wringer and left two hundred grand to a Welsh corgi. The only good thing she ever did was die and give her body to science. I feel sorry for the schmo who gets her heart. It's empty."

"What?"

"Her heart. Sherry was an organ donor. Now what did you say your name was?"

Marta tried another number with a new attitude. "Is this the Walters residence?"

"Yes," said a woman's voice. Someone was playing piano in the background. "But I'm giving a lesson now."

"Just one minute, we're checking our records. Is it true that one Ronald Walters passed away four years ago?"

"Thereabouts. Yes."

"Was Mr. Walters an organ donor?"

"Why, yes."

"Thank you very much," Marta said and hung up.

57

Christopher's stomach was killing him. Pain shot through his gut like buckshot. He'd never had cramps like this before. He gulped his coffee but it didn't help. He wanted to roll over and die.

"Let's deal with the testimony, friends," Ralph was saying. He stood at the other end of the conference table and drew in Magic Marker on a wipe-off board on an easel. The thick black lines wiggled before Christopher's eyes and he blinked to bring it back into focus. It looked like a star or a triangle or something. The lines wouldn't stay put.

"Ralph, what is that?" Christopher heard himself say. His voice sounded weak, and Megan looked over with a concerned frown.

"You okay, Christopher?" she asked, and he nodded.

"Sure." It hurt to talk but Christopher didn't want them to know that. He'd get sent home or kicked off the jury or who knows what would happen. He had to stay here and convince them. "You were saying, Ralph?"

Ralph pointed to the easel with his finger. "It's a diagram of the carjacking. Point A shows where Steere stopped his Mercedes. Point B is the pillar under the bridge where the carjacker was hiding. The testimony is that this is a distance of five feet at the most. Correct?"

The jurors nodded. Christopher watched their heads bobbing like a herd of horses. He felt so damn sick. He took another swallow of coffee, avoiding Megan's eye. She really looked worried. Lainie had never looked that worried about him.

"Now," Ralph continued, "what I'm saying is that if I were the driver of the car and somebody jumped out of the pillar that close at me, I couldn't even think about what to do. There would be no time, like that Marta Richter showed us."

"I agree with you, Ralph," Mrs. Wahlbaum said. "You'd have to react in a split second. You wouldn't have time to think. You wouldn't have time to consider your alternatives."

Christopher struggled through the pain, which was worsening. He wanted to grab his stomach. He was supposed to be convincing the jury to convict Steere.

"You sure as hell wouldn't," Ralph said. "Not with a knife at your throat."

"It's a natural instinct," Mrs. Wahlbaum added, nodding her gray head. "Flight or fight. Even animals have it."

Mr. Fogel smirked. "A zoologist now. Is there anything this woman does not understand? Any area of science, mathematics, or philosophy that she's not an expert in?"

Mrs. Wahlbaum's head wheeled around and she finally exploded. "So what do *you* think, buster? Every day for two months I've listened to you criticize me. All you do is criticize. You never say one thing for yourself. You're all negatives and no positives."

Christopher looked between Mrs. Wahlbaum and Mr. Fogel. Don't fight, we have to convict, he wanted to say. Don't be tired. We have time. His gut twisted like a wrung-out rag. He opened his mouth to speak but no sound came out.

Mr. Fogel blinked behind his thick glasses. "You want to know what I think, Miss Know-It-All? I'll tell you. I'm the expert on just one thing. I'm the expert on *time*. And I, for one, have given enough time to this trial. I have been here seventy-two days, two hours, and"—Mr. Fogel checked his Timex—"twenty-three minutes. The way I see it, that's too much time!"

Ralph clapped heartily. "Hear hear!"

Support seemed to embolden the watchmaker, who stood up at his seat, tall and straight as an hour hand. "I'm not giving a day more of my time. Not an hour more, not even a *minute* more. I want to go home. I want to drive my own car. I want to talk on my own phone. I want to go into my shop and fix Mrs. Millstein's clock, which I owe her from September. We listened to the witnesses, the lawyers, and the judge. Now it's time for them to listen to *us*." And then Mr. Fogel sat down.

The jurors started applauding, Gussella loudest of all. Megan clapped, too, less enthusiastically because Christopher wasn't clapping. His face was turning gray and he leaned to the right. "Chris?" she said softly.

Nick's lower lip began to tremble. "I wish I could see my wife. I want to go home, too."

Mrs. Wahlbaum patted his suit sleeve. "I miss Abe. He has a hard time all by himself, the shopping and the cooking. It's his knees."

"Lord, I got to see my little grandbaby!" Gussella shouted, so loud that Wanthida jumped.

"We all want this over with," Wanthida said in accented English, "and we think Mr. Steere innocent. We should vote and go home."

"Not all of us would vote for acquittal," Ralph said, though he couldn't have been happier. The war was almost won and he'd taken out the opposing general. The only problem was Kenny Manning. Time to attack, when his enemy was weakest. "Kenny, what do you think? You still would vote to convict?"

"Why wouldn't I?" Kenny said, cocking his head.

"It's up to you, friend. I'm the first one to say that we all respect your right to vote however you want. I'm not tryin' to put pressure on you. If you want to talk about it longer we will. I'm here to tell you that you have a right to satisfaction."

Christopher saw it all slipping away. Marta. The conviction. Somebody was pounding hoof nails through his stomach. Megan was saying something to him but he replied only with a gurgling sound the jurors didn't hear. They were all looking down the table at Isaiah, who suddenly cleared his throat and hunched over the table, meeting Kenny's glare head-on.

"My fiancée's pregnant, man," Isaiah said, his voice low. "If I don't get outta here soon and get her down an aisle, she's gonna get her heart broke. And her momma's. She don't want to be showin' in front of the whole church, and I don't blame her neither."

"Shit, man," Lucky Seven said, hanging his head. "Why'n't you say somethin'?"

"She told me last night, durin' the visit. I'm sorry, Kenny, I'd like to go with you. I know how you feel about convictin' Steere, and you might be in the right. But I don't blame the man and I can't stand with you, bro. I can't even take the time to fight with you about it. I got to take care of my family. I got to get home."

Kenny just glared back; then his dark eyes slid over to Lucky Seven, who threw up his hands like he'd been held up. "Don't look at me, man," Lucky Seven said, from between large palms. "It's up to you. I go with you, you know that."

"Christopher?" Megan said in alarm. She rose to her feet and was almost at his side as a wave of agony wracked Christopher and he collapsed in his chair.

58

Ten phone calls later, Marta sat at the edge of the futon, her thoughts racing. "So what have we learned?"

Judy sat slumped into the white cloth cushions. A carton of milk was wedged between her legs. Crumbs were sprinkled across her gray sweats. "We learned that we're terrible people, intruding on the privacy of the bereft."

"What else?"

"That all the people we called are dead."

"And all died violently or by accident."

"Yes. In the City of Brotherly Love."

"And all died a little over four years ago. And they were organ donors."

Judy took a slug of milk. "A file of organ donors. That's why it didn't show up on the computer fields. The whole file is of organ donors."

"What do you mean?"

"In Pennsylvania, you can tell by someone's driver's license if they want to be an organ donor." Judy crossed to the counter, retrieved her wallet, and handed her driver's license to Marta. "See? It says right there. I'm an organ donor. Aren't you?"

"Of course not." Marta looked down at the small plastic card. Under an unflattering photo of Judy it said in bright green letters, ORGAN DONOR. Like a grisly caption. "How disgusting."

"No it isn't. Everyone should be a donor. You know how many people die each day waiting for an organ transplant? I signed up at City Hall. They have an organ drive every year."

"City Hall does?"

"Sure. It's run by the mayor's office. It started when the mayor was D.A."

"When did you sign up?"

"A long time ago."

"When, exactly?"

"Must have been five years ago. They had a big drive. The whole office went. We were at Stalling and Webb then, Mary and I."

Marta felt suddenly antsy and rose from the futon. Her ribs were killing her, but she had to pace to think more clearly. She had her best ideas pacing or in the shower; if she could pace in the shower she'd be attorney general. "Let me get this straight. You're telling me the mayor's office has a list of organ donors in Philadelphia."

"I guess. The donor drives are a high-profile thing. The city runs it with the local organ donor organization."

"The mayor can monitor deaths of organ donors in the city?"

"I suppose so. City Hall could tap into a network of organ donors. I think it's a public organization that runs the network. I doubt it's even confidential information."

Marta paced back and forth. "Assume City Hall connects up with the network, so they know when an organ donor dies. Some of the donors die right before the mayoral election. Their deaths get reported because their driver's license says they want to be donors."

Judy followed Marta's line of reasoning. "Their deaths don't show up in enough time to take them off the voter registration rolls. City Hall finds out first because they're hooked up with the information." The associate paused, momentarily stumped. "But why would they do that? Why would they care?"

Marta's eyes met Judy's. "Ten to one, Mr. Swenson and Mrs. Minton voted in the last election. And Jacobs and Walters. All of them, on all those driver's licenses. They all voted even though they were dead."

"How? How would they physically go and vote?" Judy frowned and Marta resumed pacing.

"Good question." Judy was more able than Marta had realized; it was almost better working together. "Maybe somebody pretends to be them and votes for them."

"Not possible," Judy said, shaking her head. "There are women and men. Some are white, some are black. They're all different. You can't vote without somebody seeing you."

Marta froze. "Yes you can. An absentee ballot. Somebody makes out absentee ballots for them. Somebody finds out they're dead before anybody else knows it—because of the donor card—and makes out absentee ballots for them. They have their signature right on the license, and they forge the ballot. That's why they need the licenses on file. Because the licenses have the *signature* and they have to sign the ballot."

Judy's mouth fell open. It all fit together. "Street money."

"Somebody gets paid to file an absentee ballot in the name of the organ donor."

"Eb Darning would be the somebody."

"Bingo," Marta said quietly, and suddenly she saw it all. Steere's scheme, perfectly planned and executed, years in the making. Steere had paid Eb Darning to file absentee ballots in the last election, undoubtedly voting against his enemy, the mayor. But Steere didn't anticipate that Eb would keep his own proof of the deal. Darning must have been blackmailing Steere, and Steere killed him for it. "Get the file and notebook," Marta said. "We have to get going."

"What? Where? To the cops?"

"No time for that. To court."

59

Bennie sat sweltering in her parka, growing increasingly impatient as she and Emil waited for Jennifer Pressman in the chief of staff's office. There was no alternative to waiting, but it went against Bennie's nature to sit on her hands. She'd excused herself twice already to prowl the corridors of City Hall, opening office doors and checking the room where the mayor had held his press conference. The conference had ended, and Jen Pressman was nowhere to be found. "Maybe she's home by now," Bennie said, nudging Emil with her elbow. "Ask the secretary to call again."

"No." Emil flipped through the glossy magazine he'd found on the coffee table. "We just called. Behave."

"Ask her."

"No. Jen will be in soon, she has to be. It's her job. She's dedicated."

"I can't wait any longer. You want the story or not?"

Emil snapped the magazine shut. "You try me, Bennie."

"Thank you."

He dropped the magazine on the table and walked over to the secretary's desk. "Flossie, do you think we should call Jennifer's home again?"

The secretary stopped typing and looked up from her keyboard. "It hasn't been that long since last time."

"I understand, but this is an important matter. Would you mind very much? I consider it a great favor to me."

"You know—," the secretary hesitated, then her voice softened. "To tell you the truth, Emil, it won't do any good to keep calling her at home. I don't think my boss made it home last night."

"What do you mean?"

"You know what I mean. I don't think she *slept* at home last night."

Emil colored. "I see."

"You didn't hear this from me, right?" the secretary said, lowering her voice.

"Right."

"You'd never print anything we talk about, right?"

"Of course not, Flossie. We're friends, you and I."

"Well, I think she went to see her boyfriend last night. That's the only time she pulls a disappearing act. She hasn't taken off much lately, so I thought it was over. Maybe not, though. Guess they reconciled and she couldn't get out of bed."

"Love weaves a spell when you're young," Emil said, and back at the couch, Bennie wanted to throw up.

"Oh, this isn't love." The secretary leaned over confidentially and whispered, "I think he's married."

"No," Emil said, with genuine disapproval. He was the most traditional man Bennie knew, and she would have bet that he wasn't the one frying the grape leaves.

"Yes. I'm sure of it. In summer, she used to take off early on weekends. She'd come back tan and wouldn't say who she went with. She never brought back any pictures."

"Can she be reached? Who is this man?"

"Damned if I know." The secretary leaned over farther. "You know, I tried to find out once. I was curious and finally I just asked her, straight out. 'Are you seeing anyone?' I said to her. Just straight."

"Good. It's best to be honest and straightforward."

"Sure it is. I've worked for her for two years now, and we never talk or anything. You think she'd have lunch with me? Never. Anyway, know what she said when I asked her? She said, 'I don't discuss that with subordinates.'"

Emil's face fell. "How unkind."

"Tell me about it. 'Subordinates!' She said she was quoting somebody named Sun Zoo something. So I said to her, 'Who the hell is Sun Zoo? It sounds like a suntan cream or something.'"

Back on the couch, Bennie's ears pricked up. Sun Zoo? Where had she heard that lately?

"Sun-Tzu?" Emil said. "He was a Chinese philosopher. A general."

"That's right. That's what she said. I told her, 'I don't know from Chinese generals, honey, but I know common courtesy and you don't have any.' Imagine! I'm gonna transfer back to the prothonotary's office as soon as they post it."

Suddenly Bennie remembered. In the conference room at the office, when she was talking to Carrier and DiNunzio. What had Carrier said? *If you spend any time with Elliot Steere, sooner or later he hauls out Sun-Tzu.*

Bennie sat bolt upright on the couch. The picture came into instant focus. Jen Pressman had a secret boyfriend, but he wasn't married. He was Elliot Steere. She'd have to keep it quiet because he was the mayor's nemesis. In that moment, Bennie realized the whole scam. It wasn't exactly the way she thought. In fact, it was quite the opposite. But there was no time left. She jumped up and headed for the door.

"Bennie?" Emil asked, turning.

"Gotta fry some grape leaves, Emil," she said, and bolted out the door.

60

Judge Rudolph was presiding, though when he looked down from the mahogany dais he didn't see a packed courtroom, he saw a running track with hurdles. The finish line was straight ahead, marked by a fluttering red, white, and blue banner that read JUSTICE HARRY CALVIN RUDOLPH. At the defense table, Elliot Steere watched him intently, and the prosecutors looked alert. In the stands, all eyes were on him. Everyone was quiet and waiting for the starter's pistol. On your mark, get set, go! *Crack!*

"Gentlemen," the judge said, "I called you here because of an emergency that has arisen in the jury. One of the jurors has taken ill with a stomach virus and had to be sent to the hospital. The Court has been informed by another juror, acting as substitute foreperson, that the jury may be very close to delivering a verdict in this matter. The alternates have already been sent home, and by now have undoubtedly been tainted by exposure to publicity. Therefore, the issue before the Court is whether the jury should be permitted to proceed to verdict without the juror who has fallen ill."

Elliot Steere sat at the defense table and not a muscle on his body moved. His juror had acted. His acquittal was assured. His victory was complete. He breathed slowly, in and out, and his heartbeat thumped steadily. In his ears he heard the rhythms of his own life force. Sun-Tzu taught that victory goes to those who do not miscalculate, and Steere had not miscalculated. He had prepared for this victory and so it was at hand.

"Under Pennsylvania law," Judge Rudolph continued, "the jury in a murder trial may proceed to verdict with a vote of less than twelve jurors only if the defendant and the Commonwealth agree. The defendant had a constitutional right to a verdict by a jury of twelve, and such right can be waived. The Court is holding this hearing this morning in order to determine how the parties wish to proceed."

At the prosecutor's table sat Assistant District Attorney Tom Moran, and this time he was wide awake. The district attorney of the City of Philadelphia, Bill Masterson, was seated on his right, so close their padded shoulders grazed. Masterson was basketball-player tall, big-boned and ruddy-faced, with a thatch of gray-blond hair and fierce blue eyes. Nobody could sit next to Bill Masterson and be unaware of his power, especially a young father of twins who had already fucked up once. Tom needed his job, now more than ever.

Judge Rudolph prepared to jump the first hurdle. "Mr. Steere, you are the defendant in this matter, and this court has at every juncture been careful to safeguard your rights under the law, especially since you have chosen to proceed as your own counsel. Do you have any questions so far?"

"No."

"Do you understand the question that is being put to you? The Court must determine if you wish to waive your right to a verdict rendered by a jury of twelve."

"I understand that, Your Honor."

"I will conduct the required colloquy to confirm that you understand your rights, but would you like to consult with an attorney before we begin? I see that Mr. LeFort of the Cable and Bess firm is in the gallery." Judge Rudolph acknowledged the expensive lawyer with a nod. "If you wish to consult with Mr. LeFort or one of his partners, the Court would be happy to recess for fifteen minutes."

"I do not wish to consult with Mr. LeFort, Your Honor. It's a straightforward question. I can give you my answer right now. I want my case to proceed to verdict as soon as possible, Your Honor, even if that means I accept the verdict of less than the full complement of jurors. I wish to waive my right to a verdict by a jury of twelve."

The gallery burst into excited chatter. Judge Rudolph's gaze slipped to the back of the courtroom and he banged the gavel. *Crack!* "I'll have none of that in my courtroom. Keep a lid on it, ladies and gentlemen, or there will be expulsions. Mr. Steere, do you understand that you have the right to ask for a mistrial?"

"Your Honor, I do not want a mistrial. I do not want any further delays in my trial. I have been in prison for a long time. I have a business to run when I am released."

"Thank you, Mr. Steere." Judge Rudolph imagined himself leaping over the first hurdle and landing on the other side without breaking stride. One down, one to go. The judge turned to the prosecution table. "Mr. Moran, I see that you are joined this morning by District Attorney William Masterson. Welcome, Mr. Masterson."

"Good morning, Your Honor," Masterson said.

Judge Rudolph acknowledged the powerful lawyer with a nod. The judge knew that the D.A. wanted his job and had kissed enough of the right asses to get it when the judge ascended to the Supreme Court. Without a word being exchanged, both men knew a baton would pass, but only if the judge won his final leg of the relay. "Mr. Masterson, will you be speaking for the Commonwealth this morning or will Mr. Moran be doing the honors?"

"Mr. Moran will," Masterson boomed. He grinned broadly and made a note on a legal pad. "I'm just here for the ride. Mr. Moran likes my company."

The gallery laughed and the reporters scribbled. Judge Rudolph smiled indulgently. Very funny. Take my job, please. "Fine." The judge prepared for the second hurdle. "Does the Commonwealth have any objection to this case proceeding to verdict with less than twelve jurors, in view of the circumstances, Mr. Moran?"

Tom was about to object when he felt a nudge at his elbow. He glanced over, and Masterson was looking thoughtfully at the dais, the flags, and the judicial seal of the Commonwealth of Pennsylvania. His hammy hand rested on a legal pad that said:

AGREE, TURKEY

Tom didn't even have to think twice. Fuck it. He'd worked his ass off on this loser. The mayor had gotten his indictment, but nobody had promised him a verdict. No matter that the Commonwealth had a chance of winning, Tom knew where the pacifiers were. He said without hesitation, "The Commonwealth has no objection to this case proceeding to verdict at this time, Your Honor. The Commonwealth is as interested as the defendant and the Court in bringing this matter to a swift and certain conclusion."

Judge Rudolph watched himself leaping the last hurdle. Sprinting for the finish line. Leaning into the tape. Splitting it like a spiderweb. The crowd roared. The banner flapped. He had won. It was over. Somebody handed him a flute of champagne.

And a brand-new robe.

61

Marta and Judy churned down the street, racing toward the Criminal Justice Center. Snow whisked from the sky and lay in a thick layer over sidewalks, buildings, and cars, as if someone had tossed a white comforter over Philadelphia. Stores and businesses were shut down. No one was outside. The stillness and silence were complete except for the whistle of the wind, a fluted note blown from the chill gray ether.

Marta panted as she ran in the heavy clothes, struggling to keep up with the younger and fitter associate; she was almost hyperventilating by the time they reached Broad Street. "Judy," she called weakly, and the associate ran back through the snow. Marta doubled over and braced her hands on her knees, trying to suppress the soreness in her torso. "I have to stop," she said, gasping. "I can't keep this up."

"You have to. We have to keep going."

Marta felt dizzy. Blood rushed to her head and it throbbed. She couldn't find the strength to straighten up. "Aren't there any cabs?"

"No. No cabs, no buses, nothing," Judy said, scanning the deserted street. She was panting, too, and her breath made large clouds of steam in the frigid air. "We gotta run for it."

"How much farther?"

"Five blocks." Judy squinted through the snow at the old-fashioned yellow clock atop City Hall, with its ornate Victorian hands. Her heartbeat quickened. "It's one-fifteen, Marta. We gotta go. Come on."

"I'm too old for this." Marta panted heavily as she stood up. Her chest felt like it would explode. "You go ahead. Take my purse. The evidence is in it."

"No. They won't believe me without you, you're lead counsel. Come on. Straighten up. Move your ass."

"You just like bossing me around," Marta said, panting too hard to smile.

"That too," Judy said, and ran off toward the courthouse.

62

Bennie climbed the snowdrift to Carrier's stoop, brushed snow off the brass buzzer, and leaned hard on the black button to ring the associate's apartment. She buzzed and buzzed, but there was no answer. Damn. Bennie hit the buzzer for the ground-floor apartment. It was marked by a card that said HILL-SILVERBLANK, but the Hill-Silverblanks weren't in either.

Bennie banged on the front door in frustration. Snow shook from the door panels as she pounded. She had trudged all the way here to stop this kid. She wouldn't be turned away now. She banged harder, hoping Judy hadn't already done something stupid. She could land all of them in front of the disciplinary board and put Rosato & Associates in the toilet.

She stepped away from the door and looked up at Carrier's windows. They were empty and dark. Where could she be? Bennie climbed down the stoop and into the snow at the sidewalk. Then she saw them. Tracks in the deep snow, messy footprints that led from Carrier's stoop and down the sidewalk, then

438 — LISA SCOTTOLINE

traveled beside a row of buried cars and disappeared around the corner.

Bennie peered through the blowing snow at the tracks. She could follow where they led. The footprints were easy to see in the deep snow. In some places it looked more like legprints than footprints. Bennie smiled. Lawyer tracks. Cloven pumps. They wouldn't get far on foot.

She clambered down the stoop, careful not to kick snow on the fresh footprints, when it hit her. There were *four* footprints, not two. Two people had left Judy's apartment—Judy and Marta. Either that or the Hill-Silverblanks, out for a stroll in a blizzard. Bennie knew in her bones which was more likely. She had a hunch Judy and Marta were heading for the Criminal Justice Center. She bounded after them.

The lawyer tracks ran down Twenty-fourth Street through the residential neighborhoods. Bennie picked up the pace, running directly through them. She hadn't slept all night, but she always enjoyed a run in cold weather. Her legs felt strong. Her wind came easily. Bennie hadn't rowed since the storm and she needed to stretch. It was the golden retriever in her. She got rammy when she didn't get to fetch the ball.

She followed the tracks down the snow-laden sidewalk and fell into an easy stride. Bennie had always been the fastest on her crew, and running the benches at Franklin Field every week since then had kept her in shape. She still regretted not trying out for the Olympics, but there'd been a mother to support.

Bennie checked the tracks as she ran into the snow. Deep trails marked the snowy sidewalk, like slugs. She would overtake them in no time. She had to, before they ruined all of them. Bennie picked up the pace in the next few strides and sprinted down the street.

63

"It's D day, troops," Ralph called to the other jurors. "Time to vote." Ralph was officially the foreman of the jury, but he felt more like an undertaker at a funeral parlor. He strode around the conference table, handing a sheet of legal paper to each downcast juror. They were in a funk since the scene with Christopher. It'd been like a soap opera, with Megan hugging Christopher while he flopped around on the floor like a hooked trout. Christopher kept trying to talk, but Megan had kept him quiet until the ambulance arrived.

Ralph had started pushing for a final vote as soon as the judge ordered them to resume deliberations. If Kenny wouldn't go with the flow this round, Ralph would get him next round. It was just a matter of time. Ralph handed a piece of legal paper to Megan. "Time to vote now, young lady. The sooner this is over, the sooner you can get to the hospital."

"Thanks," Megan said, accepting the paper shakily. She stared at the blank paper. She didn't want to convict Steere even if it meant disagreeing with Christopher. Poor Christopher. She did want to visit him, at least to make sure he was okay. Megan hurriedly wrote *innocent* on her paper and folded it up.

Mrs. Wahlbaum bent over her paper, with one last glance at Mr. Fogel, who was writing with a speed that didn't surprise her. He'd vote not guilty, and Wanthida, who sat beside him, would vote not guilty, too. Mrs. Wahlbaum tried to recall what Christopher had said after he changed his mind, but all she could remember was him writhing in agony on the stretcher. It must have been appendicitis. She wrote *not guilty* and turned her paper over.

Nick trembled at the lined sheet in front of him. His nerves were shot. Christopher's stomach attack was the last straw. What if Nick got a stomach attack, too? His belly was already burning him. He gulped down some water and didn't even care if his thumb showed. He wanted to go home before he caught whatever Christopher had. He couldn't stain again. Nick grabbed his pencil, clenched it tightly, and wrote *INNOCENT*.

Lucky Seven hunched over his paper, feelin' like he used to feel in grade school when they gave tests. Everybody was writing and he wasn't. He could hear them all, scribblin' away. Everybody was finishin' before him, foldin' up their papers, handin' them in. It was like they had all the answers. Well, this time he had the answer.

Lucky Seven was feelin' bad for Isaiah and his

girl, and he was gonna stand up for what he though
no matter what Kenny said. Hell, after this case wa
over, he'd never see the dude again. It wasn't lik
they'd be hangin'. Lucky Seven wrote *not guilty* o
the damn sheet just as quick as he could. He wasn'
even the last one finished.

"Everybody done voting?" Ralph asked, takin
his seat at the head of the table. He slapped the pad i
front of him and casually wrote *NOT GUILTY*. Lik
it wasn't worth $100,000 to him. Then he looked up

"I didn't vote yet, man," Kenny Manning said
evenly, at the opposite end of the long table. All th
jurors looked at Kenny, except for Lucky Seven, who
looked pointedly away.

"That's okay," Ralph said. "Hold your papers
people. Don't pass 'em in yet. Kenny's entitled to take
his time." He glanced at his watch. 1:25. "Take all the
time you need, friend."

Kenny picked up his pencil and looked out the
window. He didn't need their shit. He could take hi
own goddamn time. Didn't need no Ralph Fuckin
Merry to tell him that. Didn't need no go-ahead from
that pig face. Kenny made them all wait, lookin' ou
the window and watchin' the goddamn snow. Takin
his *own* damn time.

At a hospital across town, Christopher lay agonized
on a gurney as it sped down a corridor. He kept trying
to tell the doctors to call the cops, but the nurse and
an emergency room doctor ran with the gurney on

either side, ignoring his grunting. Pain ripped through Christopher's bowel but he kept trying to talk.

"Nuh . . . grr . . . stop," he managed to say, but they hustled the gurney into a cold white room. Everybody was rushing around in half-masks and gowns. The gurney lurched to a stop under a blinding beam of light.

"No . . . wait . . . whoa," Christopher grunted. He put his arms up to shield his eyes. A doctor held his wrist and started to put a plastic mask over his face. No. They couldn't put him to sleep. He had to call the police. He had to save Marta.

"I said whoa!" Christopher shouted, and marshaling all his strength, grabbed the startled doctor by his white lapels and wrestled him onto the table beside him. Nurses gasped in shock as the two men fell to the cold tile floor and Christopher screamed in the doctor's face, "Call the police! Now!"

64

Marta got her second wind as soon as she spied the Criminal Justice Center through the driving snow flurries. The building was modern with Art Deco touches, trimmed in gray marble and tan. Fresh snow outlined its geometric ledges and decorative windowsills. It was a beautiful building and she'd take it by storm. Marta panted with exertion and excitement as she ran.

Judy knew without a word what Marta was thinking. They were on the same page. They had the evidence against Steere. They would turn it over to the court. Judy ran faster. The ethical problem nagged at her, but every time she felt a doubt she thought of Mary lying in the snow. Bleeding almost to death. Mary might not survive, and Judy couldn't even be with her at the hospital because of Elliot Steere. She owed him exactly zip. Judy hugged Marta's purse under her arm and kept her legs churning.

But something was wrong. Odd. The heart of

town should have been deserted. City Hall and the Criminal Justice Center were closed because of the blizzard, except for the Steere case. The street should be as dead as the rest of town, snowed in for the duration. But it wasn't.

Bennie squinted through the snow as she ran. She had lost their tracks when she reached the business district and followed her hunch the rest of the way. Three blocks ahead of her, two figures were running down the sidewalk past Market Street toward the Criminal Justice Center. Judy and Marta. Bennie recognized Judy's bright yellow shell. The associate was a rock climber with a full wardrobe of pricey gear. Besides, who else would wear a color like that?

Bennie took it up for a few strokes, running hard. Power strokes, at the beginning of a race. Cranking up the stroke to launch the scull smoothly, then taking it into full stride, full bore. She narrowed the gap between them. Two blocks, then one. She watched Judy and Marta reach the Criminal Justice Center and the fringes of a crowd collecting there. There was activity. Commotion. Oh, no. Bennie took up the stroke until the scull began to fly.

Judy was aghast as she ran. People were collecting at the mouth of Filbert Street. Something was happening at the Criminal Justice Center. News vans with colorful logos had parked crazily in the plowed snow. Blue-and-white police cars thronged at the corner of Filbert Street. "We're not too late, are we?"

Judy asked anxiously, panting as she ran. She looked over at Marta, whose expression showed strain and alarm.

"No. We can't be."

"The TV stations are here. The cops. Maybe it's the verdict."

Marta shook it off. "It could be the jurors, arriving from the hotel."

"But it could be the verdict. They could have delivered it already."

"No!" Marta shouted hoarsely. "We're not too late! Now run!" She gritted her teeth and ran harder. She wouldn't be beaten by Elliot Steere, not after last night. Not after the guards, and Mary.

Judy peered through the snow flurries at the scene. The crowd got closer and closer. They dashed past the shadow of City Hall and rushed down the block to Filbert. At the back of the mob stood black-jacketed cops and reporters in green parkas and snow ponchos. The noisy crowd was dotted with black police hats, baseball caps, and golf umbrellas. A hundred people filled the narrow street, talking excitedly, their breath making a collective cloud in the cold air.

"I can't see anything, can you?" Marta shouted, out of breath. She was at the edge of complete exhaustion.

"No. The crowd's too big." Judy peeked from behind an overweight cop. "Officer, what's happening?"

"Just got here myself, lady," the cop said. His

nose was red and leaky. "They called for crowd control."

Marta yanked down her hood so she wouldn't be recognized and shoved past a reporter in her way.

Bennie dashed the last hundred feet to the crowd. It was the final kick. She gave it all she had. Her legs hurt. Her lungs ached. She reached the Criminal Justice Center just in time to spot Judy's yellow hat disappear midway through the crowd, with Marta pushing ahead of her.

65

Marta stood near the front of the crowd, riveted at the sight. Elliot Steere was free. He stood joking with reporters on the sidewalk in front of the Criminal Justice Center. Cameras snapped his fake grin. TV lights bleached his features white as a cadaver. He was *free*. She was too late.

Judy pushed next to Marta from behind. "Oh, God," she moaned, instantly sick at heart. Tears welled up in her eyes. Her body sagged with defeat. Steere had gotten away with murder. Judy wiped her eyes with a wet, snowy mitten.

Marta was too horrified to speak. She could see only her own fury. The man had used her. Used the court. Killed people. She seethed as he smiled for the press and raised his arms in victory. Steere would go free and prosper. It couldn't happen. It couldn't be permitted. Then Marta remembered.

The pritchel. A long iron spike with a tip as lethal as a dagger. Did she still have it? She slipped her hand into her pocket and felt the cold metal. The pritchel. She held it, feeling its heft even through her glove. It struck Marta as the perfect solution. She was already ruined. She had already killed. She had nothing more to lose. She stepped forward in a sort of trance, leaving Judy and the world behind.

Back at the middle of the crowd, Bennie began pushing harder. "Excuse me!" she said, elbowing past a cop. She spotted Steere at the front of the crowd, being interviewed by reporters on the sidewalk. So he'd been acquitted. At least Marta and Judy hadn't been able to interfere with the trial. But where were they?

Bennie scanned the crowd and spotted Judy's yellow ski cap among the black police hats. Where was Marta? She would be furious at seeing Steere walk. Bennie felt panicky without knowing why. She jostled her way forward from the right side where the reporters were fewer.

Marta stopped two rows from Steere. Snow fell on his fine overcoat and sprinkled his padded shoulders. She was so close she could see the hand stitching on his lapels. She gripped the pritchel in her pocket. Her heart pumped in her chest. Adrenaline pounded in her ears, drumming behind Steere's voice.

"I always knew the jury would find me innocent," Steere was saying to a TV reporter holding a black bubble microphone. "Never doubted it for a minute."

Bennie pushed through the crowd and finally spotted Marta. There. Right near Steere. Marta was standing still, a faraway look in her eyes. What was she doing? Bennie would have shouted to her but the crowd was too loud. "Comin' through!" she said, pushing her way to Marta.

Marta stood a foot from Steere, her face obscured by her hood. She imagined the pritchel piercing his chest. Staining his camel-hair topcoat with hot red blood. She waited for the right moment. The TV reporter was still in the way. Marta inched forward, the drumming louder in her ears, waiting for the reporter to move.

Bennie saw it then. What was happening. Marta was closing in. She must have a weapon. Would she really kill Steere? Oh God. She had to be stopped. She couldn't do that. Bennie couldn't let her. She bulldozed through the crowd.

The TV reporter moved suddenly aside. Steere looked around for the next interview, smiling. The path in front of him was momentarily clear. Marta's world froze. The crowd stood still. The reporters fell mute. The motor drives stopped whirring. The only sound was the drumbeat pounding in Marta's ears. She stepped into the breach and drew her hand from her pocket.

"MARTA, NO!" Bennie shrieked.

The scream broke Marta's trance. The world came screaming back to life. What had she been thinking? Was she crazy? Strong arms grabbed her. It was Bennie, alarmed. She wrenched the pritchel from Marta's hands and searched her eyes for sanity.

Suddenly sirens blared at the edge of the crowd. Cops shouted. Reporters yelled. Cameras clicked.

Video cameras whirred. A phalanx of cops and detectives charged through the crowd toward Steere. "Mr. Steere!" shouted one of the detectives, pointing. "We have a warrant for your arrest."

Steere started to edge away, but a ring of black-jacketed cops blocked his path. There was nowhere to run, nowhere to hide, at least for the time being. His expression remained composed as they shackled him, and the cacophony of the reporters drowned out his requests for his lawyer.

66

It took Emil Gorebian all day to interview lawyers, police, and the employees at the election commission. He sat tapping at his keyboard in the press room at City Hall. It had finally stopped snowing. Leftover sun struggled through the dirty window next to him.

Emil was hardly tired even after such a long day. He wasn't old enough to retire, he was still going strong. He had the entire story in his head and it poured out as smoothly as olive oil. It would be all over the front page in the next edition. His first exclusive in ten years.

Emil tapped away. Elliot Steere and Jen Pressman had been lovers. They used the organ donor scheme to file absentee ballots with forged signatures. They paid Eb Darning to forge and file the ballots, but Eb began blackmailing them and had to be silenced. Emil had spent all day reading election records and reviewing absentee ballots filed in the last election. There had been at least two others who were paid to file the fake absentee ballots, and he figured there were many more. Gorebian would explain the scheme in a sidebar, so readers could understand.

Emil kept tapping. The best part of the story was that the forged votes hadn't been filed against the mayor, they'd been filed *in his favor*. Almost ten thousand votes filed on his behalf. Elliot Steere and Jen Pressman were trying to set the mayor up, so they could leak the driver's license file right before the election and pin the voter fraud on him. Pressman had planned to betray the mayor and go her merry way. Steere would have defeated his biggest enemy and the price of historic properties would soar. The Philadelphia Renaissance would never blossom.

Emil sipped tea as he skimmed the half-finished story on the computer monitor. He would emphasize in the conclusion how the lawyers had worked to bring Steere to justice and how Bennie Rosato had risked everything to protect a client. The story would take the cloud off Bennie's law firm and show her to be a hero. The young Turks called it spin, but that wasn't what Emil called it. He called it truth.

Emil finished the story, tying up the loose ends. He imagined winning a Pulitzer and would settle for reinstatement to the day shift. Emil always knew he was a better reporter than Alix Locke. Sneaking into the chief of staff's office and stealing her purse. Using Pressman's keys to get into Steere's beach house. Emil shook his head. No one had any morals anymore, any scruples. That was the problem today.

Emil hit the PRINT key and sighed happily.

❖   ❖   ❖

John LeFort watched the telephone lights blinking from his desk chair in his office at Cable & Bess. Sunlight poured through the windows and glinted off the Waterford tumbler in his hand. LeFort never drank during the day, but today was an exception. He heaved a short sigh and picked up the phone. "Hello?" he asked, as if he didn't know who it was. As if he didn't know who any of the blinking lights were.

"John, Mo Barrie. I'm at home watching television. Did you see? Did you see it on the news? Steere's been rearrested. Conspiracy to murder, for hiring a hit man. Vote fraud, trying to rig the mayoral election. It's a scandal."

"I know. I was there."

"We're calling the notes, John. We're calling the notes right now. All of them. Those properties are for sale as of this minute. I'm ringing the city right after we hang up."

"I understand," John said. He sipped his drink. Mo could be as hysterical as Bunny. How foolish. It was only business.

"All of them, John. Consider them sold, John. As of now. Right this instant. It's a house of cards, John, and it's about to come tumbling down."

"See you in court, Mo," LeFort said, and hung up. He took another sip before picking up the next call.

❖   ❖   ❖

Elliot Steere sat behind the wired glass across from his new criminal lawyer. The glass was scratched and smudged, and the interview room at the Roundhouse was far dirtier than the one at the Criminal Justice Center. Steere's surroundings didn't matter to him right now. "You'll plead me innocent of all charges," he said to his lawyer, who wore costly rimless glasses and a Zegna suit.

"But they have an excellent case for conspiracy in the murder of the security guards. They found Bogosian's magazine, and there were papers in his apartment linking him to you. They'll get his phone records and bank accounts."

"Bogosian will never testify against me."

"Bogosian is dead. The New Jersey police found his body on the beach."

Steere paused. "All the better. Then he can't testify."

"But Richter will. Carrier will. They have a computer file from your beach house. They're impounding your boat. They have records from Darning and a suspect in the DiNunzio shooting. He used a stolen car." The young lawyer consulted his notes. "I expect indictments on vote fraud and election rigging. They're talking about obstruction of justice, but I don't know if they can prove it."

"I am innocent of all charges against me."

"You'd be lucky to be offered a deal."

Steere smiled, amused. "Luck has nothing to do with it. Nothing at all. Did you ever hear of a general named Sun-Tzu?"

67

In an anesthetized sleep, Christopher dreamed he was cantering a horse across a snow-covered field, under a warm sun and a crisp blue sky. A fog hovered over the snow, so the horse appeared to be cantering on a bed of clouds. In anyone else's dream the horse would have been white, an Arabian, but Christopher thought white horses were for show-offs, so it was a brown quarter horse. A large gelding with a white blaze, over sixteen hands high.

The horse's hooves crunched through the snow as its canter accelerated without warning to a gallop. Though Christopher hadn't kicked the horse to gallop him, he didn't object to the change of pace until horse and rider were racing toward a wooden rail fence that appeared from nowhere. The fence was high, almost four feet, and Christopher didn't know if the horse could jump it.

The horse's hooves reached farther into the snow as it galloped full tilt, nostrils flaring, straining against the bit. The fence raced toward them. It was crazy to jump at this speed, but if Christopher halted he'd fly over the horse's neck. He lifted into position and tightened the reins, but the leather slipped from his hands and flapped against the horse's wet neck. The jump zoomed up to meet them. The horse leapt into the air. They'd never clear the fence.

"No!" Christopher shouted, waking up. He looked around him. Everything was white, but it wasn't snow, it was a hospital room. He wasn't crashing into a fence, he was lying on a hospital bed. And the touch on his hand wasn't a loose rein, it was a woman. Megan Gerrity, the redhead from the jury, was sitting at the edge of his bed. Christopher blinked, groggy, and cleared his parched throat.

"It's all right, Christopher," Megan said. She squeezed his hand, and Christopher squeezed back, easing into the soft pillow with a sigh.

"You almost stabbed Elliot Steere! Do you realize that?" Bennie said as she stormed down the long hospital corridor. The late afternoon sun glowed through the large windows, but its residual warmth was lost on Bennie. On either side of the hall hung polished plaques listing the names of hospital benefactors, but she couldn't have cared less. Bennie was walking so fast she didn't notice anything and was so angry she didn't care if Marta could keep pace.

"I agree, it never should have happened," Marta said, bedraggled, as she rushed along. Her boots squashed and her snowpants rustled with every step. She felt whipped, out of gas. She had spent a long day at the Roundhouse being questioned by the cops, and the night before that had been eventful even for a criminal lawyer. "I'm sorry. Sorry for all of it."

"*Sorry?*" Bennie didn't break stride. "For *attempted murder*? You can't say you're sorry for attempted murder. There are lots of legal excuses for attempted murder, but saying you're really really really sorry isn't one of them. If the cops had known what you were up to, you'd be in the slammer right now. And if I hadn't palmed that fucking knife—"

"Pritchel."

"Gesundheit."

"No. It's a pritchel, not a knife."

"What? What the fuck do I care?" Bennie fumed, her jacket flying as she charged ahead. "What the fuck difference does it make? You tried to stab the man!"

"I wouldn't have gone though with it. I didn't, did I?"

"Oh, please. Only because I stopped you. You could have stabbed *me*!"

A passing nurse glanced over nervously and quickened her pace. Marta whispered, "I didn't even know you were there. How did I know you'd jump in front of him?"

"I wasn't gonna let you *kill* him." They reached the elevator bank and Bennie punched the UP button. "You could have known that, couldn't you? First rule of solo practice. Do not kill the clients. They don't come back, for one thing."

"I already said I'm sorry. What else can I do? Open a vein?"

"I should've left you in jail. In another hour they would've brought out the rubber hose. *I* would have brought out the rubber hose."

"I said, 'Thank you.'" Marta rolled her eyes. "Listen to me. 'Thank you.' 'Sorry.' 'Please.' I'm like a fucking Hallmark card."

Bennie started hitting the elevator button like a video game. It made a *clikclikclik* sound. "I should've let you rot there." *Clikclikclik*. "Let you wait for a public defender." *Clikclikclik*. "Thrown you to the press." *Clikclikclik*. "Sent you up for Bogosian."

"That was self-defense. They knew it, they were just working me over."

"And what about the jury tampering, huh? You owe me big-time on that. Community service?" *Clikclikclik*. "You know what, I'm charging you. I'm billing you for my fucking time." *Clikclikclik*. "Where is the goddamn elevator?"

"Okay, fine. Bill me, no problem. Thank you, thank you, thank you," Marta said, meaning it. She'd have a lot of time on her hands in the next few years. She might buy a house, fix it up, and actually live in it. But she'd need to do a little legal work on the side, if only to prevent ring rust. "You know, I've been thinking that you might need help getting the firm back up on its feet."

Clikclikclik. "If I even have a firm anymore."

"You do. You will."

Clik. "Hmph."

"Maybe I can make it up to you. Help rebuild Rosato and Associates. It's the least I can do. Draft briefs. Teach the associates." The elevator arrived and the doors slid apart. "Behind the scenes, you know."

"You?" Bennie's mouth dropped open. "You? Stay in Philadelphia?"

Marta began to laugh as the doors closed, and the sound of her laughter echoed all the way up the shaft.

Marta and Bennie stood at the threshold to Mary's hospital room. The associate had been moved out of intensive care and her condition was finally stable. Mary looked drawn against the thin hospital pillows, and an IV snaked to a shunt in her arm. The DiNunzio family surrounded her like an embrace, and Judy sat among them. She grinned tiredly when she saw Bennie and Marta. "Hey, guys, isn't this cool?" Judy said. "Mary's alive."

Bennie smiled with relief. "Wonderful. That's how I like my associates. Breathing."

"It's the only way they get any work done," Marta said, leaning against the doorjamb. "By the way, they are hired back, aren't they?"

Judy held her breath. Mary blinked.

Bennie thought a minute. What ran in her veins, ice? "If they got a license, they got a job," she said, and Mary smiled to herself.

It's not a job, it's an adventure.

ACKNOWLEDGMENTS

Rough Justice is a work of fiction, but a number of people helped enormously with the research and I want to thank them here. Any mistakes are entirely my own.

First and very special thanks to Mayor of Philadelphia Ed Rendell and his former chief of staff, David Cohen. I am a huge fan of these two men, who have worked wonders for my favorite city and inspired all of us. They permitted me access to the mayor's office and to other areas of City Hall for this book, and David Cohen gave generously of his time, energy, and intelligence, as is typical of him. Thanks, too, to Robin Schatz, for the insider's tour, and to Ginny Kehoe.

Thank you to Larry Fox, president of the Litigation Section of the American Bar Association, who helped with the ethical questions herein, and thank you to criminal defense experts Frank DiSimone, Glenn

Gilman, Burton Rose, and Mike Trigani for their on-the-spot advice.

Thank you to the detectives of the Homicide Division of the Philadelphia Police Department, who continue to help me in so many ways and gave me the coolest sweatshirt ever. Thanks to Mark McDonald of the *Philadelphia Daily News,* who took me through the lovely press area in City Hall and spent time teaching me about newspapers and how they work. Thanks to Dr. Andrea Hanaway, an emergency surgeon who taught me the details of some truly heinous injuries.

Thank you to Richard Clark, Jr., a farrier who answered all my stupid questions while trying to reset the shoe on a cranky mare. Thanks to all at Thorncroft Equestrian Center, for all of their good work, and especially to Diana Johnson, who teaches me about horses and life.

Thank you to Kevin Sparkman of the DVTO, who helped me a great deal. Also, thank you, Chuck Jones, for your friendship, hunting advice, and general expertise. I also want to acknowledge a fascinating translation of Sun-Tzu by J. M. Huang, which served as a source for *Rough Justice.*

Equally important as the research is the writing, and I had experts to help with that, too. Heartfelt thanks to president and CEO at HarperCollins, Anthea Disney, to my editor,

Carolyn Marino, and to my agent, Molly Friedrich of the Aaron Priest Agency. I marvel constantly at the brilliance, talent, and generosity of these women, who are like literary Power Rangers. They improved this manuscript in countless ways, and supported me throughout all. I am the luckiest author in the world to be able to tap their time and expertise. I can't thank them enough and won't bore the rest of you by going on longer here.

Thanks, too, to Paul Cirone, Molly's assistant, for his hard work and terrific sense of humor, and to Carolyn's assistant, Robin Stamm, who understands the importance of the comma. Special thanks to production editor Andrea Molitor, who cared enough to get it right.

Thank you to Gene Mydlowski, associate publisher, for his efforts and eye, and to Laura Leonard, publicity manager, who, besides being a dynamo on her job, is one of the sweetest people in the world. Thanks to Laura's assistant Caroline Enright, too.

Personal thanks and love to my family and friends, as well as my husband, Peter, and daughter, Kiki. They had to put up with pizza for dinner while I wrestled with this book and, worse yet, they had to put up with me.

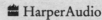